Avenge Us All

A Novel

Pamela King Cable

In a world where over two billion people profess Christianity, I lost my religion before my twenty-eighth birthday. I had lived with fire and brimstone until it scorched and burned any spiritual covenant I had. The church destroyed my faith, deceived those I loved, and delivered me to the brink of destruction with no lifeline. Meeting my sin-sick soul head-on, I left the church in its entirety to find God. To this day, I cannot enter a house of worship without experiencing symptoms of PTSD. Though I found a new personal relationship with Jesus Christ, I don't belong in the evangelical community. I doubt I ever will.

— Pamela Cable

ISBN: 978-1-962754-04-0 Paperback
ISBN: 978-1-962754-05-7 eBook

10 9 8 7 6 5 4 3 2 1

Manufactured in the United States of America

Televenge Trilogy:

TELEVENGE
AVENGE US ALL
VENGEANCE IS MINE

Other books by this author:

SOUTHERN FRIED WOMEN
A collection of short stories

THE SANCTUM
*A coming-of-age Southern tale dusted with magic
and set in a volatile time in America
when the winds of change begin to blow.*

Lynn Andreozzi ~ Many thanks for your incredible attention to detail and professionalism in designing the re-release covers of this trilogy. We are truly grateful.

Julie Murkette ~ Thank you, friend and mentor, for your tireless work in book design, and for your counsel. This trilogy would not have been possible without you.

For Michael, as always

Names of God

Adonai-Jehovah: The Lord Our Sovereign

El-Elyon: The Lord Most High

El-Olam: The Everlasting God

El-Shaddai:
The God Who Is Sufficient for the Needs of His People

Jehovah-Elohim: The Eternal Creator

Jehovah-Jireh: The Lord Our Provider

Jehovah-Nissi: The Lord Our Banner

Jehovah-Ropheka: The Lord Our Healer

Jehovah-Shalom: The Lord Our Peace

Jehovah-Tsidkenu: The Lord Our Righteousness

Jehova-Mekaddishkem: The Lord Our Sanctifer

Jehovah-Sabaoth: The Lord of Hosts

Jehovah-Shammah: The Lord is Present

Jehovah-Rohi: The Lord Our Shepherd

Jehovah-Hoseenu: The Lord Our Maker

Jehovah-Eloheenu: The Lord Our God

Beware of false prophets,
which come to you in sheep's clothing,
but inwardly they are ravening wolves.
Ye shall know them by their fruits…
Not everyone that saith unto me
Lord, Lord,
shall enter into the kingdom of heaven;
But he that doeth the will of my father
which is in heaven.
Many will say to me in that day,
Lord, lord,
have we not prophesied
in thy name?
And in thy name have cast out devils?
And in thy name done many wonderful works?
And then will I profess unto them,
I never knew you.
Depart from me,
ye that work iniquity.
—Matthew 7:15-23 KJV

Dearly beloved, avenge not yourselves,
but rather give place unto wrath:
For it is written,
Vengeance is Mine;
I will repay, saith the Lord.
—Romans 12:19 KJV

We are each of us responsible
for the evil
we may have prevented.
—James Martineau

Out of suffering have emerged the strongest souls;
the most massive characters are seared with scars.
—Kahlil Gibran (1883-1931)

I recalled Harry's words —

After opening Mavis's apartment door, I followed a trail of blood. With the bedroom door ajar, I saw her; the sight knocking me to my knees. Someone had raped and beaten her so severely that she was scarcely recognizable . . . Andie, whoever slit her throat, nearly removed her head from her body.

I walked into her bedroom by myself.

The air was dank; they had shut off the electricity, but sunlight streamed through the windows. The room smelled of antiseptic, cleaning fluids, and paint, and I stared at an area near the foot of her bed. The place Harry said he found her. I dropped to my knees, running my fingertips across the floor where Mavis had lain, dying.

〜

The grave's timeless smile creases every skull, but her smile was gone forever. They laid the cremated remains of Mavis Grace Dumass at the base of a monument placed above new tobacco fields. It was the most majestic and yet the most lonesome grave on earth.

No burial was more impressive. The air was spiked with the smell of fresh-turned earth as the mourners broke the silence of the lonely Dumass farm, singing low, sorrowful songs and weeping in the muted, slanting light. I leaned against an oak tree, my flip-flops and bare legs spotted with mud. I closed my eyes, imagining an angel standing in our midst—a real Arch Angel of flesh and blood, full of the Spirit and fraught with anguish, wielding a vengeful sword at his side. I felt close to God then, knowing Mavis was home and no one would ever hurt her again.

Almost as silently as they assembled, the hushed crowd slowly broke apart. Looking for Mavis's father, I turned to walk the long path back to the house in my bare feet. I hadn't seen him during the funeral. But there he stood, alone on a grassy knoll. He spoke first to his folded hands and then to a silent horizon before approaching me.

Pulling me into a hug, he whispered into my ear. "Be careful, Andie." He made little sense, and I didn't ask, but the strength of his arms was firm and persuasive, and I kissed his soft, tear-stained cheek. His sweet concern for me was unimportant.

I was on my way back to Salisbury to pack and leave Joe for good.

Chapter 1

Everything I Want

Andie ~ July 1975

Packing what little I owned, I hauled three carloads to Winston-Salem and into my parents' garage. Back in my old bedroom, I needed a purging release from Joe. But for weeks afterward, I endured his continual telephone calls at all hours—begging—pleading for me to return to our trailer at Shady Acres. Beseeching calls from my mother-in-law woke me every morning. An endless supply of roses arrived every payday. Cards and letters, all from Joe. He wooed me endlessly, and I had to admit, it felt good. And yet, I held firm. Primarily because of Dixie, truth be told. My mother had a knack for making a persuasive argument.

But on the day of my appointment to see an attorney and file for divorce, Pastor Tony DeSanto called. I didn't care to hear from Calvin Artury's Assistant Pastor, and I couldn't imagine why he bothered. Then he explained he had counseled Joe for months and agreed I had every right to divorce my husband because of his infidelity and inability to grieve with me over the death of our baby. "Joe's trespasses are many," he said sympathetically. "But what about forgiveness, Andie? How many times did Christ tell us to forgive?"

"Seventy times seven," I answered sheepishly.

"Withholding forgiveness and love is not Christ-like, Andie. God would forgive *you*. He's forgiven Joe. How can you do less?"

I canceled my appointment at Currier & Dunn, Esquire.

The following morning, Joe appeared at the front door on his knees in full-blown tears and a new and improved declaration of love. Gripping a handful of freshly picked roses from somebody's garden, he held up the bouquet and said, "A peace offering." This time, his promise included working toward *my* goal of a better place to live. I wanted to believe my husband's new confessions of love and devotion. I wanted it more than anything. Standing in the doorway with my arms around Joe, I looked back at my parents inside the house. Daddy shook his head, gave me a look, and walked away.

"She's a glutton for punishment," Dixie said.

☙

That same day, I returned to Salisbury and our trailer in the unbearable summer heat. Two dozen pink roses and a Hallmark card sat on my nightstand. When I lifted the roses from the box, a large thorn pierced my ring finger, drawing blood. It dribbled down the back of my hand, and I froze, watching it forge a path through the hair on my arm. I remained mesmerized by its tiny trail until I heard Joe hollering for me to get the lead out and help him unload the car. He needed to hurry and pack. It was Friday— time for the next Calvin Artury Miracle Crusade.

Left alone, my mind swirled with images of Mavis. I disappeared down endless corridors of the past five years, drowning in recurring memories and rediscovering the blessed comfort of food. Never one to indulge in the unacceptable behavior of alcohol and drugs, I treated myself to an addiction of carbohydrates, fat, salt, sugar, and caffeine. As Joe continued to work at Coot's garage during the week and travel with the suddenly famous Reverend Calvin

Artury to miracle Crusades across the country on the weekends, it allowed me to overeat as much as I wanted and whenever I wanted.

And to appease my husband, I found a job serving the lunch crowds at Newberry's, a popular southern restaurant chain with a kindhearted cook who sent me home with boxes of leftovers. Occupying my mind four hours a day at the restaurant resulted in feeding frenzies every evening. I refused to answer the phone, watched non-stop TV, inhaled massive amounts of local cuisine, and then fell into a coma until it was time for work the next day.

Watching Joe pack another suitcase, I twirled my ponytail around my fingers, sighed, and trailed behind him from room to room like a forlorn puppy. "Can't Calvin find an assistant to help you? Give you a weekend or an evening off? For crying out loud, Joe. He doesn't pay you a dime for what you do for him."

"You don't get it, do you? You never did. I'm Christ's disciple. My reward is in Heaven. Besides, nobody knows the audio equipment like I do. I *can't* take time off. Monday is trio practice, Tuesday choir, Wednesday the men's quartet practices until midnight, Thursday I edit tapes, and every Friday we leave for another weekend Crusade. It's harder on me than it is on you, Andie. Once I'm a full-time employee, it'll ease up. I promise."

"We need to talk about moving to Winston-Salem. Or even Kernersville. You said we'd talk about it."

Joe slammed the lid on his new sturgeon-leather suitcase, a gift from Calvin. "Then *you* find a better job. Or wait until I'm making twice what I make at Coot's garage. That's when we'll talk about it." He kissed me. "Go spend the weekend with Mama. At least she has an air conditioner. See you Monday."

Sitting on the bed's edge in the quiet, I cursed my inability to get on with my life, then looked at myself in the mirror. Moments later, I slammed the trailer door behind me. It was bargain night at Hoggy's Barbecue.

Libby said she knocked several times before she panicked and drove to the nearest pay phone to call our mother-in-law, who arrived at my trailer moments later with her spare key and a bad attitude. Maudy had never learned to hold her tongue around Libby. "Andie? Where the heck are you?"

When my imposing sister-in-law opened my bedroom door, Maudy pushed her out of the way and gasped, "Lord, sugar, wake up! It's noon. You sick?"

"She's not sick, Maudy. She's hungover!"

"Hungover? Libby! Andie doesn't drink. Ain't a drop of liquor touched those lips as long as I've known her. You may guzzle it up in the Catholic church, but House of Praise people don't touch the stuff!"

"Not booze. Food. Look at this place!"

Candy bar wrappers, Krispy Kreme boxes, and KFC carry-out tubs littered my bedroom. I had amassed piles of empty soda bottles, an assortment of Burger King bags, and pizza boxes in the kitchen. My refrigerator and freezer were bare except for a half-eaten two-gallon butter pecan ice cream container. Since the trash overflowed, I had stashed empty pie pans from the restaurant and Styrofoam containers from the past week's lunch specials in the sink. My otherwise spotless single-wide smelled like rotting fruit.

Rolling over in my sweat-soaked bed, I opened my sleep-filled eyes and wiped my cottonmouth. "How'd you two get in?" I heard Libby rooting around in the kitchen.

Maudy cupped my face with her hands. "Sugar, you need to get up, shower, and come home with me and Al for a few days. Get away from this stinking depression you're in."

Libby stomped back into the bedroom. "This place smells as bad as you look. Andie, get out of that bed and into a shower, and I'm not taking no for an answer. Have you seen yourself lately? You look like shit—sorry, Maudy—but she does."

I sat up and glared at Libby. "Stop it! What do you know about what I've been through? You've got a good man, a college education, a pretty house, and a great job! And you wear a size two! Did you lose a baby and your best friend lately? What do you know of suffering?"

Libby walked around my bedroom, picking up trash. "Quit feeling sorry for yourself. You're a food junkie, and *you* are still alive. But you won't be long if you don't stop. Your heart's going to give out before you're thirty. And you can still have more babies. Mavis would be ashamed of you! How dare you destroy her good name and memory like this? Have you visited her dad since the funeral? Rupert needs to hear from you."

I flopped back on the bed, moaned, and buried my face in my pillow. Libby knew her words were the shot in the arm needed to rouse me from my sugar stupor. My pillow muffled my words. "I've been eating like this since I married Joe."

"Don't blame Joe," Maudy said.

Libby snickered. "It wasn't Joe who put the fork in her mouth, but he caused her pain. Where is he now when she needs him? Go home, Maudy. I'm taking Andie to my uncle's farm with me for a while. She needs to sober up, do some actual work, and lose weight."

Maudy dug her fists into her fleshy hips. "Libby! I—"

"—Thanks for bringing the key, Maudy."

Maudy looked at me, trying to pull myself out of bed. "Hmmm. Well, you know where to find me if you need me, Andie." She leered at Libby, the Catholic daughter-in-law she didn't like. "So, Libby. Now that you've taken over, I suppose you'll stick around and clean this vomit-smelling mess of a trailer, too?"

"Already working on it," Libby said, ushering our incensed mother-in-law out the door. Libby then called Newberry's restaurant and informed my manager that I had quit.

I sat wide-eyed at the kitchen table. I couldn't believe Libby did that. "I can't quit my job. Joe will be furious!"

"So what? If he cared one iota about your health, he'd be here, trying to save you instead of letting you dig your grave with your fork. Besides, that restaurant's turning you into Porky Pig, and I'm not about to watch it happen."

Libby flung three Hefty bags full of garbage into Shady Acre's dumpster that swarmed with flies before writing Joe a note: *If you want to speak to your wife, she's with me at the Stewart farm in Burlington for a couple of weeks. If you have a problem with that, take it up with Ray, not Andie. Love, Libby.*

Then she stuffed my suitcase and me into her truck.

For weeks, dark skies had skipped off to the northeast, leaving the dry Rowan County dirt begging for rain. I found it strange the rain arrived in torrents the day I rode out of Salisbury with Libby. She stopped at the Exxon station on the edge of town to gas up her truck and call Dixie. My mother told Libby to keep me until I was well. I knew what that meant. Dixie couldn't deal with me. Not like I was. I gazed through the rain. My stringy hair lay smooshed against the truck window. Dark rings of sadness circled my eyes. My body had morphed into a boated mass of fat and flesh, with bands of grief twisting around my head that cut off my ability to reason.

Thankfully, Libby drove as if we were both in our eighties and not our twenties. Riding to Burlington that day in her old truck, my stomach and bowels churned from massive amounts of food and soda. Still, she had to stop twice so I could vomit on the side of the road. "I don't believe in God anymore," I said, my face chalky and lips swollen.

"Yes, you do." Libby handed me a tissue.

I wiped my mouth. "Then why doesn't God do it?"

"What? What do you want Him to do?"

Wiping away tears with my shirt sleeve, I spoke as if I were alone. "Why won't He make Joe love me?"

It was the first time I'd seen Libby's tears. "Damn him," she said.

We rode in silence. Libby had become more than a sister-in-law. She was suddenly my friend. My only friend.

"You want kids someday?" I asked her.

"Ray and I both want children. In a few years. After my veterinary fellowship, and he's passed the bar. And after we move to Virginia to live near my parents."

"You *both* want children. What beautiful words. I envy you. I have to warn you, though. They paved the road to motherhood with blood and tears. I feel like an old woman."

"I know you do," Libby said. "You've lived a lifetime already."

I rolled back to the door and leaned against the window again. "What's your family like? I know little about the Stewarts besides meeting them at your wedding. Since you kidnapped me to stay with you awhile, the least you can do is tell me about your family." I yawned, slid down in the seat, and propped my knees against the glove box.

Libby smiled. "Not much to tell, really. Raised Catholic, as you know. Baptized as a baby. My family never ate meat on Fridays or missed a Sunday confession or Mass. But they never criticized those who did. Saturated with religion, the Stewarts are quite like the Olivers in that respect. But they love Ray. I think Maudy and Al preferred Ray marry a girl like you."

"I'm not sure how to take that," I said.

Libby sighed heavily. "Don't take it wrong. Ray and I are on your side. Like Ray says, over and over, he and Joe will always be brothers. I don't have answers for you, Andie, and I can only offer you a place to stay while you clear your head."

"And get sober," I said.

Libby winked. "Yeah. And get sober."

Ray and Libby had moved into the "extra" house, as they called it, at the back of Byron Stewart's property. The ancient farmhouse, painted white and standing in a grove of oak and poplar trees, rested near a stream that eventually emptied into the Haw River. Libby's uncle gave his niece free rein to fix up the place. So while Ray studied for his law degree, he also worked hours to infuse new life into the 100-year-old extra house, repairing its woodwork, heart-pine floors, and drafty windows. The blessing for Libby was the large, enclosed porch that Ray had turned into her veterinary office.

Libby drove up her uncle's gravel driveway toward the house, passing fields layered with fresh manure. Near the tool shed, Byron worked to unclog a geriatric spreader, and in the pastures, his horses nosed for grass. I spotted a couple of paints moseying toward the barn. As Libby parked the truck, I laughed at her orange cat with one chewed ear, sitting on the tilted porch with a mouse in its mouth. I hadn't laughed like that since before Mavis died—it surprised me.

A simple life, and I wanted it. *My* life had paralyzed me with grief and so much sorrow at times to even weep. I fell asleep early that night with no supper and slept hard. My first dreamless sleep in months.

Early the next morning, a weak moon shared the sky with a rising sun, casting skinny shadows behind Libby and me. Walking up the brick path to the horse barn, Libby chattered as if she'd been awake for hours. Opening the barn door, she grinned. "Grab a shovel."

Twice the length and breadth of the main house, the barn's small windows, when opened, allowed drafts of warm air to stir scents of sweet hay, alfalfa, and of the animals. For days, I cleaned stalls, piling manure high, while Libby shoed, walked, brushed, and walked the quarter horses again. Insisting I follow her on rounds to nearby farms, we often trekked a mile or two around the barnyards. Watching my tiny sister-in-law lay hands on sick animals, performing her own healing capabilities, I became a captive audience, along with her big yellow dog.

"We got a cow about to give birth tonight. You interested?"

"Are you kidding? Count me in," I said.

Outside the glowing warmth of the birthing barn, the chilly night air pressed fingers of rain against the windows. As the temperature dropped, a smoky fog covered the ground. I pressed my fingers against the cold glass, remembering the stormy night I gave birth.

The grunt and bellow of the calf beckoned me to where the newborn curled in the straw at its mother's feet. Watching the proud mama lick her baby clean, I experienced a peace I'd not felt in a long time.

Exhausted but triumphant, Dr. Elizabeth Stewart-Oliver patted the cow's nut-brown rump. "You have a beautiful baby boy, Thelma Lou. Good job." Libby picked up the obstetrical handles she'd used earlier, and I leaned against the wall, staying out of the way. Watching the calf, after several unsuccessful tries, wobble to his feet and root for milk, I didn't want the evening to end. Babies of any kind moved me like nothing else, it seemed.

Libby maneuvered in and around the barn stall and was even more stunning in her Levi's, scuffed boots, and denim apron than her church clothes. Descending from old money and a long line of horse people, Libby's family history had little to do with her career choice. She simply loved animals.

"You're incredible," I said.

"And you're crazy. Working in cow, pig, and horse shit all day is *not* incredible."

"Not just that, Libby. You live on this wonderful farm, you're a doctor, and you have Ray, who adores you. It's incredible because it's everything I ever wanted and can't have."

Libby scrubbed her hands and glimpsed over her shoulder. "Ray and I will always love you, whether or not your last name is Oliver. So here it is, all wrapped up in a pretty bow. You chose the wrong man, that's all. The sooner you accept that, the sooner you can get on with life."

"Maybe. Sometimes, I think a demon has dug its claws into me."

Libby shot me a smirky look. "Now you sound like the pious Reverend. *You're* the one who won't let go. What Ray and I have right now is all we need. Even if he never passes the bar exam, we'll be content. We want that for you. Contentment."

"Thanks, I know you do. You put up with me."

"Right, I do. Now, hand me my medicine bag. Let's leave this girl alone with her baby. I'll check her in the morning before we head out on rounds at five."

"In the morning? Are you serious?"

Libby laughed. "You want breakfast, or do you want to sleep in?"

❦

A week later, after another particularly long night watching a broodmare deliver her shiny black colt into Libby's competent hands, I opened one eye when I heard a knock at my bedroom door. My showered and dressed sister-in-law poked her head inside and said, "Morning, beautiful. Want to have breakfast with Ray or go on rounds with me? Miss Verbeena's got a sick cow."

I didn't hesitate. I'd come alive on the Stewart farm. Country and clean air—a life I loved. I hated punching time clocks in drab, tacky offices—stuck under fluorescent lights, stapled to a desk chair, glued to a typewriter. And I hated waiting tables of foul-mouthed truckers or happy couples with children in highchairs. After throwing on my clothes, I bolted down the steps, stuffed a biscuit into my mouth, grabbed a coffee, and waved goodbye to Ray at the table before I ran out the door after Libby.

We rode five miles down a dirt road and turned left at a sawmill. Verbeena Crawford's farm spread over the next hill with a driveway full of ruts that snaked between fenced pastures. Several dozen Guernsey stood in the fields, swatting flies with their tails.

Libby downshifted her truck. "You received a phone call last night?"

"Yeah."

"Was it Joe?"

"No."

"You want to talk about it?"

"No." I rubbed my neck and craned my chin to the side.

"Your business. Don't mean to pry." Libby parked next to the barn. Her dog hopped out of the truck bed to chase a few of Verbeena's chickens. We followed the sound of the sick cow to a straw-filled stall; Verbeena had brought her in early from the pasture. Libby squatted, resting her butt on her heels. She pressed her ear against the cow's belly and groaned right along with the cow.

"What's wrong?" I asked.

"Shhh," she said, patting its taut tawny hide. "I'm hearing—" Libby placed her stethoscope on the cow's abdomen. "I can't tell for sure, but I think it's twins."

"Twins." A shiver shot down my spine. "Lucky girl."

"Don't say that," Verbeena answered grimly. "Twins might do her in."

Libby rose and flipped through a notepad she carried in her apron. "She's due in six weeks. I'll be by in a few days to check her for Toxaemia. In the meantime, monitor her. Call me immediately if she refuses to eat or won't move when you herd her to the barn." Libby handed Verbeena directions on adding supplements to the cow's feed to increase her energy. "See you in a week, Miss Verbeena."

"Send me a bill," she hollered as we left the barn.

"Will do," Libby yelled. With a shrill whistle, she called her dog, and like the great yellow Labrador, I obediently followed her to the truck. Libby's gift was in her voice—able to calm the skittish horse, soothe the injured dog, or ease the wounds of her disheartened sister-in-law. Libby in action was pure magic, and I was dumbfounded by it all.

Chapter 2
Return To Oz
Andie ~ August 1975

In waking early, eating balanced meals, cleaning stalls, and daily walks around barnyards and pastures, I had lost fifteen pounds in a month. My mental attitude brightened living in the rolling hills of Alamance County. Joe had called twice to check on me. But it seemed to make no difference to him I hadn't been home in a month, and he sounded less than enthused when I told him I was ready to return to church.

Finding Libby in the barn feeding the horses, I knew our next conversation might be our last for a while. "I don't think Joe wants me to come home yet."

"Oh, but wait until he sees your new body," she said, grabbing my baggy jeans at the waistline.

"I need to lose another fifty before he notices. I've done this to myself."

"Just be happy. That's why I brought you here, to get happy again."

"I am," I said with a troubled smile. "I appreciate what you and Ray have done for me." I paused. "But—"

"—But what?"

"I told Joe I'm going back to church."

Libby foraged for the right words. "I'm not sure that's a good idea." She worked her pitchfork faster as sweat rolled down her face. "I suppose I see things differently than you," she said as she stopped and leaned against the barn door. "Damn, Andie, what happened? Why?"

Frustration crept up my neck like a feverish hand, and my throat tightened. "It's not that we don't see things the same, Libby. We're married to brothers who are totally the opposite of each other. I see your side. I do. Especially since you brought me here. I left Joe after Mavis died because I thought my marriage was over. Then, after spending time here with you and Ray, I realize I want my marriage to work more than anything."

Libby turned to walk away from me, but I grabbed her arm. "Listen to me, Libby. Locked inside Joe somewhere, is the man I married, and I'm determined to find him. It's true I almost lost my sanity, hoping to find some shred of evidence that he wasn't lying to me again and that he really loved me. But my marriage is far better when I'm in church than when I'm out. Calvin Artury called me here."

"That's the call you didn't want to talk about?"

I nodded. "He assured me if Joe is to be successful for the Lord, we shouldn't have children. He said that's why the baby died, that it was God's will. Reverend Artury wants me to return to church, get involved in the ministry, and maybe even work for him part-time. He said God would heal our marriage. I want you to know I'm no longer putting my life with Joe at risk, and I'm not having kids. Ever."

Libby yanked her arm out of my grip. "Are you crazy?" She didn't buy it. "You're a natural-born mother. Even more than me! You've wanted kids all your life. Why—"

"—It's more than just about Joe! I shouldn't expect you to understand. You didn't grow up in Calvin's ministry. You've never had him lay hands on you and shriek in your face that you'll blaspheme the Holy Ghost if you leave the church. That's been inside my head, Libby, since I was a kid! Nobody's ever called *you* on the phone and told *you* that you're doomed to Hell if you leave your husband. I live with that and the threat of missing the rapture every damn day! I wake up every night in a sweat with Calvin's voice inside my head. Do you know what it feels like to have a personal prophecy screamed in your face? Calvin has made the House of Praise the air we breathe. As much as I hate saying it, I've never had a life outside the walls of that church!"

I glared at Libby, inwardly fuming. I knew she had never experienced the full measure of Calvin Artury's power.

"He prophesied to me on the phone. He said if I left Joe again, I'd die a lonely old woman in a mental institution. That God showed him my death. Calvin repeated three times Hell is my destiny if I lay out of any more church services or abandon my duty to return; he said he saw it in a vision."

Libby shook her head, furiously. "He's out of his mind!"

"Calvin might be a mindless monster, Libby, but how do I know for sure? How do I know? You've seen the miracles happen in his services. So tell me. How do I know it's not me who's got it all wrong? He's controlled our souls, minds, and bodies all our lives. So you tell me, since you're so stinking smart and got it all figured out, how do I stop it now? How!?"

Libby's eyes narrowed, and her face flushed red. "No one would dare manipulate me like that. Nobody controls my life, and I refuse to live in fear! Thank God for my sane family."

"Damn it, Libby! I'm happy for you. But I'll never have what you have here. And if God can forgive Joe, then so can I. I can't give up on him! I just can't! This is the life I've chosen, and it looks like it doesn't include kids. Joe's put up with me staying out of church all this time. He has remained married to me even though I left him with no intention of going back to him. I owe him this."

"YOU OWE HIM? I repeat, are you crazy?! I think you're the one who's put up with *him*! Hasn't he slept with more women than you can shake your fist at?"

Tight-jawed and trembling, I shouted in my defense, my hands and arms flailing. "He's all I got, Libby! Joe is all I got left! I have to make this marriage work, and if Calvin is offering to help me do that, then I'm returning to that church, crawling if I have to, and asking God to forgive me in front of that entire congregation, pledge my loyalty, and say or do anything he wants. I'll kiss Calvin's bare ass if I have to! Don't you get it?"

"No. No, I don't. You *are* crazy. You talk out of both sides of your mouth. You're not who I thought you were." Libby threw her pitchfork into a hay mound and hoofed it into the house.

I called Dixie and asked her to pick me up and drive me back to Salisbury. Leaving the House of Praise for good meant leaving Joe *and* God. I wanted things back the way they were when we were first married. Repenting would either make Joe happy or piss him off because he'd have to make it work. Calvin and I, together, would give him no choice. And better to err on the side of righteousness, just in case. The years I'd fought against Calvin and the church worried me. It was time to get right with God.

⁓

I did exactly what I told Libby I'd do. I returned to the following Friday night church service at the House of Praise. Weakened by my losses, I wept uncontrollably in my seat. When Calvin finished his fiery blast from the pulpit, he called for the sick and afflicted to come forward and form a *healing line*. But as the line formed, he whipped around and pointed in my direction. I stood instinctively, knowing he pointed at me. Instantly, two male ushers rushed to my pew to lead me to the altar of salvation.

Calvin's hands shook above his head as he wailed. "The angel of the Lord stands beside me, speaking into my left ear. He's bidding you come. Come, child, come back to Jesus. Walk down that aisle. Your sins have found you out, and now is your day of repentance. Though your heart is black as coal and your trespasses are scarlet, the Lord will wash you white as the perfect snow. Oh, sinner, come back to Jesus! Backslider, come home to Jesus! Cry holy unto the Lord! His mighty power can set you free. There's power, power in the name of Jesus. Come home, come home, ye who are weary, come home."

Bone-deep instinct from two decades of marathon church services moved me forward. In the tradition of thousands I had watched over the years tread down that aisle seeking salvation, I staggered forward like the broken woman I was. My knees buckled by the time I reached the altar rail. Raging grief tore through my heart with one question. *Why? Why, after losing my baby and then Mavis, why do I have to go through this, too?* I swallowed the scream that rose in my throat. It was not sorrowful repentance, but hope that made me walk that aisle. Hope for love, adoration, and all the good things in life that had evaded me from the moment I married Joe.

"Lift your hands, my dear sister. Mean this prayer, and God will hear you, Andie." Throwing his head back, he directed his prayer heavenward, and I repeated him word-for-word.

"Oh God, save my soul. Take away my heavy load. I'm sorry I sinned against you, but I'm coming back. I'll serve you, Lord, for the rest of my life. Deliver me from all my sins. Set me free, Lord Jesus! I believe You died on Calvary for me, and I believe in Your shed blood. There is power in the blood to wash away my sins—all my sins!"

Swinging his arms, his chin quivering, and stomping his right foot, Calvin hesitated to touch me, as if the moment he laid hands on me, God would send a thousand volts of electricity through him. "Now, Andie, say come into my heart, Jesus. Come in, Jesus!" With an ear-splitting, high-pitched hoot and a holler, he slapped my forehead, and I fell to the floor, screaming for Jesus to forgive me. Forgive me for what, exactly, I wasn't sure, but I felt strangely compelled to cover all my bases, knowing it was required of me.

"If you meant it, Andie, He has come back to you. Jesus is yours. Hallelujah! A backslider has come home!" A victory for Calvin, he reveled in his conquest, jumped up and down, and sang like a squeaky hinge, *"Victory in Jesus . . ."*

Instructing the ushers to raise me to my feet, Calvin grabbed my hands. "Do you want to say anything, my dear, dear sister?"

With tears streaming, I said exactly what I knew he wanted to hear. What they *all* wanted to hear.

I promised loyalty to the cause of Christ, and I swore to assist the ministry as Joe traveled for the Lord with *Reverend* Artury. I confessed into the microphone that *Reverend* Artury was the chosen one to save the world for Jesus and that he was God's vessel for mankind's last hour. Without being coaxed, I even went so far as to say that I believed *Reverend* Artury to be the thirteenth Apostle. Having never called him *Reverend* in the past, I almost choked on the word, but my statement sent up praises and shouts from the members like I'd never experienced in all the years I'd attended his church.

When the crowd settled down, he asked me to promise to submit myself to my husband, and of course, I promised. Calvin then reached out and folded me into his arms, hugged me, and called me his little lost lamb. I felt as if I might suffocate or really and truly faint.

The time and attention he spent with me, I never recalled him spending on anyone else—ever. But it shocked everyone when he called for Joe to join me at the altar, pulling him from his post in the audio control room.

Joe stood next to me at that altar as Calvin laid hands on us, blessed our union, and told us to embrace and show our love as man and wife. Joe smiled, hugged me, and kissed my cheek. I detected his sigh, and yet I dismissed it. I dismissed it because I wanted, more than anything in the world, to believe it was the beginning of a great healing. Healing for soul, mind, and marriage.

A tremendous weight lifted from my shoulders as the congregation cheered for the marriage miracle happening right before their eyes, though few had known it was in trouble in the first place. Like a chemo treatment, Calvin burned out any remaining evil spirits by slapping my forehead one last time. I fell backward because I knew, once again, everyone wanted it. Two male ushers who stood close by gently lowered me to the floor as the congregation sent up more shouts to God for allowing the wayward and backslidden sinner, specifically me, another chance to return to the fold.

As I lay on the carpet, I knew Calvin stood on the altar at my feet. Slightly opening my eyes, I watched as he crossed his arms against his chest and pointed a finger at the congregation. "This happens when you fail God, people. If she had died in a car accident on the way here tonight, she would've raised her eyes in Hell."

Once again, the congregation shouted thanks to the Lord for saving me, but Calvin continued his warning. "She almost didn't make it back. She almost lost Heaven. God almost turned His back on her." He lifted his arms high, threw his head back, and shouted at the ceiling, "Thank You, Jesus! Thank You, that You saw fit to save our Andie from the gates of Hell and the fire of your damnation!" He sang again, *"There is power, power, wonderworking power, in the blood of the Lamb . . ."* making his way to the line of sick and suffering people who had stood patiently for over an hour to receive their miracle.

∽

After my humiliating return to Christ, I followed Joe out the back of the church, my eyes avoiding the stares of those still condemning me for failing God to begin with. Certainly, Julia and Evan Preston were the last people I wanted to see in the lobby. When Calvin elevated Evan to Chief Operations Officer of the television ministry, Julia also elevated herself. I had heard she ran the mailroom and several other megachurch departments.

Joe walked away to speak privately with Evan, his boss, as zipper-thin Julia smothered me in a honey-bun hug and sweet-roll smile. I had no choice but to endure it. I guessed we were the same age, yet she appeared much older with her beige updo that wouldn't budge in a blizzard. Mascara-caked eyes—everything about her was overdone—makeup, perfume, double-knit pantsuit, and square gold earrings the size of tithe envelopes. Nothing about her spoke the truth. I suspected gaudy Julia was a carefully veiled loose woman from her tongue to her toes. Like Maudy always said, *a woman who skipped the chit-chat and strapped a mattress to her back to snag a man like Evan Preston.*

She giggled. "I swear, Andie, you are the most beautiful thing I ever laid eyes on." Overpowering described anything to do with her, and that included flattery. From his pulpit, Calvin once said Julia was a fine example of a Proverbs 31 woman, a woman we ladies should all aspire to. I rolled my eyes every time I thought about it.

Behind Julia loomed Sylvia Turlo, the head usher and wife of Silas Turlo, Chief Financial Officer of Calvin Artury Ministries. A decade older than Julia and myself, her black and white usherette uniform matched her black and white hair, teased and sprayed reminiscent of her high school graduation picture, I was sure. I couldn't imagine two more depressing women. Sylvia's icy scorn flickered in her eyes. "Welcome back, prodigal daughter, to the army of the Lord."

I summoned a smile, albeit a weak one.

Sylvia hugged me like someone would hug a leper, but her deep, man-like voice dripped with honey. "Silas said you were back, and it thrilled me to hear it." A loyal spy for Calvin, she kept a close eye on the lives of House of Praise employees and volunteers should anyone make a move to retreat, quit the church, or slack off in their duties. "Julia and I have prayed for you every day for a year. Haven't we, Julia?" Excusing herself, she had important church business to attend to, she said.

I had always looked at Julia and Sylvia as martyrs. Megachurches, I heard, were full of them. Both sneered at any activity not church-related. The church was their very existence, and they expected the same from all ministry team wives. I heard Julia give her testimony once. She openly admitted to being so busy recruiting volunteers she had no time for picnics, parties, or social events. She spent any free time she could find in prayer, fasting, and submitting to Evan. Everyone laughed when she said it, but I knew she meant every word.

"You ready?" Joe had waited long enough for me to finish my conversation with Julia and wanted to go. She flashed a smile at Joe, then cupped one hand around my chin. "Andie, call me next week. The Praise Buffet serves free sweet tea in July, and we can do lunch. Maybe you'd like to volunteer at the studio or in the mailroom. I think you might like to work in our new state-of-the-art kitchen. I hear you're a wonderful cook."

"Sure," I said, elated to have returned to my husband's arms and heart. But not necessarily to be back in Oz.

∽

I only saw Libby and Ray on a few brief occasions after my return to the House of Praise. It wasn't long before Maudy told me Ray had passed the Virginia bar exam, and they had moved to Richmond. I received a phone call from Ray occasionally. Still, my declared devotion to the House of Praise had created a rift between Libby and me, and I wondered if we would ever be friends again. The Oliver family had fractured a little more, and a little more of my heart broke off in the process.

Chapter 3
A Well-Conceived Plan
Andie ~ March 1976

For three years, Joe had traveled from Salisbury to Winston-Salem and back, eating up gas money, working weeknights, and leaving every weekend on faith-healing Crusades, hoping Calvin would hire him full-time on the ministry team. Even as a volunteer, Joe never took time off. He attended every service and made himself available at a moment's notice. I couldn't fathom why Calvin kept putting it off. It perturbed me only because it kept Joe in a foul mood. Calvin dangled Joe's potential church career like a carrot on a string in front of a jackass.

In the spring of 1976, Calvin Artury scheduled himself and Evan Preston to fly to Nigeria, Africa, for two weeks on business. Prior to their departure, during an unscheduled staff meeting, Evan announced they would begin hiring the all-volunteer traveling ministry team upon their return with one caveat. As a condition of full-time employment, Reverend Artury required a vasectomy of every male employee. He suggested the team use the two weeks of Reverend Artury's absence to notify their current employers and complete the *procedure*.

Joe bounded into the trailer that evening as if he had won an Olympic gold medal. Unable to repress his excitement, he lifted me in his arms and twirled me around the living room. To look at his face, wholly absorbed in pure happiness for the first time since our wedding day, I couldn't help but share his exhilaration. No shadows of sadness crossed his face, and for the moment, I felt enormously relieved that I had made the right decision to return home. Then he told me about the *procedure* and that he had already scheduled his surgery.

But what Joe didn't know was that a few days prior, Julia Preston had taken me to lunch and *let it slip* about Evan's trip with Reverend Artury to Africa. More of a means to boast their hierarchy in the church than anything else. But she believed the team could use those two weeks at home as *vacation* time. A rare gift to an exhausted ministry team.

When I *let it slip* to Maudy, she finagled an invitation for Joe and me to visit her brother, Dodrill, in Atlanta for a week. I'd lost my pregnancy weight since spending the previous summer on the farm with Libby, and I'd put a patch on our marriage by staying in the church and keeping my mouth shut. With Maudy's persistence and resolve to use those precious two weeks to strengthen her son's marriage, Joe reluctantly canceled his surgery and agreed to take me to Atlanta instead.

On our first-ever vacation since our two-day honeymoon, that time away from the pressures of the church was like winning money and prizes on a game show, a trip to Disney World, or front-row tickets to a Bee Gees concert. Driving the six hours to Uncle Dodrill's house, I felt no burdensome chains of grief choking my thoughts for the first time in years. My tears evaporated in the onrushing wind, riding along with the windows down. Courage and determination were like a rock inside me again, begging for a slim chance of genuine happiness.

Dodrill Lee stood on his front porch, bald and covered with freckles. I waved from the car as Joe parked between rows of live oaks and crepe myrtle. Looking at Dodrill was like looking at Maudy. Twins who descended from old money, mostly gone, Dodrill inherited the house and land and had squandered the rest of it, Maudy had said.

After catching up, Uncle Dodrill showed us around the house and grounds and said to make it ours for the week. Spacious and clean, the antebellum two-story resembled the house I grew up in, only run down and desperate for a woman's touch. He employed a Black maid and a Mexican gardener. An "illegal immigrant," he said with a smile. Dodrill gave us a room with a connecting bathroom and pointed out the entire house was air-conditioned. In my estimation, it was better than a cheap motel.

By suppertime, Joe held my hand and stroked my back. He took deep breaths and sat in one place for over five minutes without needing to do something work-related. A miracle. But he'd been confrontational for so long that I found responding to his sudden show of affection challenging. I had forgiven him, but forgetting what he had done to me wasn't easy. Nevertheless, I knew if I wanted to remain married to Joe Oliver, I'd have to find a way, once again, to live with the past and stay submissive in my future.

Exploring the hundred-acre farm after supper, Joe pulled off and parked the car in a meadow of tall grass. We sat and listened to the wind and the shrill song of a Whip-poor-will.

"Makes me sleepy," I said.

Joe picked up my hand from the car's seat and kissed it. "Makes me want to forget about so many things," he said. Not wanting to break his sudden spell of euphoria, I didn't ask what he meant.

Like a cathedral ceiling of glittering colors and light, an archway of live oak covered our stroll as we explored a world different from the one we knew. Softly fragrant and chocked full of sweetness, the air blew cool and refreshing. I had forgotten how good country air made me feel.

Warm and in full bloom, spring had come to the Deep South. Joe and I climbed a steep ravine packed with kudzu and knotted as tightly as a latched mat. Laughing and tripping over tree roots, we heard water to our left. A creek tumbled down a gentle waterfall, spilling over skillfully placed river rock. We stood on that hill, holding each other, taking in the quiet and peacefulness of a moment we had never experienced together, and I wondered. *Did he never realize there is freedom outside of Artury's church?*

Walking back to the meadow where we had parked, we stepped over and around thick underbrush that lay nearly impenetrable on all sides of us, as if God had spread an enormous swatch of deep green velvet over the ground. Wildflowers sprouted from every dip and mound, and I picked a bouquet of Queen Anne's lace for our room. Joe pointed to webs with giant spiders asleep in their silken hubs, and as always, the ever-present hum of cicadas rode high in the treetops.

The idea of a life like the one Mavis led was no more a part of me than moving to Antarctica. The daydreams of my youth flooded my head again. Dixie had always called me an old soul. I was born for a country life, a slower pace. I wanted it for both of us. I hadn't thought about it in a long time, but I imagined our dream house again. Closing my eyes, I saw it sitting inside its picket fence at the back of Dodrill's property, where the woods opened up, and the creek swelled into a swimming hole.

At sunset, I held Joe's hand while we lounged on the veranda, gazing across a pond at the bottom of a long slope of dogwood and mimosa. Trout heads nipped the surface for food, creating ripples that floated to the water's edge. Vibrant sunrays bounced off the glassy pond, shooting hundreds of sparkles into the air. The fireworks continued until the sun sank behind the tree line. We heard Dodrill call his dogs for supper. A night heron sang, and I watched lightning bugs glow golden in the dark. I had all but stopped thinking about my life in Salisbury.

That first night, Joe and I crawled naked into a soft, cool bed. It felt glorious not to move from a sweat-soaked spot to a dry one. Air conditioning was a luxury we couldn't afford at home. Joe had said if his parents did without it for years, so could we.

It wasn't long before Joe pulled a rubber out of the suitcase and laid it on the bed. I stared at it. Pill or no pill, when it came to birth control, I knew Joe would never trust me again. When we began having sex again, he took no chances and always pushed me away unless he had on his rubber.

"Why do we have to use that?" I asked.

He shook his head. "We've argued about this for years. You know why."

"That's not what I mean."

Joe sat on the side of the bed. I could count his ribs and see the sharpness of his hip bones. Having just finished another twenty-one-day Bible fast, he had wanted his constant praying and fasting to send a clear message to God—to speed up his hire date with Calvin. Joe's piercing green eyes swept over me as he reached for his Trojan. "Almost ready," he said.

"What I mean is, I hate how that thing feels in me. I always have. It hurts."

He stopped priming himself. "Damn it, Andie. You sure know how to throw ice on the moment. Can't you talk dirty or something?"

Glaring at his silhouette through the dim light from the bathroom, I scarcely heard him. All I wanted was a child to love. Just one child. He had carved a niche for himself with Calvin and his band of marauders. Joe found his reason for living. And as much as I didn't want to believe it, I knew it wasn't me. Hiding my anguish, I took the rubber from him. "Can this piece of latex really keep me from getting pregnant? A girl at the bank said she got pregnant even though her husband used these."

Joe yanked it out of my hand. "Unless they're defective, they work fine."

"But it's so thin. You're sure it works?"

He ignored me. I wanted him to know I tolerated it. That it was painful, not pleasurable. After a minute of watching my face wince while he thrust away at me, he stopped. "It really isn't good for you, is it? You've already been pregnant. How can this still hurt you?"

"It just does. It's uncomfortable. I told you, I've always hated them."

"We haven't had sex in a week. You might pretend to enjoy it, at least."

I watched Joe peel off the Trojan. I suspected he liked how my body felt, like when I was eighteen; the only difference was a few faded stretch marks and the thin purple scar that traveled from my navel to my pubic hair. Pulling me on top of him, his hands on my bottom, he sucked at my breast like a giant, red-spotted puppy. I felt the tip of his bare penis slide between my legs, and my thoughts became tangled with desire and those of motherhood.

Despite my feelings, insecurities, and all I had realized about my husband, I knew if Joe were gone, there would never be another man in my life. Refusing to consider I might make the same mistake twice, I allowed my desire to take over. I also knew my chance for another baby was gone forever after Joe had his vasectomy. Holding my breath to keep up my courage, I forced his penis inside, and something happened. I moved into positions I never had before, giving him the erotica I was sure he fantasized about. He wrapped his arms around me, making no attempt to pull out. I became determined to give him the best sex of his life, better than any woman he'd been with.

It seemed I succeeded. His hands explored me as if I were new to him, parting me, sliding into the depths of me. I trembled and gasped. He moaned as he entered me, again and again. I pulled him tighter between my thighs and arched my back. The soft roundness of my breasts pressed against his chest, and he shuddered in the dark. In the past, Joe had never felt the need to kiss me during sex, yet I gave myself freely to the passion of his mouth, the first such passion I'd felt from him since our first few weeks of marriage. I claimed every kiss, and afterward, he kept on kissing me softly.

"Andie?"

"Yes?"

"Did you?"

"Did I what?"

"Enjoy it."

"Yes. Very much."

"Did you—?"

"—Come? Yes."

But I didn't. Joe never waited long enough for me to have an orgasm. Only a few times in our marriage had I experienced it. What I really wanted from him was love and a few minutes of his time. At that moment, however, it didn't matter. I had something else on my mind. "Why can't we go rubberless every time?" I asked.

"No way, Jose'. We can't take another chance like that."

We can't because YOU don't want children.

I rolled next to him and trickled my fingers down his back. "I'll douche it out. It won't stay in. It's much more enjoyable for me when it doesn't hurt." Snuggled beside him skin-on-skin, I had offered him the believable repetition of perfect sex from a new and improved wife.

Joe nodded like a schoolboy. "Go do it now. Get it all out. I don't want any accidents. But I suppose you're right. It is nicer for me when you're not lying there like a corpse."

Returning from the bathroom, having done nothing to remove the possibility of a child, my cool skin covered him like a sheet fresh from the line, my eyes wide and pleading. I kissed him again. "No rubber. Just on vacation. A few days, and that's it." I watched him nod, yawn, and close his eyes. Overwhelmingly victorious, I smiled in the dark, cool room as the drone of the air conditioner lulled us both to sleep.

Away from home, Joe woke every morning in a grinning, pensive mood. I reveled in it. We ate well, and he put on weight. His skin tanned again, and I felt certain every available woman at the next Crusade would attempt to attach herself to him like lice on a first grader. I worked hard at enticing him to stay an extra day. But as the end of the week neared, his mood changed. Of course, he refused to talk about it, but I knew him well. He had thought about his job, the church, and of losing his position. The fear of it constantly plagued him.

Joe's anxiety took us home a day early. I suspected unless my husband walked Calvin's straight and narrow, he would one day find they had replaced him as Chief Engineer. Joe's longing to return to work proved he never intended to wander far off that path. He had a relentless fixation on his job, and as long as his youthful stamina held up, Joe would remain faithful to his beloved Reverend.

But I'd seen tough men turn tender around their children. I had to believe Joe could, too, if he had a child who loved him. The first anniversary of our infant son's death had just passed. What better way to repay the demons who stole our first child than to conceive a second one? I was sure Mavis agreed. Those precious few weeks before Joe's surgery were my last hope for motherhood, and the one thing I knew how to do best—was hope.

Chapter 4
Aunt Wy
Andie ~ May 1976

The original volunteer ministry team, including singers and musicians, began full-time employment on May 1st. Evan Preston had delayed it a month to ensure everyone got their *procedure* done, as it was not an option within Calvin's inner circle.

Knowing his congregation wouldn't entirely approve, Calvin insisted it remain hush-hush. He never mandated the *procedure* from the pulpit to the membership, but I knew many of the young, engaged men to be married at the House of Praise. Some had a vasectomy after private counsel with their *Reverend*, and some, I heard, flat-out refused.

Joe had insisted on re-scheduling his surgery before we left for Atlanta. But I held Joe off until Calvin agreed to pay for it. Medical insurance was not an employee benefit at the House of Praise. Also, like many other megachurches, the House of Praise did not withhold social security. Calvin informed his staff not to worry. The rapture would take place before we needed retirement money.

Finally, Calvin's secretary called me, and I relayed the news to Joe.

"Fannie told me to send the bill to the church. When I contacted the clinic they indicated the doctor's schedule is full until the end of May," I said hesitantly.

Joe leaned back in his recliner and crossed his feet. "Do you realize I'm out of a job until I have this done? Hopefully, Coot will keep me on at the shop until then. I'm holding you responsible if Reverend fires me before I even start! I shouldn't have listened to you and re-scheduled it myself."

"We don't have the money to pay for it, Joe. It costs five hundred dollars. I needed a payment commitment from your employer. We discussed this."

"No, you waited until I had to scream at you to make the damn appointment!"

I ignored his hissy fit and washed the supper dishes. I had missed my period in April and wanted to have unprotected sex as many times as possible. A missed period in May meant only one thing. My wish had come true.

"By the way, Andie. When are you getting a job? Reverend isn't paying me enough for you to stay home."

"No kidding," I mumbled. I had discovered Joe agreed to an income from the House of Praise that wasn't much more than he made working for Coot. Joe had wanted to work for his *Reverend* for so long that he took whatever they offered.

"I found a job," I said.

"What?"

"I said I got a job. Candace Cooper hired me. Part-time."

"The Shady Acres whore? That trashy woman still owns a beauty shop in town?"

"Yes, and she isn't trash. I used to think so, but people aren't always what they seem. Besides, you liked her plenty until you discovered her age. She's been sweet to me since our baby died. And she moved her shop. She's renting space by the Kmart. Asked me to work three days a week. Answer phones, make appointments, and sweep up hair. Simple stuff. And Julia Preston wants me to volunteer in the mail room at the church the other two days."

I dried the last bowl and wiped off the dish rack. "If you need me, I'll be across the street talking to Candace about my new job. Before I forget, your mama's having a surprise party for you next Thursday night to celebrate your new hire with Calvin. Act surprised." I slammed the door behind me. I'd been in a pissy mood for days. I had no desire to help Maudy with Joe's party and didn't care a bit about Joe's crossover into full-time employment with Calvin. In fact, I didn't plan to attend the celebration at all.

The women worked around the large table like quilters at a quilting bee. Outside the mailroom, office doors stood open, and conversation spilled out to the hallway, creating subtle and pleasing background noise.

Kitty peered across the table. "I love attending the miracle Crusades, don't you, Andie?"

You'd have to drug me and drag me. Opening the mail, I ignored her and did as Julia had instructed. Placing prayer requests in one pile and letters that contained offerings in another, I could not answer her honestly. I had no desire to see Calvin act a fool in Atlanta, Philadelphia, Nashville, Chattanooga, Little Rock, Memphis, Boston, Cleveland, Denver, Los Angeles, or any other city where he'd parked his pretentious pulpit. My commitments, promises, and tolerance had faded in the weeks since my chastisement in front of a bloodthirsty congregation.

I sat across from Kitty Childress and Maxine Pruitt. Proud ministry team wives who wore their lonely lives as medals on their lapels and had created their own club—a sympathetic group of Joe Oliver supporters.

Kitty seemed determined to capture my attention. "I'm sorry, Andie. Have you been to a Crusade?"

"No. Not yet."

The two team wives eyeballed each other.

"I've gone back to work, and I'm too busy on the weekends," I said.

Maxine's cheesy grin nauseated me. "Do you miss sex when Joe's out of town?"

I nearly fell off my chair. *It's none of your damn business.* I nodded politely. *Do you miss having a brain in your head?* I had kept my weight down, and although Joe was not as attentive as he'd been on our trip to Atlanta, we made love at least once a week.

"Maybe, Andie; if you went to a few Crusades, maybe you and your husband would be happier."

"What do you mean?" I asked sharply.

Kitty poked her friend in the side. "Hush, Maxine."

Shoving my unopened stack of mail to the middle of the table, I pressed my piles of prayer requests and offerings into the provided folders. Like an underground newspaper, gossip ran rampant in this church that preached so adamantly against it. I couldn't endure another minute in the stuffy mailroom with my insolent mail-opening partners. I carried my folders to Julia Preston's office. "I'm going home, Julia."

Julia's shoulder held a phone to her ear. A quick flick of her wrist signaled her goodbye as if I were nothing but a fleeting shadow crossing the room.

I flicked my wrist back at her and rolled my eyes, hoping she saw me. Living in a constant state of irritability was not like me. Every damn person at the House of Praise got on my last damn nerve. Cussing like a truck driver was not like me either, but fuck that shit. I picked up my coat and purse and walked out without saying another word. I couldn't help but wonder if Kitty and Maxine traveled to the miracle Crusades only to keep a watchful eye on their husbands.

Opening my car door, I glimpsed down at the volunteer clearance badge that had caught on my sweater. I had forgotten to turn it in. Turning around, I ran back into the mailroom in time to hear my name spoken, which stopped me in my tracks behind a row of metal shelving units.

"Poor Andie," said Maxine. "She has no idea her husband doesn't love her." Maxine dumped a new mailbag of letters on the work table. As unattractive as her personality, she had big hair, a big butt, and an even bigger mouth.

Kitty poured a cup of coffee at the snack table. "How do you know that?"

Maxine settled her wide rear end on a mauve-colored secretary chair, smiling as if she were privy to secret information. "Joe told my husband last week, and my husband tells me everything."

"My Earl adores *me*," Kitty believed out loud. "But why doesn't Joe love Andie?"

"Andie Oliver will never get right with God. Can't you tell? She's not into saving souls. Not like us. Not as dedicated to the ministry. She won't go to even one Crusade. Reverend will find Joe a proper wife someday. Julia said that Evan told her that Reverend wants the congregation to see Joe as the good husband that he is. When Andie backslides again, and you know she will, their divorce will be her fault. She will have failed God for the last time, and Joe will be free to remarry. Reverend will see to it."

"I never want that to happen to me and Earl," said Kitty.

"It won't, honey. We support Reverend Artury; we've sacrificed for the ministry's good. Given our husbands to the Lord. A wife like Andie, who can't decide if she's in or out, that girl deserves the hell she's headed for."

I threw my badge on the floor and retreated to my car. My life went around in circles of regret.

✑

Maudy's surprise party was mild compared to Coot's keg party for Joe the night before his surgery. Against the instructions of Joe's doctor, Coot and the old gang from the pool hall bought Joe enough beer to drown his sorrows for a month. The following morning, my hung-over husband paced back and forth, cracked his knuckles, and bit his nails to the quick. Calvin gave him three days off to recuperate. I had no sympathy. I hoped it hurt like hell and told him it probably would.

The clinic had scheduled Joe's *procedure* for nine a.m. After a quick kiss goodbye, I left Joe alone on a table, his penis taped to his stomach, his legs draped and spread as if he were ready for a pap test. I giggled all the way to the women's clinic on the opposite side of the building.

"I'm Andie Oliver, here for a pregnancy test." The grin never left my face.

Dr. Eshelman had moved his practice to Charlotte, so I was searching for a new obstetrician. One who accepted payments. I figured the outpatient center was an excellent place to start. I peed in a cup, and they confirmed my suspicions in a short time. The clinic doctor examined me internally, finding my uterus naturally swollen for an eight-week pregnancy. He handed me a slip of paper with a due date—on or around Christmas.

I was officially pregnant.

I paid my bill, received my lab results, and walked to the outpatient waiting area. Two hours later, a nurse wheeled my woozy and nauseous husband to the recovery room.

"How are you feeling, honey?" I held his hand as he weaved in and out of consciousness.

"I should've stayed away from the beer last night. How long was I out?"

"You weren't out; you just don't remember it. But long enough."

"Andie?"

"Yes?"

I stood beside him, his hand in mine, waiting for him to say, *I love you* or *thank you for coming with me,* but he didn't. Known for his meanness when drunk, Joe became a monster when drugged. "Fuck you," he said, slurring his words. "You'll never have a baby now. Not by me, at least. I'll never have to worry about it again. Despite what you did to me before, I won. You get pregnant after this—it ain't mine, and you can fuck off." He laughed a sick, feeble chortle, reeling from pain medication mixed with the previous night's alcohol.

My eyes narrowed, and my anger seared hot. After the previous week's ridicule from team wives in the church mailroom, I wasn't about to take it from Joe. Not anymore.

I leaned over and whispered into my husband's ear. "Do you remember what Dr. Eshelman said at my last appointment? You were with me, remember? He said I wasn't to take birth control pills for a while. To give my body time to heal. And do you also recall you haven't worn a rubber during sex for the past two months? I mean, I sure as shoot couldn't put one of those things on you. You remember all that?"

"Yeah, so?" Suspicion sparked in his eyes like torches in a cave.

"Calvin knows I'm not on the pill. You told him, remember? You tell him everything about us."

Joe breathed deep, long breaths and squinted like he was about to be struck in the face.

"See this piece of paper?" I shoved the lab results in front of him. "I had a pregnancy test in this clinic. Today. While you were getting your nuts cut off. I'm eight weeks pregnant. Due on Christmas. Must've got pregnant down at Uncle Dodrill's. So, guess what? This time, I guess it's *both* our faults. Calvin will be happy, don't you think?"

Staring with a potent mix of horror and disbelief, Joe grabbed my wrist; his eyes rolled back in his head. He nearly passed out before I pulled out of his grasp. I stuffed the paper in his shirt pocket on the recovery room door, then stood at his feet, away from his reach. "I called Maudy. She's coming to take you to her house. I don't want to wipe your nasty ass. You never offered me so much as a hug after my accident and losing our baby. Stay with your mama until you're on your feet. I'm going home. See ya."

A Kleenex box flew past my head as I walked to the door, missing me by a thumb's width. "You fucking cow!"

I spun around.

Blood dripped down his chin. He'd obviously bit through his tongue or lip. His nostrils flared with fury, and his eyes blazed. A sinister smile spread across his face when Joe laid his head back on the pillow. His lips thinned. *"Vengeance is mine, saith the Lord,"* he said.

I sauntered back to him, keeping my distance, and threw my next words like rocks. "I'm sorry to be so insensitive in your hour of need, *dear*, but I might as well tell you. The doctor here, the one I saw today, he heard two heartbeats in this cow's womb." Raising my hands, I mockingly tilted my head toward Heaven in praise. "The Lord's seen fit to bestow His vengeance on you a second time, Joe. With twins."

A nurse at the clinic scribbled several doctor referrals on a piece of paper, and when I arrived home, I glanced at the list, spotting a name I knew. *Wylene Rose Oakley, M.D.* It was my aunt. It had to be. I didn't know she was a doctor. In fact, I was completely unaware she was alive. Dixie hadn't mentioned her in ages. Wylene Rose wasn't a name one heard often.

So I called.

A pleasant female voice answered the phone. "Greensboro Medical Group."

"Um, hello. My name's Andie Oliver. I found out today that I'm pregnant. I'm looking for a new doctor. I'd like to make an appointment with Dr. Oakley."

"I'm sorry, Dr. Oakley is not accepting new patients."

"But—she's my aunt. I think. Please, may I speak to her? Tell her Andie Parks is on the phone. She'll know me by my maiden name."

"Please hold."

The seconds passed like hours. As I waited, I thought about Joe. Maudy probably had him propped up on pillows. She hadn't asked me to join them for supper, but I had every intention of showing up while Joe convalesced in his old bedroom. I wanted to break the news to the Olivers while they babysat their son. I needed their help to soften Joe on fatherhood before I had to deal with him alone. It pissed me off I had to *deal* with him at all. But I would not go through another hellish pregnancy with him. Not again.

I waited on the phone.

Maybe I'd jumped the gun. Maybe Wylene didn't want contact with our family. It had been over twenty years since any of us had seen her. Suddenly, I regretted calling.

Wylene's scratchy voice interrupted my thoughts. "My God, is this really Andie Rose Parks, firstborn of Dixie Anne?"

I giggled. "Sure is. It's nice to meet you again, Aunt Wylene, even if it's on the phone."

Wylene rushed to the point. "So, you need a doctor?"

"I'm eight weeks pregnant. Confirmed this morning, and yes, I need a new doctor."

"You had an old one?"

"Dr. Otis Eshelman from Lexington. He moved to Charlotte."

"Know him. Great doc."

"Yes, yes, he was."

"So, you have a little one at home?"

My pregnant pause pulled on my heartstrings. "He passed away shortly after birth."

My aunt said nothing momentarily, then cleared her throat. "I'm sorry to hear that. Then, by all means, you need to see me. I'm the best."

"That's good to know."

"Well, bust my hump! I'm finally talking to family! I'm putting you back on the phone with Debbie, my receptionist. Make an appointment."

"Thank you. Thank you so much, Aunt Wylene."

"You're welcome, darlin'. By the way, are you married?"

"Yes, ma'am. Nearly four years now."

"Good. See you soon."

Debbie miraculously found a cancellation slot for the next day. My excitement at meeting the infamous Wylene Rose kept me awake all night. Determined to avoid Dixie's wrath, I decided not to break the news to my parents until after my appointment with my new doctor.

In a medical building annexed to the hospital, Wylene's office smelled like cough syrup and mimeograph paper. I signed in at the receptionist's window and sat on one of the green vinyl chairs in a sparse waiting room next to a metal rack of dog-eared magazines and a plastic fern.

Flipping through a back issue of *Redbook,* I glanced up at the peeling plaster. That's when the door opened. She had come to fetch me on her own. Filling the entire doorway, the full-figured, big-bottomed woman with reddish-blonde hair hinted at a sharp tongue and a flaming temper. A prominent, undisputed doctor whom none dreamed of disobeying. My mother once said her sister's husband died early in their marriage. I saw no ring on her man-sized fingers. It didn't take a brain surgeon to see what kind of woman she was. Holding a cigarette in her hand, her face wreathed in smoke, Wylene appeared curious. The creases in her forehead gave her the look of an intelligent woman. One who spent too much time in deep concentration.

"Aunt Wy?"

Wylene's eyes shrunk to tiny brown dots, and she nodded. "Come on in. Let's take a look."

I walked to my aunt, kissed her plump, splotchy cheek, and followed her inside.

Wylene told her receptionist to clear the rest of the morning. My aunt sat behind her desk and sighed. "I'll be damned. You look like a smaller version of me when I was your age. Except you got them big blue eyes. I never understood how you ended up with blue eyes." She held up her Virginia Slim. "Hopefully, you've taken better care of yourself than I have. You know what they say about physicians being the last to heal themselves? Damn, these cigarettes will kill us all in another twenty years."

I brought my aunt up to date on the family. I talked about my sister, whom Wylene had never seen. But she recalled Mavis as a little girl. She remembered I shared a crib with Mavis at Dixie's house when Rupert and Loretta Dumass visited. Wylene took a deep breath when I relayed the chilling details of Mavis's death. And then of my child's.

"Hope you don't mind," she said. "I drove to Lexington last evening. I know the office manager there. Doc Eshelman and I go way back. He hasn't moved his entire office to Charlotte as of yet, so I was lucky they still had your chart."

"I'm glad you cared enough to actually go get it."

"Andie, this is my dream come true, to see you again. You were two, maybe three years old, the last time I laid eyes on you. I hope our relationship as doctor/patient will be okay with your mama."

"Dixie doesn't know I'm here."

Wylene smiled. "It's interesting you call her Dixie."

"Caroline and I always have."

"Well. It's up to you, darlin', whether or not you tell her about me."

I shifted in my chair. "What happened, Aunt Wy? Can you two ever forgive each other?"

My aunt sat back in her chair. "In my youth, I saw life in black and white. The shades of gray came after life had kicked me around a few years. I'm willing to bet Dixie still sees everything in black and white. You need to remember this, darlin'. Sisters never forgive one another. Usually, they just pick up where they left off. What happened was Dixie's temper. And mine. We said things we didn't mean. Made from the same mold, us two. But we're as different as we are the same. The flamboyant sister that I was and am, I think Dixie cringed with shame around me. And her jealousy didn't help our situation."

"What do you mean by that?" Aunt Wy's story had me glued to my seat.

"My foster parents, who eventually adopted me, lived on the wealthy side of the tracks. They allowed me the privilege of attending college and medical school. Dixie had numerous foster parents, none of whom were kind or wanted to adopt her. But hey, she ended up with Bud: that's worth all the degrees hanging on my wall over there. Then your little brother died—it was a bad time for all of us." She sighed. "When Dixie's baby died in '56, I decided to become a doctor, specifically an obstetrician. Now, here I am."

I nodded. "My mother never talks about her life as a girl. It's taboo."

Wylene cleared her throat and pulled her rimless glasses down from the top of her head, changing the subject. "I see you haven't any health insurance. Is that still the case?"

I told her the short version of Joe and his employer, Reverend Calvin Artury.

"We won't worry about payment until after your baby is born. Or babies, as the case may be. Right now, let's head down the hall to the exam room. I need to examine you internally." Wylene shook her head and then spit it out. "Good God. How did you get hooked up in that god-awful church? I've heard stuff about that place. Seems like half my patients go there. No, don't tell me. Dixie dragged you to Sunday school as a kid. We'll discuss it later."

I followed her down the tiled hallway. "I want to go natural."

"You sure about that?"

"Aunt Wy, I want to be awake and see my babies born. The natural way."

"That's a tall order, darlin'. I've studied your chart. You suffered during the birth and death of your first child. I'm taking the safest route to deliver your twins—if that's what you've got. I'm not saying it can't be done, just that it's risky."

I suspected my aunt was not in the habit of arguing with her patients, but I wasn't any old patient. I was family. And clearly bull-headed, like her.

An advocate for natural childbirth, Wylene made me promise to follow a strict diet and exercise routine—to the letter of the law. Her law. She drilled explicit instructions into my thick head. If I missed one appointment, there'd be Hell to pay. My pregnancy was considered high-risk because of my medical history. She'd never lost a patient and said she wasn't about to start with me.

Under normal circumstances, Wylene would've referred me to a colleague. But it appeared I wasn't normal by a long shot. And I had no money, no health insurance, and a set of twins on the way. Considering the trauma I experienced the previous year, the good doctor would not risk leaving me in anyone else's hands. I also suspected she'd inquire about my deadbeat husband later. Having no children of her own, her eyes filled with tears before she left me alone in the exam room to undress. "I'm happy you're here," she said.

Gratitude swelled in my chest. Aunt Wylene had returned to my life, and Dixie could like it or lump it.

∽

"Okay, let's see what we got." Wylene closed the door with her foot, then covered my knees with a warm blanket, keeping my top half draped and bottom exposed. "I'll agree with natural childbirth, at least for now. I may change my mind as we progress. You understand that?"

"Yes, thanks." I believed if I were fully awake and there, nothing wrong would happen to my babies. The cold table shocked my bare back. Spread eagle, feet in the stirrups, I shivered.

Wylene snapped on her latex gloves. "You understand the risks?"

"Yes."

"Good." Sighing heavily, she palpitated the outside of my abdomen before laying a freezing stethoscope on my skin. "Yep, two babies! Heartbeats sound good. Blood pressure looks good. Drink lots of water and take those vitamins. Is that clear?"

I nodded and sucked in a breath as she inserted two cold, jelled fingers into my vagina. I tightened up. She laughed and said, "Hold still, darlin'. We're just getting started. Ah, Doc Eshelman did a fine job on you. I must commend him. The cervix feels normal and looks good."

Wylene finished examining me and patted my bare butt. "All done. Get dressed."

"Aunt Wy!"

"What? I remember the last time I changed your diaper; from where I'm sitting, your lily-white behind still looks the same to me."

I got dressed and then opened the exam room door. Wylene's heavy footsteps stopped at the door frame. She leaned against it, her large hip forming an armrest for her man-like hand. She had powdered her face and applied fresh lipstick, a frosted pink that only emphasized the lines around her mouth. Her brows looked like brown caterpillars, and her big, round brown eyes made her face appear doe-like. She wore more white under her white lab coat, from the enormous bow holding back her long, wiry hair to the stacked heels sticking to her swollen feet. She was one giant snowball. A wall of white polyester. *How did she get through medical school?* I imagined her piss-and-vinegar attitude was a fortress of self-defense against the young and privileged men in her residency program.

Wylene removed her lab coat and suit jacket. Her slip strap fell to her elbow. The dark brows rose, and she spit her gum into a nearby wastebasket. "I'm going on a smoke break. Want some lunch?"

Chapter 5

SURRENDER

Andie ~ May 1976

After spending the morning and afternoon with my aunt, I slipped on a T-shirt and cut-offs and drove to the Oliver's house. Opening the back door with a hesitant smile, I flopped into a kitchen chair and rubbed my eyes with the flat side of my hands. It had been some time since I'd visited my in-laws, which made this visit even more difficult. Al appeared dusty and tired, his overalls tinted with rust. Maudy's familiar housedress, wrinkled and worn, was missing a button.

Maudy nodded coldly. "Andie."

"Joe in the backroom?"

"Uh-huh," she said, sipping her coffee.

For the first time in my life, they did not welcome me with warmth. Even the house felt cold, like a basement in winter. I tiptoed down the hall to Joe's old bedroom at the back of the house and found him, as I suspected, on a feather comforter. His eyes closed; he had guzzled several bottles of Coke, read a stack of Hot Rod magazines, and laid open his Bible on the nightstand.

"Joe? You awake?"

He opened his eyes but did not return my smile. Instead, he rose on his elbows like a dog sitting on its haunches and motioned with his head for me to come near as if he might kiss me. Surprised, I side-stepped to the bed's edge and leaned toward my husband.

Quick, like a cobra, he spit in my face. "Get away from me!"

I jumped back, spun around, sprinted down the hallway, and fell into a chair beside Maudy. Grabbing a napkin from the ceramic daisy napkin holder, I wiped a fair amount of saliva from my face and hair.

Maudy's tone softened, knowing what Joe had done. "What did you say?"

"What did *I* say?" I held out the napkin. "After he literally spit in my face? Are you serious? You coddle him any more than you do, and I'll find you breastfeeding him the next time I come over."

"Andie!"

"You baby him, Maudy. You always have! He's a grown man! I'm eight weeks pregnant in case he forgot to tell you." I stood to leave. "By the way, it's twins."

"Twins?" Surprise drained the blood from Maudy's face. The tension lessened. Maudy took in a sharp breath. "Ah, now, he'll change. This is wonderful news, sugar. I'm sorry. I don't understand why you wanted him to come here instead of taking him home to care for him. Isn't this good news, Al? Twins."

Al nodded and raised his eyebrows, but said nothing.

I swallowed my despair. "He'll change? When, Maudy? When will Joe change? What is a Christian man supposed to act like? Do they all spit on their pregnant wives? He's cruel and insensitive, and the worst thing is—he knows it! You keep saying he'll change, but he's worse. Maybe you can talk some sense into your son. And some manners."

Al wiped his mouth with a napkin and then closed the door to the hallway so our voices didn't carry to where Joe moaned with an ice pack on his groin. "I've had enough," Al said. "I'm calling Reverend. This nonsense has to stop. Andie, I assure you, next time you see your husband, you can take him home where he belongs and get the husband you deserve."

Standing at the open back door, I wiped well-deserved tears from my eyes. "After all this time, I doubt it. I'm not sure I can live with him any longer. But it's my fault as much as it is his. I should've never gone back to him after Mavis died."

Maudy's mouth dropped open. "Please, Andie, a baby needs his daddy. Don't give up on Joe."

I shook my head and crossed my arms.

"Oh, please. Stay for supper, sugar. I got smoked sausage in the skillet and lima beans in the pot, one of your favorite meals." Maudy's feeble apology was like trying to heal a child's boo-boo with a kiss.

"Thanks, but I need rest. I start a new job tomorrow. Please drive Joe home by Wednesday. I'm sure Calvin wants him better for next weekend's Crusade."

Maudy had drawn a hard line. She was no longer my confidante. I sensed a noticeable difference in my mother-in-law's affection toward me. Blood was, after all, thicker than water.

Al had indeed called the church, as he said. Word got back to me by Maudy that Calvin was furious with Joe and that her beloved son had spent the better part of an hour on the phone cowering under Calvin's rage, leaving him humiliated and quiet with defeat. On Wednesday, Maudy drove Joe home to Shady Acres. But my attempt to talk to him was fruitless.

Joe scowled at my light-hearted talk and turned away. "Stop, Andie," he said. "Just—stop. Your fru-fru bullshit conversation does not make me feel better. I'll never be what you want. But

Reverend made me see that it's both our faults. Let me get through this on my own, and quit talking to me non-stop. I've got a lot on my mind. Reverend told me to accept it. I said I would try. So you got what you wanted." His hand swatted me away like I was an annoying insect buzzing about his head. "Now, leave me alone."

Chapter 6
A Date That Will Live In Infancy
Andie ~ December 1976

Working at the Tease Me salon for Candace was a breeze. Macrame plant holders filled with dusty silk ferns hung around the shop's perimeter like ratty ponytails. The windows dripped with humidity, and she had covered the walls in posters. Large headshots of models sporting the latest perm, cut, and color. Glass and chrome shelving separated my workspace from four stylists, two sinks, and a manicuring station everyone shared. Although the wage was minimal, Candace's playfulness and sense of humor got me through the first trimester, the sick part, filling my days with laughter and free regular haircuts.

"Walkin', after midnight . . ." Hearing Candace bellowing out *Patsy Cline*'s song before she opened the door made me smile. The last words fell tunelessly from her lips as she hollered a *howdy-do* to somebody in the parking lot. Still the queen of poufy, her bleached hair curled down to her Barbie-doll breasts, which bulged above a lace brassiere that showed through her too-tight T-shirt. Tar Heel-blue stretch pants clung to every curve in her tiny butt and long legs, and her signature western boots clicked on the tiles as she wiggled through the door with coffee and a box of Krispy Kremes.

Glaring at Candace, my skin felt hot and tight. Embarrassed and annoyed, I'd already gained forty pounds. I smoothed back my hair and ran my palms over my stonewashed denim tent, second-hand and, like a lukewarm Christian—covered in spots and wrinkles. My entire pregnancy wardrobe had come from a local thrift store in Fashion Maternity Hell. Ungracefully, I pushed my big-bellied body out of my chair and stood. "No more donuts; what'd I tell you?"

Candace set the box on the counter and picked up a rat-tail comb to scratch an itch on her head. "Oh, stop. You look good."

"Yeah? Well, your belly's flat enough to iron my dress on. What do you know?"

Kicking inside the fertile cave of my uterus, the babies grew quickly, like a tiny rosebush with two buds. Pregnant all over, especially in my legs, I walked with a back-and-forth gait, like a penguin, unable to balance the mass of *baby* taking me over. Joe had yet to accompany me on a doctor's visit to see Aunt Wy. He met her, finally, on Thanksgiving, a day of firsts. The first time Joe had seen my parents since the death of our son and the first time Aunt Wy enjoyed a holiday meal with her family in over twenty years.

Dixie and Wy indeed picked up where they left off as if no time had passed between them, and Joe promised Wy to accompany me on my next appointment. Later, I called Daddy to commend him for his civility toward Joe. "I figured you've walked on enough eggshells, Rosebud. Besides, football got me through it. Thank God for the Cardinals and the Cowboys."

Aunt Wy's receptionist read me Joe's rambling, panicked message as I signed in. *Please tell my wife and her aunt I had a church emergency and can't make the appointment. I've got to catch a plane. I apologize.*

Blushing as I stepped into Wylene's office, I stood there, not knowing what to say moments before her phone rang. Wylene waved *come on in,* excusing herself to take the call. Relieved, I parked myself in a chair. After she said goodbye to *Doc,* who was obviously a colleague, she mashed out her lipstick-smeared cigarette and unleashed a coughing fit. Getting herself under control, she pushed her chair back and wheezed in quick breaths. "I'm down to a pack a day," she said. Shuffling through a few files before drawing her eyebrows together into a frown, she looked up and said, "So. Where is the little bastard?"

"There's a meeting somewhere. They had to catch a plane."

Wylene leaned over her desk and ran the tip of her tongue across her lips as if to collect her thoughts. Her face reddened into angry blotches that traveled fast down her neck. Then calmly, she said, "When I first laid eyes on your husband, I thought, what an attractive young man. He's polite and cordial and even uses the right fork. But hell's bells, Andie. He's shallow and selfish. I don't want him in labor and delivery. Hear me. You need love and support in that delivery room, and he has none."

I shrugged. "I can't imagine why I expected him to show up."

"Did you really think this pregnancy would save your marriage? It didn't work the first time; why did you think it would *this* time?"

"I'm selfish, too, I suppose. I wanted a child. I tried not to want kids, Wy. I did. It was useless. Now, I have no choice but to pay the price for *these.*" I shivered at my words. "I hoped if he were with me during the birth, he might, oh, I don't know—change? Find some love in his heart for his children. For me." My tears fell on my aunt's desk.

Wylene tossed me a Kleenex. "We'll talk about this later, after you're on your feet. You don't need Joe to bog you down mentally right now. Find a labor coach. Anyone but him."

I sniffed and blew my nose. "I've asked my friend, Candace. Somehow, I expected this."

I also expected to someday watch my aunt rip Joe a new one. In fact, I thought I might enjoy it.

At twenty-two weeks, the babies had grown so big that Wylene had to sew up my cervix. At thirty weeks, the stitches started to snap. Except for doctor appointments and trips to the toilet, I was on mandatory bed rest to ease the possibility of premature labor. Thank God for Candace, who lightened her schedule at the salon to care for me. According to Wylene, the twins would've had more room if I had stayed on the prescribed diet, a challenging request considering my sweet tooth. And then the contractions started around week thirty-one, as many as twelve an hour. With only medicine and sheer will holding the babies inside, my uterus went about its business contracting, releasing, and preparing for the blessed event.

At week thirty-seven, my pains started again. Excitement and fear reached new heights as I lay in bed, listening to rooftop lullabies from the morning's pelting rain. It shimmered in stripes of light under the streetlight. As the next pain hit, I screwed up my face and bore down, watching myself turn crimson and purple in the mirror over my dresser. Twelve minutes later, at the next contraction with the veins distended in my neck, I called Aunt Wy, then Candace, and finally, I called Joe at the church.

I met Joe at the door in mid-contraction with my suitcase in hand. Forcing a smile, he appeared concerned as his eyes met mine. Until he opened his mouth. "You picked the worst day for this. I take one afternoon off to help Coot pull an engine out of a tough-looking '68 Stingray, and then you call me at the church. Fannie had to phone me at Coots." Clearly irritated, he excused himself to take a shower. Which irritated *me*.

Joe took his time in the bathroom. I couldn't wait any longer. I walked through the steam to use the toilet. "My pains are ten minutes apart, but my water hasn't broken yet."

He offered no compassion. "Don't flush," he said. "Wait until I'm out of the shower."

"If you didn't want to take me to the hospital, why not stay at Coot's garage?"

Joe stuck his head out of the shower. His look of exasperation raked my skin. "Don't start that crap," he said. I heard him sigh deeply, as if trying to compose himself. "Have you picked out names for these kids?"

His contrived sympathy got on my last nerve. Amid a strong contraction, I clicked my tongue. "Did you think I would wait until the last minute? The last time I waited for you, you weren't around. I named Brian by myself. Daddy and I picked out names for the twins last week. *Not* to worry!"

Joe stuck his head out of the shower again to glare at me.

I met his eyes and flushed the toilet.

"Damn you!" he screamed, flinging an empty shampoo bottle at my head. I ducked, and it hit the bathroom door. "I swear, you were born to torment the hell out of me!"

Wanting to respond with a vindictive ferocity that fully matched his own, I bolted out the front door instead. As fast as my impregnated body could move to the car, I had to calm myself down. Sitting and waiting for him to drive me to the hospital, I had only two thoughts. My babies took priority over the abused woman I had allowed myself to become, and Joe could suck it.

I didn't bother to give Joe the look of pure infuriation I'd planned after he threw my suitcase into the trunk and slammed the lid. I wanted to get there in one piece. He drove to the hospital like a taxi driver—without saying a word or giving me any sign of his feelings. It felt strange and sad in some cosmic sense; I sat next to a man I called my husband and, at that moment, couldn't see him, feel him, or care. I tried to relax and concentrate on my breathing. In. Out. Each contraction hit hard, the pain unleashing memories of my previous labor.

Clouds, the color of a deep bruise, built on the horizon. Rain-covered cars approached from the other direction with their headlights on, and as we drove into Greensboro, the squall hit. Goose bumps covered my arms from the cool air of the defrost. The windshield wipers slapped back and forth as the rain stirred up more terrifying memories of the crash, the flash flood, and crawling out of the deep ditch, injured and in the throes of hard labor. But Joe only stared straight ahead, wrapped in his thoughts, while I timed the prickly silence between us and the minutes between my pains.

My contractions were eight minutes apart when Joe wheeled me into the emergency entrance. I fought against the seismic urge to tell him to *go to Hell*. Smiling with relief when Candace appeared in the waiting room, I let go of my urge and focused instead on the miracle inside me. Candace stepped beside my wheelchair, her boots clicking out a familiar beat on the hospital floor. "Let's do this!" she shouted.

A nurse took the wheelchair from Joe and pushed me down a long, polished hallway to an elevator. Sweat dripped from my forehead and clung to the short hairs pulled from my ponytail. I looked up at Joe and sighed. Standing there, he watched the nurse roll me into the elevator and nodded something meant as a quick goodbye, allowing the doors to shut between us.

My babies took their own good, sweet-patootie time. More sweat plastered my stringy hair to my neck and cheeks as Candace blotted her face first, then mine, jumping from one subject to the next and hollering, *breathe!*

"Baby number one is all wampy-jawed," Candace said, as I winced in pain.

I looked inquisitively at the nurse, who took my blood pressure. "Face up instead of face down," she explained.

One hour rolled into the next as vicious contractions sliced through my groin. I shut my eyes while my hands crawled over my stomach and the inside of my thighs. When the umpteenth contraction ended and my eyes opened, Dr. Wylene stood overflowing in her shoes by my bed, surrounded by young nurses. Poised in a lime green suit under a white lab coat, her face oily, a pen over her ear, and her hair frizzed out of its bun, she said, "Are we enjoying our beautifully, wonderfully, totally natural experience yet?"

I stuck out my tongue and gave her the finger. She threw her head back and roared with laughter, rotating on her heel to leave the room. The nurses quickly smothered their smiles and followed her, but at the door, she turned back, and for a quick second, she smiled and said, "Strong women, Andie—may we know them, may we raise them, may we be them." After blowing me a kiss, she left the room.

The following two hours passed in a blur. I remember little other than the nurses transferring me onto a rolling bed, clicking the rails into place, and wheeling me under the searing lights of a ball field. I reached for Candace. "Where are we?"

"Surgery. Everything's fine," she said, holding tight to my hand.

Wylene, in full surgical gear, examined me. "Andie, sweetheart, I'm giving you a spinal block now. Then we'll see what happens."

"Just get them out!"

My aunt laughed and patted my belly. "Not only are we getting them out, but you also get to watch the entire performance in living color!"

Candace helped me sit on the side of the delivery table, my legs dangling. "You've got to be having a contraction when Wy inserts the needle, honey." She encouraged me to hang on. I dug my nails into the shoulders of the nurse standing in front of me, anchoring me through the procedure. Her sympathetic eyes sparkled above her green mask that covered her nose and mouth. Bearing down, I felt like I was sitting on my baby's head. In seconds, my water broke, pouring to the floor and into the nurse's shoes.

Candace hollered. "The dam burst over here!"

I lay back on the delivery table, my pain unbearable. Closing my eyes, I tried to conjure my vision of the hands. Those peaceful hands beckoning me as I suffered from the pain of Brian's birth and death. I kept my eyes closed tight, yearning to see them again. The hands with the missing left ring finger. The hands that soothed me amid utter sorrow.

Listening to the footsteps of nurses marching in and out of the delivery room like a Marine battalion, I felt the numbness take over. From the waist down, I didn't exist. The nurses carried out their orders. They draped, swabbed, and quietly relayed my vitals and that of my babies to Aunt Wy. What seemed like days was only a matter of minutes when twin number one turned, and everything around me shifted into high gear.

I saw Candace thoroughly enjoying the moment, asking dozens of questions until I wanted to stuff her facemask in her mouth. The laughing and joking quickly subsided when Wylene sat at my feet. She was all business as slippery baby number one, crowned and cracked through the shell of my womb. It was more than a beautiful experience. The room exploded in blinding white light for one split second, letting me know I had once again laid at death's door to give life.

A boy. In minutes after his birth, my baby boy lay against my heart, and I counted his fingers and toes, traced the precious curve of his puckered ear, and thought of Brian. Blowing a kiss to my sweet new son and rubbing his back, I felt tears run down the sides of my face, pooling in my ears. Without warning, a nurse snatched him off my stomach, and I reached for him, calling him back the moment before the next contraction hit.

"Next one's coming down the chute. No time to stop now!" Wylene shouted orders like an Admiral at the helm. Bearing down again, I groaned deep and long as another little head crowned. Within minutes, my baby girl took her place on my stomach.

"A girl! Candace, look, a girl!"

"A big girl. This lil' piglet's got more meat on her than her brother," she said.

My fingers gently stroked my baby girl's face and tiny hands.

Candace pulled her mask down and kissed my cheek. "How blessed you are! One of each. Your heart's desire." And there it was. The one word that suddenly blared inside my head. *Heart.*

I panicked. "Check their hearts, Wy, please. Tell the nurse to listen to their hearts!"

"Andie, these babies are fine. We'll give you a full update in a minute. I did not detect any heart arrhythmia prior to birth, nor do I suspect any now." Wylene ordered the nurses to report the date, time, and birth weight as soon as they had it.

"December seventh, ten thirty p.m. for baby boy, and ten fifty-two for baby girl!"

Wylene laughed. "December seventh—a date that will live in infancy!"

I listened for shouts from the nurses. "Baby boy is six pounds two ounces, six pounds six ounces for the girl." Almost thirteen pounds of baby in my body.

Wylene patted herself on the back. "Ain't bad for one day's work," she said, stitching me from the inside out.

A few minutes later, a nurse shouted from the next room where my babies were trying out their lungs. "Apgar score of nine for each baby, Dr. Oakley!"

"See there? Near perfect, I'd say!" Wylene peeled off her gloves and dropped them on the delivery tray littered with gauze pads, bits of suture, and a little piece of umbilical cord. She cut off the middle fingers of her bloodied gloves, stuck them inside her bask, and handed them to me. "A souvenir," she said, kissing my forehead. And then my aunt whispered into my ear as she smoothed the hair off my brow. "We were lucky, Andie. I won't be able to patch you up again. Be happy with these two, darlin', because you're done."

"I know. Thanks, Wy. I owe you."

The nurse asked if I had the babies' names for the record.

"Dillon Wayne and Gracie Mae," I replied.

Horribly bloated from the pregnancy and pee-yellow from an adverse reaction to the spinal block, I lay enormous and unattractive against hospital-white sheets. My wedding rings cut into my sausage-like fingers, my bangs hung in my eyes, and my long, scraggly hair fell tangled on either side of my cream-puff face. But my ears were open way before my eyes, listening to the soft shuffle of nurses, Candace's constant questions, and the cries of babies from down the hall.

Candace's voice sounded dry and sharp as two sets of footsteps entered my room. "Hey, Joe." She paused. "And you are—?"

"—Pastor Tony DeSanto."

Joe spoke up. "Pastor, this is Candace Cooper."

He filled the air with well-chosen words. "Nice to meet you. I understand we have you to thank for assisting her doctor in delivering the babies the way God intended when they said it could not be done."

"It was in God's hand from *conception*," she said.

"Where are they?" Joe asked. "Where are the babies?"

Someone stepped toward my bed. "Is Mrs. Oliver sleeping?"

Candace knew I'd be in no mood for the feigned concern of my pastor. "Off and on."

"She looks like she's had a rough time of it. Don't wake her," he said.

"I wasn't planning on it."

Joe's voice rang with agitation. "Candace. I repeat. Are the babies in the nursery?"

"No, Joe. They walked down the street to order a pizza. Hell yeah, they're in the nursery. Where do you think they'd be? Obviously, Candace was in no mood to watch her language, either. I kept my eyes shut but imagined Pastor DeSanto and Joe exchanging glances of disgust.

"Excuse me, Pastor. I'm going to the nursery," Joe said, attempting to smother his Southern accent.

"When you're done staring at the babies you didn't want to have, get back here and be kind to your wife," Candace said curtly as she left the room.

Joe cleared his throat. "She's Andie's friend. Not mine. And she's not saved."

The brazen pastor whispered loud enough for me to hear. "Satan has covered that woman in spiritual darkness. I suggest getting your family back in church and keeping them there. Watch Andie—what she does, where she goes. Keep her safe in the fold." His words, veiled as a request, were more of a subtle demand.

But then, the Tasmanian devil blew into my room. "Joe, get your butt to the nursery and see them babies of yours." I cracked open one eye. Aunt Wylene, her eyes ablaze, stood with her fists nestled so deep into her fleshy hips they all but disappeared.

Joe bolted out like a third-grader summoned to the principal's office.

"The little ones?" asked Pastor DeSanto. "They're doing well?"

"So far, so good. A nurse can show you to the nursery window if you'd like." Wylene examined my chart.

Pastor DeSanto grinned. "I can't believe I'm standing next to a famous female doctor, who I understand might be the next Hospital Medical Board president. You—"

"—Don't patronize me, Pastor. I don't care for your contrived flattery, and I don't play ball with pretty-boy preachers. Furthermore, I'm not about to go to your church or give you one damn dime. I answer to a higher power than your buddy, Calvin Artury. If you'll excuse me, I have patients to attend to."

I opened both eyes and smiled. "I see you met my Aunt Wylene."

Pastor DeSanto stood slack-jawed with his Bible in his hand— as if bitten by a junkyard dog. "She doesn't hold anything back, does she?"

"Nope," I said. "That's why I love her."

❧

Dixie and Daddy arrived the following day and wheeled me to the nursery.

"There, Daddy," I said with a smile, pointing to my twins behind the glass. "Dillon Wayne. You did well naming him."

"You don't mind if I named him after Matt Dillon and John Wayne?"

"Course not. You love those old cowboys."

"Rupert will love that you named Gracie after Mavis Grace," he said.

I thought of Mavis then, hoping she could see my babies. "They're good names, but aren't they the most beautiful babies you ever saw?" I watched my parent's reflections in the window.

Tears fell down Daddy's face and onto the nursery window ledge. He smiled. "Almost as pretty as you were."

"Prettier," said Dixie.

Chapter 7
Double Your Pleasure
Andie ~ March 1977

I had wedged a changing table next to the kitchen table and shoved a tiny chest of drawers against the trailer's back door across from the bathroom. Dixie slept on my couch five feet from the babies' crib, which I had squeezed into a living room corner. Exhausted by the end of the week, Dixie called Daddy to take her home. Caroline, newly married and pregnant with her first child, helped a few days after Dixie returned home. Our mother insisted she get some on-the-job training.

And then Maudy came to help. During the day, she was a blessing, but at night, I worked solo. Consumed by the constant care of my infants, I had finally filled my life with purpose and meaning as my days and nights became indistinguishable.

My weight climbed to new heights as the pregnancy had taken its toll on my body. I felt stretched out, like an old leather shoe. Purple stripes lined my underarms, stomach, and back, and the fat on my abdomen jiggled like a tub of sour cream. Swollen with milk, my breasts leaked while my joints ached from giving birth to twins. I felt, in a word—ugly.

Meanwhile, Joe used every excuse imaginable to stay away from home, becoming increasingly indispensable to the House of Praise. He held the babies for pictures Maudy insisted on sending to Uncle Dodrill, but quickly returned them to me afterward. He often worked around the clock at the church or followed Calvin every weekend to whatever city booked the next big Crusade.

I forced myself to church on Sunday with no one's help, only to keep the peace while winter dragged on. The four-hour services were simpler to manage in the nursery, where I claimed one of ten cribs lining the wall. The large glass-enclosed balcony above the sanctuary served as a perfect buffer between the congregation and me. They had piped in audio, but with screaming babies, nobody listened intently. Sitting upstairs in that soundproof room, I ignored the whole church ordeal, but I showed up as promised to my husband, his parents, and Calvin.

At home, glass bottles boiled three times daily in the sterilizer on top of the stove. My babies created buckets of dirty diapers. The only hope for clean ones was sending them to Maudy. Al became my deliveryman for everything from laundry to groceries while I spent the first cold, dreary months of 1977 inside my trailer at Shady Acres.

By March end, Maudy and Candace took turns babysitting while I packed as many errands into my time alone as I could handle. My world of bathing, feeding, and diapering my twins included long nights with either Dillon or Gracie or both crying for hours. Joe learned how to sleep through their endless nights of bawling, but I walked the floor with a tiny one in my arms, a baby cheek to my lips, acquiring little sleep myself.

When I could sleep, I didn't. Instead, I stood at the crib with its mobile of smiling, bald-headed moons and watched every move my babies made. For months after I brought them home,

I imagined Mavis and Loretta bending over Heaven's balcony, totally captivated by my twins. In time, the hole Brian left in my heart healed over. All that remained was a ragged scar, sensitive and tender, but no longer painful.

Spring came, and then summer rolled in with its blast of heat and bright blue skies. Dillon and Gracie grew into chubby, squealing babies who demanded their mama's attention and got it. Joe insisted I return to work. But Candace had sold her beauty shop to the highest bidder to stay home and care for her teenage daughter, who needed her. The thought of office work nauseated me, but I had to try. Promising Joe, I'd look for work; I checked the classifieds every Sunday and mailed resumes I'd typed on a borrowed manual typewriter. *It won't be so bad,* I told myself. *I'll never move out of this trailer otherwise.* Cramped beyond belief, I yearned for more space.

The twins were healthy, full of energy, and filling lots of poopy diapers. Their drooly smiles lifted my spirits, eliminating thoughts of Joe and my plans to leave him. My babies were my life; they were my loves, and Joe observed it all from a distance until one day when he thought no one was watching. Whispering sweet words to each baby, like he once did to me, he picked each one up. First Gracie, then Dillon, touched their little head and kissed them.

It was that moment, that tiny shred of hope, that once again turned me on my heel. I would stay with him a while longer.

The call came. "Andie, we'd like you to start work on Monday." Southern States Insurance Company reviewed my resume. After a telephone interview, they hired me for essential clerical work. A full-time position paying six dollars an hour, and I accepted. Then something grabbed hold of my heart and twisted it. How could I leave my children with a stranger?

I tiptoed into the living room, where Gracie and Dillon shared a crib. Their milky-white hands curled like pudgy little paws against a freshly laundered sheet. *The Long and Winding Road* played softly on the stereo. The twins filled every void in my life with their chubby legs and perfectly shaped heads. I couldn't get enough of them. I touched their soap-scented skin with the tips of my fingers. Their cherry cheeks, vanilla eyelids, and entire bodies constantly reminded me of the miracle that had occurred within me despite the odds.

Exhausted, I sat on the floor, leaned against the crib, and nodded off while the summer's warm breath billowed through the curtains around the open window.

While Joe had yet to change a diaper, I juggled childcare between two days with Maudy and three days at the Methodist Church Daycare in Lexington. My strength gave out by Friday. I filled my Saturdays with washing clothes and diapers in a Hotpoint wringer washer on the Olivers' back porch. Maudy had long ago refused to buy a washing machine. The grueling work of hanging every piece on the mile of clothesline that zigzagged in the backyard by Al's shop drained my energy. Pampers were a luxury saved for church.

Daddy drove to Salisbury every Saturday evening, bringing bags of groceries and gallons of milk. My mother showed her love by sending along homemade pies or cakes. A diet became an impossible project for me, knee-deep in babies and working full-time.

I was a married, single mother. I said goodbye to Joe every Friday, while my overwhelming impulse to ask for a hug or a word of kindness hit me like a brick in the chest. Starved for attention and any love I could drag out of him, I desperately hoped he didn't notice the effect he had on me. Over a year had passed since having any physical contact. Other than accidentally touching arms or shoulders, we squeezed through our small living space like roommates who didn't like each other. But watching his car pull out of the driveway on Fridays, my reality didn't take long to sink in. I had babies to care for. They took priority over Joe, my self-pity, and his incessant need to follow the illustrious Reverend Artury around the country like a puppy dog on a short leash.

Chapter 8

JIM JONES MASSACRE
Andie ~ November 1978

I turned up the volume on the TV. At almost two, Gracie fussed and squirmed while Dillon tugged on his ear in the crib. Both babies had developed upper respiratory infections. After wiping my daughter's little nose, I placed a bottle in her mouth, gently rocking and patting to quiet her. The evening news with Walter Cronkite brought the first shockwaves to the world that religious leaders and their megachurches could be deadly.

"Today, followers of American cult leader Jim Jones and the Peoples Temple died in a remote South American jungle compound in British Guyana called Jonestown. They shot some members and forced others to drink poison, but most willingly took part in what Jones said was an act of revolutionary suicide."

The hair on my arms stood straight up.

"California congressman Leo J. Ryan received many complaints from his constituents regarding family members who were followers of Jones. He responded with an investigation. Having received permission from Jones, Ryan traveled to visit the group's compound. The congressman toured the settlement and met with Jones. Yesterday, Temple members passed notes to Congressman Ryan's

party, requesting to leave with them. Ryan agreed. Under Jones's orders, gunmen from Jonestown ambushed Congressman Ryan's party at an isolated airstrip. They immediately fired on Ryan and four others, killing them instantly. Some of the Ryan party escaped into the jungle."

"Jones then ordered the 'state of emergency' he had so long expected. A carefully rehearsed mass suicide took place. Everyone, except the few who escaped into the surrounding jungle, committed suicide, or were murdered, including over 280 children. Authorities found Jones in Jonestown, fatally wounded by a gunshot to the head."

I shuddered as fearful images built inside my head.

"Jim Jones began his ministry in 1953 as an independent minister in Indianapolis, but by the end of 1971, he had moved his congregation to California. His main church remained in San Francisco, but he opened a second church in Los Angeles. The Peoples Temple peaked earlier in this decade to include 8,000 members."

"Jones was once a popular community activist who contributed cash and coordinated volunteers to support causes and political leaders."

A cold wave of familiarity pulsed through me.

"Jones recently appeared with many prominent politicians, including State Assemblyman Willie Brown. In 1976, Mayor George Moscone gave Jones a seat on the San Francisco Housing Authority Commission. Governor Jerry Brown had also attended church services at the Peoples Temple. Today, after the 914 tragic deaths at Jonestown, Willie Brown said, 'If we knew then he was mad, clearly we wouldn't have supported him...'"

If we knew then he was mad. If we knew then he was mad… the words played repeatedly inside my head.

Calvin's House of Praise had grown steadily as he and his ministry team traveled the world, now spending as much as six weeks away from home at a time. Every week the television mega-ministry flourished, and the renowned Reverend's popularity increased by mega-leaps and mega-bounds.

But apparently, he was as cautious as he was charismatic and had no intention of starting a commune in a third-world country. He assured his congregation at home and his TV audience that he believed Jim Jones to have been demon possessed.

Calvin Artury would never make the same mistakes as Jim Jones. Yet this news had struck me silent, leaving me with one question: *Could Calvin be worse?*

Chapter 9

OPPORTUNITY KNOCKS
Andie ~ August 1979

I was to celebrate my twenty-fifth birthday in two days. The twins were approaching age three, and life in Salisbury remained the same—cramped, poor, lonely, and hot.

Working a full-time job, I learned quickly I could not support two children and myself on my pitiful salary alone. Though I despised Calvin all over again, I knew he was the one person holding my marriage together. As long as I showed up for church every Sunday, he would not allow Joe to leave me stranded, and I needed my husband's entire paycheck more than anything else from him.

Years before, I made the horrible mistake of staying in a loveless marriage. I found myself in a vicious circle. A predicament I couldn't get out of. A bed I made that I now had to lie in.

Interrupted sleep had become part of my life for the past three years. I had no time to challenge Joe, the church, or my long-forgotten dreams. I felt fortunate to find my purse and car keys in the morning. But I charged into every new day, believing God's rising sun would somehow light my path to a better tomorrow.

☙

August temperatures hovered in the nineties, and with humidity, you could drink. Dillon and Gracie fussed at night, rolled on sweat-soaked sheets, and repeatedly woke for water. I took a long weekend off work, hauling the twins and twin paraphernalia to my parents' house to escape the high temperatures of the trailer park for a few days.

Arriving at noon, I spied Daddy with his banjo on the front porch with his dog at his feet. The old dog fidgeted and settled his gray jowls on crossed forepaws. His hoary eyebrows twitched, keeping tabs on the world around him.

I reached down to stroke his long back. "Hiya, Pitch." At the sound of his name, the dog—which resembled a lean bloodhound with sleek black fur—looked up and wagged his tail despite his infirmities. I rubbed his silky ears and wondered if Pitch ever had hopes and dreams. What did he hope for or dream about? Maybe all Pitch knew how to do was wait. Patiently. For food, shelter, and love. I knew something about that.

I flopped into the wicker chair next to my father. "I can't take it anymore, Daddy. I've got to have a house with trees and an air conditioner. Somewhere the twins can play outside on a swing set, in their own yard, under a shade tree. I'm sick of doing laundry at Maudy's house and can't afford the laundromat. I've got to move to Winston-Salem, get a better job, and find a house. If one twin sleeps in the crib, the other sleeps with me in the bed. Joe, since he's not home much, well, he gets the couch."

I was not about to say it'd been over three years since we had any physical relationship. Obviously, Joe got his needs met elsewhere.

"What would Joe say if you proposed moving to Winston-Salem?" Daddy asked.

"He insists on staying where we are. Says it's all we can afford. Of course, he's never there. He travels in air-conditioned buses and stays in spacious hotel rooms."

"Let me give this some thought. You know Caroline and the baby are moving in with us? And she's pregnant again."

"I heard. I'm sorry things have gone badly for her. Little Bonnie isn't much younger than the twins. It's awful what Caroline's going through." But as far as I was concerned, fighting alcoholism in a man was far easier than fighting a man's god, especially when that god was Calvin Artury.

Pitched blinked his soulful eyes and yawned. He shifted but didn't stand, his hips so painful that he moved only when my mother made him. She declared he was an animal that Daddy should carry down behind the shed along with his shotgun. Indeed, Dixie only saw life in black and white. You worked hard and lived well, then you died. There was no gray area. But I knew Daddy loved Pitch. He'd never shoot his dog or allow anyone else to do it. Suffering was a divine calling for him and Pitch, and he was bound and determined to prove his point. I saw myself following in Daddy's footsteps, not in the physical sense, but in the spiritual.

The next evening, I relaxed, grateful for my parents' help with two fidgety, inquisitive, and perceptive three-year-olds. I treasured my children's innocence, their clean smell, and the taste of their peachy-soft cheeks on my lips. They kept me in a sane boat tied to a solid dock when, otherwise, I would've drifted far from the rocky shores of rationality and sensibility.

Gracie clung to me, but Dillon's curiosity and spirit of adventure kept me running. Eventually, the weight melted off my size 18 body. No one noticed as I shrunk. The excitement of looking attractive seemed as silly and frivolous as accent pillows and ankle bracelets.

I walked out to the porch where Daddy played Cripple Creek on his banjo for the twins until Dillon crawled onto his lap, begging to hear another ghost story. Gracie held tight to my legs and tucked her bashful face behind them. My little girl had become a thumb-sucking growth on my side.

"Gracie," said Daddy, "c'mon over here and listen to Grandpa's story."

She walked in front of me with her hands behind her back, then leaned into me again. "Go on, honey," I said. "Go sit by Grandpa. I'll bring you some cheese, okay?"

When I returned from the kitchen, Gracie had perched herself on Daddy's knee and about sucked the skin off her thumb. Daddy tilted forward, looked each grandchild in the eye, lowered his voice, then burst out with a *boo!* As always, Gracie shrieked while Dillon squealed for more.

I set a slippery plastic pile of yellow cheese near Gracie. She held her slice by the end, taking a tiny bite of cheese and then dropping crumbs on the porch. I started cleaning up after her when Dixie stepped out to join us.

"Let the child eat. I'll sweep it up later."

Guarded, I watched my mother tickle Gracie's belly, who pulled up her little knees and folded in on herself, squealing and giggling. I sat in amazement as Dixie kissed Dillon all over his chubby face again and again. I suspected she loved her grandbabies far more than Caroline or me, as I could not recall a time when she showed that kind of affection toward either of us.

"Your daddy and I have been talking." Dixie collapsed in the chair next to Daddy the way she always did. As if she wanted you to know relaxing wasn't something she did or that any woman should do. "You know we love these babies. I agree with Bud— even though Caroline is moving in and costing us a small fortune, we need to give you a down payment on a house."

Moved to tears, I lifted Gracie back onto my lap. "Oh, Dixie, I—"

"—Hush. It's our gift to you, not Joe. The house has to be in your name only. We're not so sure Joe will be around in the future, and I don't want the two of you fighting over it. These children need a home, something other than the junkyard you've lived in for the past seven years."

My emotions were mixed as we worked out the details. I was grateful for my parents, who cared enough to rescue me from poverty, yet embarrassed that I needed *rescuing* in the first place. Unfortunately, I understood it would take Joe's paycheck and me working overtime to pay for a house.

Three days later, I asked Maudy to babysit moments after Joe called to tell me choir practice was canceled and he was on his way home to get some much-needed sleep. This rare opportunity to talk business with my husband, whether or not he wanted to, needed to be seized immediately.

The conversation quickly turned bitter. I fought hard against the tears and bit my lip to stifle the outcry, but it was useless.

"I need security!"

"I don't give a damn what *you* need. You need your head examined if you think I'm moving closer to your parents!"

"Do you sincerely believe we can raise our kids in this trailer? We've got to give them a place to play other than a patch of dirt in a trailer park!"

"You should've thought of that when you brainwashed me into not using a rubber!"

"You should've thought about brainwashing when you went to work for Calvin!" I bolted to the bedroom.

"Good God, Andie!" Joe showed no sign of relenting.

I clenched my jaw to kill the sob in my throat. My skin prickled with resentment at the detachment that ran clear in his voice. Lying on the bed, I had not finished pleading my case. I stood, and my feet hit the floor like meat pounders. I stormed back into the kitchen, where Joe sat at the table reading Calvin's latest book, *The*

Deceived and The Damned. He had taken to reading Calvin's books and tracts like a starved animal.

He looked up. "What now?"

I felt pain and loss twist inside me again. "I'm not stupid, Joe. You've been unfaithful to me since the twins were born and before that. Why does Calvin excuse it? Do you honestly think God winks at your carefully hidden infidelity? Your adultery?"

With a visible force of will, Joe's composure surprised me. His lips twisted into that cynical smile he had perfected, and he raised one brow. "Have you not heard a word of what I've told you these past few years? I used to worry about a lot of things I didn't understand. Not anymore. Reverend speaks the gospel truth. He is my Shepherd. I am his sheep. He preaches private sermons to the ministry team when we're on the road. That's why you're so deceived. The enemy has saturated you with darkness; you don't listen or care about what God has to say."

"I care what *God* says, not Calvin!"

"Okay, how about this?" Joe quoted scripture, his voice dry and emotionless. "*And David took him more concubines and wives out of Jerusalem.* The men of the Bible had many wives. God allows men things women cannot have, according to the scriptures. Women are not even supposed to preach. Did you know that?"

"You can't be serious!"

He spoke with quiet iron control—his face almost unrecognizable. "Your fat ass is staying in this trailer in Salisbury, and I want you to leave me the hell alone about it."

Quoting scripture one moment and cussing the next came naturally to Joe. His insults were no longer shocking, and I forgot about them almost as fast as they flew out of his mouth. I simply swallowed my hurt. "Then what about *our* children? They cannot grow up here!"

Once again, he gave me that disturbing smile. "Like I said, you should've thought of that long ago. You accuse Reverend Artury of manipulation, but everything you do is to manipulate me into something I don't want." Then he did what he always did to win an argument. He stood, grabbed his car keys and jacket, and stormed out.

A war was going on in Joe's accent as he battled to unload his redneck persona. To my knowledge, he had stopped smoking and drinking. He'd become a religious zealot. Quiet and cold as always, Joe had submerged himself further into the teachings of the church and its leadership. His whereabouts were unknown to me for weeks at a time, only calling home occasionally from Crusades all over the world. And since Calvin despised public scandal of any kind, I suspected he gave Joe no choice but to play the role of husband and father in front of the world.

At home, Joe rarely spoke. But when he did, he told me I spoiled the twins. *Ridiculously overprotective* were the words he used. I didn't care what he thought. I knew every crease in their necks and every dent in their knuckles. My life with my children was profound and inseparable. The twins and I had our own secret language—a dialect Joe heard but didn't care to learn.

Chapter 10

PANTS IN THE FAMILY

Andie ~ October 1979

Saturday morning's air chilled with the season's first frost. The real estate agent arrived at Daddy's house early. Mrs. Greer—the only name she gave—waited in the car. I left the twins with Dixie, who made me promise to get back before noon so she could finish the second coat of wax on her floors.

We headed to Turner Street in Winston-Salem, driving past poor, stunted homes that hadn't seen a fresh coat of paint since Eisenhower was in office. Houses that didn't concern themselves with lush lawns, pretty porches, or roof repairs. Mrs. Greer's car coasted until it came to the *for sale* sign on the corner, where a small red brick house stood stiff and alone. The place looked forlorn and run-down: the painted white trim and eaves peeled like blistered skin, and the porch sagged in the middle.

I pictured a tired, swayback nag. "It said *rambling ranch* in the classifieds," I said. "Looks like it's about to ramble on out of here."

Ignoring the goose bumps that prickled my arms, I stood at the front door, pushing it wider as Mrs. Greer followed me inside, wrinkling her nose at the musty smell. Glancing back at the open door before moving deeper into the living room, I thought I should forget this one. Cold, dark, and dank, the air reeked of a thick, nauseating odor of something dead, decayed, and forgotten. Instinctively, I reached for the light switch. Nothing happened.

Faded wallpaper curled and peeled away in places, revealing cracked and crumbly plaster underneath. The floor creaked beneath us. I raised my eyebrows. *I could clean it up. Make it livable. Maybe.*

Mrs. Greer put her hankie to her face, covering her nose. "The old man who lived here had cats. Lots of them."

"No kidding," I said. Blanketed with yellow spots, the ceilings reminded me of my tear-stained pillow. "This house has a story."

"They repaired the roof last month," Mrs. Greer said. "But that's all they've done."

"You think?" Despite the cracked walls, stained ceilings, and ancient picture window with wavy glass, the room suddenly appealed to me. I imagined a splendid tree with a thousand twinkling lights and shiny ornaments in the cobwebby corner to my left.

"Try to see the possibilities," Mrs. Greer said, then coughed.

"Can I see the kitchen?"

I sighed at the sight of no appliances, and from the looks of it, squirrels and mice had dined on a bag of grits left in the cupboard. Rodent turds rolled everywhere. "My mother would pitch a fit if she saw this. She's meticulous about her kitchen."

I wandered through the rest of the house. "Hmm, and a dead bird, too." A torn-up bird with its brown feathers scattered over the god-awful gold carpet caused Mrs. Greer to visibly shudder. "At least we know where that putrid smell is coming from," she said. Then she poked her head into the only bathroom. "Needs work, too."

I tried to remain optimistic. Admittedly, the place was a wreck. I had hoped to get a little more for Daddy's money.

"Mrs. Oliver, you need to know the owners are Lester and Effie Gerber. They'll carry the financing. They'll have to. No bank will loan on the place. But it's got potential, doesn't it?"

That was what I wanted. Potential. An enclosed breezeway of windows connected the garage to the kitchen but I stopped at the back door, frozen. "A fenced backyard. It's big. Look at that enormous tree. I can see a tire swing, a picnic table, and a puppy back here."

Pointing to a large barn-like building against the fence, Mrs. Greer glanced down at her notes. "Notice the backyard shed is nearly as big as your one-car garage."

I couldn't imagine what I would need a shed for. There was plenty of storage in the thirteen-hundred square feet of house and garage. Certainly more than I had the past several years inside a trailer.

Mrs. Greer called my attention to the cabinetry, woodwork, and hardwood under the nasty carpets. The walls, floors, and ceilings needed to be stripped, and either repainted, re-papered, or refinished. The thought of it made me more tired than I already was. It was once someone's home, though. The question was, could I make it mine?

Standing outside, I spied the elementary school at the top of the hill, within walking distance. I let out a sigh of resignation. "I'll make an offer. I have to talk to my father first and get him to agree. After all, he's doing most of the work and donating the material. But he told me to get a fixer-upper, and this certainly is one. Maybe I can get it livable before my husband comes home from Africa in six weeks."

"Your husband's in Africa?"

"On business," I said. It embarrassed me to say who Joe worked for.

Mrs. Greer opened the car door for me, but I had stopped at the curb, scraping the bottom of my shoe on the grass. "Dog shit. I think somebody's trying to tell me something."

☙❧

When I arrived at my parents' house, the smell of roast chicken and floor wax hung in the air. "Sorry, Dixie. I lost track of the time."

She pointed to the study. "Your daddy wants to talk to you. The twins are napping upstairs. Next time the floors need waxing, you can do it for me. See how much fun you have with kids hanging on your legs."

Dixie was addicted to housework like her friends were addicted to alcohol and men. The best thing for me to do was walk away, which is what I did.

I found Daddy in his study. I curled up in his recliner, fingering the cigarette burns in the upholstery. Daddy leaned back in his desk chair, fired up his Zippo, and lit another unfiltered Camel. The leather squeaked slightly, and I smiled at his scruffy face. His mustache needed trimming, and his hair a shorter cut, but I adored him. He softened the pitfalls of my life.

Mustering my enthusiasm, I relayed the details of the house and then, with vivid recollection, repeated my brother-in-law's long-ago prediction. "Ray told me once I'd have to become the head of the home, wear the pants in the family." I took a sip of Daddy's strong black coffee. "I have to protect my children, do whatever it takes to provide for them."

He folded his hands across his chest. "Will he move in with you?"

"I think Calvin will make him. Publicly, the ministry team walks a fine line. Calvin won't allow Joe to leave me unless I first turn my back on the church. So, I'll continue to attend services to keep us together. I'm stuck. Unfortunately, I never consulted my budget when the pangs of motherhood fell on me. I need the money he brings in," I sighed. "It's become a marriage of convenience for both of us." I pressed both hands over my eyes. They burned with weariness. "But Joe does care about his kids."

Daddy raised his eyebrows and took another powerful pull on his cigarette.

I stood. "It's hard to believe, I know. I'm assuming he'll want to stay with me for their sake. I've been saying for years maybe someday I can get him out of Calvin's grip. I guess it's easier to hope than actually give up."

"Do you love him?"

I paused, not sure what to say. "When Mavis died, I wanted it to be over."

"That's not the answer I'm looking for."

"I know."

"Someday, those kids may need braces. The expenses get bigger when the kids get bigger."

"That's why I need his paycheck."

Daddy made his next point clear. "I won't work in that house if he's there."

I laughed. "He's never home. I used to hate living without him. Now, I look forward to him traveling. This house is for the kids and me. Not Joe. He won't appreciate it, anyway." I walked to the door.

"And I won't miss *Gunsmoke*. I have to watch *Gunsmoke*."

"I know, Daddy."

My parents' check for five thousand dollars secured the house. At closing, I had a twinge of guilt, signing the papers alone—buying a house on my own—without Joe knowing a thing about it. But the twinge didn't last long.

I quit my secretarial job in Lexington and said a tearful goodbye to Candace. Looking around the empty trailer, I knew I should've moved from Shady Acres a lifetime ago. I had packed Joe's things, what little he kept in the trailer, and hauled them, along with everything else I owned, to the refurbished house on Turner Street in Winston-Salem.

I picked up Dillon and held Gracie's hand in the doorway. The years we spent there suddenly festered inside me like an ulcer. I closed the door for the last time. Sitting in the car, I placed the new house key on the old, worn microphone key chain and said, "Mavis, you hear me? It's been a long road out of here. Put in a good word for me, will you? I'm walking on eggshells again."

On the way to our new house, I stopped at the Village Tavern—an upscale restaurant—and submitted my new employee paperwork. They had hired me as a hostess to start on Monday. I girded myself for a new life with the twins, whether Joe stayed with us—or not.

When I met Joe at Piedmont Triad International Airport, he and the rest of the preoccupied ministry team moved Calvin and his luggage swiftly to a waiting limousine before tending to their own baggage. I forced a smile at Joe's surprised look on his face. I rarely met him at the airport, only when necessary. We walked in silence to the short-term parking lot, where I broke it to him quickly.

"You did WHAT?" He threw his bags into the trunk and slammed the lid.

"Daddy gave me the down payment. Why don't we just get in the car?"

"Do my parents know what you did?"

"Yes. Al helped me move. They're happy for us. I also called the church and requested that Fannie contact Calvin in Africa, since I know he likes to be informed of everything going on in our lives. I had hoped he told you."

"No, Reverend didn't tell me! I doubt Fannie told him. He has more important things on his schedule than *your* trivial pursuits.

YOU are not at the top of his list. How could you do such a thing to me again? I told you we have to live within our means! You cannot do something like this without my consent!"

"Well, I did, and it's done. And I can't undo it. The house still needs work."

"Don't expect *me* to help."

"I won't. You now live closer to the church. That should make you happy. And it's a house, not a trailer. Aren't you the least bit excited?"

"No. I am not. Shady Acres was cramped but affordable. How do you plan to make the payments?"

"Your paycheck and mine. I've got a job. I'll handle it. As usual, I'll take care of everything."

We rode home in icy silence. He had spent the past six weeks in Africa, but didn't have a word to say about it, or even inquire as to his children. Instead, Joe walked through the new house, pointing out everything wrong with it. "I'm glad you own this rat hole, Andie. This is *your* problem. Not mine. Where are my clothes?"

"Why do you stay with me, Joe? You don't love me; why does Calvin force you to stay with me? Do you even love Dillon and Gracie?"

"Don't ask me stupid questions like that. I need to take a shower and rest. Do you have the faintest clue how long it takes to get home from Africa?"

"I want to know—do you love your children?"

Joe's face radiated an image of contempt. "Of course I do. It's why I'm here."

"Then why don't you get a better-paying job, for their sake?"

Joe threw his suitcase down the hallway, leaving black scratches on the wooden floors I had polished to a mirror shine. "You have no regard for how I was raised, do you? None. It's all about you; what *you* want. You've used the kids to get it. You've used them to keep me. Well, it's worked. But I will NOT quit my job because *you* want me to, or so the twins can get a few extra toys, a new bike, or a trip to Disney World! I work for the church because I'm concerned about their souls. And if that means living in a lesser house, driving a lesser car, or a few missed meals, then so be it! You will not use one red cent of our tithe or pledge money on this house! Get that through your thick head!"

"Got it," I said. "I think I finally got it."

Calvin had always preached that God wanted his children to have the best life could offer. But the fancy suits, custom buses, expensive restaurants, and plush hotels awarded to the ministry team did nothing to feed their families at home. It was all presented to appear like God heaped every good blessing from above on Calvin and his team.

I listened to him unpack, cursing, tearing through the house, and looking for *his things*. Joe muttered under his breath—his footsteps thundering down the hall.

The newly varnished hardwood felt cold and smooth beneath my bare feet as I tiptoed to the backyard and sat silently on a lawn chair. Wild grief slashed through my chest wall, landing on the painful knot I called my heart. I placed my hand on my breast. My long-ago vows choked me as memories of a kinder Joe flickered behind my closed eyes, holding back more tears.

Joe walked out to where I curled myself into a wounded heap. He ignored me and stood gazing at the storage shed. I somehow got into my car without allowing my tears to fall. The raw sores of my aching life needed something equivalent to the healing balm of Gilead. It was time to pick up the twins and get on with my life.

Chapter 11

MONEY COMETH

Andie ~ April 1982

With the house finished as much as I could afford, I experienced, for the first time, a sense of pride in my home. But I could no longer depend on Daddy to help me with house repairs. He had taken sick with asthma, and his doctor forbade him to breathe fumes of any kind. My parents were suddenly at each other's throats, but that didn't stop Dixie from hiding Daddy's cigarettes.

I needed a better job. I'd decorated each room with gently used furniture purchased from street sales and thrift stores, all while Joe continued traveling the world for Jesus on extended trips to Africa, Asia, Israel, and Europe. My focus had turned from food to fixing up my home. I had exchanged one sin for another, and our measly paychecks were insufficient funds to pay my maxed-out credit card.

But the good news was that I was once again on speaking terms with Libby. Ray and Libby knocked on my door one morning, holding a housewarming plant and a box of glazed donuts. After a quick tour, we drank iced tea on the patio. Ray raised a glass to me, and I blushed. "It's not The Biltmore, but it'll do," I said.

"I'm more than impressed with your gumption, Andie. You've hung on to the strings of a marriage and built a proper home in the meantime. That takes strength. Mama said the house looks great, but we had no idea you could do this." Ray's words made me smile, and I exhaled a long sigh of rare contentment.

Libby spent time in each room, asking me where I purchased such pretty woven rugs and how I got the floors the color of elderberry honey. Sunlight flooded through the new picture window as I showed her my second-hand couch and chair, reupholstered in a faux chocolate suede. "It's comfortable and wears well," I said.

"Andie, the house is lovely. You and your mama definitely have a knack for decorating. It's spotless and cozy, and I swear, it looks like you paid a fortune for some of this."

"Not at all. Garage sales. Every Saturday morning. Even Gracie's upright piano. We bought it at an estate sale last month."

The conversation eventually drifted to Ray and Libby's new farm in Richmond, the latest escapades of the twins, and life with Joe. Finally, over coffee, Ray asked me the question I dreaded. "What about you, Andie? What are your plans for keeping this place? We all know Joe is not dependable."

I blinked, then cleared my throat. "I want to be my own boss. The entrepreneurial bug has bitten me. There's been no sign of a raise for Joe, and I don't expect one. I need to make up the difference. Running a business is a better way to survive than what I'm doing now. I need to build something for my children. I'm tired of working my butt off for pennies and making someone else rich. With no college behind me, I'm stuck in minimum-wage jobs. I also need to keep the kids near me while I work."

I blew my bangs off my forehead, then bit into a donut. "I can make these, you know. My cooking skills—I don't mean to brag, but I'm a damn good cook. Common sense, I got. It's the business experience and capital I lack. I need a break."

Ray smiled. He looked at his wife. Libby nodded. "I have what you need," Ray said. "I've got the capital. It's a risk, and I'm not sure about you taking on a business; it's more work than you can imagine. And I may never see a return on my money, but if you can do with a business what you've done to this old house, we might break even."

I don't think I slept for a week after Ray and Libby left that day.

Again, Joe didn't care to ask what I was up to. He never thought to question my interests, what I did when he was gone, or what my dreams or goals in life might be. His life was separate and apart from mine. My wants and needs took a back seat on a big bus. I forged ahead, secured a commitment from Mavis's Aunt Lula as my partner, and transformed myself into an entrepreneur, even if I wasn't exactly sure what it entailed. Out of necessity, I became a business owner and quit my job at the Village Tavern to put my business plan together.

Over the following weeks, Oak Hill Cafeteria was born—a mixture of soul food and good Southern cooking. Lula and I rented a postage-stamp-sized storefront off Miller Road, near Baptist Hospital and Business Route 40. We worked non-stop, converting the old store into a country restaurant. A breakfast counter with naugahyde-covered bar stools stood at the back, and I filled the front area with mismatched wooden tables and chairs. Lula hung antique lace curtains in the large windows by the door. I knew the cafeteria's old-fashioned charm would draw customers almost as much as our good cooking.

We opened daily for business from 6 a.m. to 8 p.m. except Sundays. Breakfast and lunch consisted of whatever Lula or I had a notion to fix for the day. Cream cheese French toast, shrimp and grits, chicken and waffles—whatever sounded good. Customers selected from three main entrees, and lunch included a slice of Lula's special cake or pie, for which most women chucked their diets. I wrote the breakfast and lunch menus on two large blackboards at either end of the dining room.

At suppertime, we served a family-style buffet. Customers didn't need to order, and there was no need to keep track of who ate what or how much. I worked at the counter while my only employee, Janice, served beverages and bread, keeping the country buffet and salad bar full. Patrons served themselves until they had eaten all they could hold: one price fit all and no doggie bags.

After a rocky start, the cafeteria earned a reputation both Lula and I were peacock proud of.

Chapter 12
EYES ON THE PRIZE
Reverend Calvin Artury ~ June 1982

I was furious with Joe Oliver. I had instructed my ministry team to control their wives' spending habits and loose lips. To keep them busy working for the church's good. But from the day he married her, Joe proved, again and again, his inability to rein in his wife. I called Joe into my office when I discovered Andie's frivolous business venture. Oh, the heartache of the prophets! For thousands of years, we have endured the trials of fire. Mine grew hotter every time I had to deal with the Olivers.

He sat across from my desk, averting his eyes and massaging the tension out of his palms. To be so coy and ostentatious with women, Joe shrank around me like a penis suddenly gone flaccid.

"Do I have to fire you?" His empty stare didn't faze me. "Every time you go away, she buys a house, a car, and now a business! The materialism of your wife has sucked up the money you should put into the work of God! She finagled children out of you, which *has* and *will* cost you a fortune, and now she controls *all* of your purse strings! And I won't even mention her erratic church attendance."

"I hate to confess this, Reverend, but no matter how much I yell at her, I can't stop her. I didn't expect her success," he said, barely audible.

"Do you envy her? Her success?"

No response. Another blank stare. I crossed my arms and waited, bristling at his cowardice.

Joe squirmed in his seat. "I hate that you're making me stay married to her. My life is here, with you, in the church. Not out there playing *Father Knows Best*."

The seriousness of his tone provoked a change in my strategy. "We're all feeling the stress of the ministry. Evan and I have set you apart, pulling you into the more *private* projects."

"I appreciate it, Reverend. It's just that—"

"—Just what, Joe?"

Joe turned his head. "Nothing."

I stood and walked around to the front of my desk, lifted Joe's hands, and held them in my own. "Well, let's see if Andie tithes the profits of her business. I'll leave it alone for now. You must remember, you are a mighty warrior. The Lord has called you into His service. These hands of yours—they're anointed. I think you know, there's no middle ground in serving God. You're in or out— no teetering on the fence. *Many are called, but few are chosen.* The Almighty Jehovah chose you to do battle for Him. Keep your eyes on the prize, Joe."

I kept my features deceptively composed. I wanted Joe to feel only my authority mixed with the tenderness of the Lord. "I have not heard from God as to ending your marriage. Andie is not to be put in harm's way. The wrong attention will bring the enemies of God to our doors to destroy the ministry. Don't be responsible for that."

When I wasn't preparing for the next sermon, leading staff meetings, or stuck in a barrage of business meetings, my mind drifted to the delicate situation surrounding Joe and Andie and how much Andie knew. Satan besieged me with thoughts of them day and night, robbing me of much-needed time in prayer and supplication before the Lord.

The powder keg had shifted from Mavis and now rested on the Olivers' shoulders. Joe did not know I would've given my right arm to secure Andie inside the ministry's walls rather than him. Oh yes, it was a delicate situation.

Chapter 13

Into The Future

Andie ~ July 1984

At six years old, my twins were all arms and legs. They loved wrapping themselves around their daddy's waist and neck, and it thrilled me to watch them do it. My heart warmed whenever I found Dillon and Gracie in Joe's arms or on his lap. More often than not, unfortunately, Joe arrived home frustrated and short-tempered from lack of sleep and who knows what else. He spanked the twins for trivial things, and I had difficulty keeping my mouth shut. One afternoon, it was for leaving their bikes in the driveway.

"Don't look at me that way," he said. "They're my kids, too! I will not spare the rod or spoil them rotten like you do!"

Naturally, Dillion and Gracie ran crying to me. I hugged them both and told them to play quietly in their rooms for a while, then walked back to the garage to find Joe loading boxes into the backyard shed. "What are those?"

"Nothing of interest to you. Extra sound equipment I occasionally need, more easily stored where I can find it than at the church."

"Oh." I followed him back into the garage.

"Look, Joe, you have a right to discipline our kids, but you've got to balance that with love."

"When I'm home, I tell them I love them. They may whine and throw fits around you, but they'll not grow up to be heathens. Not around me."

"They're not heathens. They're kids." Nothing I said mattered. Restless and irritated, he ignored me as usual. When Joe hadn't slept in days, any clamor, creak, or stifled voice might rile the father they barely knew—a man who smiled one moment and screamed the next. He was a shouter, a weary man with constant headaches who insisted the Old Testament way of bringing up Christian children was the only way.

On Friday nights, as the sun set behind the church, the ministry team and their families gathered around the big, shiny buses to say their goodbyes. The twins' teary eyes watched the man they called *Daddy* load suitcases into the luggage compartments and joke around with other team members. Joe's rare displays of affection toward his children included cold hugs and half-smiles. Two little Oliver kids, trying hard to be brave, careful not to make a sound or embarrass him when the air smelled like diesel fuel, when silence was their secret game and gift to him. When all they wanted and hoped for from him—was a show of love.

It broke my heart and tore my nerves to shreds.

Joe said I needed to knock them down a peg or two, and that I let Dillon and Gracie get away with too many childish pranks, but all too often, I stepped in between them and their daddy. I had to. Shielding them from his dogmatic doctrine and relentless refusal to allow them a normal childhood with secular music and Friday night sleepovers and birthday parties became a common occurrence.

I swear—as far as Joe Oliver was concerned, God put the twins on this earth to walk *his* walk and talk *his* talk. Become Calvin clones he could be proud of.

In time, the twins avoided him entirely. He picked on Dillon and scared Gracie to death. So I took them to the cafeteria rather than ever leaving them with Joe. He possessed no paternal instincts—just as Dixie had predicted many years before.

Thankfully, my little restaurant thrived. It surprised everybody. In the time it took to transform the fledgling idea into a reputable enterprise, my business relationship with Lula blossomed from our shared love and memory of Mavis into a strong friendship and partnership.

"Praise be, you jus' like Julia Chiles!" Lula said.

My life at Oak Hill Cafeteria bore about as much resemblance to *Julia Child* as my legs did to *Cybill Shepherd's*. But the rules for owning my restaurant were clear. I set my routines like a cherished old recipe and knew how to follow them.

The seasons of my life came and went. My work was time-consuming and often grueling, and I frequently despised my vendors and the long hours of paperwork. But the restaurant eventually turned a small profit. I believed if I worked hard, I could retire by my fiftieth birthday. Maybe.

It was time to put my nose to the grindstone, continue working my ass off for the next few years. And that's precisely what I did.

Chapter 14

The Darwoods
Andie ~ June 1987

The Darwoods lived upstairs over the drug store, across the street from the cafeteria. The small apartment was home to Henry and his wife, Velda, and their two children, Lloyd and Drema. Henry, a bus driver for Winston-Salem, and his family were our friends and regular customers. They enjoyed meals at half-price, and I sent leftovers to Velda almost weekly. For that, the Darwoods loved us back and considered us part of their family.

Dillon's friend Lloyd spoke with a lisp, and I adored him. His sister, Drema, played the piano and taught Gracie to read music. Watching Gracie and Drema play together was like watching old reruns of Mavis and me. Typical ten-year-olds, the boys tormented the girls until Gracie screamed into the cafeteria for Aunt Lula to stop them.

But at the end of the day, Dillon and Gracie finished homework, read, or watched TV on the small black and white in the back room while I scoured pots, mopped floors, and prepared menus for the next day.

"Dillon?"

"Ma'am?"

"Turn off the lights, pull the blinds." Ten o'clock. The day was done.

As alike as they were, my twins couldn't have been more different. Dillon's hair sparkled golden in the sun with waves that hung in his gleaming blue eyes. Gracie's pale and washed-out tresses were pencil-straight. Dillon was G.I. Joe in a little boy's body. But there wasn't a tomboy bone in Gracie's frilly four-foot-two inches. She was a girly girl. Gracie's blue eyes, with lashes tipped in pixie dust, shone so brightly I saw them glisten from across the room.

Fortunately or unfortunately, depending on how you looked at it, the twins developed no real attachment to Joe. It bothered me he never thought to talk to them about his travels, ask if they had questions about his job, or inquire about their day at school. They had long ago learned when Joe arrived home from a Crusade to go straight to their rooms. Gracie had no problem with that. She loved school, and her grades reflected it. She'd learned to read by age four, and had she not been so tiny, the school would've started her a year early.

On the other hand, Dillon inherited my love of daydreaming and had no time to learn when the outdoors called him. He loathed sitting still in church. He hated memorizing scripture, opting for the easy ones. I tried to help him, but I knew his sense of adventure meant he belonged outside kicking a soccer ball or riding his bike. He barely squeaked by in school. Something we all kept hidden from his daddy.

Joe and I had settled into a relationship where I raised the children, and he remained absorbed in church work. I attended services every other week for appearance's sake and to keep the peace. Pretending Joe loved me got me through the worst of it. Most of the time, we hid in our respective corners. The awkward truth was, for years, I used my children to ward off the loneliness of being partly abandoned by my husband. I had resigned myself to the life I lived. Even Libby had stopped bugging me to leave him.

Like so many women, I lived a comfortable lie.

Only Aunt Lula asked why I didn't leave him. It's hard to explain unless you've lived half in and half out of a marriage. There were the children to consider, of course. And there was always the threat of *what if Calvin is right,* hanging over my head. Hell was as real to me as Heaven. And though I didn't understand why Calvin intruded into our marriage, I had no reason to doubt the healings and miracles I had seen with my own eyes. I had no reason to doubt Calvin Artury was who he said he was. A prophet of God. And so, I walked on my own tightrope, continuing to use Joe's income to help us survive.

And yet, I didn't know why Joe stayed with *me.* Lots of men left their families. I suspected it had something to do with his position on the ministry team and Calvin's code of ethics. My only question was, *how long would it last?*

My life revolved around the twins and the propaganda I dished out to the public: that we were a typical Christian American family.

After five years of backbreaking work and little time to think about myself, my weight hovered at an all-time low. One hundred twenty-five pounds. At thirty-three, I looked better than ever. That is, whenever I found the time to fix my hair and makeup, slip into a dress instead of blue jeans, and shove my feet into heels instead of flip-flops.

Joe's inconsistent behavior had worn on me throughout the years. He wanted sex from me when I was thin, but ignored me like a fat woman in a freak show whenever I gained the least amount of weight. My life, as always, ran according to his moods. A rare kiss when I smelled fresh as a daisy turned into a contemptuous look of disgust should I arrive home haggard and exhausted from a sixty-hour workweek.

By our fifteenth wedding anniversary, Joe's attention was more often focused on our new black lab, Prissy. And only the puppy paid attention to his tirades. Prissy-girl was the better listener.

"A trip to Hawaii? Are you serious? I can't leave the cafeteria."

"Lula can take care of it. You'll only be gone a week. It's Reverend Artury's first miracle Crusade on the islands. He suggested I ask you to attend," Joe said.

"Why?" The thought of attending my first Crusade in Hawaii, no less, excited and sickened me at the same time. But once again, there I was, hoping for a miracle where Joe was concerned.

"If you don't want to go, fine. I thought you might like a nice trip since it's our wedding anniversary. God's promised a special anointing to those who attend this Crusade."

"Oh, you mean God will tell the poor souls who can't afford to travel to Hawaii, '*Too bad, sucker, no anointing for you!*'"

"Your sarcasm is sending your soul straight to Hell. You know that, don't you?"

I had ignored the religious comments of my zealot husband for years. Especially his attempt to repeat Calvin's doomsday prophesies. "How can we afford it, Joe? All I make goes back into running the cafeteria. You know that."

"Reverend paid my way, as usual. I cashed in a life insurance policy for you."

"You did what? Joe! It's all we had if something ever happened to you! With all the flying you do?"

His eyes flashed. "Who cares? Your daddy will take care of you. What difference does it make in the grand scheme of things how you get to go?"

"But, I—"

"—There's no hope for you. Forget I asked," he said as he walked away.

I blew out an exasperated breath and tugged on his arm. "Don't be an ass. I'm sorry. I apologize. Sure, it would be nice to get away," I sighed. "Maybe we can spend some time alone?"

Joe moved in closer and gave me a quick kiss on the cheek. "Yeah. Maybe so. Besides, you look great; it'd be a damn shame not to show you off before you balloon back up again."

⁓

"The Darwoods are here!" somebody shouted toward the kitchen.

"They's a nice-looking bunch." Lula peeked out the pass-through window while dishing collards into a large serving dish. "'Cept Velda. No self-respectin' Black Baptist woman I know wears pants in public."

"Be nice, Aunt Lula," I said. "I've got to ask them to take care of the twins for a week while I go traipsing off to Paradise with Joe. I feel so guilty."

"You hush. You deserve this trip. Leave this place to me. Iffen I need 'em, I gots a lady or two at the church to hep me."

I put my arms around Lula. "Thanks. Dixie's got her hands full with Daddy. He's been so sick. Maudy and Al are too old to keep up with the twins. Libby and Ray live so far away. At least with the Darwoods, the kids will be with their friends."

It was a first for me on many levels. The first time I'd been away from my children for more than a day, the first time I saw the ocean, and the first time I attended one of Calvin's miracle Crusades. Little did I know it would be the last time.

Chapter 15

A GRIEVED SPIRIT

Reverend Calvin Artury ~ June 1987

Rigid behind my palatial desk, I felt like the President granting an interview. I put down my notepad, admiring my spacious television studio office. It encompassed 500 square feet of the new building and exuded nothing less than an aura of perfection. My old office in the church didn't compare to this in size or décor. Plush and pristine, this luxurious suite was long past due. Persian rugs covered marble tiled floors. My designer had arranged priceless artwork, stately leather chairs, and elegant tables built by skilled craftsmen. Lamps made by a world-renowned artisan were a gift I graciously accepted. Around the room, collected treasures from well-wishing judges and politicians cemented my place in the hierarchy of religious celebrities.

Secure as if the righteousness of Christ pulsed through my veins, I sat poised in my crisp Dior shirt and tie, then turned to scowl at Evan like Almighty God at the Great White Throne Judgment.

"Relax," he said. "Joe got her commitment to attend."

"Good. She needs deliverance." I made my fingers into a steeple, something my mother always did. *Here's the church, there's the steeple, open the door, see all the people.* All the people. All the people except Andie. Resting my elbows on my armchair and peering across the desk, I reminded Evan that Mrs. Oliver had slacked off in her church attendance. It alarmed me.

"She'll be in Hawaii. Don't worry."

I leaned back against my three-thousand-dollar chair. "What do you think she knows?"

"There's been no sign that Andie knows anything, Reverend. You've followed her for years. I could use the manpower elsewhere. Besides, wouldn't she have played that card by now?"

"Maybe. Maybe not. But I feel the tug of the Spirit. It's grieved within me. Either way, I want her in church all the way or—not at all. It's the only way I can be sure. I'm done with her sporadic church attendance, and Silas reported she's paid no tithe since 1982."

Evan shot me a look of concern. "If she knows—I trust you'll deal with it."

"If she knows, I will put my trust in the Psalms. *Be merciful unto me, Oh God, be merciful unto me: for my soul trusteth in thee: yea, in the shadow of thy wings will I make my refuge, until these calamities be overpast.*"

Evan did what he always did when I quoted scripture in private. "I have to make a call, Reverend." He found an excuse to leave.

Chapter 16

Aloha Crusade
Andie ~ July 1987

Three weeks later, I sprawled across a lanai beneath a sluggish paddle-bladed fan. The Hilton Hawaiian Village on Waikiki Beach was more like Paradise than I had ever seen. At the end of our ten-hour flight, the pilot banked the plane over the island of Oahu. I glued my face to the window for my first glimpse of the ocean. I wasn't about to miss the volcanic island and its molten, sunlit sea lapping around its beaches. Great green mountains and bluffs jutting toward afternoon clouds; the view held me captive like pineapple slices in a punch bowl. The giant, sun-bronzed city of Honolulu hugged the island's edge and took my breath away. All I wanted to carry home from that trip was a head full of treasured memories.

I sat up and grinned at Joe. "Let's go to the beach. I want a suntan. It's the only souvenir I can afford."

"You go. But you need to show up this afternoon at the orientation. Only thirty couples from the church volunteered to help on this trip. Believe me, they'll notice if you're not there."

"I don't care about orientation. Why do I have to go? And I don't want to go to the Crusade service either," I said.

"We talked about this. You have no choice," he said, shoving paperwork into his briefcase.

"They'll never miss me. I hear they're expecting record crowds. Over ten thousand people. Why do I need to sit in church when there's all of Oahu to discover?"

"Because you're a ministry team wife. Don't be stupid."

"I'd rather have my thumbs crushed in a vice and my butt crack sewed up."

"Don't give me any ideas," Joe said.

Before we left home, I glanced through the brochure Evan instructed Joe to give me, *Rules of Conduct for the Ministry Team and their Wives*. I promptly threw it in the trash and thought no more about it. Dressed in a modest two-piece bathing suit, flip-flops, sunglasses, and a straw hat, I tucked a beach towel under my arm and headed to the beach. The white sands of Waikiki awaited me just outside the lush gardens surrounding our hotel. I giggled, knowing Joe had to work in the heat to set up for the group's orientation later that afternoon in the hotel ballroom.

Flat-out on the beach, the sunrays soaking into my skin; I rolled over on my beach towel as an image of Mavis filled my head so quickly and clearly it almost spooked me. The New York police never found her killer. There were no fingerprints in her apartment. Whoever murdered and raped her left no trace of himself. With no apparent motive and no evidence, the case went cold. Mavis's friend, Harry, who found her body, had moved on. To California, I heard. Rupert had become sullen and quiet, toiling daily in his fields. Daddy visited him sometimes in the evenings, but Aunt Lula took him supper most days. Mavis's father had allowed his farm to run down, and I grieved for Rupert almost as much as I did Mavis. Old and worn out, Rupert's reason for living had seemingly gone out of him.

"Oh, Mavis," I said out loud. "I wish you were here with me." A rushing wind rolled up on the shore fast and forceful. The sand stung my skin, and I grabbed my hat to keep it from blowing away. But the only sound I heard filled my head like the ocean's roar.

I am.

"You look like a tomato!" Joe said.

Sunburnt from forehead to pinky toe, I twisted my ponytail into a knot on the top of my head to keep it from touching my back. "Just don't touch me. I'll be okay. Let me get into this sundress and meet you in the hotel ballroom."

"I won't be there. Evan's in charge of the orientation, while the rest of the ministry team meets with Reverend in his suite."

"Figures," I said.

I sat in the last row, my back not touching the chair, thinking how ridiculous. It was too much like church. Calvin preached we were to come to Hawaii for an anointing, but I'd come for the sun, the beach, and the macadamia nut pancakes. Gazing around the room, it became apparent why Joe had roped me into that trip. No other woman sported a sunburn, a skimpy sundress, a flower in her hair, or a lei around her neck. No other woman looked like me. Demure fashion for House of Praise women, though classic and often elegant, never fit me.

Evan stood at the microphone to make his do-it-or-else announcements. "I hope you've settled into your rooms. Shuttles will be available to take you to the Aloha Stadium tomorrow, one hour before the miracle Crusade begins. I need all ushers to report two hours prior. If you did not read *Rules of Conduct for the Ministry Team and their Wives,* copies are available on the front table."

I rolled my eyes.

"Please remember," he continued. "If you plan to enjoy the ocean, you are to wear cover-ups walking to and from the beach, and under no circumstances are the ladies to wear revealing bathing suits. We represent the Lord and our church. Remember, though we live *in* this world, we are not *of* this world. I want to speak to Andie Oliver after our orientation this afternoon, please."

"I'm busted," I told the little old lady beside me.

"Maybe it's nothing but a message from your husband, dear," she said sweetly.

"No. It's assuredly not that," I said. They were out to threaten me with my husband's job for ignoring those rules of conduct. Suddenly, it hit me: I was being watched. I winced as my burnt back touched the chair. Me getting Joe fired would give him the perfect opportunity for the divorce I'd ducked the past fifteen years. I'd lose my house and the cafeteria. Even though Ray had kicked in extra cash, the problem was I had squeaked by for months. I needed Joe's entire paycheck more than ever.

Evan droned on. "Also, Reverend Artury wants to ensure everyone read the rule about sleeping in the same room with your spouse. We do not permit it on Crusades, including this one. Remember, the team is working; this is not a pleasure trip. Professional sports team wives do not room with their baseball-playing husbands. We are certainly better and more important to the Lord than a sports team."

"What!?" I shot to my feet and shouted. "It's MY pleasure trip!"

Every head turned and stared at me like a demon had appeared in their midst. I swept an angry glare around the room, silently confronting each church member before returning to my seat.

"If anyone has a problem with that, they should see me afterward," Evan said. "Men stay with men and ladies; please room with another lady. Remember, this ministry team and the volunteers must pray before every service and consecrate their minds to the Lord. We need mental preparation for the miracle services. There are souls at stake."

"Mental brainwashing bullshit," I mumbled. And then, without thinking, I did something I had never attempted in all the years I sat under Calvin's ministry, bristling against its dogmatic teaching. I stood again and shouted. Again. Louder. "But what does sleeping with your spouse have to do with preparing for the service? Can't you pray with your spouse in the room?"

"Mrs. Oliver, we can talk about it after orientation."

"Evan, this is my fifteenth wedding anniversary. Are you serious? I'm not allowed to sleep with my husband?" Joe had asked me to come to Hawaii, and I came, hoping for a thread of reconciliation with the man I married.

"We plainly stated the rules for this trip in your pre-registration packet. If you had read them, you could've saved money and stayed home."

I yelled back. *"What God has joined together, let man not separate!"*

Volunteers and team wives gasped and murmured, breaking the dead silence in the large, carpeted ballroom. Several couples nodded and seemed to agree. Still, most stared at me with eyes like a deer in headlights that I dared to defy the distinguished Evan Preston.

Evan motioned to the back of the room, and a tall, beefy male usher grabbed my sunburnt arm, forcefully pulling me out into the hallway.

"Let go of me, or I'm pressing charges!" I yelled at the man who, had he been green, could've passed for the Jolly Green Giant, only he wasn't jolly either.

"You need to wait here for Evan," he said.

Struggling free, I faced him furiously, my eyes blazing. The bulging man backed away. I won the stare-down. Thankfully, the orientation ended quickly. The volunteers and team wives filed out, whispering and glaring at me, huddled near a wall divider of potted heart-shaped anthuriums. Waiting for his next instructions, the giant guarded my every move like a Roman soldier. Within minutes, I saw Evan bolting toward me with two ushers flanking him.

"Andie, care to step over here out of the way?" Evan led me to a more obscure corner in the luxurious Hilton lobby, out of the view of inquisitive eyes. "First, you misquoted scripture. You did not quote from the King James, the only accurate translation of the scriptures."

"Okay then," I said. *"What therefore God has joined together, let not man put asunder!* Mark the tenth chapter and ninth verse." I never read my Bible willy-nilly. I knew my Bible.

His yellow eyes narrowed with self-righteous annoyance. Evan grabbed me by my other sunburnt arm. "Let me tell you something, Mrs. Oliver. We will not put up with your attitude and defiance toward God. You will keep your mouth shut, or His wrath will definitely fall upon you and your family right here in Paradise. You don't want that to happen, do you?"

I couldn't believe it. This high and mighty Christian man had threatened me. He *threatened* me. I yanked out of his grasp, meeting his icy gaze straight on. "Let me tell *you* something, Evan Preston. You touch me again like that, and I'll not call the cops; I'll call my daddy's relatives. For a six-pack and a twenty-dollar bill, they'll do far worse to you than what you'd like to do to me!" It'd been years since my first encounter with Evan, having thrown up on his fancy suit, and I never liked him since. His self-appointed deity was unconscionable. I felt liquid fire flow through every part of me as my hands twisted into fists.

But Evan only smiled, leaned in, and spoke slowly through gritted teeth. "Get this through your head, pretty lady. Jehovah-Elohim will eliminate you and your family from the face of the earth in one swift breath from His nostrils if you *ever* disrespect me again. Woe be to the inhabitants of your household!"

"Now—your actions here today may cost Joe his job. Knowing you wouldn't read the brochure clearly stating Crusade rules, Joe should've *told* you about the sleeping arrangements. So listen up. This being your first Crusade, I'll spell it out for you. First, you and Joe will stay in separate rooms. Second, you either show up at the Aloha Stadium for the Crusade, or Joe will need to seek employment elsewhere when he returns to Winston-Salem. You will not bring further reproach upon this ministry. It's that simple. And one last thing. Reverend Artury has requested a private meeting with you and Joe in his suite the night before we are to return home."

Evan smiled another cruel smile, turned, and walked away with his guard-dog ushers following close behind.

☙

I staggered to the nearest water fountain and wet my face with cool water. I was ready to get on the next plane home. But I couldn't. Evan's threats, though absurd, were serious and real. That much I knew for sure. *What do I do now?* I found my way to the hotel and took the elevator to the ninth floor. The sounds and smells of the island and ocean floated through the open sliding door into my room. I didn't care. I ran as cool a bath as I could stand and filled it to the top. Sinking into the water, I entered a long, troubled night of soul-searching.

Joe could sleep with a hundred whores during the Crusades, but not with his wife? It was no longer a ministry. It was pure bedlam. No doubt, they had followed my every move, so I decided to make it as easy as possible for myself until I could get home. Lie

117

low, do as I was told, go to the Crusade service, and visit Calvin in his suite on Friday night. Saturday morning, I would get the hell off the island. That was the only plan possible.

I crawled between the sheets after wrapping myself in a thick terrycloth robe. Homesick, I had never felt more foolish. Like electric impulses, my memories dredged up incidents from the past that began to make sense. Suddenly, I realized I had not seen the depths of Calvin's power, which frightened me. He had manipulated Joe and me for years, even in our bedroom. And I had allowed it.

I couldn't sleep. At three in the morning, I rolled over to my stomach and stuck my fingertips through the headboard slats, touching the wall behind it. "I'm in Hawaii—HAWAII, and Joe is on the other side of that wall." Sighing heavily, I got out of bed. I didn't have to share a room with anyone. Joe had at least allowed me that courtesy when he moved to another suite with his tail between his legs. They had obviously told him of my blatant protests and admonished him. I walked out of my dark room to the lanai. My arms folded, I sat on the plastic woven chair and propped my feet on the glass-top coffee table. The moon's shadows on the beach below were no longer mesmerizing.

Was it courage or insanity that kept me fighting for Joe, no matter what it cost me?

⌒

I woke with a migraine. Joe phoned my room and told me to meet him in the hotel restaurant. I eased my sunburnt self into a tiny strapless dress and slipped a pair of funky sunglasses over my puffy eyes. Walking barefoot past the *Reverend* and Evan, eating their breakfast in business shirts and ties, I wanted to spit in their coffee. Instead, I found Joe at a nearby table, wrestling to say something that wouldn't upset me. "Couldn't you find anything decent to wear?"

"Let 'em look."

A hostess handed us menus. Joe returned them and said, "Just coffee."

Neither of us wanted to eat.

"Please, do as you're told, okay? I can't lose my job because of you. And don't embarrass me again in front of the members. Go to the service tonight. Try to have some fun during the day. But stay away from church people."

I shouted, "Fun? Have some fun? I've come all this way—"

"—Shhh, lower your voice!"

I started over. "I've come all this way. We've spent money we didn't have. This trip has ruined the excitement I've had for weeks, hoping you and I could find time to talk like married people. All because you didn't have the guts to tell about this separate bedroom crap."

"For God's sake, don't let anyone hear you. I didn't know Calvin would enforce that rule until the day before we left. In past Crusades, they looked the other way. Besides, you had the rules; you should've read them. If I lose this job, my soul is in danger. Yours already is. And *if* I lose my job, I will have blasphemed the Holy Ghost and sold out. The church will no longer protect me. You don't know, Andie, you don't know what that means. It will destroy me. I could lose my life! Please do what they want, like you always have. For me. For us."

My slit-eyed fury at Joe's drama softened. "What do you mean, lose your life? That's ridiculous. What are you involved in, Joe?"

He sighed and looked away. "Never mind."

"Well, if you can't tell me, then there's *nothing to tell!*" His blown-up church-drama tactics irritated me to no end; always using it to get me to kowtow under. "Prepare yourself; if Calvin yells at me during that meeting in his suite Friday night, all you'll see of me is the back of my head. I won't sit there and take his crap."

"I don't have a choice," he said. "I have to take it."

Too stunned to move, I forced my lips together and blinked, whispering. "What's going on, Joe? Tell me."

He slumped back in his seat as the waitress brought our coffee. After another deep sigh, he said, "Your explosions will bring permanent consequences, Andie. Please," he shrugged. "Please get through this without another outburst."

Joe's plea tugged at my heartstrings, but misery throbbed in my gut. An old familiar bruise, misery, it restrained the words and the reaction building inside me. I nodded instead, fully aware that my agreement rendered a temporary peace. "We have to talk when we get home."

"Fine. In the meantime, act like a good team wife is supposed to act. How about it?" He kissed my cheek, then stood and walked away. Evan was expecting him at the stadium for sound checks.

I ambled toward a line of gift shops selling adventure tours, shark-tooth jewelry, and snorkel gear. Hawaiian print T-shirts, bikinis, and flip-flops hung on sidewalk racks. A woman behind dark sunglasses appeared from nowhere. "Can I help you with anything?"

I jumped. "No. No thanks." I suddenly didn't trust anyone.

Chapter 17

Paradise Lost

Andie ~ July 1987

The sun sank into the Pacific, dyeing the world crimson, but I didn't care once again. We could've been in war-torn Cambodia; it all looked the same to me—a wasted trip to Paradise. I found no beauty in my surroundings; I just wanted to go home.

I didn't ride on the provided shuttle to the mammoth Aloha Stadium; I caught the city bus instead. Avoiding anyone I knew seemed the right thing to do. Dressed in proper church attire and carrying my Bible, I found a seat as far up and away from the stage as I could climb.

A line of volunteer male ushers sat in metal chairs on special flooring in front of the makeshift altar. They held plastic buckets with gold crosses stenciled on the front and wore dark slacks, ties, and frumpy white shirts. But Evan beamed with the presence of a politician, his navy suit crisp and tailored to fit his slender GQ frame. I prayed the lei of fresh lavender orchids circling his neck turn into a noose.

Facing the assembly with his sleek, cordless microphone wrapped around his head, he greeted everyone with a ringing shout. "Aloha, Children of God! It's time to give your love to Jesus!" Evan led the crowd in songs, prayer, praise, and an offering that lasted over an hour. Behind him, the service played on a gigantic TV screen for us in the cheap seats. It was like sitting in the front row. I'd never seen anything like it.

When the quartet ended their last Southern Gospel song, applause spread, slowly at first, then soared to a deafening roar throughout the stadium. Evan bounded across the stage and hollered, "Please welcome your pastor and evangelist to the world, Reverend Calvin Artury!"

In the distance, his white suit sparkled in the bright stadium lights. Pressing his way toward the pulpit from the back of the nearly filled arena, he shook hands with those in the VIP section—invited government officials and celebrities who came from the islands of Hawaii and the nations of the Pacific. He wore an open-ended ti-leaf lei, captivating those who touched him. Surrounded by bodyguards, Calvin avoided the thousands of ordinary people who couldn't take their eyes off him. A woman with a white plumeria flower in her hair screamed, shook, and fought through the crowd, desperate to reach him. Finally, the ushers dragged her limp body out of the stadium. I watched the giant TV screen as staff trampled the flower that fell from her hair to the ground.

The mob moved in, making it difficult for him to reach the stage. Forty minutes later, Calvin pushed through the crowd amid unrelenting applause and shouts of praise. As his feet hit the sweeping fifty-foot platform, he twirled in a circle, his arms out from his side. I recognized his familiar dance in the Spirit. *Going into the vision*, as he called it. His voice reverberated as though it were echoing through the Grand Canyon, adding to the mysticism of the moment.

"Satan!" He bellowed and spoke as a god. "You have no power in Hawaii!"

The crowd roared.

He screamed again. "Pagan gods who once held the souls of those living on these islands will bow to Jehovah-Nissi tonight!"

When the applause waned, he exhorted further. "Demons in the minds of God's people are like parasites that infiltrate the bodies and blood of their victims, sucking out every drop of holiness until you become like the walking dead. By using the nine gifts of the Spirit, I, Calvin Artury, God's chosen vessel, will uncover the atrocities of Satan!"

"Pentecostal fire will fall in this great stadium tonight! Before this mighty service of God is over, I will bring to light the most inconceivable invasion in the minds of men and women—complete and absolute Devil possession!"

As the people jumped and shouted, Calvin held his Bible in the air, spoke in tongues, and pranced back and forth across the platform. Whirling around, he stopped at the edge of the stage and pointed to the crowd.

"God is a rewarder of them who diligently seek Him. This same God who liberated the three Hebrews from the fiery furnace will deliver you if you tirelessly seek His face. I tell you tonight, deliverance is at hand. Demon-possessed people are sitting in this grand stadium, but God will set them free through *my* hands. Miracles and healings will take place in this very service. The signs of Jehovah follow those who believe!"

His arms flailing, body jerking and twisting, he moved as if a demon possessed *him.* Calvin wailed for what seemed like hours. The people swayed, entranced by his every move. They shouted when he shouted. They screamed when he screamed. I felt sure the ear-piercing crowd noise rivaled any football game ever played in that stadium. When Calvin grew quiet, standing solemn and still, you heard nothing but the wind and the buzz of the lights. Haunting in his speech, Calvin stood as one in a deep trance.

His services at home in Winston-Salem didn't compare to the eeriness of what I witnessed that night. The people in the Aloha Crusade had opened themselves to his charisma and showmanship. I questioned whether the honest-hearted mass of humanity admired Calvin, esteemed him, or worshipped him. Ignoring the time on their watches and the crowd surrounding them, everyone, it seemed, believed in him. Everyone but one woman sitting way up in the cheap seats.

"He's pissed off about something," I said to myself. I had hoped he wouldn't notice me in that nosebleed section, but Larry, Curly, and Moe showed up in the next few seconds. Three more bulky male ushers stood like Polynesian warriors behind me. Calvin glared up at the high balcony where I sat. "Bring her down!"

Two of the ushers motioned for me to come forward.

"I can't believe this!" But as quick as I said it, a burst of wind blew in from somewhere, and the same voice I heard on the beach again filled my head. A voice louder than the applauding congregation of thousands. *Tell him what he wants to hear. Get off this island.* For a split second, it terrified me. I turned, thinking someone had spoken to me. A familiarity of Mavis caused my arms to gooseflesh. I sensed raw fear in one awful moment, but then I heard it again. *He has not given you a spirit of fear, but of power, and love, and a sound mind. You can do this, Andie.*

Smooth like a satin blanket, a warm peace covered me from the top of my head to the soles of my feet. I stood. Winding my way down the long stadium steps, I walked slowly, without fear, between two ushers escorting me forward. They led me through the gawking crowd and up to Calvin, who immediately grabbed my head. His thumbs on my temples, his fingers wrapped tight around the back of my sunburnt neck, he moved my head back and forth, speaking to the congregation. "This woman has fought God for years. Demons bind her mind, and she lives in darkness. I speak to the demons that bind her! LOOSE HER, Satan!" He screeched with the force of a man gone mad, his body and hands shaking me, pressing me to the floor.

I fell backward and remained still on the floor, covered with a large cloth as I had on a dress. With my arms crossed over my eyes, I pretended to cry. Time melted away, and I saw myself as a little girl, pulled into the House of Praise by Dixie's gloved hand. I smelled the old church before hired decorators installed the carpet and velvet draperies and before a local artisan gold-plated the organ, piano, and pulpit. I felt the heat and humidity of those long-ago church services before the addition of air conditioning when Daddy fanned my face as we sat in the pew, with me asleep against his arm. I heard the church of my youth, the doctrine that had overtaken my life, wishing I had never stepped foot in that place. And then I heard—*him*.

"Slain!" Calvin shouted over the swell of the organ. "Slain in the Spirit!"

Brought back to the present, I had gladly fallen to the floor, sensing if I lay there long enough, they might leave me alone. I kept my eyes shut tight and waited, humiliated in front of thousands, except this time, only the ministry team and a few volunteers knew me. I stayed on that hard, dirty floor, my arms crossed over my eyes until I sensed Calvin had moved on. There were far too many people vying for Calvin's attention for him to linger over me.

Within the hour, I pulled myself up and escaped, reaching the upper deck just in time to see the third usher sitting in my seat.

"Let me guess. They sent you to watch me."

The young man appeared to be a local. He threw up his hands and slid into the seat next to mine. "Whoa, lady. This isn't my style, man. These people are crazy, if you ask me."

He reminded me of a Hawaiian cop I'd seen on *Hawaii Five-O* reruns.

"My grandmother asked me to volunteer here. The woman goes to church a lot and watches this Artury guy on TV. I'd rather be at Waimea Bay. Big waves are coming in tonight. Man, if these people want to see God, all they have to do is surf the North Shore, and they'll see Him."

I smiled at the large Hawaiian. "Then do yourself a favor, get to the North Shore, and see the real God. I won't tell anybody. Your granny won't miss you in this crowd."

"Thanks, lady. I think I will." He winked. "Mahalo." He stood and grinned, giving me the hang loose sign with his massive hand.

"You take care." I waved, envying him as he left.

The sweet Polynesian boy walked out under the exit sign and was gone.

❦

Calvin awarded *free time* to the team for the last day of the trip. Two hours before meeting with the *Reverend*, Joe and I walked the beach and found a straw mat left behind by a sunbather. Away from the eyes and ears of the church, we plopped down under a palm tree to gaze at the ocean.

A family twenty feet to our right built a sandcastle. The father, a tan young man, laughed and coaxed his two children down to the water. Hoisting them into his muscular arms, he walked into the ocean as they clung to his neck and back. It wasn't long before the mother, golden and beautiful like her husband, followed her family into the waves. All four splashed and frolicked in the surf as we watched in silence.

I glanced at Joe. His face distorted; he looked like he had started the next world war. Regret oozed from his pores. I could almost smell it. Slipping my arm through his, I laid my head on his shoulder, something I seldom did. I wanted him to know I cared about him and he could confide in me. But he felt rigid and unresponsive. In a voice strange and distant, he leveled his stare at the ocean and repented. "Sometimes—sometimes, I wish I could start over. Learn how to love all over again."

"What would you do differently?" It was a Joe I had never seen before.

126

"It doesn't matter. I can't go back and undo it."

For the first time since the death of our child, Joe clenched his jaw, and tears welled on his eye rims. It bewildered me. He hadn't forced those sudden tears. A large one spilled out of his right eye and dropped into the sand. "I have no choice."

"Yes, you do."

His gaze shot back to me. Embarrassed by his show of emotion, he grabbed my arms and squeezed tight, shaking me and hurting me. "No, Andie, I don't! You don't understand!"

I wanted to ask him what I didn't understand, but a young boy stepped in front of us. "Picture?" He snapped his Polaroid camera and handed me the photo before I could say no. I slipped him a dollar, and he took off down the beach to his next unsuspecting customer. By then, Joe had already sprinted halfway back to the hotel without me.

The hour of reckoning had arrived. Evan opened the door and pointed to a long, gold brocade sofa in the middle of the room. "Come in. Sit over there."

My mouth flew open. Spacious and filled with finery, the Presidential Suite at the Hawaiian Hilton Village, reserved for kings, presidents, and royalty, conveyed an almost museum-like appearance. Island artifacts, statues of Polynesian Kings, and large vases of exotic flowers and tapestries filled the room.

Reluctantly, I moved forward; my body felt stiff and awkward. *This place must've cost a fortune.* I longed to see the reaction of the House of Praise congregation if someone leaked how elaborately their *Reverend* traveled.

Several rooms noticeably made up the suite. A door led into what I assumed was the bedroom, but it was firmly closed to my curious eyes. Suddenly, the room smelled of heavy doses of

Drakkar cologne, so I knew he was there. On the top floor of the Tapa Tower, the breathtaking view of Diamond Head loomed in the distance.

Joe and I stepped further into the room, which stretched approximately forty feet in length and twenty feet wide. The outer wall, a sheer expanse of glass, offered an unobstructed view of Waikiki Beach. Island sounds floated upward—crashing waves and tourists playing on the sandy shoreline. The sudden scent of salt drifted into the air, filling the room.

Before the trip, I had meticulously crafted a list of places to visit. Yet, during my wretched week in Paradise, I abandoned my planned excursions to Chinatown, the Polynesian Village, and Pearl Harbor. The week I was to *celebrate* my wedding anniversary. A week I had secretly hoped to rekindle a spark in an otherwise loveless marriage. And a week I had yearned to prove my sanity for holding on so long, for so little.

A door opened, and Calvin approached us wearing a pressed white shirt and linen pants, grasping a stack of folded shirts. He was obviously packing. Evan was packing, too. He stood like a war hero in the corner, with a Colt .25 automatic in a leather holster under his jacket. He made sure we saw it. I recognized the gun. My daddy was not only an avid hunter but a gun collector as well. Calvin repeated Evan's request. "Please, have a seat."

Shoulders back, I tried not to think of the sermon ahead. We sat in the center of the room on that gold sofa, facing the beach and the view of Diamond Head. It was my saving grace because, just that quickly, I moved from Paradise into the fires of Hell.

Calvin tossed the shirts on a chair and said, "Don't speak unless I ask you a question. When you are called, I expect a respectful answer and to be addressed as Reverend Artury. You are not to ask to go to the restroom, nor are you permitted looking at each other."

Around and around the sofa, he stalked us as he preached. "I have heard from the Almighty regarding your conduct and behavior. You will *not* mock God! He has a message for you. Jehovah-Shalom is a jealous God, and He wants your attention, and by everything in me, He's getting it, if only this one time, in His presence."

His slow, interrogating-like gait, meant to intimidate us, infuriated me. I glanced at Joe, who stared straight ahead and shook like a wet puppy. The coward.

Making a run for it crossed my mind, but I didn't. I endured it for one reason and one reason only. To return home to my children without further incident. Antsy, I wanted to end the torturous crawl out of that room. I started to fidget, smoothing my hair and dress, staring in the other direction, and tapping my toe on the floor. On carpet as thick and velvety as pineapple marmalade.

"I said to sit still! *Be still and know that I am God,* saith the Lord of Hosts!"

I crossed my ankles, pulled my legs under me, and immediately determined it was the last time I would ever sit under the agony of Calvin Artury.

Calvin suddenly stopped circling us and stood directly in front of me. Like a ravenous wolf waiting for a meal, he licked his teeth. I fought the trickle of a chill on my neck as his left hand trembled, raising his arm to prophesy over me. Slobber leaked out over his lower lip, and I heard something I'd never detected in the past—a low growl in his speech, like that wolf ready to devour both of us.

"Andie. You've left your mind open to the Devil. You're saturated in sin, carrying your own self-centered thoughts, Satan's thoughts. I had hoped you found deliverance again in last night's Crusade service, but you have not. You should know I did not learn my vast knowledge about God from any university or even the seminary I attended; Jehovah Himself came down and taught me. With the gifts he has given me, I have discerned your spirit. You think you possess salvation, but you lay out of church. Your haughty spirit rules over your husband instead of submitting to him. You have no respect for the Shepherds of God's sheep. Darkness has overtaken you, and this is, I assure you, your last and final chance! God will not give you another! If you fail God tonight, after I have taken the time to counsel you privately, He will destroy you. I stand here, in His presence, to testify that you will meet with a fate worse than death. You must decide. Either stand for the oracles of God or land in the bowels of Hell."

"Joe, you have disappointed God by failing to reel in your wife. You've let her go off and do whatever she wants. She deceives you and gets pregnant. Then God takes the baby, and you allow her to become pregnant again. She is your cross to bear!"

Calvin continued on, but I couldn't take it anymore. I prayed silently. *God, if Calvin truly possesses Your voice, let me hear every word from his mouth. If he is not Your mouthpiece, then Lord, close up my hearing and allow me to enjoy the beauty before me.*

In the next moment, Calvin's voice faded like an echo at the end of a long hallway as I watched the sunset. Brilliant on its perch and glorious in its divine presence, the sun warmed the island and hotels of Oahu as it sank into the ocean. Something drew my attention to a group of children playing with a Frisbee on the beach. A couple meandered down the sidewalk that wound around tropical gardens and out to the ocean. An older man with a cane, wearing Bermuda shorts, socks, sandals, and a funny-looking hat, combed the sand for treasures. Seagulls, the first glimpse of the moon, the lights of an airplane landing, or maybe taking off. Lucky them. The wind picked up, the palm trees swayed, and suddenly, I had to shake myself, realizing he was waiting for an answer to a question I had not heard.

I raised my eyebrows, surprised that Calvin's tirade had ended. Wringing wet, his shirt dotted with sweat, he had delivered his last blast of fire and brimstone, a private sermon for two, and he was staring a hole through me.

"I'm sorry," I said. "What did you say?"

I think it was then he saw me swallow a yawn. His voice strained; he twirled around and grabbed his Bible from a table behind him. In one quick flip of his wrist, sweat flying from his hair, he flung the thick leather Bible across the room, breaking a lamp. Raising his hands, he screamed, "I asked you, are you prepared to miss the rapture! Listen to me, Andie! You will miss it if you continue on this way. It is imminent! I am pleading for your soul!"

He could have beaten me over the head with his hefty King James and still not have made the impact he wanted to make. I sat with a blank stare on my face, waiting for his sideshow to end. I figured if Moses threw the Ten Commandments down the mountain, Calvin's fast pitch with his Bible wasn't so bad. I'd get through it. The fact was, God had opened my eyes. Many of the miracles I had witnessed over the years were real, but not because of Calvin. They were real because of the faith of the one receiving the miracle. Calvin had used God to build a congregation rooted in fear and false prophecy. After all my years in his church, I finally had my answer. He was nothing but a charlatan.

Having puked up his last few words, he nodded to Evan, leaned back on his heels, and stomped off to another part of the suite. Evan rushed over and stood in front of us. He dismissed me, but Joe had to stay.

Chapter 18
TIME TO CHOOSE
Andie ~ September 1987

Pulling into my parking spot behind the cafeteria, I hit the sidewalk with a skip in my step. On the short drive to work, I had filled my hope bucket to the brim. Since Hawaii, I hadn't returned to church, not once. Having received no backlash from Joe about slacking off in my attendance, I prepared an intimate supper of roast pork in my slow cooker at home. His favorite.

It was my night to pull hard on my rope. I felt my tug-of-war ending. If I gave Joe an ultimatum, I hoped he'd choose his children over his church. Not that I was using the children to *keep* him—I was using them to *save* us as a family. I was prepared to live without companionship, without love, but I wasn't ready to watch my family fall apart. Children need a father. The marriage was still intact, and I wanted to keep it that way. For Dillon and Gracie's sake. Foolish—maybe. But I had witnessed his remorse on the beach in Hawaii, a moment of regret, perhaps, but clearly evident. Clearly there. And I meant to find it in him again.

Brisk autumn air had shoved summer aside with a blustery gust. Cool enough that flies were easier to swat, and mosquitoes no longer feasted on my exposed flesh. The leaves hadn't turned, but the city had that change-of-season look.

I walked by two young boys on the sidewalk, gently tossing a football. I could see an occasional boy or two hanging around whenever Gracie made her presence known at the cafeteria. She had plastered the cafeteria windows with the previous year's Halloween decorations and a few of her newest creations. Gracie lived to decorate for any holiday. Lula usually had to pull on her reins, or she'd have every square inch of the windows covered, which meant Lula couldn't see outside. If anyone in town wanted to know the latest gossip, they ended up at Oak Hill Cafeteria talking to Lula Pudrow.

The bell jingled above the door as I rushed through. Several regulars at the counter swiveled on their stools and nodded or waved a slight hand. Oak Hill served as the breakfast destination for every construction worker and road crew within a five-mile radius. Men who needed a gallon of caffeine and one of Lula's pork chop biscuits to kick-start their day.

I sat at the counter to open the morning's mail.

Janice slipped her apron over her head. "Hey, boss." Janice Oliver had the same last name but was no relation. "We been busy; that's good, huh?"

"Yeah, that's real good," I winked.

God did not bless Janice with many natural graces. Her limp brown hair stuck to her forehead, and her clothes hung off her wiry frame, but she was a bundle of restless energy. And Janice was dependable. She never called off work. Her sixth-grade education and fear of unemployment motivated her to work as many shifts as possible.

Lula set a cup of her special brew in front of me. "You missin' all the excitement."

I glanced out the plate-glass window behind me and sipped at my coffee. "What's going on across the street?"

A beehive of activity swarmed the building next to the drugstore. No one in the cafeteria took notice; the customers' eyes, all male, were on me. I'd learned to ignore them politely since I knew most of their wives they went home to.

It amused me, watching Lula swipe at the counter with a worn rag and straining her neck to get a glimpse of our new neighbors at work. Her eyes tapered to dark slits, and the little pink fleshy parts of her lips fluttered as they always did when her mind schemed. "Looks like we gots new neighbors. Couple of fellas stopped by a few days ago, then again yesterday. Say they's preachers. Before they lef', they had the nerve to ask me if I needed saving. I huffed at 'em. Told 'em I belong to the biggest Baptist church in the city." Shrugging, she patted her iron-gray hair. "Seem like nice enough fellas, though. All Black mens, nice looking, and friendly. Pastor name is Clete."

"First name basis already?" My smile turned into a chuckle. Lula, always looking for a new lover, watched as the men made several trips from a white van to the storefront they were changing into a house of worship. "Why don't you take the morning off, Lula? I'll finish the breakfast and lunch shifts. I need to be out of here by two, though."

Lula didn't argue. She shed her apron and handed it to me. "I'll be back by two. Orders are in, jus' need to bus the tables. I think I'll mosey over there and invite them new preachers to Oak Hill for supper. Maybe I can get Clete to carry me to the grocery, then fetch me back here. Might be a little forward, though."

It took Lula only seconds to cross the street and approach our new neighbors with a wave and a warm smile. The men had loaded their arms with what looked like black Bibles or hymnals. I shook my head and opened another past-due notice. *That's all we need—another evangelist in the South.*

⌇

I stopped at the house to check my roast before heading to my counseling session with Joe. After the Hawaii Crusade, Calvin insisted Joe and I counsel with his Assistant Pastor every week. I knew it was a ploy to get me back to church. Although I wasn't about to return for any reason, I *was* determined to wage one final, fierce battle for the only marriage I knew I would ever have. I'd endure a few more counseling sessions only because of Joe's rare display of grief on Waikiki Beach. *'I wish I could learn to love all over again,'* he had said. It rang in my head day and night as a cry for help. But nobody could drag me back to the House of Praise for a church service. Not ever.

Sessions with Pastor Tall, Dark, and Annoying lasted only minutes before he and Joe began discussing church business. I was willing to bet losing Calvin to out-of-town weekend Crusades had been a breath of fresh air for many in the congregation. And Pastor DeSanto, like a pack of Rolaids, spelled relief. Taking over with shorter sermons, no healing lines, and less pounding on the pulpit, DeSanto had become a favorite to many at the House of Praise.

Live broadcasts of *The Calvin Artury Hour of Power* television show aired daily from the studio complex in Winston-Salem to the world, whether or not Calvin was in town. But Pastor DeSanto, the Ed McMahon of religious broadcasting, became a celebrity in his own right. His TV spotlight grew brighter each week. Christian talk shows were all the rage—top-rated hits with evangelicals around the globe.

Frustrated, I looked around Tony DeSanto's office while they talked. Put off by their church chatter and mind-numbing talk of a newly purchased satellite, I interrupted with, "I hate this, Joe." My words exploded as if I'd spit out a hot pepper.

Joe's defiant eyes set his countenance into a hard, firm, *shut-up* expression. Feeling unimportant, I studied his chilly appearance, searching for warmth, some hint of the regret he had so aptly displayed in Hawaii.

As I expected, both simply ignored my comment.

With a sigh, I leaned back in my seat, fighting the onset of tears. I was sick to death of my long list of sins, made public and thrown in my face regularly. Can't submit to authority, no dedication, a lying tongue. Calvin had even likened my previous weight problem to an obsession with drugs or alcohol and explained that I needed deliverance from the gluttony demon to ensure I never became fat again. They related every fault and flaw to some hellish, tormenting demon attaching to my soul, causing my misbehavior. And, as always, the wrath of God was imminent.

They laid no faults at Joe's feet except his inability to control me. Evidently, since it happened years before, his sin of adultery was to be forgiven and forgotten. I sat thinking about that fact with my hands clenched in my lap while Joe communed with Pastor DeSanto. As if I weren't there, as if nothing were more important than a new satellite.

I glanced around at the plethora of books and materials on DeSanto's desk, all written by Calvin Artury. On end tables, bookshelves, stacked in corners—everywhere I looked lay Calvin's edicts. Bible tracts, cassette tapes, the church magazine, and full-length books delivering the power and majesty of God, the forces of demonology and demon possession, and the so-called anointed messages of prophecy spoken by the infamous *Reverend*. But nowhere did I see a shred of paper that could tell a husband and wife how to return to their first love and forgive each other. To sympathize, compromise, and appreciate each other. To believe in the sanctity of their union, conquer their fears, and rise above the hurtful words they'd thrown at each other for years. To love each other as Christ loved them, as I had loved Joe at one time: unconditionally. Finally, my longsuffering had arrived at an end.

After years of religious domination, my tolerance for the evangelical lifestyle had not just worn thin; it had worn out. I had also come to the end of my fraudulent counseling sessions.

"I am not afraid of him," I said, soft in my bitterness. Their silly babble about television equipment and taping schedules bored me to tears. I no longer believed in the power and magic of Calvin. In Hawaii, I'd had my epiphany, revelation, and anointing. I smiled then, which caused DeSanto to cease his chatter with Joe, and unwittingly turn his attention to me.

"What did you say?" The pastor's face flushed with a grin.

Joe shook his head with a sly sneer, and I heard him breathing hard. His embarrassment of me showed on his face.

I drew straighter, lifted my chin, and endured their feigned amusement. With flaming cheeks, I repeated myself without hesitation. "I said—I am not afraid of him."

"You shouldn't be. You should never be afraid of your husband. You're to honor him—"

"—Not Joe. I'm not afraid of Calvin Artury!"

Everything had just become a great deal more complicated. Pastor DeSanto's face turned bone white. His eyes skittered everywhere except my way. He slammed his Bible down on his desk, knocking over his chair as he shot up and stormed out.

Joe followed but first glared at me with the hostility of a rabid dog. I sat motionless, amazed at my own words.

A minute passed when Pastor DeSanto walked back in alone. "I once led a violent life," he said. He cleared his throat to find his *pastor's* voice. "I revert to it when confronted with disrespect and a blasphemous tongue. Most women I know would love to be in your position, the wife of a man who works close to Reverend Artury. Go home, Andie. We will keep working on your attitude."

My anger stirred as I thought about my wasted trip to Paradise. Suddenly, I emerged from my corner with my fists raised. "*My* attitude? We're trying to save a marriage, and you and Joe spend our entire session discussing work."

He glanced upwards for a moment, as if seeking heavenly intervention. "Joe wants to include you when he talks about his work. He thinks you aren't interested and have no respect for what he does." Unmistakable loathing churned in his words. He wanted to resort to his *violent life*; I could feel it. "Please remember," he said, "this counseling is free of charge to you."

I stood, threw on my jacket, and turned to the door. "Joe's had plenty of opportunity to talk to me about his job. The past fifteen years, in fact. So that's a load of crap. And it's never been free of charge, pastor. I've paid for it repeatedly. I've paid for it every day since I married the man. Thank you for your *free* time, but I won't be back."

Pastor DeSanto spoke like a well-oiled defense lawyer, halting me at the door. "Your accusations about Reverend Artury are absurd, you know. We've heard what you've been saying. As a minister, I must advise you to be careful. The Bible says it angers the Lord when we speak evil of one another. Jesus Himself said He will hold us accountable for every word we speak. If you have a problem with Reverend Artury, I suggest you examine Matthew eighteen and fifteen and handle it biblically."

I heaved with tears. My voice seemed to come from another mouth, and as hard as I tried, I could not stop even one word from spilling out. "Yes—yes, I know that one. *Moreover, if thy brother shall trespass against thee, go and tell him his fault between them and him alone.* Of course, just like he never did with me. Sure, I can abide by scripture. But there's one little detail you're missing. Every single word I've ever said about Calvin Artury—is true. So let's think for a moment, shall we? If God smites me for telling the truth, then His word is untrue. Am I correct?"

"But you're a liar."

I hadn't intended it to go that far. Rage rose in my throat and nearly choked me. It roared in my ears. "I'm not a liar! But I *am* an idiot for following Calvin as long as I did. Now, you want to sling some *more* mud at me?"

"The Bible is clear! *Touch not mine anointed, and do my prophets no harm!*"

"Oh, but it's okay for him to harm us? To impose himself in our personal lives? He's not a prophet, Tony. No more than either of us. He's a fraud."

With a thunderous crack, Pastor DeSanto's fist landed on top of his Bible.

I jumped, and all but fell back into my chair.

"Get out, you whore!" The shock of his words sent me spinning before I could brace myself. It took everything I had not to let him see me stagger.

"Now, there's a lie if I've ever heard one!" I spoke slowly and shook my finger at him like a mother would to her two-year-old. "You're giving yourself a stroke, Tony. Here's a scripture for you. *O give thanks unto the God of Heaven: for his mercy endureth forever.* I think you can find that in the Psalms. I thank Him for His mercy. I'm *sick* of living in fear! Do you hear me? I'm sick of it! I don't fear God because He might throw the next lightning bolt my way. I fear Him because I love Him. Like a child loves a good daddy."

"The scriptures command you to fear the Lord!"

"Hoo-boy, maybe you need to return to seminary, Tony."

"You're walking a straight path into Hell, sister Oliver." I think he grew quiet, hoping I'd attack him physically so he could call the police. But I knew there were cameras in the offices. Joe had told me. So I stood there, shaking my head and zipping my jacket.

Finally, my defiant posture had melted like a forgotten burning candle. I turned toward the door, grabbed the knob, and twisted, but I couldn't leave it there. With my last longsuffering sigh, I turned around and found his face had darkened to blood red. "You keep pushing that fear, preacher. It'll keep folks in the pews and plenty of money in the offering bags. But I am *not* afraid of Calvin. Not anymore. You tend to forget that God and Calvin Artury are not one and the same."

I'd spoken the last word and quietly closed the door on my way out.

We arrived home separately. My pork roast had burnt, and the sweet potatoes in the oven had withered to the consistency of shoe leather. I tossed the potatoes into the garbage and stood at the stove, picking at dried pork crusted and hardened on the stainless steel pot.

Joe nearly yanked the breezeway door off its hinges as he stormed into the kitchen. After slamming his briefcase on the counter, he grabbed my arm and spun me around to battle face-to-face. "What—what the hell were you doing?"

I kept fragile control over my composure and words. "It's time to choose, Joe."

"Reverend was always fond of you through the years, always taking *your* side, always concerned about your soul, and this is how you repay him?"

"Fond of me? About as fond of me as what? A boil on his butt?"

"He knows you want our marriage to work."

"Oh, that's nice. But the question is, what do *you* want? Do *you* want our marriage to work?"

He didn't answer.

I turned to the sink and ran soapy water into the roasting pan. "I'm never stepping foot in that church again. Never. Not for counseling, not for church, not even for a funeral. Never."

"Then I guess I have to choose, don't I?"

"Yes. You do. But I'm begging you, Joe. Let's keep our family together. You can be just as happy working for another company or church. You've got lots of experience now. Billy Graham is always looking for good technical people. Charlotte isn't far from here. We can move—"

"—Just—just stop, Andie. I think you know my answer."

"You'll actually leave your children?"

"They can stay with you, but I'm not leaving them. I'm leaving you."

My stomach tensed, my heart skipped a beat, and I broke out in a sweat. I knew this day would come. I had longed for it and dreaded it, yet, for years, I held out for a miracle. I had hoped above everything that something I did or said would soften his heart. Make him want me for more than a quick sexual release. I had hoped he saw how hard I tried to keep us together by staying in church when he *knew* I didn't want to be there.

I heard Lula's car in the driveway. The breezeway door opened. Gracie and Dillon walked into their parents' showdown, dragging their coats and backpacks behind them.

"Go to your room," Joe said. "Your mama and I are having a discussion."

"A fight," said Dillon.

"I said go to your rooms. Don't ask questions."

The children's expressions broke my heart. They instinctively knew this was the end, and I watched them position themselves around the corner.

Fuming, I looked firmly at Joe.

"It's time, Andie, for *YOU* to choose," he said. "Life without me, or life with all of us in church."

I knew he didn't *want* me. In *or* out of the church. Joe gave me the choice to appease his pastor, hoping I'd give him the answer *he* longed for. I weighed it on my mental scale. Life with

Joe at the House of Praise destined me for more years of barely getting by financially, a loveless marriage, and a doctrine I loathed. I'd lived that life for fifteen years. But an existence without Joe was certain inescapable poverty. Yet, it meant rescuing my children from the cult's grasp and offering *them* a choice.

"For a fleeting moment when we were on the beach in Hawaii, I saw regret in your eyes. I saw it, Joe. Whatever you're afraid of, it can't be bigger than both of us. Talk to me!"

"I'm fine, Andie. The only thing I regret is marrying you. And those kids will go to church with me while I'm still in this house."

At that bit of news, Dillon ran into the kitchen. "No! I'm staying with Mom!"

I knew my son was suddenly in for a whipping if he didn't stop. To distract Joe, I reached for his briefcase. As I opened it, I saw a photograph sticking out of the top of his Bible. At the same time, from the corner of my eye, I saw Joe lunge for Dillon. Quickly, I picked up Joe's Bible, pulled out the photograph, and thrust it into his face. "What's this!?"

A young woman posed against one of the ministry team's buses, her name *Gloria* and phone number scribbled on the back.

"Give me that!" Joe yelled.

I had uncovered him in front of his children.

"Yeah, Daddy, what's that?" Gracie pointed, not knowing what she was pointing at.

I held Joe's Bible in my other hand. He reached for it, but the Bible and more pictures of the same woman fell to the floor.

"You bitch!" Joe dropped to the floor, gathered his snapshots, and yelled one obscenity after another.

I stood in silence, staring at my husband's collection of *Gloria* spread out on my kitchen floor. I purposely left the red lace panties inside his briefcase. Finally, it hit me like a brick to my head. *My God, our marriage never existed in the first place.* A soft gasp escaped me, along with the suffocating tears of my past.

"I'm moving to the couch, then out of here," he said.

Ushering my twins back to their rooms, I crawled into bed with Gracie. Her nightmares started weeks before; she had already seen and heard too much.

My tug-of-war was over. I lost.

Chapter 19
TIME TO LOSE
Andie ~ February 1988

"Andie! Turn that up!" Libby pointed to the tiny black-and-white TV in the cafeteria's kitchen.

The local television station interrupted *Days of Our Lives* with breaking news.

"Jimmy Swaggart, one of America's leading televangelists, has resigned from his ministry after revealing he consorted with a prostitute. Before his congregation of seven thousand in Baton Rouge, Louisiana, he confessed to 'moral failure' without giving details. Swaggart's confession is even more scandalous since he unleashed fire and brimstone against rival televangelist Reverend Jim Bakker a few months ago for committing adultery with secretary, Jessica Hahn. Bakker was subsequently defrocked and fired from his multi-million dollar Praise the Lord TV station."

"This time, it was Reverend Swaggart's turn to repent after officials from the Assemblies of God Church were given photographs showing Swaggart taking a prostitute to a Louisiana motel. Rival televangelist Martin Gorman, who was also accused by Swaggart of 'immoral dalliances' in 1986, turned him in. Gorman, who ran a successful TV show from New Orleans, launched an unsuccessful

ninety-million dollar lawsuit against Swaggart two years ago for spreading false rumors. He also said Swaggart was attempting to undermine rival TV shows."

"Over two million families watch The Jimmy Swaggart Hour, and donations raise about one-hundred-fifty-million dollars annually. After the Bakker scandal, donations from the faithful dropped dramatically, and the same is likely to happen to Swaggart's show."

"The resignation will also displease Republican presidential contender Reverend Pat Robertson. He is drumming up support in the Bible-Belt Southern states ahead of Super Tuesday primaries on March eighth. Reverend Robertson has threatened to sue anyone who calls him a TV evangelist and prefers to be described as a businessman."

"Enough!" Libby reached across the counter and hit the *off* button. "When will it end? Calvin Artury is probably worse than all of them, yet there's not one scandal about him." I loved it when my sister-in-law came for a visit. I missed her. She spun around on the stool. "It has to hit Artury, eventually."

"Yeah, but Calvin is way more careful than these guys," I said. "Exposing a rotten televangelist is not as easy as it sounds."

Libby shook her finger in the air. "People are so damn gullible. The problem, I hear, is that TV evangelism raises billions of dollars. This is good news for Artury. He knows the money-giving evangelicals who followed these TV preachers will seek a new one who appears honest, with the backing of the Almighty. The church body, as a whole, will probably lose a few because of men like Swaggart and Bakker, but Artury's ministry is in a prominent position. Swaggart and Bakker's loss is his gain."

I served Libby a grilled pimento-cheese and tomato sandwich with a glass of sweet tea. "In the meantime, my family falls apart." I sighed, contemplating the poison wrought by televangelists and the people who worship them. "Some evangelicals have a lot to answer for."

"Aren't all holy-roller churches the same? Complicit with whatever their pastor says or does?" Libby asked.

My Catholic sister-in-law was one of the most intelligent women I knew. Still, as knowledgeable as she was about Catholicism, she had no clue about the depths of spiritual abuse in the evangelical megachurch.

"There are different levels of megachurch people," I said. "Some attend a few services and are no more visible to the ministry than a fly on the wall. They flitter from church to church. Nobody cares who they are past a welcoming handshake."

"Then there are those who come and get saved, maybe receive a healing, and someone notices they've given a nice offering. Their money is important, so the pastor throws them a heartfelt thank you from his pulpit. But for the most part, they're invisible. Some stay, and some move on because they don't like the marathon hellfire and brimstone sermons. Nobody cares about them, either. There's always another to take their place."

"Others who can sing, play an instrument, run a TV camera— they come to get noticed. These people, with or without a talent, volunteer for everything from driving a church bus to teaching Sunday school to becoming an usher. They give a lot of money because they have jobs outside the church and know little of what goes on behind the scenes. They're valuable enough that the pastors consistently praise these folks and make them feel needed. So they stay, raise their families in the church, and look the other way when hearing gossip about Calvin."

"And then there's the ministry team and their spouses. The inner circle. The elite. Hired men and women who live at the edge of Calvin's spotlight and are likened to the apostles. They're charismatic. And the majority are childless. Bold in their faith, they toe the line and slave for untold hours with little reward. Two men in the quartet quit six-figure jobs for piddly ass House of Praise wages, but that's a small price to pay to work so closely with their *Reverend*. And their God. Still, every employee is required to tithe and give offerings. They're addicted to admiration, praise, and secrets. Calvin's ministry team knows everything and reveals nothing. They have a lot to answer for. And yet, they're constantly under a microscope. Nobody gets away with a thing but what it's used against them. Calvin took great pleasure in holding Hell over my head as I lied my way into parenthood, crash-landed into a business, and quit the church while determined to take Joe with me."

Libby shook her head. "It's worse than I thought."

"You have no idea. Seventeen no longer seems old enough to drive a car, yet that's how old I was when I married Joe—because Calvin said our marriage was *God's will*. He wanted us in the inner circle from the beginning."

"You also loved Joe, Andie. You tried harder than anyone I know. Your marriage would not have lasted as long as it did if Joe hadn't been out of town with Artury every week. Your lives went separate ways, but you tried everything short of slitting your wrists to change him into husband and father material. I don't mind telling you, there are better men out there than my brother-in-law."

The truth made me into an idiot. "Please, Libby. Stop."

Libby sipped her iced tea. "I'm sorry, but it's true. Not all men abuse their wives."

"I'm not interested in another man. Never again. It wasn't only Calvin Artury who wanted me to marry Joe. Everyone did. Nobody but Mavis tried to talk me out of marrying him. And I'm not perfect. I realize that. God knows I've made my share of poor decisions."

"Joe being the worst. And don't say you'll never be interested in another man again. You've got a beautiful heart. Some wonderful man might get lucky enough to have you someday." Libby wiped her mouth with a napkin. "Is he still sleeping on the couch?"

"When he's home, and that's not much. We never speak."

"You need to kick him out. It's *your* house, after all."

"I know. But, damn. I really *need* his paycheck."

"Here. This should help." Libby handed me a check for five hundred dollars.

"Oh, Libby—I—"

"—Forget it. Ray and I will step up when we can. Thanks for lunch." Libby kissed my cheek and left the cafeteria to drive back to her uncle's farm only moments before the phone rang.

It was Dixie. "Andie Rose, your daddy's sick. Can't breathe a lick. Wylene is with me. We're on our way to Baptist Hospital."

"What can I do?"

"Call your sister; she's a mess. They pray, honey. Don't come to the hospital yet. I'll call you when I get home tonight. Wy thinks they'll keep him. Run some tests."

I felt the tears puddle in my eyes. "Please call me as soon as you know anything."

On top of everything, those damn cigarettes were killing my daddy.

⁓

Over the winter, Lula Pudrow had fallen in love with Pastor Cletus Owens, the evangelist across the street. Pastor Clete had set up shop and worked to pull in as many new members as any new evangelist could. Finding Lula was his fortune. She began attending Sunday services in the little storefront Pentecostal church, inviting several of her lady friends from the Baptist Church. In time, Pastor Clete, whom I hated to admit I liked, asked Lula to marry him.

Lula married her pastor on a sun-drenched March afternoon. Members of the Mount Zion Baptist Church and Pastor Clete's small flock filled Oak Hill Cafeteria to capacity. Janice and I cut and served a buttercream cake decorated with dogwood blossoms while Gracie poured tea and coffee. Lula threw her wedding bouquet into Janice's hands before the happy couple left on a four-day honeymoon to visit Pastor Clete's relatives in Birmingham. But before the ceremony, the good pastor promised me he would never stop Lula from working at the cafeteria. At least, not until the Lord called him to preach elsewhere. My fervent prayer was for God to keep the little storefront church across the street alive and well for a good long time.

Hours later, I covered my kids with their jackets as they lay on opposite ends of an old couch I kept in my storeroom. I sent Janice home at midnight with a piece of wedding cake to put under her pillow. After cleaning up and preparing to open by myself in the morning, I was ready to faint from exhaustion.

Turning off the dining room light, I then locked the door. Standing in the darkness and peering out to the sidewalk lit with the muted yellow glow of the streetlights, I stepped closer to the window as the wind blew away a heavy cloud, revealing a full moon. As I watched, another cloud floated across the sky, blocking the moon from view. A brief glimpse of happiness. Just like my life.

Joe hadn't left the house as he'd threatened, and I didn't know why. *Libby's right. I should kick him out.* Except I knew I couldn't. Feeling myself dip into depression, I chewed at my lip. Money was tighter than ever. Recent vicious rumors about my cafeteria drifted inside with the patrons—bugs in the soup and hair in the salad. Those were the worst. The battle to keep my business afloat had just begun.

Chapter 20

Truth Out Loud

Andie ~ September 1988

Daddy walked around with an oxygen tank dragging behind him. Aunt Wylene had moved her practice to Charleston, South Carolina. Unless she was on call, Wy drove back to Winston-Salem every weekend to help with Daddy's care. And Dixie, as usual, got on everybody's nerves.

Either Lula or I visited Rupert once a week during the dog days of summer, with its deafening whir of cicadas. We stocked his cupboards and Frigidaire with a week's worth of groceries, a cold jug of sweet tea, and a pie. I figured the man was determined to work himself into an early grave, but I'd not let him go hungry doing it.

Rupert only left his farm to visit Daddy and his oxygen tank. Rupert stayed on Daddy's front porch since Dixie's fancy house made him edgy. The end of summer's heat blast had dried out Rupert's tobacco fields before they had a chance to thrive. The two men shared cigarettes and passed the evening playing the banjo, reminiscing about old times, and discussing the dry crop season.

And then there was still Joe to deal with. Joe never arrived home until after midnight when the ministry team was in town.

But in the morning, after a shower and a few words to the twins, he'd drive off in his new truck without uttering a single syllable to me. At least every weekend, we were free of him. Dillon and Gracie adjusted to their daddy's brief appearances. At eleven years old, the adolescent pull of school, friends, and sports occupied their time. The twins refused to attend church with Joe. But I knew with eventual visitation rights, Joe had every intention of taking them back into the church. In the meantime, I tried to keep them busy and away from the pull of the House of Praise.

The popularity of Oak Hill took a nose-dive when a customer's severe case of food poisoning made it into the newspaper. A customer, we discovered, who attended Calvin's church. Overnight, the cafeteria sunk into the red and struggled to survive. Monday through Friday, few customers trickled inside. Fortunately for Lula and me, our loyal Saturday customers kept us busy.

Patrons stood in Saturday's buffet line heaping their plates with butterbeans, baby peas, squash, collards, fried okra, ham, scalloped potatoes, slow-cooked roast beef, homemade applesauce, cornbread, buttermilk biscuits, sliced fresh tomatoes, fried chicken, and more. Gracie, her tiny body wrapped in a flowered apron, bustled out from the back. She swept through the dining room, pausing at every table, "Y'all doin' okay? You want lemon with your tea?" She poured coffee and water, scanned the tables, and moved on, calling toward the kitchen, "We need them biscuits out here, Aint Lula!"

"Comin', chile!" Lula hollered back, bringing smiles to the customer's faces.

Despite the rumors, another couple from the House of Praise had mysteriously started eating at my cafeteria on Saturdays. Lula said it was because they lived a few blocks away. I doubted that was the real reason. When Calvin's congregation ate out, they usually ate at his Praise Buffet next to the television studios. But paying customers were paying customers.

Claiming a table by the front window, Leonard Culver, a nettlesome man, loaded his plate with roast beef and potatoes. Babs, his wife, with silvery hair carefully coiffed, chose a slice of tomato from the platter in front of her.

Leonard found time to taunt me between bites of food while I bused tables. "Babs, Mrs. Oliver needs to close this place and start cooking at the Praise Buffet. Why, with her good cookin', loyal customers would follow her and find true salvation. Think they got any more of them butterbeans back there?"

I walked to the kitchen, ignoring my arrogant customer. "Gracie, baby girl, take a bowl of butterbeans out to the Culvers. How that man can eat and talk non-stop is beyond me."

"I ain't a baby, Mama."

"You used to be," I assured her. After a quick pat to her behind, I watched her walk to the Culver's table with a large bowl in the crook of her arm.

"More butterbeans, Mr. Culver?" Gracie asked politely.

Leonard nodded. "Thank ya, kindly." But then he smiled and said, "Hey, little gal. I heard your mama doesn't go to church anymore." His obnoxious chortle startled a few of my customers.

"Where'd you hear that?" Gracie cocked her head. Her eyes narrowed.

"Everybody knows." Leonard winked and adjusted his smudged eyeglasses while he chewed.

Gracie set the bowl on the buffet table. "My mama is busy, that's all."

Leonard stuck his fork in his wife's uneaten chicken wing. "Not the way I hear it. I heard she's got herself into a peck of financial trouble. What's that scripture, Babs, about rendering unto Caesar?"

The entire room heard him, including me.

I flew out to the dining room and steered Gracie back to the kitchen. Moments later, I ambled toward the Culvers' table, gathering plates and smiling before saying my piece. Quietly. "Bad news always involves a former House of Praise churchgoer, doesn't it, Leonard? House of Praise members shouldn't persecute folks who leave. It's still a free country. You want to discuss my business; you talk to me, not to my children. And frankly, my business is none of *yours.* Please don't bring your church dirt back into my restaurant again. Furthermore, Calvin can't afford me. I don't work for peanuts like the rest of his staff."

The voices in the dining room grew quiet amid the clinking of silverware as I bussed a few more tables and headed to the kitchen.

"What happened out there?" Lula asked.

"Nothing a good ass-kicking wouldn't help," said Gracie.

"Gracie!" I tried to hide my approving grin.

Lula winked at me. "Folks 'round here, feed on trash talk. They's a mean bunch, that House a Praise. My Clete wouldn't put up with it. Pastor Cletus loves his people. What few of us they is."

I scrubbed especially hard at a few pots and pans in my galvanized sink. "Sometimes I think the entire church is out to get me."

Lula nodded. "Sho' looks that way, doesn't it?" She ladled chicken gravy into a serving boat. "You thinking 'bout talking to that man, Artury? Give him a piece of what for?"

"No. What can they do besides start more rumors? I'm staying put." I had no choice, really. Pouring myself into aching, mindless work was my only option.

Lula flipped more chicken in the massive cast-iron skillet. "Whole thing sounds fishy to me."

Gracie sliced more warm biscuits and laid them in a basket. "What's going on, Mama?"

"Don't you worry, baby. You keep getting good grades and leave the church gossip to your mama and Aunt Lula."

"Law-hep-me-Jesus," Lula said. "Amens to that."

"Time to serve their pie, though," I said.

"Cain't you do it? Janice will be in soon; she can do it."

"Be sweet, Gracie. Keep your mouth shut and show the Culvers you're not afraid. Hopefully, they'll leave you a nice tip."

"House of Praise people don't tip, Mama. They only tip their preachers. I wish they'd all eat at the Praise Buffet and leave the rest of Winston-Salem alone."

"Fat chance," I replied. "Fat chance."

Monday started another long workweek, and I wondered if my customers would return to the cafeteria. A handful showed up for the lunch special—pork chops and potatoes au gratin. I couldn't bear to let the curtain fall. Filled with conviction to make it work for my children's future, I ignored the fear in my gut and prepared Tuesday's menu.

At midnight, I fell into bed, exhausted. Again.

During the night, I felt his hand on my hip. I stirred. My mattress creaked in protest as he slid between my sheets. The warmth from him, now strange, gently reached for me. *Why?* I rolled onto my stomach, hoping to convey the oblivion of sleep.

His fingers drifted through my hair. His seductive whisper sounded almost affectionate. "Once more? For old time's sake?" But he spoke to the dark as if his mind lingered elsewhere. I clawed at the sheet, knowing he couldn't see my face. My mute lips refused him. A memory faded—a time when I adored him beyond reason.

Why would a husband try to make love to a wife he intended to divorce? Libby would say he tried because he could. Because I had not changed the locks, barring him from entering. Libby would declare it was my fault. I should've known he'd attempt to bed me one last time. To dominate me once more. To prove he was special to God, cunning, and worthy of a better woman than me.

He had never loved me. Not as a husband should love his wife. I understood that. There was nothing, no tears, nothing left. In the silence, I felt the same cold, untouchable heart that had possessed him for years. I was done with deal-making and hoping for that last drop of love to show up. Joe had thrown me at the wall of despair and tormented me with the *hope* of love for years, ruthless enough to use it against me for sex one last time.

Repulsed by his presence, I cut myself loose. I wasn't sure where my new life without him would take me. I wasn't sure how I would survive, even without his paycheck. But I knew, without a doubt, that Joe had lost himself, his conscience, and the love of his children before I completely gave up on him.

Love, I learned, didn't conquer all. It forced me to see the miserable parts of my past, denying me a clear path to revenge. I stopped believing in a life that made sense and that God had my best interest at heart. Love was nothing but an exhaustive, brutal joke. It was not, nor had it ever been, greater than hope or faith. Not for me.

The gossipmongers had made their rounds, and eventually the dirt they shoveled got back to me. The entire congregation was told to *pray for Joe.* Calvin wanted it to appear as though *I* had ended the marriage. That's why he insisted Joe remain in the house. To make it appear that Joe had done all he could to *save me.* And yet, I knew Joe had no intention of leading me *back to Jesus* and that the full impact of his rage had yet to descend on me.

I was also aware ending my dreadful marriage would come at an awful cost, like a vulture ripping away at my flesh, piece by piece, exposing me to the muscle, the vessels, and the bone. It would attempt to steal anything left of my hope and leave me with crushing grief and no peace. It would cause me to doubt my salvation and the faithfulness of God and to question my belief in the Almighty Himself.

It didn't matter. Something went out of me—the addiction of a lifetime. I'd been weak, gutless, and pathetic, and Joe had been that wretched habit I finally found the courage to break. It was time to tell the truth out loud.

I turned onto my back and hiked myself on one elbow, glaring down into his soulless eyes. Forever the hypocrite, Joe smelled of alcohol. His naked body, stretched over my bed and blankets, repulsed me. I found my voice. Quiet, solemn, uncompromising through clenched teeth. "Get out. Get out of my bed. Get out of my house. Get out of my life."

His fingers, still fondling my hair, gave it a vicious jerk, yanking out a handful as he sat and swung his legs over the bed's edge. "With pleasure."

The room's darkness shifted, turning from silky grays to patchy, watery blues. Joe ran his hand across his face, stood, and then walked back to his temporary bed on the couch, leaving behind the faint smell of his cologne on my pillow. A smell I had come to despise.

The moonlight sliced through the curtains when he closed the door behind him. That same moon had appeared on my wedding day many years before and followed me. The moon's blemished face, worn and sad, shone outside my window under a dense canopy of stars. I felt kin to the moon.

I rubbed my head, the sting of him still painful. But he had stung me for the last time.

A framed photograph sat on my nightstand. A picture of me, pregnant with a son I never knew, and of Mavis. Our arms locked around each other, we stood in front of the Mount Zion Baptist Church. Two friends, broken, battered, and torn apart. It sickened me. That picture had yellowed and aged, with cracks that burrowed deeper into my heart and memory every time I looked at it.

I crept into Dillon's room. Nine years had passed since we left Salisbury and moved to Winston-Salem. My children remembered little about Shady Acres trailer park. For that, I was thankful. But I wasn't sure how many good memories they would ultimately have about their childhood.

Sleeping hard with his back to the wall, my son filled his bed. I sighed, looking down at him. Breathing heavily with his mouth slightly ajar, Dillon was my delight. I brushed his bangs from his face and kissed his cheek, savoring his presence.

I was grateful to God for my children. Nothing gave me more joy.

Dillon shifted onto his back. A warm sheet fragrance rose in the room, carrying the scent of his clean pajamas, sweet skin, and shampooed hair. A cheerful aroma, reminding me of him as a newborn. It was the smell of home and of all things good. It was the promise of a better tomorrow, a different life than we had. His voice ascended in a whisper. "Mom? Everything okay?" The words, a precious smile on his lips.

I hesitated. "Everything is fine. Go back to sleep, baby."

I knew he would not remember I had slipped into his room. After covering his feet, I walked into Gracie's room. My twins were my life; they were my loves and always would be. I could go forward as long as Dillon and Gracie lived in my shadow. I would make a better life for them, for me. I would thrive in this new life; I had no choice.

Crawling into the warm nest of Gracie's little bed, I molded myself to my daughter's back and breathed in the scent of her tiny body. I brushed my fingers against her hair. It felt as it always had. Infant soft. Her baby face, creased with sleep, moved only slightly. I sensed the warmth of her love, and my heart eased. I fell asleep within seconds.

☙

In the morning, I listened as he went about his routine. When I heard his truck back out of the driveway, I found the strength to get up. I opened the curtains, and the sky greeted me with a lush throng of blue and a fresh sense of direction. Guided by some inner compulsion, I looked down the long highway of my destiny.

It's time to pack him up, move him out, and change the locks. It was time to live again.

Chapter 21

WORKHORSES

Andie ~ October 1988

"Andie?"

"Hmm?"

"You remember my sister, Donna Beth?"

"Sure do. She attends the House of Praise, poor thing."

"Well—" Janice hesitated an unusually long time. "She had an abortion last month."

I dropped my paring knife into the vegetable bowl and stood frozen momentarily. Janice, who loved to talk non-stop, had been quiet all morning.

"Why?"

"I wish I knew."

In her twenties, Janice looked fifty. Nothing but freckles and bone; she'd lived a hard life, a life a dog shouldn't live. Residing in a single-wide condemned in the '60s, Janice wandered into the cafeteria shortly after Lula and I opened. At first, we expected her to walk out after the lunch crowd. To our surprise, Janice was a workhorse and one of our best business decisions. After I fixed her hair and explained essential beauty tips, she turned out pretty under her ragged exterior.

We continued working. The clatter of pots, pans, and a knife chopping vegetables filled the kitchen. Then, slowly, Janice walked to my side and blinked. "Is abortion wrong?"

I stirred the soup and chose my words carefully. "Some folks think so. I believe it's horribly wrong if you're pushed or forced into it. Ultimately, it's a decision every woman makes on her own. I think it's personal between her and God and, hopefully, the child's father. But then, I'm not the one to ask," I sighed. "I have a question, Janice."

"Sure. Shoot."

"Did Donna Beth's husband get hired at the church? I recall the last time we talked about your sister, you said something about her husband applying for a janitorial position."

"Yeah. They hired him months ago. The thing is, Roger and my sister don't make diddly squat between them. Didn't have money for a proper doctor. Some man who called himself a doctor all but killed her. Donna Beth ended up at Baptist Hospital; she nearly bled to death. She cain't have kids now."

"I'm so sorry, Janice. That's awful."

"Donna Beth ain't but twenty-two. I'm dern sick about it."

I slid my arm around Janice's shoulders and squeezed. "Please give her my best. Tell your sister to call me if there is anything I can do. Take them this pot of soup tonight."

"Thanks, Andie."

"Sure. You know I don't go to the House of Praise anymore."

"You and Joe left then?"

"I did. Joe's still there. We're separated."

"Oh. Ain't he still living in your house?"

"Yes. But it's temporary. He's moving out soon. Only a matter of time."

"I'm sorry. I've heard rumors, I admit."

"It's okay. I'm ready for it to be over." After pulling more carrots, celery, and kale out of their bins, I slammed the refrigerator door with my foot.

Janice ran water in the sink and kept talking. "I hear things. Bad things about that church."

"Like what?" My ears were wide open.

"Donna Beth volunteers in the offices, making copies and stuff like that. She's a good cook and wanted to work in their fancy Praise buffet, but she's having second thoughts. My sister said they asked Roger to get fixed. They don't realize she cain't have kids now, anyway. Nobody from the church came to see her in the hospital or even asked why she was *in* the hospital. What's going on there, Andie? You and me never talked much about that church. Why don't they want women to have babies?"

Hoisting myself up on the counter, I sat, wiped my hands on a towel, and pulled a pack of Camels out of my purse. A pack Dixie gave me to hide from Daddy. I lit up and took the first drag from a cigarette since high school. I coughed and noticed Janice staring at me. "It's a long story. According to Calvin, you must divide your time between your kids and the church if you have children. It's difficult to work the long hours they require and raise kids at the same time. If you have children, you spend money on your kids instead of tithing and giving it to the work of the Lord. Calvin wants all your attention and money. He's created a business with a false front and calls it a church. That's the short version, anyway."

"Oh," said Janice as she sliced potatoes.

My thoughts turned to church members I had known for years. Trapped. Afraid to leave for fear of failing God. I suspected some had marriages similar to mine but stayed in the church. Fear of the unknown. It was no way to live.

After I coaxed a simmer from the soup, I sat at the counter, coughed, and finished my cigarette. "Janice?"

"Yes'um?"

"You go to church anywhere? Are you saved?"

Janice tapped a fingernail thoughtfully against her cheek. Her face blushed, and she nodded. "Came close. Nine times. In different churches. I'd cry, and my tongue stammered. I walked down every aisle and had my name written in The Lamb's Book of Life. But I stumbled out afterward, still unsaved, I think. I like to read the Bible, though, especially Revelations, all about rivers of blood and the Lake of Fire. Shit like that." She winked.

Biting my lip to stifle a laugh, I looked away. "You keep going, Janice. It's not that hard. *Believe, and ye shall receive.* It's called faith. You don't have to feel anything. Some pastors make it harder than it is. You believe you're saved. Believe it. That's all."

"That's all?"

"Yes." I smiled as I handed Janice a tray of ketchup and mustard bottles. "Salvation is a gift. All you have to do is accept it. You don't work for it. He takes you as you are. You don't need to belong to a certain church or straighten out your life before accepting Jesus into your heart. You can get saved at home."

"Honest?"

"*Just as I am,* like the old song says."

"Wish I had known that." Janice fidgeted with the tray. "I should tell you, Donna Beth heard you were in a backslidden condition."

"Tell her not to believe what she hears. In fact, get your sister and her husband out of the House of Praise if you can."

"It's a pisser."

I tried to keep a straight face but failed and laughed out loud. "Yeah. That's a good word for it."

࿇

Gracie and Dillon were due home from school soon, and they'd be hungry. My eleven-year-old twins grew faster than I had the money for. Rag-tag clothes were in style, and I was happy for that small blessing. Consignment shops and thrift stores were all I could afford.

Remembering Mavis's fantastic sense of style always made me smile. But the memory faded when the same old disturbing questions surrounding her death surfaced. Every time I tried to free myself from the grip of the past, I couldn't break the fire-hardened chains of that horrible day, thirteen years before, when someone had raped and murdered her in her Manhattan apartment. The case had died, as well.

Life with Joe remained a constant, uncommunicative nightmare. I had boxed his belongings and left them on the porch, then changed the locks on the house. It was *my* house, after all. But my futile attempt to force the inevitable only made things worse. After Joe beat the front door into splinters with a sledgehammer, my call to the police resulted in embarrassment.

Legally, it was Joe's home, too, and until we divorced, I was told I had no right to force him out. I couldn't fathom why he insisted on remaining in my home when I knew he hated living there. He said it was for the sake of his children, but I suspected Calvin had something to do with it. So I gave him one key. A key to the *new* front door that I made him pay for.

A bitter silence ruled the scraps of our relationship. He informed our twins their mother was on her road to Hell. Ironically, I thanked God he was only home a few days during the month. Something I used to complain about had become my biggest blessing.

Daddy's breathing worsened every evening as the sun went down. Dixie continued to hide his cigarettes and prop him up with pillows to sleep. Somebody needed to prop Dixie up every morning. God did not make my mother to care for the sick.

We all thanked God for Aunt Wy, our doctor in the family. But nobody, not even Rupert, Daddy's best friend in the world, could stop Daddy's disease from worsening. Dixie nearly drove Caroline, Aunt Wylene, and me to drink. But I had a cafeteria to run, children to care for, and a heart to mend. An empty heart, emptied of tears. Nothing, it seemed, kept the world from turning.

Chapter 22

A RIDICULOUS DELAY

Reverend Calvin Artury ~ November 1988

Do you want the truth? Here it is. Living perfect before God isn't easy. Something was missing. My ministry was under constant scrutiny. I fought to contain every scandal, never allowing one syllable to seep through the walls of my church and into the media. It often seemed not one staff member cared but me!

I collapsed into the deep hotel tub; steam rose and swirled, ghost-like, then clung to the marble tiles, gilded mirrors, and the crystal chandelier. I needed to soak the tiredness out of my aching joints.

I was a minister of the Gospel, a prophet, an evangelist, a pastor, and a faith healer. I had seen blind eyes open, witnessed the lame stand from their wheelchairs to run across my altars, pulled my fingers out of deaf ears that suddenly heard their mother's voice for the first time. Casting out devils, delivering the unsaved into the arms of the risen Savior, I'd seen it all. But I questioned God. My body was aging. Anointed men of God were not supposed to age! *Rock of Ages, cleft for me, let me hid myself in Thee!*

My ministry had grown to crowds far more significant than any televangelist in modern history. Tourism in Winston-Salem and the cities of the Triad had developed faster than any area in the country because of the massive crowds I drew to my Friday night miracle services. The church renovations were near completion. I possessed money and power. I was on top. I had rid my ministry of every threat; they either were dead or in exile.

I churned the soapy water with my hands. Sweat poured down my forehead and neck. It pooled in a deep scar across my chest, under my nipples. Every plan was precisely on time, as Jehovah-Elohim had intended. But something was missing.

I longed for peace and privacy. A warm body to hold me, tell me I was a wonderful lover. I wanted to kiss passionately. Hump like a wild dog, feverishly. I was, despite everything, still a man of the flesh. Maybe the cold ritual of living in hotels was getting to me. A hotel had performed essentially the same role as a prostitute. In, out, and on to the next Crusade. It wasn't enough.

My blue eyes sparkled in the mirrored wall across from me. A bottle of the hotel's best sat next to the tub. I poured a tiny cup full. The warm drink soothed me from the inside out. I wanted to hole up for a few days. Spending time at the feet of God in prayer, fasting, and reading the scriptures, I had not slept over four hours a night for years.

I had watched too many TV news shows. Every evangelical Christian was interested in the news. My end-time prophecies needed to reflect the day's politics, comparing world events to prophetic scriptures, yet remaining neutral on many topics plaguing my congregation. I danced around moral issues and insisted if one lived holy before God, these things took care of themselves.

In the old days, nobody questioned me. Proving my sovereignty over and over, I grew tired. Like children, my staff had become problematic. Every morning, I assembled the team in a large circle before taping the day's program. Praying over them, giving a word of stern prophecy to anyone who had allowed their loose lips to create friction within the inner circle. I had built an empire on the threat of Hell. *The Calvin Artury Hour of Power* reigned as the number one Christian talk show, and I wasn't about to let that slip away. But my past—my past plagued me, day and night.

Peace and privacy finally surrounded me as I sank under the water in the cavernous tub. Silence. The silence of death. I shot to my feet like a man out of a cannon. Dripping wet and shaking as if afflicted with palsy, I bounded toward my towel and shoved my almost-white hair back until it fell in drenched locks down my neck. In seconds, I had wiped the mist from the mirror and stood gazing at my sagging body.

A harsh light swirled in the steam behind me. My tormentor appeared, the face hideous. I held my privates and laughed at him. "Satan, you have no power over me. I rebuke you."

Satan couldn't hold me prisoner. I had no fear of the Devil. But if Andie Oliver held any evidence, any proof Mavis may have gotten to her, the effect on my ministry would be catastrophic. My eyes wide, I refused to entertain the demon with my phobia any longer.

Wrapping myself in a towel, I walked to the bed and sat on the edge, shivering as my skin glistened from the hot bath. "I miss you, Mama. Please, if you will, tell Vivi I miss her." I groaned for my long-dead wife. "Vivian," I spoke her name like speaking to the highest-ranking angel. "You and I could've ruled the world. You were my best friend. My only friend."

Within the hour, I entered a waiting limo outside the Ritz-Carlton—my body poured into a girdle, my boots polished to a black diamond shine, and my Armani suit tailored to a flawless fit and a new shade of blue. They had matched the dye specifically to my eye color.

My driver's voice echoed from the front. "Shall I take you to the Metrodome, Reverend?"

I hesitated, questioning if the sun had set because it seemed to have vanished behind cold, dense clouds. City lights filtered through the limo's tinted windows. It was time to put pressure on Andie Oliver and end the ridiculous delay. Waiting on one piece of country trash to show her hand—ludicrous! I spoke to my driver. "Minneapolis is waiting to see the power and glory of God, Percy. Let's go."

Chapter 23

SON OF A BITCH

Andie ~ November 1988

The bell jingled above the door. I surmised the man and woman weren't interested in the Today's Special. I recognized the woman from somewhere. They wore business suits and unreadable faces.

"Andie Oliver?" The man extended his hairy hand. "Are you the current owner of Oak Hill Cafeteria?"

"Yes. That's me. Mrs. Lula Owens is my partner. She's not here right now. Can I help you with something?"

The woman laid her business card on the counter. "We're from the Health Department, here to investigate a complaint against your establishment." Her plum-gray suit matched the color of her skin and the streaks in her hair.

"Excuse me?"

"This will only take a few moments, and then we'll send you a report."

I looked at the woman and laughed. "Who complained? No, let me guess. A House of Praise member. Right?" I crossed my arms. "Don't I have a right to know what it is?"

"We address the complaint in the report we send you."

I squared off and blocked their way to the kitchen.

"We can do this easily and quietly or return with the Sherriff."

I stepped away, regretting I had left the kitchen in a mess. I tapped my fingers on the counter while the health inspectors rummaged through my back rooms. After fighting the rumors for weeks, one after the other, losing customers, and struggling to keep my doors open, it had come to a showdown.

A half-hour later, they huffed out the door, giving me no sign of their findings. I grabbed the phone. Joe's extension rang twice at the television studio. "Joe! So you've lowered yourself to siccing the Health Department dogs on me?"

"Why would I do that?"

"To ruin me!"

"Don't be stupid. I had nothing to do with it."

"Well, just in case you did, I will fight the whole damn church if I have to! I can make a few calls myself, you know; I—"

Click.

"Son of a bitch!" I slammed the phone on the receiver.

The report read worse than I thought. They forced me to shut down until I corrected a list of ten items—all of which took lots of money to complete. Things like my ovens were old and hazardous, and my refrigerators needed replacing because of faulty wiring. The report also mentioned bugs.

When I called the Health Department to complain, they agreed it was an unusual repercussion for a first-time offense and that they typically issued fines. Still, the inspectors suggested we close the cafeteria until we rectified their findings. They advised me to get an attorney. *Yeah, right. With whose money?*

After a little back-door investigation of our own, it all made sense. Pastor Cletus discovered both inspectors attended the House of Praise. But I had no choice. I did as instructed.

Closed for repairs. The sign on the door drove away my remaining loyal customers to new restaurants. Janice went on unemployment, and my reputation went down the drain while more rumors spread that roaches had taken over my cafeteria. Lies all spawned from the House of Hell itself.

Lula and I had taken pride in our cleanliness, ensuring that even our worn utensils and kitchen appliances were spotless. On most days, you could eat off the floors. But we forged ahead, scraping together enough money to fix the items on the list. Unfortunately, a non-existent advertising budget did not help our situation. Most of our customers came to the cafeteria by word of mouth. I kept wishing for my customers to return and spread the good news that our tiny establishment was open.

But the war waged on, and the rumors continued.

Why are they doing this? What do they want? I turned my attention to my children, buried in homework at the counter. The thought of it made me weak in the knees.

In the following weeks, Lula and I gave it our best. We worked the hours using Dillon and Gracie's help. Six weeks of closed doors had nearly ruined us for good. Lula insisted I stop paying her for a while. She even kicked in a little money to keep things afloat. Nonetheless, we'd taken a tremendous hit, and our vendors were calling for payment.

Chapter 24

OVERWHELMING ODDS
Andie ~ November 1988

My feet were cold, but it took too much effort to untangle the blanket and cover myself. I turned my head to the right to see the alarm clock on the nightstand. *Noon already.* I'd taken the day off. The cafeteria would have to do without me. I needed to think. I needed good sound advice. I needed to get out of bed. I rolled onto my back and stared at the ceiling instead.

Dixie, consumed with a sick husband, all but ignored me. Aunt Wylene, knee-deep in a new medical practice, seldom called. Maudy and Al, in-laws who had once been my rock, avoided me like a severe case of the flu. I'd seen Coot once or twice since my move, and someone had told me his garage was for sale. My sister lived a miserable life of her own. Caroline popped out babies with husbands who spent their time in unemployment lines or at Alcoholics Anonymous meetings. Ray and Libby's professional careers in Richmond had no time for my problems. My brother-in-law had done enough by setting me up in a business with start-up money. But that business was failing. How could I face him? I hit the bottom of my list of confidants and came up empty.

I felt as if I had dared to risk what few women do. My family raised their eyebrows when I told them I'd bought a cafeteria; they expected me to fall on my face. Instead of realizing I was trying my best, they ridiculed my foolishness. *An uneducated woman owning a business—whoever heard of such a thing.* Of course, they would've taken some of the credit had there been any success in the venture.

Since the Health Department fiasco, I spent my time sitting at a makeshift desk next to the refrigerator in the back room where past-due vendor bills, bank statements, and piles of paperwork gnawed me to death. I didn't have a clue what I was doing.

I shifted onto my side, closed my eyes, and imagined God shaking his fist at me again. My breathing echoed in the quiet room, planning my next move. Wanting to get out of bed. Hoping I could.

I'd spent a gazillion hours at the cafeteria. My life as an entrepreneur didn't make it easy to find friends or keep them. Up to my nose hairs in running Oak Hill Cafeteria, it was easy to get by day after day and not think of myself as lonely.

Time stretched out like an empty road before me, a heavy burden rather than a glorious gift. Mascara marks and tear stains covered my pillowcase. I hadn't changed the sheets in two weeks. Despite my overpowering fatigue, I hadn't meant to lie in a dirty bed until lunchtime.

I forced myself up and walked across the cold floor, wandering from room to room. Dust, clutter, and piles of laundry consumed every foot. *The Health Department should've come here instead.* I had kept my little cafeteria spotless. Far cleaner than my house.

At four o'clock, I could add cranky kids into the mix. The mess pressed on me like a weight, sending me back to bed and onto the cold side of my pillow. I crawled between the covers, pulled the blanket to my chest, and curled on my side again. The lists were endless. There was too much to do, and I had neither energy nor desire to do it.

◌⌒◌

Lula's husband apologized but said he'd heard the call—from a new church, a bigger one. Pastor Clete packed up his wife and his hymnals and set out for his hometown of Birmingham. Lula cried, hanging her arms out the van window, reaching for me one last time. "I'm worried 'bout Rupert. He's been feelin' poorly. You look in on him, Andie?"

"Of course I will. Bye, Lula. You two take care of each other." The rusted-out white van pulled away. I knew Lula didn't want to leave. But the duty of a pastor's wife was to follow her husband. So she did.

Somehow, I drove to the cafeteria every day, only to have a few customers wander in and complain the buffet wasn't what it used to be. I had become a hostess, waitress, cook, server, and cleaning crew. I hated it. Instead of eating, I smoked and stared out the front window at nothing I hadn't seen a thousand times before. Not noticing, and still less giving a damn, that the window was greasy, and the floor needed to be mopped. Life was mostly empty. I'd close up early, and the entire nonsense repeated the next day.

Daddy gave me a steady supply of Camels—the extra packs Dixie wouldn't let him smoke—since I couldn't afford them. Nerves. I felt them skittering along the top of my skin. Joe occasionally darkened my door long enough to wash his clothes, talk briefly to his children, and pack for his next trip. He had become nothing but a boarder who slept on my couch and deposited money into my account twice a month.

It all affected me as a mother. I felt the twins' embarrassment. I wasn't like other mothers. I had serious problems. Believe me when I say the House of Praise ensured the lies spread beyond the church's stained glass windows. The other mothers in the neighborhood did not include me in school activities. However relieved I pretended to be, it hurt knowing they all pointed and stared. But my life had become too ominous and full of pain to care.

Chapter 25
An Appeal
Andie ~ November 1988

Sadly, I prepared to close Oak Hill Cafeteria with bankruptcy as my only option. Before delivering the bad news to my principal investor, Ray, I felt desperate to make one last appeal.

I needed money. Breaking my own rule, never to return to the House of Praise, I decided to ask Calvin for help. Help for Joe's children, at least. His threats to leave and divorce me were now over thirteen months old. I thought perhaps I could buy a little more time before I lost Joe's financial help altogether. I'd agree to work at the Praise Buffet as a cook, maybe two days a week, and pay back any financial loan with interest. It was a genuinely good plan. I reasoned many mothers down through the centuries worked in the face of evil, made great personal sacrifices, and appealed to their persecutors just to feed their children. I was no different.

My phone call to Fannie landed me an appointment the next day. I requested no one be in the room except Calvin.

Nailing a sign on the door, I closed the cafeteria for the week. Nobody would miss it except the Darwoods across the street. They had been there for me to watch the twins and eat at my humble establishment. Their children playing with Dillon and Gracie on the sidewalks—treasured memories that made me smile despite it all.

On the day of my appointment with Calvin, I borrowed Caroline's spare Honda because my Monte Carlo sat in the repair shop. My old car seemed to cost more money for repairs over the years than the monthly payments.

When I pulled into the parking lot at a quarter to five, employees, volunteers, and Praise Buffet customers occupied every parking spot. The management, namely Calvin, did not permit parking in the church lot except during service hours, so I circled the other lots several times before parking across the street at McDonald's.

Fannie greeted me in the reception area of the television studio. I took a seat, recalling the first time I waited to talk to Calvin in his old office at the church. Pregnant with my first child, I remembered my knees knocking. He scared me to death back then.

This time, the wait was considerably less. Calvin opened his studio office door. "Andie." The barest of smiles cracked his lips. "Come in," he said with an imposing jerk of his head.

I stood and ambled toward him. "Thanks for agreeing to see me, Reverend Artury." Stepping aside to let me pass, he quickly closed the door. I heard him sigh as he leaned against his fancy desk and crossed his arms. My eyes swept around his extravagant office in one swift glance, but I didn't bother commenting. I felt sure any of his collected art pieces would pay my bills for a year.

Instead, I zeroed in on his pricy gray suit. I'd seen him wearing it on TV that morning. His tie knot was still tight on his shirt collar, and his eyes blazed like buffed turquoise stones. His hair streamed to his shoulders and glowed almost white in the light from the window behind him. A pair of diamond cuff links sparkled like the diamonds in his ring.

I didn't need to imagine what his second sigh implied. He pushed back his shirt cuff to check the time on his shiny gold watch. Obviously, his precious schedule was a tight one.

Calvin moved to his desk chair and sat slowly. "Was there something specific you wanted?" he asked, irritated and indifferent. "If you weren't a ministry team wife, I would not have squeezed you in today. I understand Joe is still in your home?"

Nothing could have stopped the tremor of desperation that crept into my voice. "You know he is."

"What, exactly, do you want, Andie?"

I sat across from him and took a deep breath as if I were about to jump into white-water rapids. "I would like your help. Financially. For Joe's children, if for no other reason. We've not had a raise in twelve years, as you know. We have no medical benefits. Of course, you know that, too. My children need to see a dentist, and my daughter needs braces."

He made an annoyed gesture. "And your business—how is it doing?"

"You know exactly how it's doing. It's failing. We will lose everything." This wasn't the time to throw the blame in his lap. I blinked away my tears. "Joe has always escaped from our financial problems. Traveling enables him to remove himself from reality and forget about his struggling family at home. So, I figured we had two choices. Either Joe gets a raise, or I ask you for a loan, in which case I would work for you as a cook at your Praise Buffet until it's paid off." My humble pie did not go down easy. In fact, I felt as if I might choke.

"That's an interesting proposition. The way I heard it, though, let's see, how did Leonard Culver put it? Ahh yes, you said, and I quote, 'The Reverend can't afford me; I don't work for peanuts.'"

"My circumstances have changed." My driving needs to survive terrified me. I felt myself groveling. "I'd really appreciate your help." I reached across his immaculate desk, daring to put my hands on it, staring into eyes that sparked with impatience. "I have fought this ministry long and hard and am about to lose. I know that." My body slumped toward him. I froze my blind, unbelievable wish to cry, imploring him.

Then, with fury, righteous anger, and a ruined heart, I allowed my tears to fall on his pretty, shiny desk beneath me. "Please try to understand. I'm not evil. I'm not an awful person. I just don't want to attend your church. Can't you see that? Why didn't you leave us alone long ago? Let us remain a family?"

"My, my," someone said, clapping his hands behind me. "That was quite a performance, Mrs. Oliver. Brought tears to *my* eyes. What about you, Reverend?"

Evan!

Calvin cleared his throat. "I'm sorry, Andie. Evan, I promised Mrs. Oliver we would meet alone."

"Sorry to interrupt, Reverend, but I must speak to you briefly."

Calvin stood. "Excuse me." He exited quickly while Evan insulted me again with a sneer.

It was no performance. I had exposed my throat, laid my cards on the table, and begged a man I loathed for help.

Appearing distracted when he returned, Calvin sat in his chair again, crossed his legs, and leaned back. "There are technical difficulties in the studio. I need to go. Although my heart goes out to you, Andie, I must bend to the will of God, which is for Joe to do His bidding. There are millions of souls at stake. You have stood in the way of God's will for Joe all of your married life. You have hindered him, and now you beg for mercy. If you had not gone into debt with a mortgage and a business, this would not be happening to you. I pay Joe what I can afford. I warned you not to conceive children. It was *your* choice to have them. Now you complain you cannot take care of them properly. It's time you pay the consequences. My answer to you is simple. *No.* I will not help you. You have failed Jehovah-Shammah one too many times. Your call to salvation in Hawaii was your last and final chance. I thought I made that clear. Whether Joe divorces you is up to him. But I cannot see him spending the rest of his life serving God and married to you. My suggestion to him will be that he leave your home immediately. Joe knows the scripture: *Ye cannot serve God and mammon.* I'm sorry; I need to get to the studio. Fannie will see you out." He stood and walked to the door. The meeting was over.

My temples pounded, and my throat felt as dry and rough as an old dog bone. For a moment, defeat held me immobile. I swallowed my despair while mentally quenching the fire in my brain and the fierce craving to see him nailed to his own cross. And then, rage, more potent than anything I'd felt since Mavis died, swept through me with a force that pulled me to my feet. I walked toward him and stood as close as I dared. "I truly should write a book about all this someday," I said, allowing him to see my fury.

For the first time, anger showed on his face. Swiftly masked, something else followed. Something sinister. Dark. His nostrils flared slightly, and he spoke almost too quickly, too calmly. "Do you think that's a good idea?"

Seconds passed. My silence intimated him, and it felt good. I stood straight and lifted my chin. At that moment, I would've sold my soul for revenge. "No," I said. "Just a thought."

Calvin smiled an artificial smile, walked back to his desk, and pulled out a small envelope from his top drawer. "Andie, why don't you walk over to the Praise Buffet and have a coffee on me? In fact, have supper. I'll buy. Here's a meal ticket. Enjoy. We give these to employees for perfect attendance. Then, go home, accept your future, and plan your life without Joe." He opened the door, a sure sign he wanted me to leave, then hesitated. "I expect you'll allow your children to stay in church?"

Read my mind, Calvin. Not just no, but hell no! "I'll think about it," I said.

"Goodbye then," he said as he ushered me out of his office.

Numb, my mouth refused to work. Holding my meal ticket, the only thing I could think of to say was—*you can shove your free food up your pretentious ass.* But I said nothing and walked away.

I stood dazed and defeated. I'd be in my sister's car in one more minute and then go home. And do what? Pay bills? Worry and panic over which ones to avoid so I can pay those most pressing?

My stomach growled, watching Fannie get into her car; it was after six o'clock. *Oh, why the hell not?* I'd have to walk outside to get to the Praise Buffet, but that was better than finding my way through the complex and running into any studio employees I knew who had clocked out for the day.

Rain spotted the sidewalk. It was the beginning of November—*maybe Joe will stay until after the holidays, which would take care of Christmas money. Maybe. Hopefully.*

Gusts of wind picked up brown leaves and swirled them around my bare legs. I'd worn my only suitable dress but had not purchased pantyhose in months. My hair blew into my mouth and stuck to my lip gloss. A crowd had formed the dinner line waiting for an open table. The Praise Buffet had become a popular eating destination. I debated but got in line—a free meal was a free meal. Besides, I hadn't found the courage to go home. And I was hungry.

Table for one?"

"Yes, thank you."

The inner circle, which Joe had been a part of since the beginning, remained the same thirty-some men and their wives.

But the new staff, the outer circle, had grown to well over three hundred in my estimation. Too many to remember by name. The attractive young hostess with *Farrah Fawcett* hair in a short skirt and tight sweater handed me a House of Praise Bible tract to read while I waited. Calvin's smiling face covered the front of the flimsy paper. A piece of marketing magic. I balled it up and threw it in a nearby trash can.

"Our members have sacrificed to make Bible tracts for people to read." The girl had guts.

I laughed. "You'd be luckier betting at the racetrack than handing that thing to me. Can I have a menu?"

The simple-minded hostess glared at me as if I had committed the unpardonable sin in front of her heavily made-up eyes. I figured the poor thing believed Calvin walked on water.

"Menu?" I asked again.

She handed it to me slowly, as if my attitude were contagious.

"Oh wait, I've changed my mind. Can you bring coffee? I'll do the buffet today instead of ordering off the menu."

"Sure."

"If I don't see you before I leave, here's your tip." Feeling sorry for the little hostess, I shoved a five-dollar bill into her hand.

"Thanks!" she said with a polite hostessy smile.

"You're welcome. Here's another tip for you, honey. Get out of this church as soon as you can. Before it ruins your life, before you want children, and before your husband, if you have one, gets sucked into working here. Run away and never look back."

The girl nodded, turned, and staggered back to her post as if I had hit her head with a two-by-four.

Chapter 26

SET FREE BY A MIGHTY HAND

Reverend Calvin Artury ~ November 1988

There was no *technical problem*. A Praise Buffet chef had become difficult and needed dealing with. I allowed Evan to handle the young man's behavior in any extreme manner of his choosing, and then I excused myself quickly. Rushing back to my meeting with Andie, I groaned with an awakening that sent me reeling. She possessed no evidence. She knew nothing. Nothing of what Mavis knew. Otherwise, she would've played that card during our meeting. But she didn't. She didn't because Andie Oliver walked in darkness.

I had been waiting years for that moment. The confirmation I sought God for, day and night, fell into my hands the moment she stepped into my office and began her tawdry request for money. God delivered me from my oppressor, set me free of her, and it was time to set Joe free of her.

When she left my office, I walked to the recording studio with a purpose, ignoring employees who attempted to distract me in the hallways with trivial compliments, comments, or requests. Hard at work in his usual spot, Joe sat among the flotsam and jetsam of audio equipment behind the soundboard, mixing music.

I inspected the hallway to ensure our privacy and closed the door behind me. "Joe, got a minute?"

A flicker, then a flame of apprehension crossed his face. "Of course, Reverend."

I pulled up a chair and sat close to him, taking my time to get to the point. "I met with your wife this afternoon."

He clenched his fists. "What was *she* doing here?"

"She needs money."

"I'm sorry, Reverend. She's a depressing woman. She had no business bothering you."

"You're miserable with her, aren't you, Joe?"

"Horribly." He turned in his swivel chair and stared into my eyes. "I can't stand to look at her."

"It was not my will, but God's, who kept you with her all these years, hoping against hope to save her soul from the flames of Hell. She was your responsibility as head of your home. However, I realized today she took that honor from you."

I touched his shoulder, intending to relay the seriousness of my visit. "I must tell you, last night God affirmed to me in a vision everything I've discussed with you these many years. If you leave this church and go with your wife, leave my protection—" Tears blurred my vision, and I failed to stop them from falling as I spoke. "—I saw you, Joe; I saw you drop into Hell with her." I lowered my voice. "It was a vision I will not shake for quite some time. You know you're dear to me, not like some around here. You've been with me since you were a boy. You're like a son to me. Years ago, I pulled you into the private parts of this ministry that nobody but a few are privileged enough to know about. I need you, Joe. God needs you. And you've—you've done wonderful things for Almighty Jehovah no other man could've accomplished."

Joe wept. "I will never leave you, Reverend Artury. Never."

"Well, then. It's almost time to take flight, son. This is the day of your dreams. Your Red Sea is about to part. It'll be my blessing to watch you run to the Promised Land! Your prison term is almost over. Get your house in order. See an attorney and make your arrangements. The Holy Spirit tells me you can leave her for good in December. I will tell you the exact day and where to move as soon as God reveals it to me. You have my blessing. And I am sure God will bring the right help-mate into your life."

I patted Joe's arm, then stood to leave. "It's a good thing you confiscated the envelope Mavis mailed. Since nothing else has emerged, the ministry is in the clear. Messes like that often take many years to tidy up to ensure nothing surfaces. You've paid for your mistakes. Time to end it and brighten your future."

I cemented my relationship with Joe. He had proven his loyalty repeatedly. In under five minutes, I had pardoned all his sins and set him free, releasing him from a woman he may have initially loved but quickly learned to loathe. And if he had any notion of staying with her for his children's sake, I sweetened the deal. Oh yes, I did indeed!

"One more thing. I'm giving you a raise. Double your present salary. But there is no sense in making your child support any more than it should be, so we will wait until your divorce is final to set that in motion. And Silas will add you and the children to the medical and dental plan."

Joe's eyes widened, his speech breaking off in mid-sentence. "We have—a medical plan? Thank you. Thank you, Reverend. My life is yours."

"No, Joe. It belongs to God."

Chapter 27

JOHNNY REBEL

Andie ~ November 1988

When I arrived at the Praise Buffet, few tables were available, so the hostess sat me at a small table in the back of the dining room next to the kitchen. A row of faux palmetto plants hid me in a relatively obscure corner. I was grateful. At least if I fell apart, I wouldn't be a spectacle.

When I called the Darwoods from a pay phone next to the restrooms, the twins begged to sleep over. I said *okay*. A night off from kids and an evening alone appealed to me.

The Praise Buffet's spread of meats, potato dishes, vegetables, salads, breads, and desserts served in chafing dishes over Sterno cans stretched the length of five ten-foot tables. This unexpected treat, presented like a feast for the starving middle class, delighted my senses. Owning a restaurant offered me little time to visit other restaurants. I timidly approached the beautifully presented buffet, carefully eyeing every selection. I felt I deserved it, though a free meal was not much of a consolation prize.

Sipping my coffee, I watched the House of Praise employees and regular customers come and go. I returned for seconds and thirds. *Why not?*

Occupying my mind, I put my feet on the chair across from me and read the newspaper as employees cleaned up before the nine-thirty closing hour. I peered into the kitchen again. I had hoped to have a modern kitchen someday—a fantastic kitchen, even better than Dixie's, like the kitchens in the magazines—like the kitchen at the Praise Buffet.

"You've been here a long time. Need more coffee?"

I looked up into the smiling eyes of a boldly beautiful young man. There was no other way to describe him. Somewhere in his twenties, he was like one of those chestnut-haired angels in paintings, only fully clothed. Perhaps it was the ringlets over his dark brows and about his neck. His long-lashed eyes were clear blue, like a perfect sky, and his lips were sensual and a little sad. Statuesque and athletically proportioned, his broad shoulders descended to an almost female waist. He could've been a rock star, so why was he serving me coffee?

"I'd love some."

"Well, hey, it's lukewarm and weak as dishwater, but what the hell, it's free, right?"

I smiled. "Did I hear you say the H-E-L-L word in here?"

"Damn!" he gasped. "Pisser—oh!" He stomped his foot and covered his mouth with his free hand. "Please don't tell on me." He giggled and wiggled like a young girl, like my Gracie. "I always screw up when I'm tired!"

I laughed. I needed to laugh. It felt good.

"I rarely bring coffee," he said as he poured. "I'm the chef today, and noticed you've returned to the buffet several times. You must've been hungry. You work here?"

"I'm wasting time. And no, thank God, I don't work here. My husband, soon-to-be ex-husband, does."

"Oh? Who's that, may I ask?"

"Joe Oliver; know him?" I took a sip of my coffee.

"Know him? He's one fine-looking man, honey."

He's gay. How long has he worked here?

"I've worked here four years and counting," he said.

"How'd you know I was about to ask?"

"Eventually, it's something you just know. They've hidden me in the kitchen, but that's okay. Oh, hell, it's a long story. Damn! There I go with the H-E-L-L!"

I laughed again. "I won't tell." Drawn to him, I smiled; I needed a new friend. "I've got time if you do. Want to talk?"

"Sure. Why not? I'm at the end of my shift. Let me finish a few things in the kitchen, and I'll be right back. I promise."

"That's fine; take your time," I said, hoping he kept his promises.

⌒⌒

Twenty minutes later, he returned. "Sorry, I had to review tomorrow's menu with the staff before they left for the day. It gets busy around here at Thanksgiving. Mind if I pull up a seat?"

"Of course not. My name is Andie, by the way." I held out my hand.

"Yes, I know. Andie Oliver. The infamous backslider."

"That would be me. Maybe you'd prefer not to talk to me after all."

"You're wrong. I'd *love* to. Mrs. Oliver, it's a privilege and a pleasure to meet you."

He took my hand and kissed it. Captivated by his expression and character, I blushed. "I didn't know I was so popular."

"Are you kidding? Your name comes up often. Especially with people who would rather stick Calvin's Bible tracts up their fat hineys than speak the truth about this place."

He kept making me laugh. "I've told you my name. What's yours?"

"John. John Rossi. They call me Johnny Rebel because I am one. Only I'm a rebel *with* a cause."

I smiled. "Let me ask you something."

193

"Only if you let me ask you something next."

I nodded in polite agreement. "Fair enough. Where are you from? You sound Southern."

"I am. I'm from the mountains, a small town west of here. Having spent my early years in a two-stoplight town, I left home shortly after high school for Harvard. My family has money—shhh, don't tell anybody. Although, after getting to Harvard, I wanted to become the next Galloping Gourmet, the next Julia Child. So I dropped out, I know—shocker. What idiot drops out of Harvard, right? But I enrolled in culinary school, and now here I am."

Harvard had failed to water down John's accent. Diluted but still country, he radiated a rare male loveliness.

"And I'm gay," he said.

"So?"

"That doesn't bother you?"

"Should it?"

"I'm not allowed to attend church here unless I confess my homosexuality sin in front of the congregation. Sometimes, I slip in the back for the sheer orneriness of it. So yes, being gay bothers most people here who know about me. Except for Pete." He winked.

"Peter Collins? Head Chef of the Praise Buffet, Peter Collins?"

He waved his hand at me as if shooing away a fly. "We were together a long time, honey. My turn to ask you something. And don't worry, they never bugged this dining room. It's too big, and I've turned off all the cameras."

I hesitated. "Okay."

"Why are you here tonight? Did you backslide from God or Calvin?"

"That's more than one question."

"I know. Sorry."

"I hate this place," I blurted. "I hate Calvin. I shouldn't hate anyone, I suppose. It's a pretty strong word. But at this moment, it's exactly how I feel. He's held on to Joe and ruled my family for—

sixteen years. Sixteen long and exhausting years." I shook my head at the sound of it. "Anyway, I've always bucked him, kicked against the pricks, Calvin being the biggest prick, if you know what I mean."

John's head flew back, and he laughed as loud as he dared. "That's one I haven't heard!"

We both laughed. It was as if I'd known him all my life. Then the laughter stopped, and we stared at each other in soundless sorrow. In that silent few seconds, we understood something far greater than ourselves had destined our meeting.

I tilted my head and grinned. "I guess I'm a rebel, too. Since my youth, I have lived in fear of Calvin and God's wrath. The problem was, I never asked him for permission to scratch my butt like everybody else does." I leaned forward, resting my arms on the table. "Today, I groveled at his feet, begging him to help me. My marriage is over. Adding insult to injury, my financial life is coming apart at the seams. You know what? My marriage never began. Calvin never gave us a chance for a normal life. What's normal? I'm not sure what that is."

John sat quietly as I thumbed tears from my eyes. He warmed my coffee again, pouring from the carafe he'd placed on the table.

"I suppose the answer to your question, John, is that I'm not a backslider. I love God. Sure, I've made plenty of mistakes and even came short of the glory several times. I don't believe God places conditions on our salvation. Legalism runs rampant in this church." I let out a small whimper. "Oh well, what's it matter? I can't change it. Frankly, I don't want to be labeled as an evangelical. Or even a Christian. Religious titles and denominations are like poison to me."

"I hurt for you," he said. "But I hear you. Your plight mirrors my own. I think you're safe for me to talk to."

"Safe?"

"Yes. Safe. There are spies here because some of us want out, like you."

"Seriously?"

"Absolutely. We've all got a story and reasons we're trapped in this place. Once you're in, they erect an invisible wall. We're not planting vegetables or having orgies in some remote Montana, Arizona, or Guyana commune. Oh, no. They manipulate you here by controlling who you love. And as you know, Calvin doesn't require his converts to lose their wealth up front. He bleeds it out, one paycheck at a time. Especially from low-level employees."

Intrigued by our common ground, I asked, "So, what's *your* story?"

His eyes scanned the room. "Okay. I'll tell you. Security knows I close late, so we're protected in here. They won't check this room until they think I've left the building." He seemed to study me thoughtfully for a moment. "I like you, Andie Oliver."

"I like you, too, Johnny Rebel." I looked at my watch, ten minutes after ten. I'd been sitting there for almost four hours. The Buffet had closed, but no one could see us in the dim corner where we huddled, hidden in the low lights of the dining room.

"You ever wonder why Calvin is so attracted to the men around here?" John asked.

I choked on my coffee. Reaching his long arm across the table, John gently patted my back while I coughed, spit, and then wiped my mouth. My eyes filled with tears. Something came unbraided inside me. A secret code broke, and the mysteries of the universe exploded open. I didn't so much as smile. Neither did John. A chill settled between us, silent and misty, like the weather outside. I glanced at my watch again. Ten-fifteen. In five brief minutes, everything I thought I knew about Calvin worsened. The fact that he preached against a lifestyle he practiced made him even more of a fake, a phony, and a liar. "Of course," I whispered. "It makes sense. How did you find out? But wait—he was married."

"Lots of gay men are married. I think he might be bisexual, with strong homosexual tendencies. Or he's obsessed with sex and anything he can stick it in. His marriage was a front. In case you haven't noticed, his personality draws both men and women. Get him alone, and he burns with a smoldering sensuality. Some women turn into puppies just talking with him. Obviously, not you." John chuckled. "But Calvin fascinated me when Pete introduced us. This man of means and finery impressed the hell out of me. At first."

He turned his head and searched the near-darkness for any remote eavesdropper. "When Calvin crossed my path, I allowed him to seduce me with his palate for the finer things in life. His Sinatra-blue eyes, long blonde hair, broad chest—he blew me away," said John. "He lured me in and held me hostage."

I watched John take a deep breath. A dam burst as he poured out his heart, and I listened, thinking Chestnut-haired angels shouldn't have to endure such suffering. But his every word mesmerized me. Every rise and fall of his voice commanded my attention. I felt his longing for freedom blatantly burning within him—freedom from the job, from Calvin, and every piece of his past.

His face reflected the low lights of the room. "Aside from Calvin's physical attributes back then, he spoke like a politician, a man used to being admired and followed, and he was addictive, even when he wasn't trying to be. I could've listened to him for hours—preach or just plain talk—it didn't matter. His Southern aristocratic drawl, the way his pinky ring flashed. And there was the way he looked at me. He met my eyes directly, as if God had truly anointed him. Duped by his false sincerity, it was an honor, I thought, to be noticed by the famous Reverend. After he hired Pete as head chef, he offered me the job of assistant chef. Pete and I had been partners for years. I didn't want to lose him. I suspected Calvin was gay, but I didn't believe he was evil, and considering the bankrolls in his pockets, I wagered no price was too high when negotiating my six-figure salary."

I choked on nothing but spit and air. "That's absurd! I'm sorry. I'm sure you deserve your salary, but Joe volunteered countless hours for two decades from the time he was a boy. When Calvin finally hired him, his paycheck barely fed us."

John shook his head. "I've heard Calvin horrendously underpays and overworks the ministry team. There's nothing, Andie, nothing you or anyone can do about that. My hire was unusual, and I drove a hard bargain. He wanted me here bad enough that I could name my price. But there's no Human Relations Department for the rest of you. You have no recourse. You get what you get. Nobody can go on strike or complain. From what I hear, he doesn't even pay into social security. There's a steep price to pay to work for this ministry."

John was right. For all my hope, my decision to marry a church boy resulted in a path of poverty set in stone from the moment I said, *I do.* But I sat dead still, absorbing every word, gesture, and sigh he made, knowing that night would change my life.

I watched John lean back, his eyes unblinking, his voice low, spilling his story over the table between us. Even though he accepted Artury's job offer, it was small potatoes compared to his experience. John worked in his own spotlight and had tackled more than a few tough jobs for his young age, which included a catered affair at the lavish home of Jim and Tammy Bakker, a one-thousand-dollar-a-plate fundraiser for Pat Robertson's presidential campaign, and as a pastry chef for a state dinner at the White House. John alluded to a godly mother who raised him and that he had embraced salvation at an early age. So, working at the Praise Buffet or joining the church wasn't a big deal.

"Within weeks after my first day here, the red flags came at me like flies on a dead deer. At first, I reasoned, Calvin wanted closer to Pete for honest business reasons, to turn the Praise Buffet into a destination attracting new church members. But the nagging warning in my head and the hint that Calvin was in love with my

Pete evolved into an all-out war. Now, I can't get Pete to leave. I've wanted out for two years, but they've brainwashed the love of my life. I had no idea Calvin would prevail in our breakup."

John's voice hardened. "I thought I knew how the televangelists of the world operated, having catered their events in the past. Their desperation to pay for television time drives those with the best intentions to the gates of Hell to make the money they need to prove they're called by God. In the end, they're high-rolling zealots—all of them. But Calvin is worse. Way worse."

"Are there any honest televangelists?" I asked.

"Maybe. I've not met one. But what disturbed me most after coming to work here was how Calvin treated his employees, and even the volunteers, as if they were disposable. He's cruelty in motion, finding fault with even their best efforts. Yet, they still worship him and bask in his god-like presence."

Resting his head on his fist, John pushed his cold coffee to the middle of the table. "My mama taught me everything I needed to know about rich men, having been married to one. Getting mixed up with Calvin Artury was the worst mistake of my life. It had *whoa, mule, whoa* written all over it, but I refused to pull on the reins. I stay on, hoping Pete will see my love for him. But Calvin's goons stalk me everywhere I go. They think they can drive me crazy. I know too much. I know Calvin's a homosexual."

John raked his finger through his curls. "Man, I sure could use a cigarette. Beware of Evan Preston, Andie. He's made a fortune producing porno films and shipping them across the country."

I choked a third time. "—I'm sorry—*What?*"

"Some time ago, Evan hired me to cater a small business meeting in his dining room at his big, fancy house in Clemmons. I arrived early. But no one was home. I knocked and discovered an unlocked back door. New and naïve, I went inside to get started and set up the room. To this day, I could kick myself. I didn't see it coming."

"What happened, John?"

"After two hours of prep work, I waited for a meeting that was never meant to be. Bored, I got curious and wandered through the house. Homemade videotapes, three high-end video cams, and a dozen photographer's floodlights filled a large bordello-looking bedroom upstairs. A huge round bed sat smack in the center, with electrical outlets every three feet around the walls. I thought, hey, this guy is kinky; he makes porno flicks! There were boxes of videotapes, all unopened. Perfect setup, really. They use the church's equipment to make the tapes and bank accounts to filter the profits or launder it by other means. Either way, it's made Evan and a few others rich. Of course, someone would first have to edit the raw tapes, but that equipment didn't seem to be in the house. Then, they'd have to send the edited videos somewhere to make them into movies before selling them to adult stores nationwide. I finally put it all together."

Crossing his legs, John breathed deep into the room's silence. I had found a poor soul like me, alone and desperate for someone to listen. Somehow, in helping John, I'd help myself. "What happened next?" I asked. My eyes met his with sympathy as I listened to the intent of his heart that mixed with the ache of his discoveries.

John cleared his throat. "I rooted through a few drawers in that whorish bedroom and found bags of cocaine. They had set me up. Minutes later, all hell broke loose. Long story short, I got propositioned. They wanted me to work in the 'porno department,' but I laughed in Evan's face. That's when they threatened my life and Pete's and beat me to a pulp to keep my mouth shut. By then, they had me trapped with my fingerprints on the cocaine bags. So, here I am, still working at the damn Praise Buffet, trying to find a way out of this mess."

"Have you tried talking to the police?"

"I can't prove a thing. They moved the porno production out of Evan's house. There's no one here I trust. I'm a gay man who has hidden it from a homophobic congregation. No gays allowed. Not outwardly. Calvin threatened me with prison if I admitted my past relationship with Pete. Without Pete, I have no one here."

Fury ignited a passion for justice inside me. I rummaged through my purse, wrote my number on a slip of paper, then handed it to John.

"You're not alone. We're both trapped and trying to find a way out."

John smiled and studied the number. "I've memorized it. No need to save the paper." He rolled it into a tiny ball, popped it in his mouth, and washed it down with the last of his cold coffee. "I'll call you. Please don't call me; they've tapped my line. They may have tapped yours, too; if not now, it will be."

He put his hand on mine. "Thanks for listening, Andie. And for your friendship. But that could be dangerous for you. Someone sliced my tires last night, and I had to walk to work today. It got serious this afternoon when I mouthed off to Evan and Calvin that I'd had enough. Again, I can't prove a thing. Who will believe this church that donates thousands of dollars to the politicians, the poor, and the community is involved in anything illegal?"

"Why hasn't Calvin fired you?"

"Let me ask you, why do you think your marriage lasted as long as it did? You have something on him, or he believed you did. He needed to keep tabs on you. Same with me. I've threatened to expose him. His homosexuality, his fling with Pete. They threaten me; I threaten them. On and on. Without Pete to back me up, I haven't got a chance. Still, they're afraid it'll leak out, and the possibility of my accusations being true would cause bad press and an unwanted investigation. By keeping me here, Calvin can watch me. Control what I say and who I talk to. Eventually, he'll use scripture and personal prophecy to justify whatever means he chooses to destroy his enemies. Watch your back, Andie."

"Destroy? What do you mean by that?"

John stumbled for words. "Hasn't he destroyed your family? I want you to remember this: Calvin has more than one judge in his pocket, members of the press, a slew of doctors, lawyers, a banker, and a host of men, professional and otherwise, who will do his bidding all in the name of the Lord, no questions asked."

"Good grief! He *is* omnipotent. Can you live with your mother? She seems like a nice woman, from what you said."

"Yes, she is—salt of the earth, that woman. But I have family who have not accepted my gay pride, if you will. Except for one brother, the others hate my guts. It's been a source of contention for years. I stay away to keep the peace. And, like I said, I'm not sure Calvin will *allow* me to leave without consequences."

"How can he do that!? Please, John. *I'm* your friend. Let's meet for coffee and support each other. Some place other than Winston-Salem. We can at least lean on each other until you leave this place. I have no one who understands what I'm going through, either."

"Sure, Andie."

Suddenly, the dining room's eerie darkness frightened me. I shivered as I glanced at the exit sign above the emergency door. That was precisely what I wanted to do. Exit. "I need to get going. Can I take you home, drop you off anywhere?"

"No. It's not safe. I'm telling you, these people are dangerous. There's more to it than I can tell you in one evening. Look, they've switched off the lights in the lobby." John stood. "We need to leave. Now. Security will be around soon. Let's go out the back kitchen door. There are no lights or cameras there. No one will see us together. That would mean trouble for you. If they knew I was talking to you—" He paused, grabbed his coat from a nearby closet, then turned to me with a strange glare. "He's a Godfather in a Mafia of holy men, Andie. Never forget that."

I'd heard those words, or something similar, somewhere in my past. "You're scaring me, John Rossi."

"I hope so. Keep your family out of here. As I said, with no proof, they'll make our lives a living Hell if we spill our guts with hearsay. Without concrete evidence, we have nothing. We start a major scandal; we're good as dead."

"Dead? John, has he—"

"—Quiet." John put his finger up to his mouth. "We'll talk more about that later. Let's go."

I slipped on my coat and shuddered. John definitely knew more than he was willing to tell me. "I'm following you home," I said. "Don't try to stop me."

"Please don't. Someone is always stalking me. They might spot you."

"I'll be careful. They won't recognize my sister's car, and I'm parked across the street. Her weirdo ex-husband tinted the windows, they won't even see me. I need to make sure you arrive home safely."

"Fine. I'm a short walk from here. I live in the Southern Pine Apartments down the block. Look at the time; we really need to go. Please stay at a distance. I'm serious. Don't even appear as though you're following me. I don't want them to link us together." He kissed my cheek, then whispered, "Welcome to the enemy's camp."

I nodded but didn't answer. I wanted to hold him. My protective urges swelled and spilled into my heart; I wanted to help him escape, take him somewhere safe. I wanted to make plans with him to expose the ministry. Instead, I slid out the kitchen delivery door behind him.

ℂ℃

John pulled his leather jacket collar around his ears and bolted across the lawns. In the shadows, under a line of tall trees, I ran to my sister's car. The packed parking lots earlier that afternoon were suddenly my blessing; it appeared as if I'd left the complex hours earlier.

I drove at a snail's pace. John had already walked the short distance to his apartment building, but I caught up in time to watch him dash between parked cars. He appeared skittish.

I noticed the tenants parked nearly a hundred feet from their building, so I backed into a long row of cars under a large weeping willow tree and switched off the headlights to hide my face in the darkness and keep an eye on John.

I waited in the car, keeping my promise to stay at a distance. Admiring what was once a charming hotel that someone transformed into luxury residences, I peered into the dimly lit garden, a barrier between the dark parking lot and the apartments. A wide driveway circled to the front entrance and wound back to the parked cars and out to the street. As I cracked open the window, the scent of rain on the pavement mingled with the despair in my throat. My stomach twisted, a knot of unease as I realized with a sudden, chilling clarity, that I had only begun to uncover the depths of the evil within Artury's ministry.

John walked into the muted glow of the garden. I saw him reach into his pocket for keys. Several more steps to the verandah of the old, remodeled building and he'd be safe. Then I could leave. But within seconds, headlights from a black Mercedes plowed into the lot. I switched off my car's ignition and sank low in the seat. The Mercedes sped past, bearing down on John. I watched John turn and stare into the car's headlights, then fall backward. He struggled to pick himself up, desperate to escape the car's path. John lunged toward the building's steps, but the car swerved around him and blocked his entrance. The car's driver window came down, and in the garden's faint light, Evan Preston appeared with a gun and fired.

In one nightmarish moment, I witnessed a flash from the silent gun before John's head exploded and his body crumbled to the asphalt. The Mercedes window rolled up, and the car flew out of the lot, speeding down the street, but not before I saw Evan at the wheel and Silas Turlo in the front seat. I would've recognized their faces in a line-up anywhere.

Peeking over the dashboard, I choked on my tears. A quiet scream climbed in my throat, and I shook violently. I remained sunken in my sister's car seat, hiding my face in my hands, terrified they might return.

I don't recall how much time passed until I finally lifted my head, turned the key in the ignition, and drove out of the lot with my headlights off. John Rossi lay in the driveway by the beautiful garden behind me. A puddle of blood pooled around his body, shimmering in the darkness. It sickened me, and I vomited into my lap.

My left hand trembled driving to the gas station on the next block, as my right hand dug into my purse for a cigarette and some change to use the phone. I lit my cigarette before dropping my quarter twice and asking the operator to connect me to the police. Holding back fiery tears, I attempted to disguise my voice and report the murder anonymously, not naming the victim or the murderer.

Mustering every ounce of caution and courage, I drove home a different route. Visibly shaken and blinded by grief, I blinked against the glare of the few headlights exposing me at that early morning hour. My fingers had gone past numb to aching from gripping the wheel.

Driving into the safety of my garage, I broke down, pounded the dashboard, and wailed, "Why, God? Why not let me die? Why did John die instead of me!?" After a good cry and tongue-lashing at God, I unfolded myself out of the car and found my way to the bathroom and bed.

My conversation with John rolled over and over in my mind until I put pieces of it into memory. *How much more can I bear? I have to come forward. But who can I trust? With all the officials in Artury's hip pocket, they might even accuse me of his murder. After all, I was there.* I reasoned Calvin believed in his divinity, but his upper crust, his top brass, used him and his church as a cover for their crime ring. Morning's first light dawned, but the image of John Rossi's body lying in his blood burned inside my head.

An undisputed truth emerged. I had to protect my children and remain silent. I knew if I spilled my guts to the police, Calvin's men would discredit or kill me before I could testify against them. Evan and Silas would walk free, and my children would get sucked into the ministry almost immediately. I couldn't let that happen. I wouldn't. Stumbling to the kitchen, I sat at the table and wrote it down as I had witnessed it. Placing my crude deposition into an envelope, I carried my evidence to the attic and hid it in the rafters.

I did not know how or when, but if God were indeed just, He would help me unmask the evil within the House of Praise when the time was right. I would never tell Joe what I saw, since I couldn't trust him. With any luck, he was not a part of Calvin's crime ring, but I had no way of knowing. My fear for my life and my children's lives locked the secret of John Rossi's murder into that impassable wasteland inside me. And only God had the key.

Chapter 28
Only God Knows
Andie ~ December 1988

As I boxed up my cafeteria and watched the local news, I stuck my hand into my pocket and discovered a loose thread. The first sign of an unraveling seam. I thought about the seams of life that fall apart when you least expect it. The real unraveling of my life began the moment I met John Rossi.

John's murder made front-page news and headlined regional telecasting. The police pleaded for the anonymous caller to come forward. John's family, who lived near Boone, offered a sizeable reward for any information leading to the arrest and conviction of his murderer. But no amount was enough to move me to call the police and risk my children's safety and future. They were my number one concern. I remained quiet.

The news reporter said although John worked as a chef at the popular Praise Buffet, his family refused House of Praise involvement in his private funeral services to be held at the family's church in Watauga County.

"Good for them," I mumbled.

According to the reporter, the House of Praise did not comment other than to say John's presence would be missed and that he was a stellar employee. Their public relations person, who I did not know, added the church had only recently discovered his homosexuality. They suggested his murder might have had something to do with the gay community. I imagined Calvin standing in his pulpit, proclaiming to the congregation that John's lifestyle had caught up with him and that God had permitted his destruction.

⟡

Three weeks later, I closed Oak Hill Cafeteria for good. My landlord had rented the space to a new owner. I worked relentlessly, packing up what remained in the kitchen and giving Velda and Henry Darwood a few large jars of peaches, pickles, and mayonnaise. I hauled the rest of my canned foods home, knowing I would need them in the coming days. Selling what dry goods I could, I put the rest into boxes for the Salvation Army. I pulled the lace curtains off the front windows and had the sign over the entrance removed. A couple more carloads, a few swipes with a rag on the counter, and one last floor sweep. I was done. Standing with my hand on the doorknob for one last look, I closed the door on that chapter of my life.

The next day, I borrowed more money from Aunt Wylene. I filed for bankruptcy, flushing away my dreams of early retirement, independence, and success. The sheer weight of my failure backed me into a corner of confusion. How could I fight the devastating sense of defeat? How long before I would have to leave my home? Why were Joe's clothes still in the closet and his tools in the garage? And I had no clue what was in the padlocked shed in my backyard. He'd told me it was full of car parts, broken audio equipment, and back issues of *Popular Electronics*. I didn't care. I just wanted him out.

Walking alone into the enormous dark of my future, I retreated to the comfort of my couch. Except for getting the twins off to school, fixing a few meals, and tucking them in bed, I remained stoic and still and mostly—asleep.

Chapter 29

THE SECOND SON

Reverend Calvin Artury ~ December 1988

On an extended European tour, I took time to counsel my ministry team at the Sheraton Grand Hotel, laying the groundwork for the new millennium. The angel of the Lord appeared in a vision saying, that I, like Christ, was the Son of God. His second son. It was the most cherished moment of my life. But there were a few knots to untangle before enlightening my staff and congregation about my most recent revelation.

I had been slow to give Joe the exact date to leave his wife, explaining I was concerned about his children and their salvation. I assured him that, in time, God would move on his behalf. If he would trust and obey, then his son and daughter would not perish in the flames of Hell with their mother. "Our Heavenly Father will reveal His plan, and they will reside safely inside the House of Praise," I told Joe. "God will leave Andie to her own self-destruction."

I did not want to witness the demise of the young girl I had desperately strived to pull into the hierarchy of my ministry. I had no desire to watch Andie's soul enter Hell. But as a minister of the gospel, I knew God would require it. I had viewed the torturous end of many souls as they dropped into the abyss of flames. It grieved me. Andie was a beautiful woman like my mother. And yet, she had blasphemed. She was nothing but a dog returning to its vomit. An apostate. It was out of my hands.

Chapter 30
More Important Things
Andie ~ December 1988

I found a job, but it was short-lived. Emerging into the brisk December wind, I pulled up my coat collar, feeling the rough, scratchy wool on my skin. My old coat had protected me against chilly North Carolina winters for years—one more thing I needed to replace.

My warm breath swirled in the cold air. I stood in the street, glancing back at the restaurant where I'd worked the past two weeks, clutching my one and only paycheck. The chef at Goddard's Steak & Ale had offered to show me his culinary techniques two nights a week if I'd wait tables the rest of the time. But the manager let me go. He said business had slowed because of the lousy economy, and people weren't eating out as much. He explained he should not have hired me. His mistake. He was sorry.

Sorry didn't pay my bills or put gas in my car. I sure could've used more notice. Walking forward, I joined the uninviting swarm of pedestrians. Goddard's Steak & Ale seemed like an excellent place to work. It would've kept a roof over our heads and food on the table, including some leftovers the chef handed out every night. Located only a mile from my house, I had planned to walk to work and save money on gas.

I grimaced and then pushed my self-pity aside. I had severe financial problems. Joe's check was all but spent. Even with my one paycheck, I had about four hundred dollars to my name. *What can I sell?* There wasn't much. I had pawned my wedding set long ago to pay medical bills. Second-hand furniture wouldn't bring more than a few dollars. My eighteen-inch TV was my sole distraction and Dillon and Gracie's only entertainment. Except for a gold mother/child ring Dixie had given me and I refused to part with, the rest wasn't worth considering.

I weighed my options. I knew there was no way to find strength or courage stretched out on my couch. The kids wouldn't be home until four o'clock. I needed to clear my head, so I kept walking.

My sister and I had tapped out our parents. Caroline's second divorce was final. She and her three little girls had moved in with Daddy and Dixie. Again. They were driving Dixie bonkers. *So where do I fit in? How can I burden Daddy with my needs when my sister is in such a mess?*

Daddy battled emphysema daily. He was not my answer. His contribution to my life was a down payment on a house and three used cars. Dixie had donated bags of groceries and babysat plenty through the years. Like everything else, I kept my poverty a well-guarded secret from the eyes of the public.

I marched through the cold air, my head absorbed in thought. *What would my life have been like had I gone to college?* However good I was at cooking, it didn't create a career to support me. In some fields, women landed well-paying jobs almost anywhere. Except it had been nearly eight years since I'd taken a test. *How would I pay for school?* I'd missed the boat to college. All I'd ever done was clean house, change diapers, and peel potatoes while I flitted from one menial, low-paying job to the next. That fact came as a shock. I'd reached the end of my rope, focusing my time and energy over the past several years on simple cooking skills. Owning a humble cafeteria was one thing, but landing a job as a chef wasn't in my immediate future. They filled the better restaurants in town with degreed chefs. All men.

I walked for several blocks and stopped in front of one of the more prominent bistros, hoping they might need help. Maybe a hostess. Or somebody to empty the trash. I went inside and asked halfheartedly if they were hiring. The manager shook his head and said they'd laid off their hostess yesterday. *Just keep looking.*

Stepping out on the sidewalk, the brisk wind kept me moving. I strolled past a convenience store and glanced down at a rack of newspapers, stopping me in my tracks. I picked up the *Winston-Salem Journal* and stared at a picture of Calvin Artury and a stunning blonde standing at his portable pulpit, addressing a crowd of Munich's most influential people. According to the article, the woman spoke of an assassin who attacked Calvin during his Berlin miracle Crusade, where she had just given her life to Christ. The beautiful woman testified *Satan had come into their midst.* She stated the assailant shot his gun repeatedly at Calvin from a distance of only ten feet, and not a single bullet hit him. *I believe an angel of the Lord protected Reverend Artury.* The police arrested the assassin.

The newspaper also reported the German police had questioned Calvin and his team regarding the incident. They searched their equipment as a matter of routine, but Calvin proclaimed God was with them. *We have nothing to hide, said Reverend Artury. We are here on a mission from God to save German souls for the kingdom of the Lord.* It also mentioned that if you sent in a twenty-dollar offering within the month, you would be the first to receive Reverend Artury's tell-all book as soon as it became available. A complete account of the evangelist's harrowing experience in Germany and the blonde woman's testimony of finding Jesus through Reverend Artury's ministry.

Focusing on the picture, I wondered how many more theatrics and lies I'd have to witness before God uncovered this madman. It appeared gullible Christians enjoyed soaking up the entire fiasco. Why else would the media plaster it across the headlines? It kept the believers convinced Calvin was a prophet as they stuffed a few extra dollars into their monthly offerings. Nobody put tears in your eyes better than Calvin. I'd sat in his services most of my life and was the first to admit he had fooled even me. Why *wouldn't* the masses believe in him? Calvin sold God better than *Tony the Tiger* sold Frosted Flakes®.

I read on. The Germans called him the *Miracle Man.* The article stated that in the next Crusade in Brussels, he had scheduled Joe Oliver, a long-time employee and resident of Winston-Salem, to testify how God prepared his life for ministry and had selected him as a young boy to win souls.

Joe? At the sight of his name, I laughed bitterly.

I kept reading, this time out loud. "Reverend Artury said Joe Oliver is a type and shadow of King David in the Old Testament, chosen in his youth to slay Goliaths."

My knees buckled, and I sat on a stack of bundled newspapers on the sidewalk. *What might the people of Brussels think if they knew Joe's children did not receive their report cards because their parents couldn't afford to pay their school fees? And that Gracie Oliver cried herself to sleep because someone had made fun of her worn-out backpack and the holes in her sneakers? And that Dillon Oliver couldn't go with his classmates on a field trip to Asheville because there wasn't an extra twenty dollars in the budget? Would our children's sorrows make the headlines in Brussels, along with Joe's testimony of becoming a high-powered follower of Calvin Artury?*

I clenched my fists around the newspaper and stood to find a hard-looking woman in a hideous hat staring at me from inside the store. She cracked open the door and pointed with her thumb to a portable black and white behind her. "Hey, gal. You want to buy that paper, or would you rather watch the news on my TV in here?"

I stuffed the newspaper back into the rack and walked on, grinding my teeth and fighting a massive headache.

Joe had separated himself from us, even though he'd not moved out entirely. Handsome as ever at thirty-five, he'd been a notorious bad boy for years, making a fool out of me and my way of life. Endless women had no doubt shared his bed since Mavis confirmed the first incident. I saw the snapshots he'd taken of his travels with Calvin that inevitably included models, actors, and debutantes. Joe had grown out of his country-boy skin, learned how to conduct himself, and toned down his twang to become nothing less than a suave and debonair evangelical pawn.

It shocked me to see him mentioned in the newspaper with Calvin. No doubt the German blonde and Joe were friends. She looked like the type of woman he always said was *just a friend*. Everything that had to do with Joe was a lie. From his fine-tailored suits and gleaming leather shoes to the Gucci briefcase, he carried walking out the door on Friday nights. As if he came from a world of privilege. All lies.

Abruptly, I turned around and started for home, reminding myself that I once again had more important things to worry about. I had to think about shelter. The utility bills were past due. Food. We needed groceries. I shoved my hand into my pocket and felt for my gloves—they'd fallen through the hole. And a better coat.

Chapter 31

Exodus
Andie ~ December 1988

In 1972, my plan had been a simple one. To grow old together, happily married, surrounded by children and grandchildren, and the blessing of our memories. An impossible strategy anyone within the House of Praise inner circle would say because darkness cannot mix with light, and sheep must separate from goats. As hard as I had tried, I couldn't become one of them. My faith did not include the Gospel according to Calvin.

I took the twins to my parents' home for a few days to enjoy a little holiday distraction. But destiny brought the inevitable just days before Christmas.

❦

It was December 22nd, to be exact. Obviously, he couldn't wait until Christmas was over. I had driven home alone to wrap a few presents for the twins. There was no end to my nightmare. My eyes burned in my head. The house felt oppressive and stale. Drifting from room to room, I assumed he was kidding when he'd said that since he wouldn't get any money out of the house, he'd take its contents. I would never assume again. The empty rooms stared back at me, gaping and bruised. Molested.

The living room had disappeared except for the couch, the Christmas tree, and the few presents I'd bought for the twins. My knickknacks, end-tables, lamps, TV, rugs, kitchen table, and the books I loved were gone. Dust balls covered the floor where my bed and dresser had been. My jewelry was missing except for the mother/child ring on my hand and the gold hoops in my ears. Carted off to some pawn shop, no doubt. Fortunately, he didn't touch my clothes in the closet or anything in the kids' bedrooms, except for Dillon's desk. He took it.

I opened the linen closet. He left three towels and a bottle of Children's Tylenol. He had boxed up and taken every bit of toilet paper and all the cleaning supplies. Joe and whoever came to help him wiped out the kitchen except for my grandmother's four antique plates on the wall, which he'd once said were ugly. He took every pot, pan, plate, cup, and eating utensil. I thought he might have left us some food, but every can, box, and frozen food container was gone except for a gallon of milk and a stale loaf of bread.

He also emptied the garage apart from a few old tools and a push mower that belonged to Daddy. The storage shed remained padlocked, but he left me a note stating he'd return for the rest of *his* things later. A check for one hundred dollars lay on the kitchen counter, and what looked like a letter he had written to Dillon and Gracie. I opened it.

D&G, I'll see you as much as possible in the future, but it's time for me and your mama to end our marriage. Dad.

The Grinch had come and stolen more than Christmas.

❧

I sat on the couch for the next hour, my mind piecing together what remained of my life. And then I panicked. I bolted to the hallway, pulled the attic door from the ceiling, and climbed the ladder. After checking for the envelope hidden in the rafters, I lifted the lid to my old hope chest and dug through it for my photograph albums tucked under Mavis's blue crocheted afghan. *All of it,* I sighed, *safe.* When I closed the lid on the chest once filled with hope, I knew it wasn't the relationship I mourned. Instead, I grieved for the hopes and dreams I once concealed deep within my foolish, daydreaming heart.

Joe's exodus was no surprise—I'd been saying *we're separated* for years. It certainly didn't devastate me. On the contrary. He had finally done something right, and I was relieved. What surprised me was that I cried. I did not know what lay in my future. The raw and icy silence between us had finally drawn its remaining breath. He had left quickly, tearing the house apart in a reckless and rebellious escape, like a mutt digging his way out of the dog pound.

A new silence broke through me. I stared at the mess in the wake of his departure, longing for someone to hold out their arms to me, but the raped house only stood in shock. Breathing deeply, I tried to shake some sense into myself.

I brought the twins home, and together, we sacked out on the living room carpet, falling into a fitful sleep in the early morning hours. Though he was the only daddy they'd known, Dillon and Gracie's relationship with Joe was tenuous. I was sure my children were relieved to be rid of the tension that had permeated every square foot of our home like the odor of rancid meat.

The next day, Dixie gave me a bed, the mattress from her spare room, and a small TV. Caroline helped me lift it into the back of Daddy's truck and set it up in my house. But not before Dixie got her digs in. "I'd press charges. Get a lawyer, Andie! I'd—"

"—Let it go, Dixie. It's finally over."

Oblivious to the holidays, the kids and I clung to each other. Despite my parents' efforts to put smiles on our faces, the holiday season melted away with only memories of rejection, neglect, and a final blow of abandonment for keepsakes.

Mouth-breathing, my lips cracked, and my tongue dry, I answered the phone with a sleepy hoarse, "Hello." I'd long since stopped caring about maintaining a brave face. Why did I sense the worst was yet to come? How could I be relieved and heartbroken at the same time? I had lost my biggest battles. Why couldn't my family understand no amount of fresh air or exercise could dispel the anxiety of the unknown?

Dixie's daily phone call prodded me with always the same question. "You awake?"

"No. It's okay, though." Always the same answer.

Followed by a sigh of relief to hear I was still coherent enough to put two sentences together; my mother intended to rescue me. "Your sister and I are shopping, and we thought of you, darlin'."

Why does her voice always make me weepy?

Hell-bent on trips to the mall, Dixie's sudden spending sprees were, according to Aunt Wylene, a diversion from Daddy's sickness. I viewed my mother as a spoiled, anal, and neurotic woman. There was a time I would've given my right arm for Dixie's undivided attention: to go shopping, paint her nails, or share a sandwich and sip Coca-Cola at a lunch counter. But clean floors and neatly pressed clothes came first with Dixie. More than once, I awoke to the smell of Murphy's Oil Soap and the sound of Dixie mopping and rearranging furniture in the middle of the night. I had once wanted to crawl back inside her womb to feel surrounded by her love, but no longer.

"It's a lovely day. It'd do you good to go out for a walk. Get some fresh air."

"Um, I reckon so." There it was again, that damn fresh air and exercise—the answer to all my problems.

"Maybe I'll call you later. You can come over for supper and talk."

"No thanks. I'm all talked out, and I've got to pick up Gracie in an hour."

Silence.

"Well, alright then. Call me if you change your mind." Dixie always fussed unnecessarily.

"Okay." More silence. "Thanks, though."

Other than the low hum of the refrigerator and an occasional moaning pipe, my refurbished house maintained its silent treatment. After sixteen years of marriage, all Joe left me was a bundle of heartbreaking memories. My plan for the future became increasingly vague as abject poverty stared me in the face.

A long time ago, I loved him so hard, and it didn't matter one bit. A tough road loomed ahead, but he was finally gone, and despite it all—I was glad.

Chapter 32
ONE FOOT IN FRONT OF THE OTHER
Andie ~ March 1989

Who's pounding? Confused and half-asleep, I opened the front door.

"I've been banging on this door for over ten minutes!"

I looked around outside, still not fully alert. Bright and slightly chilly, I felt the cool air rush at my head. *Must be morning.*

"You gonna move? Let me in, for God's sake, Andie."

"Sorry. I was in bed."

Dixie studied my face before giving me a hug. "You look terrible."

"Thanks." I managed not to roll my eyes, but it was a struggle.

"It stinks in here. When's the last time you cleaned this place?" Dixie scrunched up her nose and marched around my house, opening windows, picking up empty cups and plates, and mumbling about fat grams and calories.

"I'll do that," I protested.

"When? Next year? Go shower and pack a bag. You're coming home with me."

A shower.

"Where are my grandbabies?"

"At the Darwoods."

"How are you living? Lord knows you ain't making any money."

"I'm on welfare."

"Oh, Andie. Welfare? I never thought one of my own would—never mind. Go shower; we'll pick up the kids on the way to my house."

"Is Daddy better?"

"Yes, that's why I'm so tickled. Wylene referred him to a new pulmonary specialist who changed his medication. He's breathing easy and wants to eat!"

"That's good, Dixie. That's—so good."

I felt almost human stepping out of the bathroom. Dixie had flung the windows wide open, and the March breezes awakened my senses. I was hungry. Following noises to the kitchen, I shook my head, watching Dixie's arms work furiously, taking out her frustrations with Comet cleanser and a rag. "I thought I raised you better than this. Your kitchen is a disaster." She looked me up and down. "How much do you weigh now?"

My black stirrup pants felt tight at the waist and butt. "I don't know. I don't look." I plopped my enlarged body on a chair and sighed. "I've been such a pile of shit. I don't know what I'd do without you."

Dixie sat next to me. "I need to tell you something." Her tone had sweetened, and that alarmed me.

"Good something or bad something?" I blew my nose into a wad of toilet paper. Kleenex, paper towels, and napkins were for people who worked for a living, not welfare lowlifes.

"Good, I suppose. I've had a long talk with Wylene and your daddy. You know, darlin', we're all hoping he lives a long time; I can't stand the thought otherwise. But Wylene made me a proposition."

"Go on."

"If Bud goes before me, and barring any accident, it looks like he will, your aunt has offered me her house. To move in with her. In Charleston. I'd have to sell *my* house—"

"—Sell the house? No—"

"—Hold on, now. I'd have to sell, but Bud says that's good; I can use the money for my retirement."

"I can't imagine it!"

"I don't want to live alone, Andie. Hopefully, Caroline and you will get straightened around and won't need me so much. I love Charleston—it's my birthplace, you know. Wy's got a nice house and plenty of money. We'll take care of each other for the rest of our days."

Plenty of money. That's what it was all about. Dixie had always been afraid of poverty. Of the poorhouse. She'd been such a skinflint. Aunt Wylene meant security, especially when Daddy was gone. "It'll break my heart, but I understand. I think. I guess I'm happy for you, Dixie."

"Wy's a prominent doctor now. I hear her office in Savannah is lovely, too. Those old biddies in Charleston didn't want her around when she was young, but now that she's gone back as a famous woman obstetrician, well, you can imagine. She's the talk of Charleston!"

"You want that, too?"

"Lord, no. I want to see her enjoy it. I'll keep house while she works. We'll do fine. I'll be back from time to time. But now we're getting ahead of ourselves; this won't happen for a while. I expect to be spoon-feeding your daddy for a few more years."

I smiled warmly at my mother. She had plans, and at her age, plans were important. To know where she was going and what her future held. It was far more than I had.

"Let's go get the twins," Dixie said, squeezing my hand with an encouraging smile. "It's good to be around family. On second thought, maybe not the Olivers."

"No worries there. I can't get Maudy to answer the phone."

Dixie's give-a-shit meter dropped to zero. She never liked Maudy. "She's just an old goat protecting what's hers, and she's pissed off, is all. Promise me you'll leave the house occasionally for some fresh air. You need to go back to work."

"Pinky swear." I was already scouring the classifieds for a job. And yet, no matter how I looked at it, welfare and Joe's random support checks paid better than Burger King.

But Dixie was right. I needed to stop moping around with the ghosts of my past. My mother promised to keep Gracie and Dillon for the week, drive them to school, and pick them up so I could look for work. Tomorrow was another day, and I intended to start by confronting my estranged in-laws with the truth about their son.

⁂

Later that night, I crawled into bed with a new sense of optimism. But a harsh reality struck me as I awoke the following morning. Making a new life for the twins and myself was like finding our way in a blinding snowstorm. And yet, for the time being, the eggshells of living around Joe were gone. I turned my head. The left side of the bed was smooth, untouched. I smiled and got out of bed.

Staring into the mirror, I replayed old conversations, feeling the effects of Joe's cruelty and every truth I knew about the House of Praise. I seethed. The poison inside me I kept secret showed on my face. My nose and chin broke out overnight. Upon further inspection, I discovered lines around my eyes and mouth. I pulled back my hair, surprised to find the first signs of gray mixed in with my darker roots. It was time to get on with life before I was too old to care.

Thank God for Dixie. She gave me money to visit a salon. A few hours later, I took advantage of a two-for-one special—a cut and a highlight. My makeover also included a trip to Salisbury to ask Maudy why she wasn't answering my calls.

I drove onto my in-laws' property and swallowed hard. Al meandered out of his shop and waved. Maudy flew out the back door and straight up to my car door, wringing her hands as if finding herself at the moment she dreaded. "You shouldn't be here, Andie."

I stepped out of my car and stood under the shade of the large oak, wondering what happened to the mother-in-law I once knew and loved so dearly. "Why?"

"It's not a good idea. We must support Joe. I hope you understand."

"Joe and I have been married sixteen years, Maudy. Doesn't that count for something?"

It shouldn't have surprised me when Maudy pursed her lips. "And after all those years, you've left him little of his dignity. You've ruined him emotionally and financially, never giving him your full support in the ministry. His only peace was and *is* at work!"

"Did he tell you this? Did he tell you how many women he's slept with? How little money he makes?"

Maudy didn't listen to a word. "You should've stayed in Salisbury." It was like hearing it come right out of Joe's mouth. "You should've lived within your means," she added, ignoring the *other women* part.

I clenched my jaw to avoid snapping at her and turned instead to see Al's droopy, sad face. Whatever regrets were battling inside him had launched tears to his weather-worn cheeks. It grieved me.

Maudy clicked her tongue and sighed. "We're getting nowhere standing here, defending Joe to you. You're deceived, Andie. Go back to church and confess your sins at the foot of the cross. I'm not sure even that will get Joe back."

I jerked my head toward my mother-in-law, searching for any speck of warmth on her face. It shocked me to find nothing but a sharp-edged tongue.

"I don't want him back!"

Maudy raised her brows. Her eyes, no longer friendly, blinked hard. "Well, that's good because after a full year of separation, Joe is filing for divorce."

I shook my head, then threw my following words at her face. "I don't have the money to file, or I would've already done it! I don't understand why he hasn't, but thanks for telling me."

"Joe waits on the Lord. He doesn't jump into anything, even divorcing his wife. His children matter."

"Oh, please. Let's not go down that road. He never wanted them to begin with!"

Maudy turned and stormed toward the house like a small tornado, but then walked back and stood as close to me as she dared. "He's got an excellent lawyer. I suggest you get one, too." And then her tone softened a degree. "I ask only one thing. Please let us see our grandchildren from time to time."

I returned to my car and stood with my hand on the door. "Sure, but not in church."

"That's awful, Andie. They need Sunday School."

"They can go someplace else."

Maudy's mouth was tight and grim. Her accusing voice stabbed the air. "They'll miss Heaven because of you!"

Biting back rage, I squared my shoulders. She had put my children in the bowels of Hell because they didn't worship at the House of Praise. "My children are not bound for Hell, and you know it! Good God, Maudy! I've been a part of this family nearly all my life, and now you turn me out?"

"Andie, you should go. Like I said, you coming here is not a good idea. You've done this to yourself, don't you see? We can't side with you. It wouldn't be good for Joe. We've been told you are demon-possessed. They've admonished us to not allow you in our home again, lest a worse darkness come on us than what's on you. I can't have you here until you've made your heart right with God."

My God. They've threatened her. I crossed my arms and felt as if I were suffocating.

Al had been silent but wiped at his eyes with his hankie. He stared into my face as though sensing my conflict, then broke into a tender smile to quote scripture. *"For I hate divorce, says the Lord, the God of Israel. And I hate the man who does wrong to his wife, says the Lord of All."*

Maudy looked hard at him, then laughed a shaky, nervous laugh. "That's enough, Al." Her unexpected interruption was jarring, and I resented it.

But Al continued. *"The LORD has been witness between you and the wife of your youth, with whom you have dealt treacherously; yet she is your companion—"*

"—I said, that's enough, Al! We stand with our son—"

"—and your wife by covenant…therefore take heed to your spirit, and let none deal treacherously with the wife of his youth. Malachi two fourteen and—"

"—Al! I said, stop!"

"I'm on God's side, Maudy. I don't stand with Joe or Reverend or you on this." He moved and stood between Maudy and me, placed his rough-hewn hands on my shoulders, and looked into my eyes. "Come and see me anytime you want, daughter. You are always welcome in my shop. It seems the only place I have any authority. Kiss Gracie and Dilly Bean for me, will you? You will always be in my prayers." He kissed my cheek as if I'd never see him again.

"Thank you." I wondered if Al's back would break from the burdens he carried. He nodded, then glared at Maudy as if daring her to speak. I watched him amble back inside his shop, his shoulders slumped in defeat.

Maudy waved her hand, dismissing him. "Al forgets the covenant we made years ago to stand by Reverend Artury, to save the lost at any cost."

"And it's costing you your family. Maybe someday you'll open your eyes and see the cult you're in. Ray tried to tell you—"

"—Andie! They've warned us. Reverend is calling you the Dark Angel. Do I have to repeat myself? We stand with Joe."

I opened my car door. Tears ran into the corner of my mouth, although I didn't remember starting to cry. "How dare he call me that!" I trembled until my legs almost buckled, but I gave it one last try. "Maudy, why don't you at least investigate Calvin for yourself? Start asking questions; see where it gets you." The look on her face was as if I'd suggested they shave their heads, pierce their noses, tongues, and nipples, and convert to Hinduism.

There was nothing more to say. Maudy turned, walked inside her house, and closed the door behind her. She never looked back.

Chapter 33
Tell Me About Your Marriage
Andie ~ January 1990

Joe wasted no time after the legally required length of separation; he filed for divorce precisely one year to the day he vacated my house. The court served me with papers during Christmas week. Happy holidays to me.

My wavering faith constantly reminded me of what God should do or have done on my behalf. I can't tell you how many times over the years I asked Him, why are you allowing this to happen? But then I'd remember He had given me what I asked for. Children to love and nurture. Maybe that was the best He could do for someone like me. And it was a hell of a lot more than some women had. Every week, I pushed self-pity aside and head-butted my future with all the enthusiasm I could gather, only to find the spark of God had gone out of me. Standing alone in the middle of yet one more flood, I pressed forward like a rudderless boat.

"Caroline? Can I borrow your Honda again?"

"Sure, why?"

It's Joe. He stole my car."

"Good God, Andie. Did you call the police?"

"Can't. It's registered to Maudy. We were making payments to her, but Joe came and took it right out of my garage. He knew damn well I'd have no transportation. I got kids, for Christ's sake! Damn them all to Hell!"

"Did you miss any payments?"

"I don't know. Ask Joe. He was supposed to make them for me so I could keep the car. That was our arrangement. The only bill he had to pay. Obviously, he defaulted. Son of a bitch!"

"I'll have Dixie follow me over to your place. That old Honda just sits in Daddy's driveway. I got both cars in my divorce settlement. Keep this one until you can get something."

"Thanks. I appreciate it. I know I don't tell you that enough. Bring the girls over this week; they can help me bake again. I wish I could help *you* more."

"The way I hear it, you got bigger problems than me. At least my worthless husbands didn't rob me blind."

"Yeah. We sure know how to pick 'em, huh?"

Caroline laughed. "I should've listened to you, Andie. Gone to school. Learned a trade. Instead, I married the first man with money that came my way. Both times. And I'm still broke, divorced, and got three kids in the bargain. Hey, do you know where they're keeping your car? You got a key, right?"

"It's sitting in Maudy's front yard with a *for sale* sign. Joe called and warned me not to take it. Said he'd call the police and tell them I'd stolen his mama's car."

"God, Andie. See you in an hour. Damn, those Olivers!"

❧

I drove Caroline's Honda to my divorce attorney appointment with foreboding, pulled in, and parked in front of a row of two-story red brick buildings. They had designed everything about the place to create an image of stability and prosperity. A bank stood across the street next to a fancy new coffee shop. An upscale dress boutique had opened a few doors down as recent developments spread, and the area's bookstores, restaurants, and real estate offices flourished.

The sign on the door read *Blunden and Crocker, Esq.–Law Offices.* Daniel Blunden, Esquire's suite, consumed the second floor. When I stepped off the elevator, the office smelled like the inside of a new car. Rich leather chairs lined the paneled walls the color of cinnamon and nutmeg. My shoes sunk an inch as I stepped onto the thick, creamy carpet.

I had worn my best black trousers and a cotton turquoise sweater that had faded to a robin's egg color. Having sewed a mismatched button on the bottom, I stood helpless to stop my embarrassment. I stared at the receptionist's black pumps. Shiny as a new nickel, her shoes reflected the underside of her chair. A nameplate on her gleaming desk read *Sandra H.* I couldn't help staring at her milky skin and perfect makeup application. She had glossy black hair and red nails you could only get in a salon. Amazed at her perfect teeth and smile, I staggered a bit. It hit me how lacking I was in everything from hair, clothes, and all-around first impressions. After an unusually long wait, she finally spoke. "Name, please?"

"Andie. Andie Oliver." Covering my button with my purse, I lifted my chin and pretended to have more money than I actually did. "I have an appointment with Mr. Blunden. At four o'clock."

At twenty-past-four, Dan Blunden opened his door and apologized for being late. I followed him into a stark office, all chrome, leather, and immaculately clean. He had hair the darkest shade of red and stood at least as tall as Daddy, with a right-angle jaw and eyes the color of frozen peas—so much so I couldn't stop staring at them.

He shrugged his slim shoulders out of his suit jacket, hung it neatly on a hanger on the back of his door, then pulled a file out of a cabinet before moving back to his desk. He seldom made eye contact, but started talking all the same. "First, we need to discuss my fee. Seven hundred up front."

I took out my checkbook. I had borrowed more money from Aunt Wylene, promising to pay her back before I died. Wylene was only too happy to help me end my marriage and told me to consider it a gift for my future.

"Tell me about your marriage, Mrs. Oliver. I'm sure you know modern-day divorce proceedings focus on money, not morality. But tell me everything."

I kept my features deceptively composed and told him my side.

A few weeks later, they set a court date for the first week in April.

Chapter 34
DIVORCE COURT
Andie ~ April 1990

Dressed in a conservative blue suit and a starched white shirt, Dan Blunden scribbled a final note on his legal pad. He took a quick sip of his water and waited for Judge Landis to nod in our direction.

The judge looked impressive and leaned toward his microphone. "Mr. Blunden, you may conduct your cross-examination."

Despite trying to control my breathing, I struggled to slow my heartbeat. I glanced at Joe. Seated in the witness chair, he had leaned back and crossed his legs. His eyes were lethal and filled with contempt, glaring back at me. He turned his attention to the judge with a satisfied look.

My attorney's three months of telephone calls and his law clerk waiting to talk to anyone within the House of Praise offices got him nowhere. A fortress of closed lips and bolted doors, the church refused to budge regardless of numerous lawsuit threats. Mr. Blunden told me he'd seen nothing like it, and for the first time in his life, he was thankful for his Catholicism. They were obviously out to shield Joe and crucify me.

Sitting beside my attorney, I tapped my shoe nervously on the polished courtroom floor. Mr. Blunden rose and walked slowly to a spot in front of the witness stand.

"Thank you, your Honor," he said. He then focused his attention on his adversary.

"Mr. Oliver, how old were you when you met your wife?"

"Fifteen or sixteen."

"Where did you meet?"

"At church. The House of Praise, where I'm now employed and attend services."

"Had your wife graduated high school when you proposed to her?"

"No, we started dating seriously during my senior year. I proposed during *her* senior year."

"And you testified on direct examination that you were married on July 1, 1972, a month after your wife's high school graduation. Is that correct?"

"Yes."

"Where did you spend the first seven years of your married life?"

"In Salisbury, North Carolina. Where I'm from originally."

"Did you or your wife go to college?"

"No. I worked. She worked."

"What type of work did your wife do?"

"Um, she had several jobs. Mostly clerical or in restaurants. I worked as a mechanic and volunteered for Reverend Calvin Artury until he hired me full-time in '76."

Mr. Blunden retrieved a stack of papers from the corner of the table where I sat watching.

"Did she work more than one job at a time?"

"Occasionally. She likes to stay busy."

"Stay busy, or make enough to cover the bills you couldn't?"

"Objection, your Honor."

"Sustained."

My attorney continued his cross. "Were you also working two jobs?"

"Yes, and no. I told you I *volunteered* my time at the church while working as a mechanic for Coot McGraw."

"How many hours did you *volunteer* each week?"

"A lot. I don't know, twenty maybe."

"For the record, you stated you lived in a trailer park for seven years. Shady Acres in Salisbury, correct?"

"Yes, that's correct."

"How many bedrooms?"

"One."

"Where did your children sleep?"

"Objection! I see no relevance here."

"Sustained."

Attorney Blunden looked down at the top sheet of paper of the stack he held in his hand. "After your wife's employment with First National Bank of Salisbury, was one of her employers Southern States Insurance Company?"

"I believe so. I don't remember the exact name."

"Did she also work as a convenience store clerk three nights a week?"

"Uh, yes, for a while."

Dan Blunden's eyes flashed with a hint of fire. "Would it surprise you I have employment records showing your wife worked an average of sixty hours a week at the insurance company and convenience store *and* for the rest of your marriage while she was self-employed? Did you realize she worked sixty hours a week for over ten years as she raised your children while you traveled extensively?"

Joe shifted in the chair. "I remember we bought a couple cars, she bought a business, and she bought a house I never agreed to while I traveled to Africa on a Crusade for souls. She sure surprised me. I came home, and she said, 'Guess what I bought?' We needed to make the payments. She *had* to work hard to help pay for *her* ventures."

Blunden took a step forward, ignoring Joe's snide comments about my purchases. "Would you like to review the employment records for yourself?"

"No," Joe responded quickly. "If the records are accurate, the math should be simple."

"Do you think she made those purchases because she wanted to make you miserable or to take a risk, find the American dream, and make a better life for your family?"

"Objection!"

Joe ignored the objection of his attorney and answered. "Andie didn't care what I wanted. Only what *she* wanted. She knew we had to live within our means. Andie knew my salary; she got my entire paycheck. It was *her* job to pay the bills. She never biblically submitted to me. She did what she wanted to do!"

Blunden smiled at Joe and continued. "Do you also recall that Bud Parks, your father-in-law, gave my client, your wife, a five-thousand-dollar down payment for your new home? And that he also paid for renovations to that house?"

"Sure, and I paid for a new roof and furnace. So? Like I said, she always gets what she wants."

"Did you pay for it or did the church?"

"Objection. Your Honor, this has no relevance."

"Sustained."

I refused to look at him; he made me want to vomit. I tucked my balled fists into my jacket pockets and turned my attention to the initials somebody had carved deep into the bench beside me.

"My point is, Mr. Oliver, that you are laying claim to all the proceeds in the house sale. A house in her name only and part of her bankruptcy."

I was sure Joe never knew about my bankruptcy until that second.

"I don't want to be dragged into her financial problems."

"Her financial problems are also yours, Mr. Oliver," Blunden answered. Joe flinched and glared at me while my attorney continued. "When was your first child born?"

"In 1975. He passed away shortly afterward."

"Did she go to work afterward?"

"I believe so."

"My records show she returned to full-time work within eight weeks after your first child passed."

"And was she pregnant again when you started full-time employment with your church?"

"Yes, with our twins."

"Did she continue working while pregnant?"

"Only at a beauty shop."

"Looks like twenty hours a week, according to my records."

Joe looked toward his lawyer, an older attorney named Howard Carson. Carson offered no help as Joe ran his finger along the inside of his collar. "Whatever the records show. I don't remember exactly."

"And after the twins were born, did you insist she work outside the home?"

"Yes. I told you. Andie had to. She bought a house and a business."

"But she had not bought that house or her business immediately after the twins were born. Is that right?"

"Yes, I guess so."

"You guess, or you know?"

"She didn't buy the house or the business until the twins were about three years old, somewhere around there."

"Did Andie ever *not* work outside the home other than when she was recuperating from a pregnancy?"

"Objection!"

"I'll allow the questioning, but get to your point, Mr. Blunden."

"Thank you, your Honor. I'll ask again: has your wife always worked a job outside the home?"

"Yes, because it was *her* decision to put us in debt with a house. *Her* decision to run a business. It left us with virtually no extra income. She thought it would force me into a better-paying job. That's why she did it. And even though I make very little money, she has not worked for anyone other than herself in years. She didn't care about the risk. She wasted her time in that cafeteria of hers. I wanted her to work a normal job. I wanted her in church. She hasn't attended our church in years. She knows how important that is to me."

"How long did she own the cafeteria?"

Joe looked up and mentally calculated the passage of time. "About eight years."

Blunden nodded. "Eight years. That's a long time for some businesses to last. Sounds to me like she worked hard at it."

"Objection!"

"Sustained. Mr. Blunden, I won't tell you again. Get to your point."

"Sorry, your Honor." Blunden stood within three feet of Joe. "Have you had any other children during that time?"

"No, thank God."

My attorney laid my employment records on the table and slid another thicker folder to where he could easily retrieve it.

"Mr. Oliver, you testified you've received all your income from the House of Praise for the past fourteen years. Is that correct?"

"Yes."

"What do you do there?"

"I'm the television ministry's Chief Audio and Video Engineer."

"How many trips do you take every year with your employer?"

"Six long trips a year, usually. Three to four shorter trips a month. My income is sixteen thousand annually. I gave Andie copies of my tax returns and asked her to give them to you."

Mr. Blunden gave Joe a slight smile. "Thank you for your cooperation, Mr. Oliver. I have carefully reviewed every one of them." Then he retrieved and opened the thick folder and took out a single sheet of paper. "Are you familiar with a company called Peyton Broadcasting?"

"Sure, it's our production company."

"Are you an employee of Peyton Broadcasting?"

"No."

"Are you sure?" My attorney handed the sheet of paper to the court reporter, who marked it as an exhibit. He then showed it to Joe's lawyer, who put on his glasses, made a few notes, and passed it back to him. Blunden moved a few steps closer to Joe but did not show him the paper. "Are you J.N. Oliver, listed as employee number 7005 with Peyton Broadcasting?"

"Uh, I guess I am. I never considered myself an actual employee there."

"Yes or no will do."

"Yes."

"What do you make from Peyton Broadcasting, Mr. Oliver?"

Joe squirmed in his seat and stared at the paper in Blunden's hand before he said, "I'm not sure."

Blunden returned to the folder without showing him the document, took out another paper, and also had it marked as an exhibit. After showing it to Joe's lawyer, he handed it directly to Joe.

"What does this page from the minutes of a corporate meeting of Peyton Broadcasting directors show as your contribution to Reverend Artury's television production company?"

Joe looked down at the paper and didn't answer.

"Take your time, Mr. Oliver," he interjected. "I want you to be sure about your answer. Remember, you are under oath."

Joe recrossed his legs. "An additional twenty-five hours a week to my work at the House of Praise."

Blunden picked up yet another sheet of paper and handed it to Joe. "And what was your income from Peyton Broadcasting last year, besides your income from the House of Praise?"

"Twenty-five thousand." Joe's face grew red. "Who told you?" he sputtered. "What about the whore I'm married to? What about her? Doesn't sleeping with every guy in the neighborhood say she's an unfit mother?"

Howard Carson stood to his feet. "Objection, your Honor!"

"On what grounds?" the judge asked.

"May we approach the bench?" Attorney Carson requested.

"Yes."

Dan Blunden joined Howard Carson in front of the judge. I heard Joe's lawyer say, "I didn't know about this—"

Blunden responded in a whisper.

The judge frowned, then raised his head. "Very well. The court will be in recess for thirty minutes while I consult with the attorneys in my chambers. Mr. Oliver, you may leave the witness stand but not confer with anyone."

My attorney gathered his files. I leaned forward. "What's the problem?"

"This is good. They're circling their wagons. They need the judge to help them out of a tight spot. Your soon-to-be-ex didn't provide his attorney with all his income records. And I suspect his attorney forgot to tell him it all boils down to assets. Sit tight."

I grabbed his arm and whispered. "What about custody?"

Blunden nodded to the judge, then turned back to me. "I have to go. From what you've told me, Joe doesn't want those kids. And if he wants to fight for custody, we'll subpoena records on the length of time he's been out of town for the past seventeen years. The courts want custodial single fathers to live at home with their children."

The two lawyers followed Judge Landis to his chambers. One hour later, the judge spelled out the agreement for the record. "Mr.

Oliver will pay child support of three hundred dollars a month per child through age eighteen along with comprehensive health insurance and payment of four years' tuition at the North Carolina average for private institutions when each child matriculates. Alimony of another three hundred a month for two years or until Mrs. Oliver remarries, whichever comes first, and a total indemnification for any unpaid taxes on returns through the current tax year."

My face flushed and burned. Joe's admitted loss included no further dissection of his income or assets. He had given up the ghost. As the court reporter prepared a transcript of the settlement, it was also agreed my bankruptcy did not include Joe. I followed Dan Blunden from the courtroom.

"I'll prepare the paperwork and send it to your husband's lawyer by the first of next week," he said. "I wish I could've got you more, but we were lucky to get what we got."

"He won't pay it."

"He has to. He's risking a jail sentence if he doesn't."

Joe and his attorney exited the courtroom and retreated in defeat. They pushed past us without speaking. I recognized Joe's temper brewing. Familiar with his body language, my stomach boiled and churned; a wave of nausea rolled over me. I gripped my purse strap until my nails dug into the heel of my hand. "He frightens me," I said.

"Your husband created his bitter pill. Now he has to choke on it."

"I know, and I appreciate what you've done. But you don't understand these people. They do what they want. Joe will never pay it. Never. And Artury will never open his books to the public or anyone. They'll retaliate."

My attorney softened. "The only way they can retaliate is to file for custody, which I doubt your ex wants to do. You're right about one thing: no one even cracked the door for me at the

House of Praise. We're lucky Peyton Broadcasting isn't under the protection of the church; they *had* to cough up his records. And we only guessed at his unreported bonuses. Hopefully, you'll get your support every month and won't have to return to work at a convenience store. Go after him again if he refuses to pay. Call me; we'll put him in jail."

I sighed. "I don't have the money for more legal fees. I can't afford to fight him. Joe knows that. He'll pay what and when he wants, I assure you." Fear came up in my voice like vomit. "I haven't heard the end. He knows I'm wounded. I'm afraid all I've done is piss him off. Knowing he intended to hide all that money even when under oath makes me wonder what else he's hiding."

I stuffed the traumas of my life deep into the fractures of my past and tried to live again. Outward circumstances improved at a snail's pace. Inside, I remained dark and twisted. Constant nightmares suffocated any hope of peaceful sleep. Dixie labeled me permanently moody.

Relationships with potential future husbands became an impossible undertaking in my mind. Nothing lasted. My deep well of mistrust was bottomless. At the first sign of interest from a man, my cocky reaction scared off the aspirant suitor. I talked to Aunt Wy about it; however, the well-meaning doctor only knew how to check for beating hearts. She had no idea what to do with broken ones.

Not wanting to see Joe when he picked up the kids for visitation, I had them ready with their bags packed. My past tormented me daily—things I knew, had witnessed, and could do nothing about. It stalked me along paths of terror. Only my children and an iron determination kept me from insanity. My best hope was for the bankruptcy judge to allow me to keep my house.

Chapter 35

POSTMORTEM DIVORCE
Andie ~ October 1990

Dixie diced vegetables for soup while Caroline carried a bowl of broth into the next room to spoon-feed Daddy. Sitting at the counter reading the Sunday paper, I threw the wedding announcements on the counter. "Get a load of this."

Dixie gasped and slid her tortoise-shell spectacles from the top of her head to the tip of her impudent nose. "Selma Rodriguez and Joe Oliver married at the House of Praise in a private ceremony on the first day of September." Dixie's chin raised a notch, and her delicate eyebrow arched above her glasses, her eyes still soft gray, like rain clouds. She laughed to cover her annoyance. "It only took him five months. You think they knew each other before your divorce?"

"Maudy let it slip to the twins that Joe was seeing a girl named Selma who lived at Ilene Robey's boarding house. Before our divorce, I drove past once—at two in the morning. He had parked his truck in the street. What happened to the scandals Calvin was so all-fired about? It appears House of Praise people don't question a thing Calvin puts his blessing on these days. No matter what it is."

"There's no picture. What's she look like?" asked Dixie. "This Selma person."

"I've only seen her from a distance when she accompanies Joe to pick up the kids. She's young. I'm guessing eighteen, nineteen maybe."

"For pity's sake! She's not much older than the twins!"

"Yeah, but she's pretty, and as you know, Joe likes 'em pretty. She's attractive—in a dark sort of way. Brunette. Tall. String-bikini body. The total opposite of me. Latino. From Mexico, we think."

My mother rolled her eyes. "How does she dress?"

I shrugged. "How would I know? I don't care. The only time I saw her, she wore, you know, the kind of outfit Joe loves on women. Trashy. Gracie says she's quiet. No sass, I'm sure. I've never seen her smile. Gracie also said Selma loves her job at the Praise Buffet and never wants to have children. Good thing."

Dixie gently brushed my hair away from my shoulder. "I don't like her. She's got home-wrecker written all over her."

"My home was already wrecked. Selma had nothing to do with it."

"I mean *her* home. There is no home without children. I see no reason for pretty women like Selma to enter the workplace and forego motherhood."

"I've realized, Dixie, not every woman wants to be a mother. And not every woman expresses love with casseroles and a spotless house like you do."

But my mother wouldn't stop. "Selma will need a thick skin, more than she bargained for. Joe doesn't come with a monogamous guarantee or an instruction booklet on how to keep him happy at home. She can't return him for a full refund," she said, giggling at her comment.

"My best to the happy couple," I said, raising a glass of iced tea. "Now it's someone else's turn to put up with Joe."

Dixie shook her head; her tone turned coolly disapproving. "It's not natural to never want a baby. It's not. Where are they living?"

"Some dumpy apartment near the church, of course."

I stepped to the sink, ran hot water for dishes, and recalled those first months of marriage. When our suppers were full of leisurely small talk and nights spent, if not curled in each other's arms, at least touching—hands held in sleep, his leg flung over mine, keeping me warm. My few happy moments with Joe. The rare, fleeting memories I clung to for years. Before he sunk his teeth further into Calvin's ministry. Our marriage had spun out of control like a barn in the path of a raging tornado.

"When I called Joe to talk about the twins' report cards, he said he feels too fragile right now to talk to me. He discusses nothing other than to rub my failures in my face."

Dixie picked up her knife and chopped the head off a stalk of broccoli. "If Bud were well enough to kick his ass, he'd feel a hell of a lot more fragile than he does now."

At that moment, it wasn't my mother's loving husband and her beautiful home I envied. It was her newfound confidence. Through the power of Wylene's ceaseless persuasion, Dixie saw a psychiatrist every Tuesday. I considered it and even called a Christian counseling service. But they wanted a thousand dollars upfront. I'd have to claw my way through my problems on my own.

Tired, I rubbed my eyes. "It's time to pick up the twins from school, and the furnace man is coming. It's broken again." I kissed my mother's cheek on the way out.

"When are you gonna lose more weight? You'd look prettier as a size eight," said Dixie.

After subtracting the sum to fix the furnace from my checkbook, I grew despondent. The repairman stuffed my check into his shirt pocket. "Your warranty ran out last month. If it breaks down again, I'll let you put it on a credit card," he said. "I won't charge you for labor."

I laughed, hoping the check I wrote wouldn't bounce and that he had indeed fixed the furnace.

Slowly, the house warmed while I peeled an apple at the small kitchen table I'd bought for a song at a fire sale to replace the one Joe took when he left. My children crept in and stood behind me. I turned to see their somewhat smiling faces. My heart wrenched. They were so vulnerable.

Gracie leaned across the table, resting her pudgy hand on my arm. She'd stopped taking piano lessons since we could no longer afford them and had painted her thumbnails apricot and the other fingers a bright lime green. Her baby-blonde hair, parted in the middle and pulled back with butterfly barrettes, hung straggly below her shoulders. Tomato sauce stains from the previous night's Chef Boyardee stained her faded *Madonna* T-shirt. "You okay, Mama?"

I believed it was my job to paste a smile on my face, straighten myself with dignity, and free Gracie from worry. "Better every day," I said. That was not a total lie. I was better than the day I had the flu so bad I vomited blood. I was better than the day my water broke when Wy shoved a twenty-inch needle into my spine. And I was better than the day I felt the pain of losing Mavis would own me forever.

Dillon scratched at a scab on his arm. "Then why are you crying?"

I sighed. "Having to take care of a broken furnace, Aunt Caroline's car won't start again, and I guess I'm tired. Things like that," I told my children.

Gracie bit into a piece of my shared apple. "Did you love Daddy?"

I raised an eyebrow. Neither twin had ever asked that. "I did, once upon a time."

"I don't know how I feel about him," Gracie said.

"He's your daddy. You're supposed to love him, I've been told. But respect is something folks earn."

Dillon's eyes stared away from me and his sister. I sensed his anger.

"There's no sense in hiding that things have been tough. You're both smart enough to know we're struggling. All I have left in this world is you two. There's always a way. There are always good things waiting for you to find them."

"Are we looking for good things?" Gracie asked.

Their faces lit with hope, and I, as always, plunged toward it despite my wanting to do otherwise. "Every day," I answered.

I reached out for my daughter's face, cupping her chin in my hand, wanting to look into Gracie's eyes and then wishing I hadn't. Just before my precious girl turned away, I peered past her little-girl eyelashes into blue eyes like my own, full of jumbled emotion as though all the hurt and uncertainty inside were finally welling up and spilling over. Gracie couldn't suck back her tears, but wouldn't let them drop either. So they hung on those little lashes like heavy dew on delicate grass.

"We tried to be what he wanted." Dillon pushed back his hair and leaned forward as if the weight of my pain rested like a cross on his back. His small face knit into a frown of concern. It undid me. "He talks about God too much. And this one time, I showed him a picture I drew of Grandpa Bud's hunting gun. He said I shouldn't spend so much time with Grandpa."

"He didn't mean nothing by it, Dillon. He just doesn't like your grandpa," I said.

"Why?"

"It's a long story. It's too long for tonight. Remember, your daddy loves you. In his own strange way, he does. He doesn't know how to show it, is all. Al and Maudy loved him. Really, they did. It's just that your daddy loves Reverend Artury more than anyone. It's something we all have to live with."

"That's not fair, Mama." Gracie yawned; her tears had fallen despite her willing them not to. She wiped them across her cheeks into her hair.

I reached over and moved her bangs from her sleepy, teary eyes. "I know, sweetheart. Unfortunately, it is what it is. We'll survive. One thing you can always count on is me. I'll never leave you; no one will ever take you from me. Come on, now let's get some sleep."

I stood and walked behind them to their beds. Dillon laid his arm on my leg, too tired to sit up for his nightly hug. I kissed my son and tucked Mavis's big blue afghan around him. Then I stepped into Gracie's room.

"Are we alright, Mama?" Gracie yawned again and stroked her inner arms with her fingertips.

I paused, groping for a reason to fill my daughter with more hope. "Sure, you bet we are. Now, off to sleep."

But in the next moment, I turned my face away. Fear knotted in my stomach. I had known terror before, but it sat on the bed with me that time. I felt as though I could reach out and touch it. Feel the sting of its tentacles. Being alone in despair was one thing. Being responsible for the two little bodies that lay on their beds, with no resources but what I had to beg for, was living a nightmare I could not wake up from.

I hope God is truly just. That justice and vengeance are the same. That someday, Joe Oliver, when you look up from the pit of Hell you share with your buddy Calvin, you will fully realize what you did to me and our children. That will be your Hell.

Chapter 36
THE WEREWOLF IS ALWAYS AT YOUR DOOR
Andie ~ April 1991

I moved through winter like a piece of driftwood on the Cape Fear, paying electric and phone shut-off notices with yet another gift from Aunt Wylene. Food stamps and extra groceries from my parents kept meals on the table. I found a fresh bag of hope in the spring when I hadn't heard from my bankruptcy attorney.

Wandering from the kitchen to the garage patio, I clutched at my burning stomach and gulped the last Diet Dr. Pepper, realizing I hadn't eaten all day. I'd not eaten much over the winter, and it showed. I'd shrunk four sizes. Instead of feeding my depression, I smoked cigarettes and drank diet sodas. Had I been able to afford a more potent drink, I might have become an alcoholic. Food had lost its appeal. One thing about living in Winston-Salem—cigarettes were cheap, especially when Dixie gave me carton after carton to get them out of the house.

I fished one out of my pocket and fired up Daddy's old Zippo, imagining myself as *Ali MacGraw* in *Love Story*. I watched it every time they listed it in the *TV Guide*, wanting to be her, the most courageous girl I'd ever seen. Imagining my body wrapped around *Ryan O'Neal*, I got choked up thinking about that movie; it had nearly killed me to see the longing in his eyes after her death, his love that meant never having to say you're sorry. I wanted that from a man. My hopeless romantic self. Pathetic.

At almost seven o'clock, sitting in a rocking chair with splinters, I watched the low and pink sun hover over the horizon like an iridescent bubble. The phone rang, and I jumped to answer it. I'd been sitting for a long time. The rocker had left its imprints on my arms and legs.

Caroline's voice squealed on the other end. "Sooo—how was your date?"

"You seriously want to know?" Trying to ignore the throb of old wounds, I had agreed to go out on a blind date. I turned away from the window and dropped my cigarette in the sink, where I'd washed dishes before enjoying the sunset.

Caroline giggled. "Hickey is a nice-looking guy. He's ambitious and attractive and—"

"—Then *you* go out with him!"

"Oh, no. I married his brother. That was enough."

"See what I mean? No girl in their right mind would date a guy named Hickey, which, I might add, is what he wanted to give me. Who would name their child Hickey? Tell me, who?" I filled the percolator with water and slammed it on the counter. "He spent fifty bucks at the Salad and Steak Pit and then expected me to have sex with him in his truck bed at an X-rated drive-in. I pitched a hissy fit when I saw we were about to watch a porno. I made him take me home."

"The truck bed? Really?" Caroline burst out laughing. "Did you?"

"No!" I didn't want to have that conversation with my sister.

"I can't believe he did that."

"Well, believe it." I wanted to scream at my stupidity. "I don't believe in true love anymore. Only the made-up kind in movies. I don't need a man to be happy, just his income."

"A girl doesn't need ice cream to be happy, either. Or cheeseburgers. Or peanut butter fudge. They're comfort foods. Girls need comforting, Andie."

"I'll remember that next time you try to hook me up. I'll go to Dairy Queen instead."

Loneliness. It wrapped around me at the oddest times. I had to admit I'd tasted companionship, and I missed having some type of relationship. Caroline had meant well, even if her ex-brother-in-law was a skank. But I wasn't sure I was ready to date or that I ever would again. I'd been so wrong about Joe; how could I trust myself to find the right man for me and my children?

Hickey treated me to a lobster salad and a porterhouse the size of his truck. I was uncomfortable—a welfare recipient eating steak and lobster. He also promised me a drive-in movie where we could sit, relax, sip wine, and talk.

As I slid backward from his wooly mammoth pickup that smelled like greasy burgers and fries, I disconnected the radio by bumping into loops of wire that sagged beneath the glove compartment. He helped me climb inside the truck bed amid litter and a blanket I assumed was clean. I had felt obligated to bring the beverage, so I brought out two bottles of cheap five-dollar wine from a Harris Teeter sack. "Red or white?" I asked.

His hair was all liquored up with goop that smelled of Brylcreem; he pulled a swig from a whisky bottle and raised a quizzical eyebrow. "You mind if I drink my Jim Beam?"

When the cartoons ended, and *Tits for Tad* flickered across the gigantic screen, I quickly finished the evening, insisting I'd become ill and needed to go home immediately. Porno reminded me of Joe, and I couldn't stand the thought of it. Besides, Hickey would've broadcast his score to every bubba in Forsyth County. Mr. Caveman curled his lip and looked at me with a gleam in his eye and a disturbing growl. I'd somehow let him kiss me only once, keeping him at arm's length afterward until I made it home without a scratch.

⁂

I watched him order a Big Mac, fries, and two Cokes. Jasper Wenger, my old flame. At least, that's how I remembered him. The crush I carried for Jasper in junior high school before I met Joe unpacked itself from an attic corner in my memory. I had often wondered where he was, how he was, and if he was married. I wished I had put on lipstick, but at least my hair looked decent.

I tapped him on the shoulder. "Hey, you."

He turned and smiled. "Andie? Andie Parks?"

"Well, not anymore. It's been a long time, Jasper."

"How the hell are ya?"

He had the same pretty face, though some teeth had yellowed. I noticed he wasn't wearing a wedding band. Still, there was no certainty on how reliable a ringless hand could be. In five quick minutes, I discovered he lived in Kernersville, worked for UPS, and was engaged to Sherry Hoover. He had a little boy from a previous relationship that never ended in marriage.

His eyes were a crystalline light blue, like a spring Carolina sky, and they looked into mine as he shook my hand with a firm grip. The sizzle of the attraction sparked through me. Then he gave me the same big, broad, charming smile he had in school and said Sherry was waiting in the car. He'd best take her a Coke.

⁂

While Dixie's casserole contributions kept meals on my table, money from Aunt Wy barred the wolves from my door. Almost. Slicing bacon the next day, I put down my knife to answer the phone.

"Hey, Andie. It's me, Jasper."

"Lordy, Jasper, how'd you get my number?" I smiled to myself.

"I called your old phone number, and your mama gave it to me. She filled me in on your recent divorce."

"She did, did she?"

He coughed to clear his throat. "Andie, I was wondering, would you like to go out, have a drink, talk about some deadbeats we went to school with?"

"Why, are you suddenly fiancée free? Did she toss you out on your ear?"

"No. Not at all. Since running into you yesterday, I can't get you out of my head. I have to say, I had a major crush on you through high school. But you had your head in the clouds for that guy from Salisbury who, according to your mama, has pissed on your parade pretty good."

I laughed. As usual, Dixie gave away more than my phone number. And then I sighed. *Jasper*. What did I see in his eyes at McDonald's? He had a sunny warmth and an adoring expression—and he was an old friend. It was a pleasant feeling I'd forgotten. To have some honest attention from the opposite sex. Within seconds, I forgot about Sherry Hoover. "Sure; where can I meet you?"

We agreed to meet at seven o'clock at a double-wide with a good dose of character someone had turned into the Elbow Bar near Mocksville, a good ol' boys' saloon. And a reasonable distance from Sherry's house in Kernersville.

He dressed in ostrich skin boots, a white shirt with rolled-up sleeves, and tight creased Levi's with a big ring in his back pocket from sitting on his can of Copenhagen. He politely asked for a Miller draft and ordered me a glass of white wine as we made ourselves comfortable at the bar.

"Leather skirt?" He touched my leg and smiled another lovely smile with sweetness in it.

"Yeah. My sister let me borrow it. I'm short on nice clothes these days."

"You look great."

"Thanks." My shoulders went limp at the first compliment from a man in years.

Jasper had smooth hands, long fingers, and crinkly lines around his eyes and mouth. He couldn't stop smiling. He said he had attended a prayer meeting the past summer where he got saved. I said that was nice and asked if we could discuss something other than religion? That's when I felt his blue eyes lock on me. We drank and laughed until midnight, creating a healthy curiosity between us.

After some time passed, a little shiver of relief rolled down my spine. It felt nice. Old friends who had not seen each other in years. It didn't bother me he'd had a fight with Sherry, so he ended up calling me. He showed sincere sympathy about my divorce, expressed concern for my children, and nearly cried when I told him about Mavis, whom he remembered from school. He talked about his little boy in a way that touched my heart.

When he downed his sixth beer and I tipped back my third glass of wine, he put his hand on my leg again and suggested he follow me home. I agreed. The kids were at my parent's house, and I'd put fresh sheets on my bed.

I fumbled with my house key, turning it the wrong way in the lock as Jasper wrapped his arms around my waist and pressed his lips on my neck. My heart quickened, and I felt a tingling, both pleasurable and horrifying, like the tickle of a spider on bare skin. Finally, I opened the door. Leaning against the frame, I allowed him to explore me with his hands and mouth. Forcing my problems aside, I pulled him inside and then to my bed, complete with my favorite rosebud sheets.

He whispered in the dark. "You sure you want to do this?"

"Yes." I didn't want to think about it. I had married Joe almost as soon as I was out of a training bra. I didn't want to think about all I had missed. Nor did I wish to give in to the guilt of being the slut I knew *they* would call me if *they* found out. It struck me as funny that Joe could have countless affairs and still keep face with his family and church. But should I indulge in alcohol and a strange man on one heart-pulsing, momentous night, *they* would plaster it across every I-40 billboard from Winston-Salem to Raleigh before morning. If *they* knew.

My blouse and bra slid to the floor. As he applied a condom, I felt the heat in my cheeks as plainly as the cool night air against my bare back and shoulders.

Evidently, nobody limited sex to monogamous relationships any longer. It was an awakening. Jasper would be my secret, my chance for sex for the first time in years. He would be a prelude to a better life. Joe popped into my head, but I pushed him out, overwhelmed by a determination to get on with living, a force more potent than the memory of him and my own principles.

Jasper moved over me. My eyes closed, then opened, then closed again. Within minutes, it was over. I'd had sex with a man who wasn't Joe. My virgin voyage into the world of *other* men. My first look at a naked body I was unfamiliar with. My first sexual encounter of pure lust and not one drop of love. My first feelings of contempt for myself and the first time I hated Joe for pushing me into a world I did not want.

In the dark, Jasper finally rolled off me. He could not see my eyes tightly closed, my teeth biting into my fist to muffle a cry, and tears like fallen angels dropping from my eyes.

❦

After I fell asleep, Jasper slipped out without a goodbye kiss or even a note. In the morning, I found nothing but a used condom on the floor. My head felt like it was coming off my shoulders. I stood naked and hobbled to the bathroom. Gripping the sink, I looked into the mirror to see my face rumpled, as though I'd tossed and turned in one bad dream after another. My skin was blotchy and red; I wiped at ringed mascara and liner with a cool cloth. My eyes burned. Standing in the shower, I felt off balance. My world tightened around me, suffocating me again. But eventually, the water washed the smoke from my skin and hair, loosening the pesky bands of my past.

Later, I strolled to the mailbox in my robe and house shoes. Nothing to do but pay bills. No Mavis to call and share my secrets, my big night, and my great realization that not all penises looked alike.

By three in the afternoon, my queasiness hadn't let up. I still felt his razor burn on my cheeks as I chugged a glass of Alka-Seltzer. After resting Daddy's old cordless phone on my nightstand, expecting to hear from Dillon and Gracie, I contemplated frying potatoes and onions, which Coot swore by for hangovers.

Crazy enough, I didn't feel guilty, not one iota, about my sleepover with Jasper. He wasn't married to Sherry. The only actual guilt I mustered was over *not* feeling guilty. I wasn't willing to sacrifice my future happiness to make a deal with God and remain celibate. If Joe could do it without repercussions, then so could I.

But word traveled fast in Christian congregation circles within the Triad, and I knew that, too. Raised in a fundamental church, my profoundly ingrained morality and beliefs haunted me. Sensing vibrations of shame, my tidy world inside me unraveled a little more.

Lying on the bed, nursing my hangover, I stared at the plaster ceiling. A crack zigzagged like a road map from one side of the room to the other. I tried to rest, but sleep evaded me. The phone rang, and my heart pounded.

"Andie? How was your date?"

"Fine, Dixie. Are the kids okay?"

"Just fine? Your date was just fine?"

"Yes. We met at a restaurant, talked, and I went home. It was fine. Are the kids outside?"

"Gracie's knee-deep in homework. Dillon's in your old tree house. I'm glad you had a nice time with your old school friend. Come get the twins; I need to take your daddy to the doctor."

"Is he sick?"

"We wouldn't be taking him if he weren't. Wy's coming from Charleston this weekend to examine him, too."

The question popped out with no thought of what I was asking. "Dixie? You ever have sex with anyone other than Daddy?"

"I hope you're not thinking of that until you remarry."

"I'm not marrying again. Ever."

"Fine. Come get your children."

Just a minute before, she'd wanted details. Obviously, Dixie didn't want to discuss sex or her past, as usual. I purposed in my heart to always answer my children's questions about sex. The sacredness and the beauty of the act. The love it should involve with one person with whom you've chosen to spend the rest of your life, totally unlike my date with Jasper.

Chapter 37

THE ROADHOUSE
Andie ~ May 1991

Good thing I wasn't head over heels about Jasper. I never heard from him again. But he had aroused my sexual appetite. In one of my sister's *Cosmopolitan* magazines, I read women hit their sexual peak in their thirties. At thirty-six, I realized they weren't kidding. For all my begging God to help me adjust to a new single life, He left me with a heightened libido and a new sense of loneliness.

Though I had boldly proclaimed my mistrust in men, I wanted adventure, an escape. Above all, I needed to be held. Church, however, was no longer the obvious choice to meet men. Once upon a time, I had prided myself on faithful wife virtues and had never visited a bar alone.

Everyone makes mistakes. Sometimes more than once, whether intentional—or not.

Heads turned as I walked through the thick smoke inside the Purple Passion Bar. The yellow page advertisement made it appear upscale. Wearing my sister's black sweater dress that fit snugly in all the right places, I sat near a man at the bar and heard someone drop a quarter into the jukebox. *Friends in Low Places* played as the man stretched out a lean arm and a solid hand to introduce himself. In a low-pitched, silky voice, he said his name was Gifford.

"Andie."

"Nice to meet 'cha, Andie."

Ruggedly handsome, Gifford's granite-like face and movie-star jaw appeared tanned by the sun and wind. Earthy brown eyes, sun-bleached hair, and a tall, lithe body, he mentioned busting his butt working fifteen years on a construction crew. The silky-smooth sound of his *Sam Elliott* voice coiled around my ears with the same lazy caress of the cigarette smoke that swirled around his *Patrick Swayze* face. My brain sucked up the look of him and allowed my heart to register a few flickers of pleasure. Sipping my beer like a lady, I felt a flush in my cheeks.

I slid to the stool beside him and looked boldly into his eyes. In the dim light, they appeared russet, mysterious, and aloof. The smell of his leather and musk aftershave generated a sense of eroticism that, after two beers and a little teasing, made me braver than I really was. I plucked the cigarette from his mouth, drew a deep drag, and then replaced it between his lips.

"Thanks for the conversation," he said, preparing to leave.

"Going so soon?" I teased, my lips parting in a pretty pout. My naiveness showed. I had no experience with men, let alone men in bars.

He hesitated a moment before answering, contemplating his empty beer glass as if he were trying to word his reply with care. But it didn't come out that way. "Men are flies in a shithouse to you, aren't they, little lady? You think all you have to do is throw up some flypaper, and we'll all stick."

I sat there watching his cigarette flip up and down as he talked, thinking he wasn't as handsome as moments before. Embarrassed, I came to myself and blinked a few times, and then shot my pissed-off response in his face. "That's been my experience. The first cockroach I ever caught, I married; the rest have been little better." I took a long swig from my beer bottle.

He stood. "Nice-lookin' gal like you shouldn't be in a roadhouse like this," he said, tossing a twenty toward the bartender. "Anyway, I'm not interested." He removed the cigarette from his mouth and slipped it between my lips as I'd done to him. "I paid your tab. Last drag is all yours," he said. "Be careful on your way out. Lots of flies in here." Seconds later, his boot heels clicking the floorboards with a long, easy gait, he strode out of the bar.

My mouth curved into a humiliated smile. Another *Garth Brooks* song played on the jukebox. I sat listening to *The Dance* and talking to myself in a throaty whisper to avoid the tears. "Oh, Mister-whatever-the-hell-you-said-your-name-was, you'll never see me again in a place like this. Ever."

I took a last draw from the cigarette, smashed the butt into the ashtray on the bar, and then marched swiftly to my car. I'd never felt so disgusted with myself. But he'd done me a huge favor. I gave myself a hard, swift mental kick in the butt, tucked my tail between my legs, and drove home. Alone.

Chapter 38

KEEPING PROMISES
Reverend Calvin Artury ~ June 1991

I arrived at the Memphis airport early. My limousine driver drove through a few rural villages and suburbs on our way to the new coliseum in the city's center. Memphis had braced itself for my miracle Crusade.

Evan smiled. "The local news channels have broadcast your route from the airport to the coliseum. I purposely weaved our course through a few small towns to stay off the interstate."

"We can barely get through this traffic. Is there an accident or something?" I asked.

The limo driver looked into his rear-view mirror. "No, Suh. They're waiting fuh you to drive through. Hoping to get a glimpse of you. Suh, may I say how privileged I am to drive you in mah limo to da Peabody Hotel."

I nodded.

Evan's expertise in publicity and promotion had paid off. He was superb at stirring things up. Because of his efforts, the money rushed in like the mighty Mississippi, and my popularity flowed at an all-time high, even among those outside evangelical circles.

The intelligence of my Chief Executive Officer rivaled my own unwavering astuteness. Evan was still the same genius I'd met in 1964 in a Nashville bar.

A newly ordained preacher, I had traveled to Nashville in search of used pews for the new church I was building in Winston-Salem. I walked by a watering hole across from the Grand Ole Opry and felt the Spirit leading me inside, where Evan Preston sat alone at the bar, celebrating his twenty-first birthday and graduation from Old Miss.

He had pounded a few too many bourbon shots when I helped myself to the stool next to him. After failing to save Evan's soul for Jesus, I made a pass at him. Evan hit me square in the jaw and then apologized.

Apology accepted; I explained I was a minister of the Gospel, and although I had a few flaws to overcome, I was building a religious empire with my wife, Vivian. Evan laughed more at the fact that I was married than what I told him next: that my empire for God burned like an eternal flame in my soul. But I saw raw courage in the young graduate that mirrored my own.

Evan's laughter finally changed to serious contemplation after I revealed my plans and promised to never again approach him sexually. Evan accepted my job offer.

I had kept my promise.

Although I preached Christians must live free from sin, the one thing I knew for sure was that God could not save the world without me and that He winked at my occasional indiscretions. As long as my priority was preaching the good news to the godless and converting the world to Christianity.

I did the same for my CEO. I allowed Evan side ventures, all under the auspices of the church. And for me, Evan looked the other way. Together, we accomplished my goal—control and power over the evangelical world—and for Evan, wealth, prestige, and his pick of the world's loveliest ladies. My ruthless business partner had enjoyed his abundant life in the church and had held on to my coattails for years.

And what a magnificent ride it was.

Having pulled myself out of a North Carolina hick town and obscure poverty, I had indeed built that empire to become the chosen vessel of The Most High. My charisma reached heights unknown to the Christian world, but in creating my megachurch, my mind grew weary. I became tired of wavering faith, gossiping, and the constant backsliding of my followers. To avert the many attacks of the enemy, I gave Evan carte blanche to eliminate threats to the ministry. *The sword of the Lord, and of Gideon,* I called it. Addicted to treachery, Evan was content as long as he was on the winning end. And I had created the ultimate winner's circle. There were no losers in the Kingdom of the Lord.

Closing my eyes to Evan's methods, the swift justice of the Old Testament God vindicated me, as well as my paranoia. I knew Evan took advantage of my weakness. But riding toward Memphis that day wasn't the time to think of such a slight flaw.

Jamming the two-lane roads, a throng of people and vehicles attempted to park on sidewalks and grassy shoulders to ease traffic congestion. Sitting on their cars, in truck beds, on lawn chairs and blankets, the silent crowds gathered, clutching their dime-store Bibles and positioning their loved ones in wheelchairs by the roadside. Children on crutches, old folks on cots, and the sick and afflicted waited patiently as the prophet of God passed by in the back seat of a limo.

I wept. Oh, yes, I did. The Lord brought the scripture in *Acts* to my mind. *Insomuch that they brought forth the sick into the streets and laid them on beds and couches so that at the least the shadow of Peter passing by might overshadow some of them.* I was that apostle, the chosen one they sought that day.

As the limousine inched toward its final destination, I recognized the familiar hallmarks of small Southern towns. A barbershop with a patched screened door, a hardware store, and a local grocery where folks bought on credit. A white clapboard community center near a marble obelisk war memorial carved with the names of the glorious Confederate dead. I had traveled the world, but I had grown up in the rural south. It was for these backwoods towns that I bowed my head and prayed, vowing to take them all for Jesus.

Moments from the city's outskirts, I asked Evan the question that burned in my mind. "By the way, have you heard from Percy Turlo? Did he take the pictures we need?"

"He did. Don't worry. In time, Joe will have his kids back, and they'll be church members again."

I smiled, slipped on my sunglasses, and waved to the people on the street. "Dillon Oliver. He must be near fifteen."

Evan nodded discreetly as he looked over his paperwork. "Yeah. Good looking kid, too."

"Yes," I said. "Very. Reminds me of his daddy at that age."

Chapter 39

LORD, REMEMBER ME
Andie ~ July 1991

Dixie had become a loose cannon, listening to Daddy breathe. I stayed nights with her, hoping she wouldn't explode on my watch. Caroline and her girls had managed time away with her ex-in-laws, who were taking them to Disney World.

"Mama, do you think we could go to Disney World someday?" Gracie's sheepish look about did me in. For a fourteen-year-old, Gracie grew solid as a fireplug. She had a turned-up nose that made her look even younger than her years and high cheekbones that gave everyone the impression she was stronger than she was. A pretty face, a future beauty queen like her grandmother, Gracie had also inherited her father's athletic arms and legs. Her intelligence was often more than I could handle. God had gifted both her and Dillon, if gifted was the proper word, with my strangely compelling blue eyes.

"Someday, baby. When things are better, I've got a good job, and your grandpa is feeling better." *When Pentecostals really do fly away.* Grateful for my parent's home, I had tagged it as my place of refuge. A place I could hide and even live if I had to. But Disney World was not in our future.

✑

"Wy's coming," said Dixie, flipping through her *Southern Living* magazine. "I'm hoping she'll stay until we see what happens with Bud." She didn't know the seriousness of her statement.

"Dixie, you've got to believe Daddy's getting better."

"It's been difficult, believing. He can't climb the stairs anymore. He sleeps upright—in his recliner—in his office. All night. Can't breathe." Dixie threw her magazine across the room. "Them damn cigarettes!" It landed safely a few feet from a large Waterford crystal vase, a Christmas gift from Wylene.

The horror of losing Daddy struck me like a padded fist. My breath caught audibly in my throat. "Dixie, the phone's ringing." My voice was hoarse. "Want me to get it?"

"No. It could be the doctor. Or Wy. She's supposed to be here by supper. I'll get it." My mother picked up her magazine on the way to the phone. A minute later, she hollered from the kitchen. "Andie! It's Lula."

Lula? I had visions of her or Cletus sick, alone in a Birmingham hospital. Then it hit me like a boot to the head. *Rupert.* His kidneys. They'd been diseased for years. Since Mavis was alive. I ran to the phone. Through her frantic cries and nose-blowing, Lula reported Cletus had bought her a plane ticket, and she'd arrive in Winston-Salem tomorrow. I guessed correctly; Rupert's kidney cancer had landed him in Baptist Hospital, and he had been asking for me. He was dying.

I prepared to leave. "Do we tell Daddy?"

My mother couldn't answer. This was a bad omen for Dixie. Connected at the hip, best friends their whole lives, Daddy always said he wouldn't die until Rupert had gone on ahead of him.

"How much more can this family take?" My mother said, shuffling back to the living room. She had not answered my question about whether we should tell Daddy, so I didn't. She looked old as she fell into the chair by the fireplace. Everyone I loved was disappearing.

How much more can I take, Lord? Me—Andie Oliver—remember me?

I stood outside on the porch and gazed into the blackest night I'd ever seen. Staring at the sky, I found no trace of silver, not one star, a slice of moon, or even the lights of an airplane. I had never seen a sky so void and motionless, like a bottomless ocean. Hurrying Dillon and Gracie into the car, I knew Dixie was in no shape to keep an eye on the twins, and they didn't need to bother her with loud TV or talk for the next couple of hours. After dropping them off at the Darwoods, I sped toward Baptist Hospital.

When I arrived, I spoke to a floor nurse; death was imminent. Lula would not get there in time. Rupert Dumass had coasted into the winter of his life, running on fumes. No one had known he was bad off until a deacon who looked in on him every day or so found him collapsed on the porch. A few Mount Zion Baptist Church members had sat by his hospital bedside the past two days. Two men and one woman—all deacons—told me they'd prayed the Holy Ghost into the room. They'd said that God would raise Rupert up or see fit to take him to his heavenly home.

I thanked them for their kindness, and they left me alone with him. Someone had parted his hair with exact comb marks. The room's soft light illuminated his closed eyes. I couldn't sit or stand still, observing Rupert's thin, pale body. It distressed me because I knew Daddy wasn't far behind. Tubes and IVs protruded from every part of him. He opened his eyes and smiled.

"Andie," he whispered. "So good to see you, darlin'." For a moment, I thought he was done, but then his tender voice spoke again. "Got blood in my urine. It's my time."

"I wouldn't miss your home-going for the world, Rupert." Blinking back tears, I stepped to his bed and clutched his hand.

"Going to see Loretta tonight. And Mavis. I've missed them."

"I know you have," I said softly. "Please, Rupert, when you see Mavis, tell her I love her and I miss her so."

"Will do. I—I need to talk to you."

"Shhh. You sleep. I'll be here when you wake up."

He closed his eyes. I was where I belonged. Daddy would want me by Rupert's bedside. I wouldn't leave him until he passed. Sitting in the quiet darkness, dozing, I watched the light from the hallway pour into the room. The nurses paid no attention to me, even though visiting hours were long over. Standing, then stretching, I tiptoed to the doorway. The heart monitor near his bed gave off faint and steady beeps, breaking the silence like a lighthouse beacon. Every blip of light signified his soul—out on the ocean—searching for Heaven.

I peered down the long hospital corridor. A janitor shuffled by, rolling a bucket that smelled of disinfectant. I held my breath as the off-putting odors of urine and a dirty mop trailed behind him. I detested hospitals and every emotion they stirred within me. Sorrow, fear, and the pain of death.

Looking back at Rupert, I noticed the hospital curtain around his bed swayed as if blown by a slight breeze. There was no open window, no air vent near him. The pungent antiseptic I smelled only a moment before turned sweet, like a strawberry field or hive full of honey. I knew about these things. I'd heard Daddy talk about his mother and the angels she saw. Unlike the fabricated angel hype Calvin dished out in his services, my grandmother saw them during difficult times. Daddy swore by these accounts, and I had always believed him.

I imagined Rupert's angel had entered the room to prepare for his departure. I had no fear, only a sad anticipation of his death. Wandering back to his bed and the quiet click of the pump providing morphine to dull Rupert's pain, I was glad I was there.

We hadn't had time to prepare. All of us who loved him in the deepest, most anguished corners of our hearts had prayed for his recovery. It was always hard to let go of those you loved. It never got easier for me.

I heard him moan. "Andie? Where are you, honey?"

"I'm here, Rupert." I leaped to his bedside again. With a gesture unlike himself, he touched my hand. In a voice worn smooth, he said, "Evil—it abides—among us. It is worse—than imagined." Rupert's effort to speak wasn't a final breath deathbed statement. It was a message that left me totally shaken, and I wasn't sure I had heard him correctly. After all, they were the words of a dying man, probably not in his right mind. His eyes suddenly popped wide open. Sunken in deep lilac hollows, they darted around as he tried to talk. "Open it, Andie. Promise me—you'll open it."

"Open what, Rupert? Open what?" Frustrated, not knowing his meaning, I yearned to climb inside his thoughts.

Closing his eyes and falling asleep under the power of painkillers, Rupert opened his mouth and, one more time, simply said, "Open it."

Confused and tired, I needed coffee. Maybe later, I'd ask him again. What did he mean, *open it?* I felt around in my pocket for change. A used Kleenex, a quarter, a nickel, two pennies. Enough for coffee from the machine.

I returned to Rupert's room seconds before dawn, seconds behind the medical team that rushed in and swarmed over him like a cloud of bees. Captivated by the flat, unbroken line, I crushed the paper cup, spilling the scalding, hot coffee over my fingers and onto my coat and shoes.

I arrived at my parents' home, dragged my weary body inside, and collapsed. Too tired and sick at heart to remove my jacket, I fell head-first into the couch. In the dark, listening to my breath, yet another bleak sense of hopelessness wrapped itself around me like an old, familiar blanket. The hours ticked by. When I woke, Wylene and Dixie towered over me in their housecoats. Someone had covered me with a quilt. "He's gone," I said.

When I told Daddy, he worsened, turning gray as if on cue. He'd promised his friend that he would not die first. He had kept that promise. As I relayed Rupert's last words to Daddy, he offered no explanation. He only shrugged as if he knew what it meant. I didn't push it. I figured it was private between him and his best friend, who was now gone.

Three days later, on a rainy spring morning, we buried Rupert beside his wife and daughter in the tiny graveyard on his farm. I served a lunch I'd spent two days preparing. Other than money for food, Dixie offered no help, as she couldn't leave Daddy home alone. A few friends of Lula's and Gracie and Dillon had pitched in to serve and clean up.

After the last guest offered their condolences to Lula and Cletus, I walked the long path back to the little cemetery. As far as the eye could see, Rupert's overgrown tobacco fields rolled over the landscape. Like fireworks, memories of the Dumass family exploded inside my head, one after the other. I gazed up into the thundering clouds and cried out, "Rupert! You're home now!" The clouds opened up, allowing a single sunlight stream to flood the gravesite. He'd heard me. I was sure of it. He made it to Loretta and Mavis. Heaven.

I strolled to the house as if hugging some wonderful secret, my steps a little lighter, my heart almost jubilant.

Lula greeted me on the porch, holding a box under her arm, her eyes filmed over with tears. I paused, watching one tear fall fast before she caught it with her hankie. Another splattered on her dress. "He want you to have all this, Andie. He love you like his own chile'. Your family was good to him. Rupert and my sister loved each other a long time. Rupert had a hard row to hoe, wantin' to marry a Black woman back then. The White folk had nothin' to do with him anymore. And some Black folk turned their back on my sister. But your daddy loved Rupert and helped him buy the first sack of tobacka seed for this ol' farm." Lula wiped her eyes and handed me the box.

I wondered if Rupert meant this box when he said, *open it*. Was this what he wanted me to open? The first thing I saw was Mavis's old camera, which she bought with stolen lunch money, and a picture of her parents picking tobacco in 1970. I held the winning blue ribbon for that picture, a little frayed and faded, and choked back burning tears. Caressing it to my chest, I could not contain my grief. A whole family—wiped out before their time, but my memories of the Dumass family would never fray or fade.

The land, house, and contents were willed to Lula, who promptly put it all up for sale to pay Rupert's bills and back taxes.

Chapter 40
Live For Today
Andie ~ August 1991

I woke on my birthday with two hungry fourteen-year-olds and seventy-five cents in my pocket. Joe's child support, half of what he was supposed to give me, had dwindled. I thought about calling him. *Can I have some money to feed our kids?* But I knew where that would lead. Nowhere.

After the divorce, the twins rarely spoke his name. When they were little and heard his tires crunch on the gravel driveway, they ran to their rooms. When he left for good, there were no more threats of discipline but no extra food. Only if it came from Dixie. I tried to not to complain about their father, but undoubtedly, they'd heard me lose my temper once or twice. After listening to some fancy psychologist on the Phil Donahue show say we shouldn't talk negatively to our children about the missing parent, I tried. I really did. But I wondered how much of a saint I'd have to become to keep my mouth shut in the future.

I flipped through my wallet, looking for a hidden or missed few dollars. My driver's license, a school photo of Gracie, and a folded coupon for Prell shampoo. Nothing. Only a nickel wedged between the plastic window for my social security card and some crumbs. Credit cards were long gone; five dollars and twenty-three cents sat in my checking account.

I got busy fixing whatever I could find for breakfast. Within minutes, the twins sat at the table eating pancakes, the last of the Log Cabin syrup, and watered-down orange juice.

After opening homemade birthday cards, I hugged them both as they prepared to leave, and I reasoned it was the way of things. Every year, I became less while their friends became more.

Dillon's voice had changed, sounding more like Joe than ever. Especially his laugh. "I'm playing basketball at Bobby's today," he said, stuffing his mouth full of pancakes. I noticed his wrist bones remained boyishly knobby. He had outgrown his clothes. Tall and handsome with thick wavy hair that grew as fast as his legs and arms, his eyes were fringed with the sort of lashes only boys seem to get and girls covet. His constant companion, Prissy, barked and followed behind him everywhere he went. And, of course, Gracie tagged along. Everyone knew she had a crush on Bobby.

"Don't forget," I hollered after them, "supper at Grandma's tonight!"

But as the twins grew, they became more aware of my problems and the pain that accompanied them. They showed their love by staying out of trouble, and I thanked God daily. Despite the divorce and everything that went with it, their lives, at least, were almost—normal.

I continued to drive my sister's car, but it needed new tires. So, with a bit of *under-the-table* money I saved over the summer working for a local caterer, I headed to the Walmart Auto Center. Baking pies for the caterer was temporary work, but enough to buy two steel-belted radials for a Honda. I felt I owed that to Caroline. Although, the best part of that day was running into an old friend.

"I'll be damned if it ain't Andie Oliver!" He'd cleaned himself up, lost weight, and traded his pop-bottle lenses for contacts. I hardly recognized him as I kissed his now clean-shaven face. "Coot McGraw! What brings you this way?" I'd missed Coot and thought of him often. He'd saved my life, and I felt remorse for not calling him.

"A little shoppin', pickin' up a car part, and waitin' on my new wife." He shot me a toothless grin. "Married Candace Cooper! Last month."

I squealed and threw my arms around his neck. "Why didn't someone call me?"

"Aww, we just ran off to Myrtle Beach and got married. No big deal."

"Well, my goodness! Congratulations!"

At that moment, Candace click-clacked her way into the waiting area of the tire center, her snakeskin boots drawing the attention of every male in the place. "Whose that strange woman a-huggin' my husband?"

"Candace!"

All three of us embraced, and I made them promise to visit as soon as they'd settled into their new double-wide in Lexington. I had lived next door to Candace for seven years, worked for her for almost two, and she had coached me through labor and delivery of the twins. Underneath her floozy exterior, her first-class character surpassed most women I knew. As it turned out, Coot was the best thing to happen to Candace and her daughter.

Coot mentioned his new set of dentures, minus tobacco stains, were almost ready to be *installed*. I laughed. He said he'd stopped drinking, sold his garage, and semi-retired, and that he drove a truck two days a week for a short-haul outfit and sold Shaklee products on the side.

I smiled at my two dear friends. They were two of the happiest people I'd seen in a long time, laughing and joking as if they'd known each other all their lives.

At least someone's life has improved.

"I ain't heard from Joe fer near ten years now," Coot said. "I 'spect he's too good nowadays fer us country folk. He's done fergot where he came from, who he really is. Yer better off, Andie. Time to find yerself a little happiness. Live fer today."

"Thanks, Coot. I'm working on it."

A timeless Barbie Doll, Candace wiggled toward me in her skin-tight pants and mohair sweater. "Still doin' hair at home," she said. Happy. She used the word three times. "Kiss them babies for us," she said after one last loving hug.

"They're not babies anymore, but I'll do it." I watched Coot and Candace walk to their car, hand in hand. A miracle.

⌒

Live for today, Coot had said. Exhausting my job search, I finally succumbed to interviewing at convenience stores and truck stops. The Pit Stop Truck Stop offered me a cashier position, the only place I'd interviewed that paid more than minimum wage. Happy birthday, I told myself. I filled out the new employee paperwork and vowed as long as I had Dillon and Gracie, I'd fight depression. Have a better life, a better job, and a better place to live.

My little house had fallen apart. I thought one day I might buy a condo with a bathroom toilet that didn't leak. Maybe rent a colonial without drafty windows and uneven floors. A cape cod with walk-in closets, a sunny kitchen, and a screened-in porch where I could sit and read or talk to a friend. With any luck, I'd get to keep my current house and completely remodel it. I still squeaked out a few daydreams.

When I arrived home, the message light blinked on my answering machine. Ray's voice sounded cheerful. Libby had given birth to a baby boy. Micah. Ray invited me to Richmond for the baby's christening, but his following statement shocked me. "Daddy's ready to leave the cult, but Mama's holding on to the bitter end. Please call her. Try to talk some sense into her again. Micah's birth on your birthday is a gift. Happy birthday, Andie."

I longed to see the new Oliver baby but had no desire to talk sense into my ex-mother-in-law, who had probably replaced all pictures of me with her new daughter-in-law. Maudy had covered for Joe, enabling him his entire life. She'd shunned me for years. Any regret Maudy possessed would not change a thing, lessen my pain, or make my life easier. No. I hoped the best for Al, but didn't expect Maudy to allow him to leave the cult or even attend his new grandson's christening.

The few families I'd heard who had left the House of Praise ended up in other cult-like churches, smaller but still full of legalism and fear. I'd heard ex-addicts often return to the pain they longed to escape. It appeared many members who left Calvin's cult returned in the end. They returned because of their addiction to Calvin. They believed they had a better chance of making Heaven sitting in his church. It wasn't easy to shake off that kind of brainwashing. Certainly, none of them knew what I knew.

As for me, a church of any kind was not in my future. I would take my chances and stay home.

Chapter 41

AS COMFORTABLE AS WE CAN MAKE HIM

Andie ~ October 1991

Listening to *The Beatles' Abbey Road* album, I used music or an old movie as a sedative. Working double shifts at the truck stop, I wanted to put Rupert's death and Daddy's illness out of my mind. I hadn't seen my family in a month. When the cassette player clicked off, the phone rang. It was Aunt Wy, insisting I come for supper.

A carved jack-o'-lantern frowned on the stoop when I pulled into the circle drive that evening. As I bounded up the steps, my mother and sister stepped onto the porch. I offered my cheek for a kiss from Dixie and hugged Caroline. "How's Daddy?" An undertone of desperation slipped into my voice.

"As comfortable as we can make him. He'll be happy to see you," said Dixie. Her voice sounded strained and rather pitiful.

"What does the doctor say?"

Caroline's eyes welled with tears. "His lungs are congested, and he's been coughing up more blood. He's weak, and Aunt Wy says we haven't seen the worst of it. Wy had a visiting male nurse carry him up the stairs. No more sleeping in his chair." She tucked her arm around mine and added, "It's chilly out here. Let's go in."

Once inside, I glanced around. For a sad moment, I studied the wood floors Daddy laid himself, the banister he took so long to sand until it was the perfect color of walnut, and the oak steps of the broad stairway he polished until you could see yourself.

"Give me your coat," Dixie said, looking in the mirror and patting her hair, ensuring the wind hadn't ruffled it from its proper place. I shed my coat, handing it to my mother, who acted like everything was fine and dandy. "I swear, your coat's filthy."

I rolled my eyes at Caroline.

Dixie went about smoothing out the coat's wrinkles and laughed strangely. "Where'd you get this old rag?"

"Um, you. You gave it to me for Christmas—years ago," I said.

"Get it dry-cleaned; don't let me catch you in it again."

I studied my mother intently in the ornate foyer mirror. Then, sighing, I touched her shoulder. "I'll take it tomorrow. Promise. You okay?"

"You're worse than a man," she said, refusing to answer my question, reaching back and fluffing my bangs. "You'll wear any old coat as long as it's warm. It doesn't matter that it smells like smoke and has six buttons missing. And get your hair cut."

Wylene waddled to the foot of the stairs, carrying magazines and a medicine tray. "Excuse me, ladies."

"Oh, sorry, Wy," I said. We all stepped back, allowing her to pass.

"I assume you want your daddy awake to talk to you; hey, Andie?" She climbed the stairs without waiting for my reply.

"That'd be fine," I said.

My mother talked as if we had all gathered for a picnic. "Did Wy tell you she delivered the Mayor of Charleston's grandson?"

"No, she didn't," I said. Aunt Wy had, however, mentioned Dixie needed to see a shrink again. I swallowed and sighed. "I'm going upstairs."

"We'll be at the table," Caroline said as she put her arm around Dixie's shoulders and turned her in the kitchen's direction.

I caught the blank stare on my mother's face. Wylene was right. This was more than my mother could stand. Her mental health was deteriorating fast. Daddy's death would send her over the edge unless Wy could snap her out of it. Of course, if anyone could, it'd be my aunt.

I hurried up the stairway and quietly opened the door to Daddy's room, nodding to Wylene, who stood when I entered. "Is he asleep?" I whispered. I had nibbled off my lipstick on the drive over. Biting at my lips again, I eased the door closed, holding my breath until the click of the knob echoed in the dark room.

"You can wake him. He's been asking for you. I'll be right outside if you need me."

I grabbed her hand and asked the million-dollar question. "Aunt Wy, is Dixie okay?"

"She's a looney tune; that's what she is. But then, it runs in our family. You're a little looney yourself, Andie."

"I know. Everyone likes to remind me. Dixie sounds like she isn't wrapped right, though."

"She's started her grieving process early. She'll be fine. It's the shock of knowing. I keep nothing from her. She thinks I'm cruel. It's because I love her, and now that I have her back in my life, I'm not losing her again. I want to get her through this."

I laid a grateful kiss on Wylene's cheek. "I thank God every day we found you, Wy. Please don't leave us."

"Not going anywhere except to the hospital to deliver a baby or two. I've cut my office hours to two days a week. I'll stay here for the rest of the time. Until it's over."

My breath caught in my throat, and I stared, speechless.

Wylene changed the subject. "Hey, I moved into the TV room in the basement. I love your old Janis Joplin poster. Her hair looks like mine."

I whispered, "You can have the poster."

Wylene smiled. "Get on over there. I think he's awake, listening and laughing to himself, the old geezer. I keep telling him to get better because he's been a real pain in my ass lately. He just smiles and tells me he will belt me later." Wy shook her head. "He's nothing but a dang redneck who's kept R. J. Reynolds in business. And what'd he get for it? Emphysema. Damn, fool. But, hey, at least it's made me quit!"

"Wy, that's great! You've quit smoking?"

"Yeah. And don't let me see you with one, little lady. I can still tan your hide!" She kissed my cheek and slipped out the door.

I tiptoed to Daddy's bedside and had yet another shock. Grateful his eyes were closed, I adjusted to the change in his appearance. One month had taken its toll. He had grown not just thin, but bony. Ravished by the disease, he appeared ghostly. The flesh on his once muscular body hung loose, and deep wrinkles lined his unshaven and drawn face. A pallor replaced his accustomed tan. Daddy's thick, wavy hair, once streaked handsomely with silver, had matted and turned white as the sheets beneath him.

I smoothed out his bed sheet, straightened his blanket, and gently lifted one of his frail hands.

At my touch, he slowly batted his tissue-paper eyelids. "That you, Rosebud?" His voice sounded flat and lifeless and strangely hollow.

My tears glistened, and I raised his hand to my cheek. "Yep, Daddy, it's me." I sniffed.

"My pretty girl." A warm glow replaced his dazed look. "I'd forgotten how much you resemble your mother. You're the spitting image of her. I'm glad you're here," he said. "How are the kids?" He started coughing and brought a tissue to his mouth. I released his hand and sat at his bedside. "I've missed you, honey," he said when the spasm ended.

"I've missed you, too, Daddy. No one can scold me like you," I teased.

"Life's been hard on you, hasn't it?" Clear regret tinged his voice.

"It doesn't matter. I just want you to get well."

"I was afraid of losing you, afraid Joe would change you into one of them fanatics at that church. You don't realize how much like your mother you are. Got that same stubborn streak, like my grandpap's old mule. I was foolish, Rosebud, allowing Dixie to take you to that church years ago. I drove myself crazy thinking I lost you to that place."

"You never lost me, Daddy. You're the king of all you survey, remember?"

His attempt to laugh saddened me. "Ah, yes. I'm the king of my castle."

"I need you more than ever. I have no role model for Dillon and Gracie if you leave me. There's nobody who loves me as much as you. If you go, I'll truly be alone."

He raised a hand and cupped my cheek. "You'll be fine. I believe there's a man to come who will cherish you. You've yet to find the love of your life."

"*You're* the love of my life, Daddy."

He turned up a corner of his mouth in another attempt to smile. That's when I saw something flicker in his eyes. His countenance closed quickly, as if guarding a well-kept secret. I turned away, wearied by it all. My voice quivered. "Oh, Daddy, I'm so ashamed for disappointing you."

His anguished eyes stared into the dimness of the room. "I've got a lovely wife and two beautiful daughters; what man could ask for more? What man wouldn't be proud?"

He reached out to me, and I clasped his hand again. I peered down at one of his *Guns and Ammo* magazines by his bed, addressed to Bud Parks. "Remember when you pretended to be related to Rosa Parks?"

"You don't know this, but I named you after her. Dixie insisted on *Andie*, though. I wanted you to admire strong women who stood for what was right."

"Strong women: may we know them, may we raise them, may we be them," I said.

"That's beautiful. You make that up?"

"No. Aunt Wy said it to me once. It's by an anonymous poet."

"My mother was a strong woman, too."

"Tell me about her. I was a little girl when she died, as I recall. There's so much I don't remember about your mother. Dixie said Caroline looks like her."

"Oh my, she does. My mother had a passion for life. I can see her kissing my father goodbye at the rail station. His job on the railroad took him away a lot. But my mother taught us boys the value of hard work." Daddy's voice drifted lower as he stared a blank stare. "There are times I still hear her laughter, just as it sounded when we'd walk behind the mule during planting season. She was happy. Content in every circumstance. She died young."

"Yes, but she lived and died in peace. How wonderful! Think of all the women who grow old and never know such happiness. Such love. I doubt I ever will."

"Of course you will. When you least expect it, true love will seek you out." He smiled with a sigh of assurance. "I'm going to see her soon."

"Don't talk like that. I need you. Please, don't talk that way."

"But I'm ready. Got to rest on my mountain." Gripped with another spasm of wracking coughs, he reached for me again. I held him momentarily, propping up his frail body to ease the strain. The coughing subsided like rumbling thunder fading into the distance. His head sank back into the pillow, and he stared at his dresser as if looking for something hidden inside.

"I've got to rest. I'm glad you're here, Andie; go be with your mother. She needs you. She loves you. I know she doesn't say it, but

I've been talking to her about that. We'll chat later, honey," he said feebly. Closing his eyes, he drifted to sleep.

In the quiet room, I heard a train whistle in the distance. I stood, and my eyes clouded with more tears. "Yes, Daddy. We'll talk again."

Leaning over, I kissed his cheek, and he mumbled. "I don't want to lose you like Rupert did Mavis." I watched to see if he would open his eyes again. *He's dreaming.* I walked pensively down the stairway. Instead of chastising my mistakes, he had always encouraged me to believe a better life was just around the corner. It broke my heart.

⌒

Caroline sat in front of a blazing fire, her cheeks a pretty shade of pink. Wafts of her Sweet Honesty perfume filled the room like a cloud. She'd recently cut her hair short; it glowed a candied red in the flickering light. Blessed with ex-in-laws who stepped in and cared for her girls when needed, she had left them there for the night.

My sister's personality, even though she denied it, mirrored our mother's. Caroline possessed a natural ability to demand Dixie's attention and get it. Sitting with her arm around Dixie, Caroline was like the monkey that never learned how to get off its mother's back.

The grim set of Caroline's jaw told me she had something on her mind. Her expression radiated frustration. She had not fought a battle with weight as I had, but her three close pregnancies had taken their toll on her—mentally. When she wasn't searching for her next husband, Caroline clung to Dixie. Closer than I ever had.

Blinking away remnants of tears, I poured a cup of coffee from the tray on the table. Wilting next to my aunt, I curled around one of Dixie's embroidered couch pillows. The four of us sat in hushed solidarity. The room grew quiet, except for the crackle of burning embers. Finally, I tried to work some encouragement into my voice. "Maybe the disease will slow down, and he'll feel better."

We drank our coffee and stared silently into the fire. I knew none of us believed my hopeful prediction, and I couldn't help but wonder if we all thought the same thing. *How much longer?* Wylene stood and announced she'd take the first shift and sleep on the cot in Bud's room. Dixie staggered off to the spare bedroom with her with her lips clamped tight. I looked at my sister, who glanced sharply around the room.

"What's on your mind, Caroline?"

She hesitated, then spit it out. "How could you stay with him all those years?" she snipped. "I never lasted over two years with either of my worthless husbands." Her sharp and accusing voice didn't give me a chance to answer. "Especially when he was never home and doing God knows what to whom? Why the hell did you stay with him?" It was the first time she wanted answers from me. "I don't understand you, Andie. Why did you put up with it for so damn long?"

"And *now* you need an explanation?" I asked.

"Sorry. But yes. I do. Dixie always told me to leave it alone. Not to pry. That you'd made your bed and had to lie in it, and I know it's none of my business—"

"—Are you going to let me talk?"

"Oh, please do."

I shrugged. "It's complicated."

"Give it your best shot," she quipped.

I set my cup on the coffee table and leaned forward, searching for words that didn't make me sound like an idiot. A momentary silence fell between us, and I felt Caroline's anger spill over the edge of her patience. But then there it was, the only answer possible.

"In the beginning, I loved him beyond all reason. I quickly realized my marriage was not what I had hoped. Caught up in church doctrine, I submitted to him, believing what I was told—that submission was God's plan and the greatest gift a woman could give her husband. I was determined to bloom in the red Carolina dirt God planted me in. *All to Jesus, I surrendered.* But I ran myself ragged, trying to please both Jesus *and* Joe while chasing silly daydreams of having what Dixie had."

"I understand wanting what our mother has."

"I'm sure you do."

The warmth from the flames served to further unchain my thoughts. "You asked how I could stay with him, knowing he cheated on me. Joe had turned me into a forgiving machine. Forgiveness was an automatic reaction to every suspicion, always plugged in and ready."

The first spark of absurdity faded from Caroline's face as she poured more coffee. "I thought you were incredibly stupid or had secretly turned Catholic and become some kind of saint."

I smiled. "What I became was an expert at forgiveness. Forgiveness allowed me to believe the past was the past. That tomorrow would be different. By forgiving him, I did what Jesus said to do. So, did that make me better than him? Truthfully, it put off the inevitable. To survive, I told myself every day that Joe would one day wake up and realize I was the best thing to happen to him. Because of my faithfulness, God would intervene on my behalf. It never happened."

Caroline raised her brows and unfolded a blanket to cover her legs. "I still think you were crazy."

After a long sigh, I looked at my sister. "Maybe I was. Maybe I was crazy enough to think I could separate the adultery from the man by forgiving Joe. As if I could remove it from his body like pulling a handkerchief out of his pocket. That way, I could justify my reasons for staying with him. Here's the kicker. I always thought *it could be worse.*" I rested my head on the back of the couch. "I married him, hoping to build a home for us and our children. We both failed, Caroline. Both of us. I was a fool. That's a hard fact to live with."

We sat watching the fire, but I felt Caroline needed more to satisfy her. So I kept talking.

"Forgiving Joe didn't change him. Loving him didn't change him. Having his children, even burying one of them, wasn't enough to change him. Not even a little. Joe's heart beat only for Calvin Artury, never me. Never us." I stood and walked toward the fireplace.

"I thought someday Joe might come clean. Admit he failed us. How silly of me to think that. To confess his failure as a husband and father was a ridiculous thought. But it was my nature to fantasize until the bitter end, where Joe was concerned. I fought hard for Joe, rebelling against the church *and* God. Because of my rebellion, the threat of Hell nagged at me day and night, always afraid of blaspheming or missing the rapture. I trembled at the thought. That, in and of itself, held me captive within Calvin's church and my marriage. It was a vicious circle."

Wanting a cigarette, I stoked the red blush of the embers and added another log. Extinguishing my yearning for an idyllic life, I smothered a groan. Tightening my jaw, I turned to my sister and spread my hands regretfully. "In the end, I had nothing left to fight with. Nothing to overrule the stinking religion and the hope for Joe to change that presided over my life."

"Money was a great mistake motivator, especially since you had none," said Caroline.

"True." Staring into the fire again, as if standing at the edge of the Bottomless Pit waiting for Satan to push me in, I wanted to stop thinking about it all. "To this day, I have no power of persuasion. No way to fight the House of Praise and its pulpit."

The image of John Rossi swirled in front of me like smoke; I dared not explain to Caroline the depth of the evil twisting around religion as I knew it. "I used to bury my head in my pillow to stifle Calvin's prophesies from blaring in my brain. Joe had proclaimed in front of God and everybody the failure was all mine. In a way, it was. I allowed the insanity to go on far too long. Ultimately, only his measly paycheck kept me hanging on. Sick, right?"

"I hate him," Caroline declared, then looked away, pale and pink-eyed.

I blinked hard. "My God. Did Joe proposition you? It wouldn't surprise me."

The fire's sparks reflected in Caroline's teary eyes. "I wanted to tell you for the longest time. I couldn't. I just—couldn't. It was that day I babysat the twins at your old trailer. I was eighteen and pregnant with my first. He cornered me and tried to kiss me. I threatened him with Daddy's wrath. I never told Daddy; he'd have killed him. I never want to see him again."

I heaved a sigh of disgust. "Neither do I."

PAMELA KING CABLE

Chapter 42
Good Men Never Die
Andie ~ February 1992

Months passed. We either needed to exercise our faith in Daddy's healing, or God didn't hear our prayers. At any rate, the holidays went by in a blur as we took our turn at Daddy's bedside.

I put Prissy into the car and left Daddy with a hospice worker to go home and take a badly needed shower. When Daddy's old dog passed away, my dog, Prissy, inherited a place at my parents' house. Daddy loved her, but Dixie put up with her for Daddy's sake, so occasionally, I took Prissy to my house to give my mother a break.

I'd had little sleep, driving home only twice in the past two weeks to pick up my mail and see my children, who had been staying with the Darwoods.

Velda Darwood's gracious and kind spirit became my biggest blessing during this difficult time. She insisted Dillon and Gracie stay with her family until I could return for more than a day. But when I arrived home, I crawled into bed and sobbed. *He's only 60. He can't die this young. How will I survive without him? How will any of us go on without Daddy? Please, God. Enough.*

I couldn't sleep. Leaving my sorrow under the blankets and sheets clustered at the bottom of my bed, I crept down the chilly hallway; the dog following sleepily after me. Prissy, as always, was our protector.

The wind raged outside like two fighting cats as I walked on a sigh in the quiet, empty part of the night, feeling as if I were the only person in the world awake.

Tiptoeing to the kitchen window and gazing at the speckled shadows on the lawn, I watched the moon over Turner Street spill a waxy patina on snow piled around the driveway's edges. Like most snow in the Triad, it would disappear the next day, unlike my mood. Iced like a cake, the frost-covered boxwood laid dormant in their winter beds, and a few grand maples I loved, naked and cold, stood guard over my small front yard. The neighbor's velvety lawns rose and fell away in the night. Their tiny and varied houses—most still lacking attention—sat like silent witnesses to the goings-on in and around my house.

I felt the temporary peace of the neighborhood. All was well; I had forced my mind elsewhere, away from my troubles, for one peaceful moment.

Winter always lagged in early February. The dreary, cold, and wet season chilled me to my toes. I cranked up the thermostat, but rage burned hot in my head and my heart. I wanted to open my mouth and let it fly. Puke it up. Everything I knew all over Joe and Calvin. But I kept my secret secured in an envelope in the attic rafters, a wretched, horrible secret John Rossi created the night I watched Evan Preston murder him. I knew too much.

I longed to see the hands that comforted me as I gave birth to a dying child over a decade before. I'd never forgotten them. The thought of those hands still comforted me on my worst days, but the vision seemed like another lifetime ago. Although the left hand was missing a finger, they were beautiful hands belonging to no one Dixie nor I knew. I had briefly mentioned them to her once. She said, "You always had a vivid imagination, Andie."

In 1975, Daddy's health went to Hell in a handbasket after burying his grandson and Mavis. That's the year he started chain-smoking three to four packs of unfiltered Camels daily. His cigarette was like an extra finger—a permanent fixture on his body. Brian's death, a few weeks before someone murdered Mavis, had knocked us all flat for a while. Though my baby breathed his last breath in infancy, it was no less devastating. It surprised no one when the doctor finally proclaimed Daddy's lungs were like overcooked grits.

I dreaded the days and silent nights. It was heartbreaking to know Daddy's house, which he rebuilt, would have to be sold for Dixie to support herself through her old age.

The early morning light, soft and warm, filtered through my curtains, casting a gentle glow in each room. My garage sale clock on the living room wall chimed, its sound a jarring contrast to the peaceful morning. I yawned and sank into my recliner, remembering the day we settled Daddy into a hospital bed that we had rolled into his study downstairs.

Dixie insisted we remove Daddy's antique clock from the wall. She said every ding wore on her nerves and stole time from all of us. I refused. "It's his Federal clock. It belonged to his mother. He loves that clock. Think of it this way, Dixie: every chime should remind us there's still time for a miracle, a sound of hope." But listening to his wheezes, I doubted it. Dixie's mouth twitched at the corner. On the verge of tears, she gave me a small, scornful smile and walked away, leaving the clock's chimes to vibrate in the room.

Suddenly, I shouted, breaking the silence. "God! We've prayed our hearts out! My family has prayed their hearts out!" I lifted my head and glared at the ceiling. "Look at me, God!" I admonished Him as if speaking to my children. "Why are You letting this happen?" The only sound was my clock's pendulum, ticking back and forth like the tail of time wagging on the wall.

My eyes stung with new tears. Possessing no self-control or faith at that moment, I scolded the Almighty. "You know what? If You heal him, it'll prove we don't have to go to Calvin for a miracle!" As I expected, no answer came. Daddy would die and leave nothing behind but a wisp of cigarette smoke and the silent legacy of a man who had once lived among us.

Morning light filtered through the windows. I found myself in the recliner wearing the same pair of sweatpants I'd put on days before, thinking I should call Wylene. Reaching for the phone, I pictured her delivering a baby, her face stern, speckles of sweat across her brow. I dialed her private number at the Charleston Hospital. *What the hell? It's worth a shot.*

She answered on the third ring. "Andie?" Apprehension spilled over in her voice.

"He's fine, Wy. Worn out, but fine. I needed to talk to you. Sorry." I sneezed. And then I sneezed again.

I heard her fax machine crank and grind. "He may be fine, but you sound like shit."

I blew my nose. "I caught a cold from Caroline or one of her girls. Taking care of Dixie and listening to Daddy breathe—I'm exhausted. I'm at home. I had to get out of that house for a day."

"I'll be there early this afternoon by plane; I had an unexpected baby to deliver. I won't leave him again. Promise."

"I know. You've done so much already, traveling back and forth. It's been as hard on you as anyone."

"I'm a tough old bird; I'm concerned about Dixie." Silence. "Andie? You there?"

"It's not how I expected him to go, you know? He's drifting away, Wy. It's devastating."

"Stay strong for him, but more for your mother. Can you do that?"

"What choice do I have?"

"None, really."

I yawned. "The twins called last night; this has been hard on them, too. I have to go back later and check on Dixie."

"Don't you want one more night to yourself?"

"Maybe," I sighed. "I'm going crazy, Wy." I blew my nose again. "I'm losing my house in bankruptcy. Dillon and Gracie will probably have to change schools, and now I'm dealing with Daddy. I can't sit on my butt and do nothing."

"What about your job?"

"They agreed to a leave of absence. Until it's over." There was nothing left to say. My world was one giant catastrophe. My body ached as I ended my call to Aunt Wy. I dragged myself back to bed because only in sleeping did I find a small amount of peace. A peace that would elude me in the months to come.

❧

The next day, the sun refused to rise, casting dark afternoon shadows on the ground. I drove with my lights on, thinking my mood matched the sky. A savage battleship gray. When I arrived at my parents' house, Aunt Wylene sat like a beached walrus in the living room, reading the newspaper and wiggling her wide fingers in hello. Allowing my coat to fall on a chair, I headed to the smell of food in the kitchen. Wy had made a pot of Brunswick stew. I wanted to get my mind off Daddy. What better way than to eat a hot bowl of stew and ask questions about Dixie. Questions that had nibbled at me for years. Wy followed me into the kitchen.

"Aunt Wy, since Dixie's napping, can we talk about something?"

"About how bad her hair looks these days?" She giggled.

"No, not about Dixie's hair. About her life. I know your parents died in that truck crash when you were both little, but did you know Dixie's foster family?"

Wy's large metal spoon slipped from her hand and dropped to the floor. "No."

"That's all you can say is 'no'?"

"Didn't your mother ever talk to you about her growing up years in Charleston?"

"I wouldn't be asking if she had."

"Then think, Andie. Maybe she doesn't want you to know." Wy picked up the spoon and set it in the sink. "This isn't the time to ask these questions."

"Can't you tell me anything?"

Avoiding my eyes, Aunt Wy's fingers pushed fly-away hair strands from her face. "I don't know much."

"Then tell me what you *do* know."

My aunt sighed. "If I tell you, you keep quiet about it. Don't tell a soul. Especially Caroline. She's not ready to hear it, and I'm not sure you are either."

As I ate my soup at the table, I watched Wy grab a mop, as if she had decided to ignore me.

"Are you going to tell me or clean the floor?"

"Don't you think you're under enough stress right now?"

"It's that bad?" I shoved my soup bowl away.

"Bad enough." Aunt Wy wiped her hands on a towel and poured herself a mug of coffee. "I need to sit for this; scoot over."

I moved down the bench to accommodate my large aunt.

She spoke quietly. "Believe me, your mother's past has made her a little crazy in the head. I'm sure you and Caroline have taken the brunt of it over the years. You're smart, Andie. You already know Dixie was very young when she had you. Her early life, before she met Bud, was not a happy one. Unfortunately, I learned everything years after it happened."

"Go on, Wy. I can take it. Tell me."

"Well," she sighed, "her foster parents were country singers and played the fiddle and the banjo. They traveled the Nashville circuit in the '40s."

It answered my question of why my mother loved to sing and knew every old song ever written. I smothered a smile, picturing the couple's rickety pickup rattling back and forth to the juke joints.

Wy sipped her coffee and swallowed twice. "Word on the street was they got mixed up in gambling and drinking, leaving poor Dixie with an elderly woman across the street. Dixie was barely a teenager when the police knocked on the door. They had arrested Claude, her foster father, for murder, and her foster mother, Gladys, lay dead in Nashville. Seems Claude caught Gladys in the sack with a guitar picker who played with *Hank Williams*. Claude shot them both and went to prison. They should've strung the old geezer up. I heard he died in a Tennessee work camp a few years back."

I stared into my coffee mug. "What happened to Dixie? She always made us think she was raised to be a socialite. A debutante."

Wy shook her head, then wiped a few crumbs from the table into her hand. "That was pure survival fantasy. Dixie was never a debutante. The system threw your mother to the four winds, baby. From orphanages to more foster homes to the streets. She was sixteen when Bud found her behind a diner, digging for scraps."

I wanted to cover my ears.

"He carried her home like a lost puppy. But the worst thing was—she was well into her first pregnancy. With you."

My mouth flew open. "What!?" My heart went numb with disbelief.

"Shhh! Take it down a notch, Andie. I don't want Dixie to hear us. Close your mouth, child. Don't ask me who your daddy was because I don't have the first clue. Nobody does. Dixie's never spoken a word about him. I'm not sure *she* knows who he was. He may be dead for all we know. And don't you dare ask your mother. This is not the time, obviously. The thing was, Bud loved her the moment he laid eyes on her. I saw a few pictures of Dixie from back then. She was a sight for sore eyes."

Wy wiped away tears with a napkin and sat quietly for a moment. "So your daddy, when he found her pregnant, dirty, and half-starved, he brought her home, cleaned her up, and married her. She loved him back. They went on to have your brother, who passed away, and Caroline. It's a wonder you were born as healthy as you were, Andie. But they've always loved you as much as Caroline. Maybe a sight more. You're special. You have a mind God gives to few people on this earth. I don't need to tell you how smart you are. Well, maybe not about men, but Lord knows, you should've gone to college. You could've sailed right through. Made a better life for yourself."

Aunt Wy's hands trembled as if it suddenly hit her; she'd let the cat out of the bag, opened Pandora's box, and hauled a monster of a skeleton out of Dixie's closet. She fixed me with a steely gaze. "Don't you dare confront either of them. Let Bud die in peace. He never wanted you to know. Ever. And don't go digging for answers. You might not like what you find. Lord, it might kill your mother if she knew I told you. Dixie and I fell out years ago because I wanted you to know the truth someday. Dixie cut me out of her life for that reason. You keep this to yourself, you hear me?"

I nodded and rested my elbows on the table, pressing my palms to my forehead. After what I'd already been through, knowing I had another father out there somewhere wasn't so upsetting. "I guess it explains why I'm the only one in the family with blue eyes."

Wy's hand rested on my shoulder and squeezed gently. "I've said enough. Leave the past alone, Andie, honey." She stood, gulped the last of her coffee, turned to the sink, and stared out the window. "God is still on the throne," she said.

A heavy sigh left my lips. I wasn't pulling one more secret out of Wy. Not that day. "Wy, don't worry. Bud Parks is my father," I said. "He always has been, always will be. This isn't as upsetting as you think. Not after the life I've already lived. But you're right. It's no wonder Dixie is a bit of a fruitcake. Now I understand."

I walked to the sink, slipped my arms around my aunt's spare tire of a waist, and hugged her tight from behind.

Wy nodded. "Yeah, girl. Losing Bud might put her away. He loved her so much and took good care of her. Gave her the world. That's all that matters to me. Why don't you head on up to your old bed and take a nap?"

"Good idea. I think I will."

An hour later, I stumbled out of bed, feeling the strangeness of knowing I was not Bud Parks' biological daughter. I shook it off. Nothing would change the fact that Bud was my daddy. Not even DNA. I felt strange because I didn't care who my real father might have been. Wylene had given me a glimpse into my mother's past, a gift, and my heart finally softened toward Dixie.

The house shivered in the cold, creaking and cracking with the whirr of the furnace. No doubt, frugal Dixie was messing with the thermostat. Every room had a hospital odor, and it felt like a funeral parlor, quiet and prayerful.

I moved silently downstairs in my stocking feet and peeked into the study. The pungent mist from the humidifier hid the stench of a lifetime of cigarettes that had embedded their poison within the walls and in Daddy's lungs. He was sitting up with his eyes closed; Dixie had propped him against a fresh set of pillows. His breathing sounded gravelly, an endeavor that fluctuated with the periodic gust from the large tank near his bed, sending oxygen through the tube secured under his nose. Every time I saw him, I cried. Non-stop tears. Not a way to live. For Daddy or for me. Rushing back into the living room, I sat on the recliner across from Aunt Wy. "He looks worse."

"More of the same, I'm afraid. Exhausting, wracking coughs that bring up blood. It soaked the bed."

I heard the soothing thump of the dryer in the laundry room. "Where's Dixie?"

"She washed the sheets, then went to the grocery store. Are you still tired?"

"A little."

Wy nodded, then rolled her eyes toward the kitchen. "We're mainlining coffee these days. There's a fresh pot."

I poured a full mug and tiptoed back to the makeshift hospital room to watch him breathe. Watching Daddy breathe came second only to eating and sleeping.

"Rosebud." His croaky voice squeaked, and he panted like a dog.

"What 'cha thinkin', Daddy?"

"I'm thinking I feel damn puny if you want the truth."

I set my coffee mug on his bedside table and thought about the yellowish tar we attempted to scrub off the walls every spring. I pulled up the sheet at the bottom of the bed to massage his feet.

"Dixie used to tell me when you'd massage her feet like this."

"Really?"

"Uh-huh. You didn't know it, but I was always a bit jealous of you and your mother."

"Daddy, that's silly. Why?"

"You knew you had my attention, but you were always trying to get hers."

I couldn't speak.

He blinked. "Wish I could stand on them feet."

I covered each foot, then took his hands and held them to my lips, smelling the scent infused in his skin. All the Aqua Velva in the world wouldn't cover it. It grieved me. I chose to think of him hunched over his workbench, spreading mulch in the yard, tuning his banjo strings, peering under the hood of his car, hunting with his dogs in full camouflage—picking, tying, and stacking tobacco with Rupert. Daddy worked his whole life, rarely stopping but for a smoke. Those decades of hard work were implanted into the cracks of his hands along with the nicotine. His hands made things last. Made things better. And if it consisted of wood or metal or grew in the dirt, he made things beautiful.

But they were not the hands in my vision from years before. Misty-eyed, I dismissed the memories. Had I known how cigarettes were killing him, I would've hidden them, made him quit, and begged him to stop. Calvin had said he would die early because he didn't attend church. Calvin's curse. Maybe he was right. Maybe Calvin was right about a lot of things.

I grabbed his hands again. "Please, Daddy, don't die!" Resting my head on the bed beside him and allowing my tears to fall, I felt his hand on my head.

"Good men don't die—" His breath was too labored; he couldn't finish his thought.

Chapter 43
Avenge Us All
Andie ~ February 1992

After several attempts to force-feed my mother, I gave up, leaving her to Wylene, who slipped a spoonful of leftover stew and a Valium into Dixie's mouth. There'd be no funny business with Aunt Wy around.

"Andie, go on in and sit with Bud. I'm putting Dixie to bed, and then I'll take over for you."

I peeked around the corner and found Daddy frantic. As if he tried hard enough, he could scream with his eyes. When he saw me, he struggled to breathe, his speech quick and toneless. "Oh, good. It's you. Remember—remember my lockbox?"

"The metal box. Upstairs in your sock drawer. I remember." I opened the box once and saw it was full of odds and ends, paperwork I cared nothing about.

On the wall near Daddy's head, the Federal clock chimed eight bells. Struggling for another breath, he asked, "What time is it?"

"It's eight o'clock."

"In the morning?"

"It's nighttime. Don't talk, Daddy. It exhausts you."

"Not much—time left. Have to—tell you about Mavis."

My heart skipped a beat. I moved in closer. "What? Tell me, what exactly? What about her?"

He pointed a crooked finger. "Go up to my room. Get—my lockbox."

"Daddy, damn it, you're sweating. We can talk about it later."

"Pay attention—Rosebud! Get it. Get the—lockbox." He collapsed against the pillows. "Go!"

I jumped up and dashed out, but waited until I knew Dixie was sound asleep before I slipped in and rummaged through Daddy's dresser drawer. Minutes later, I held the box toward him as if he could hold it. I sat and placed it on the bed near his hand. The back of his fingers moved against the cold metal.

"Ah, you found it. Sometimes—your mother moves my stuff." He winked.

"Does Dixie know what's in here?"

"No. She—she never cared about this old box. Once—once, she tried to throw it away. I—told her not to. It—it was for you."

"Combination the same?"

He gave me a nod and a slight smile. "Yes. Your birthday."

I lifted the box onto my lap, unlocked it, and opened the lid. A large manilla envelope lay on top. "It's from Mavis? How? When?" My breaths short between my words, I sounded as winded as Daddy. I picked up the envelope as if it were hot to the touch. Addressed to Rupert, the envelope felt old and wrinkled and smelled like it was from another century. Definitely Mavis's messy handwriting, it sent chills through my heart.

"Rupert—gave it to me—months ago. When he knew he was dying. He had it—hidden—in his barn for years. Mavis mailed it— the day she died. Look—at the postmark. Rupert asked me to look inside. I read her letter. She mailed—the same envelope—to you. Obviously—you never got it. Thank God. They might've—killed you, too."

Daddy fought for breath as I panicked. "Daddy, you're scaring me. And please, stop talking."

"Have—to tell you, darlin'. It's time. We kept it from you—believing you'd be in danger if they knew—if they knew you had it. It got—Mavis killed. I'm sure Artury doesn't know this envelope exists. They—didn't consider she sent a duplicate to her—her daddy. They didn't think Mavis was smart. But—she was—she was." His wheezing worsened.

"Please, Daddy, stop. This isn't necessary now. I can look at it later." I sensed he teetered on the fringe of passing out from the effort of talking.

"No!" He hacked, coughed up blood, and settled back on his bed again, sweat pouring down his face. "Your kids—might be in danger now. You—have to protect—them.

"Now you're *really* scaring me!"

"I—was never sure this was the right thing—to do—show this to you. Give you this. But you've got to know—what Calvin Artury is—what he's done. This may also explain why Joe is—the way he is. Mavis didn't know how to tell you—after losing Brian—she didn't think you could handle it or would even—believe her. Your children—need you to fight for them—like Mavis tried to fight—for you. Don't let Dixie—or Wy or anyone—see what's in that envelope. Hide it—until you can use it—against him. Use it, Andie—but use it wisely."

My heart raced; I could feel the blood rushing to my head. "What's in it?"

Daddy pointed his bony finger at the envelope. "Open it."

Open it. The memory of Rupert's last words exploded inside me. My fingers moved as if I'd suddenly become old and frail myself. I pulled out a letter and a stack of negatives.

"Pull it—all out." His shaky hand moved against my arm.

I dumped out the rest and shuffled through black and white photographs: one young man after another, naked, on a bed in various sexual poses with someone. *Another man?*

"There's writing—on the back of each," Daddy said.

My eyes opened wide, staring at them. Mavis wrote on the back of every single one. "My God! It's a younger Calvin—with a boy—I recognize this kid. It's goofy Gary, the boy Joe and I used to make fun of in church. We were all in high school. Oh, my God, he's with Calvin—NAKED! My God, Daddy, they're both—naked! He's with each boy! Look at all these pictures! Some—I recognize, and some I don't. Mavis. She took these! That's what she had on him! Why they killed her! Oh, I'm going to be sick."

"Keep going," Daddy said.

"Why? What else is in here?" Before he spoke again, I saw it. The picture that answered all of my questions. My lifetime of unanswered prayers. The reason Joe and Ray were as different as peaches and black-eyed peas. It explained why Joe was obsessed with sex. I dropped the pictures and fell to my knees by the bed, burying my head in Daddy's drenched sheets. "He molested Joe. That bastard had sex with Joe!" I pounded my fist on the bed. Then I took the picture in my hand again and studied it.

"Joe appears about fifteen, maybe sixteen," I sobbed. "Mavis was Joe's age, which would've made me about fourteen. Mavis took this picture just before or soon after I met him. I think I was almost sixteen when I introduced Mavis to Joe. No wonder she had the reaction she did! How did Calvin get her to do this?" I shuddered inwardly at the thought. "This explains why she never liked Joe. She knew I didn't know about this." I moaned. "Oh, God. Calvin is a pedophile. And Joe doesn't care! He doesn't care!"

"A psychopathic—pedophile," whispered Daddy.

"Dillon! I can't let him get Dillon!"

Daddy's wheezing grew louder as he glared at me.

Stunned, I took his head and held it between my hands. I wanted him to look at me. "Why did you keep this from me!?"

He closed his eyes, and I let go of him.

"Is there anything *else* I should know?"

Daddy shook his head, soaking the pillow with sweat. "Mavis's letter—explains everything."

Hanging on to the threads of life, Daddy could no longer speak. That indisputable truth caused me to swallow my anger before I opened my mouth. "Why did you hide this from me, Dad? Why? Why didn't Rupert tell me? I had a right to know! Rupert should've given me this years ago! Tell me what to do! What now!?"

Daddy's face was a blank canvas. There was nothing left to say.

I slid the pictures, the letter, and the negatives back into the envelope and slipped out of the room and over to Aunt Wy, who sat in front of the TV, acting as if she hadn't heard a word of it. Daddy's explosive coughing echoed out to the living room. It quickly turned to choking. Wylene shot to her feet, grabbed her bag, and rushed to his side to roll up his sleeve and shoot something into his vein. His face flushed a blood red as the cough came from deep inside his chest—a phlegmy, heart-wrenching sound that turned my face to the wall.

I fled to the kitchen, out the back door, and into the middle of the yard. Standing with my arms wrapped around the envelope, I gazed back at the house, my breath forming a white plume in the cold. Daddy's home and everything in it had become forbidding and unfamiliar territory. It all seemed blurred, unreal, like a newspaper picture. Angry and ashamed, I returned to the kitchen only to find my aunt scrubbing her hands in the sink.

"He wants to see you," she said.

"He's worse off, isn't he?"

"It's progressing fast." She sat at the counter to dry her hands. "It's time for the hard stuff. If there's any forgiving to be done, do it now." Clearly, Wy had heard some of it.

My insides lurched, and I backed against the sink. Morphine—medicine to ease him over the threshold, from this life into the next.

"It'll be better for him. Better for all of you."

"Okay. Aunt Wy, but—"

"—Andie, go see your daddy, then crawl into bed." She stood and pulled me into her big, soft breasts that smelled of Ivory soap and fabric softener. "You'll feel better about things in the morning. I'll sit with him until midnight, then hospice will take over, or your mother, whoever gets there first. Dixie's getting some vital sleep for now. Caroline will be here in the morning."

Her body was warm and comforting. I didn't want to move from it. "Will you start it tonight? When do you know—"

"—Hey, now. Please leave the doctorin' to me. Deal?"

I nodded. "Deal." I hugged Wy one last time before ambling into Daddy's room again. He was awake.

"Rosebud?"

I leaned in close. "What do you need, Daddy?"

"Do something for me."

"What is it?"

Straining, he raised himself from his pillows. I felt his breath on my face. I didn't stop him from talking. I couldn't. I wanted to hear what he had to say.

"I'm—sorry. Sorry I didn't tell you—sooner. I only thought to shield you—from Mavis's fate. When I've passed—avenge Mavis's death," he said. "Promise me."

I thought for a moment or two and then whispered my life's darkest secret into my father's ear. "I knew Calvin was gay, Daddy. I did. I knew it. But I *didn't* know he was also a pedophile. I witnessed John Rossi's murder. Remember the chef at the Praise Buffet? Four years ago, I saw Artury's men kill him. I'm the anonymous caller. The caller the police have looked for. I'm the only eyewitness. Nobody knows. Except you."

I broke my secret, knowing he could never tell it. I worried he had used up what little energy he had left as his eyes drifted shut.

Then they shot open and bore into mine. Rage and regret made him a king again. He lifted his head further and bellowed what I did not expect. "Promise me," he said. "Avenge us all!"

I watched him fall back against the pillows, closing his eyes and gasping for breath.

"I promise," I said in one quick breath. "I promise."

Chapter 44

Evil Among Us

Andie ~ February 1992

Steady white flakes fell quietly through the darkness. I needed to walk despite the freezing temperatures. I stuffed my gloves into my mended coat pockets, pushed through the door to the backyard, and bolted down the red-brick path. Moonlight illuminated the walkway. Dappled with fresh snow, the winder-dark lawn disappeared near the edge of Daddy's garden.

I stood by the tire swing, watching the neighbor's chimney etch chalky white smoke onto a blackboard sky. Slapping my palms together, I blew streamers of warmth into my shriveled, chilly hands. I hadn't realized the wind chill, so I crawled into my old tree house, still solid as the day Daddy built it. I also didn't remember climbing to be so difficult. Huddled in the corner, I pulled out the envelope from inside my coat as if it were a normal thing to do.

Mavis had mailed it sixteen years before it reached my hands. Purposely forgotten by Rupert, and then at last given to Daddy to be stashed away in his lockbox. A box filled with tax receipts, appliance warranties, copies of his will, and coloring book pages from Gracie. It was a miracle Dixie hadn't thrown out the whole box. Had Daddy not demanded I open the envelope, I never would have. My children would've eventually found it in *my* box of letters, ledgers, pictures, and personal whatnots after I had passed on.

My heart stuttered. My chest hurt. My gut clenched.

It was plain manila. Dirty. Some water stains. She had scribbled Rupert's name and address in black ink. I didn't want to open it again. Holding it tight in my hand, I looked up into the shadows of the tree house, struggling for breath.

Not now. I can't deal with it anymore tonight.

But the ghosts from my past insisted. I noted the postmark in the moonlight. *April 3rd, 1975.* Mavis died on April 2nd. Harry found her the morning of the 4th. No one could have sent it but Mavis. *She dropped it into a mailbox on the evening of her death.* Why? Climbing down slowly, I had to know more. It made sense that Rupert had given Daddy the envelope. Their plan to protect me, though hard to accept, was understandable.

Inside the house, Wy talked with the hospice nurse. I walked past them and sprinted up the stairs to my old room with the envelope clutched against my chest. I pulled out the letter, recalling that Mavis was not much of a writer. She spoke far better than she wrote. Mavis had problems getting words and ideas from her head to the paper. I had written many, if not most, of her school reports because Mavis's penmanship was atrocious.

I brushed away tears, then unfolded the letter. I recognized Mavis's loopy handwriting. Smudged words on yellowed paper, and like everything she wrote—barely legible. Even worse, it appeared she'd written it in a hurry.

Dear Daddy,

I sent this letter to Andie but I not tell her I send same to you. Don't tell anyone. Hide it.

You know I go to NYC to be a singer. I do anything for it. I always say no when Andie ask me to go to her church. That cause I already knew Calvin Artury. I was 16 and driving. I stopped at his wife's pretty grave to take pictures. He seen me. He asked to lay hands on me. Get me saved. I say no. Told him my dream to go to NYC. He ask how I plan to get there? I say I take pictures too. I read up on it.

He say he pay me to take pictures. He taught me to use his camera. It's art, he say. I didn't know all these boys. Only some. He pay me a lot. Nobody knew I did this, not even the boys. Only Artury knew. Until now. I tell you and Andie.

Artury took his camera back and thought I gave him all pictures and negatives. But I buy extra film. Develop on my own.

Some are Joe. 10 boys in all. All these boys now in jail or dead except Joe. Some did it cause of who he is. He say these boys God's gift to him. For his sacrifice. A few did it cause he pay with gifts, drugs, and booze. I saw. I sorry. I so wrong.

2 months before graduation, I needed more money. He say he pay me to take more pictures, but I say no. So he say—then you sleep with me. I did. Only once. He awful. But he pay me, so I'm worse. His money got me to NYC. I was 18 and stupid. He think I never come back. He wrong.

Pay for it now. Somebody follow me. I think it Artury. Should told police. Too late now. He know I got these. God forgive me. I wanted to use this to make him let go of Joe for Andie sake. I love you. Tell Andie I love her too. I try call soon as can. Forgive me, Daddy.

Mavis

P.S. Something else to tell you, but must wait. Need to go.

Mavis never got the chance to tell anybody the rest of it.

The discovery of why Calvin murdered Mavis made my blood boil and run cold simultaneously. Calvin had her killed as he had done to John Rossi. I was sure of it.

I folded the letter with great care, like a priceless piece of history. Mavis had what he wanted. The photographs and the negatives. Now I had them.

If I threatened him or took her evidence to the police, they'd slit my throat before I made it to the witness stand. Who could I trust? No one. Somehow, I had to use them to protect my children. And I would go through Joe to do it.

What was the P.S. about? I decided I would never know.

Chapter 45

They Just Fade Away

Andie ~ February 1992

Stretched out on my old bed and dead-dog tired, I nestled myself under a comforter with memories of Mavis's death like it happened yesterday. The dream began as a remembrance, as natural as watching home movies rolling inside my head. The year I turned ten, and Mavis, at eleven and a half, had fallen in love with *Smokey Robinson and the Miracles.*

Her long legs dangled out of the treehouse Daddy had built that summer. A castle tree house. Daddy was the king of all he surveyed, and I was his princess. The perfect treehouse—it boasted a wide plywood floor nailed across two mammoth oak tree limbs. Painted white walls and real shingles on the roof, the treehouse required a wooden ladder from the garage.

Temperatures had climbed every day that week. Muggy described it. Not a dog barked anywhere. No lawnmowers roared in our ears. Just the whir of cicadas high in the trees, as if the rest of the world were taking a nap.

Dressed in nearly the same outfit as Mavis, shorts and a white T-shirt, I had pulled my hair into blonde pigtails jutting out above my ears. Scooting next to Mavis, I saw she had swept out the bugs and leaves before I arrived. Her mother had braided her fuzzy black hair with colorful rubber bands all over her head. I pulled at the back of my shorts. "Damn, it's hot. Got sweat in my butt crack!"

Mavis giggled and dug into a grocery sack. "I got apples and Clark Bars." She pointed to the corner. "Two bottles of Orange soda."

"But I got something cool," I said. I pulled up my beach bag and unzipped the top. "Three guesses."

Mavis stood to get a look, but I folded myself over the bag. "No, you guess."

"It's a new pink bike."

"That's a stupid answer. Guess again."

"The Everly Brothers. One for you and one for me."

"In your dreams, Mavis."

"Archie and Jughead comic books?"

"That's close. Shut your eyes."

Mavis stretched her neck toward the beach bag again.

"I said shut 'em!"

Mavis hemmed and hawed. "I'm hot. Jus' show me, for crying out loud."

I set my bag in front of her and pulled out a wooden box with Parks Family Bible written on the lid. Someone had tied a wide blue ribbon around the box to keep it closed. "Open your eyes!"

Mavis sighed. "It's only a Bible."

"I know," I said. "I scooted into the back of Daddy's closet, under his pressed shirts, to get it. If Dixie knew, she'd pitch a fit."

"It's Buds? Hoo-wee, he gone kill you."

"Nuh-uh," I said, untying the ribbon. "Because you're not gonna tell him. I've always wanted to see this. Looks old. Smells funny."

Someone wrote in pencil on the first blank page. I read the words to Mavis. "If God be for us, who can be against us?" I searched for my daddy's name among the pages of births, deaths, marriages, and baptisms. "Found him! Bud Jennings Parks, born July 10th, 1932—like a page from a history book. Pretty Bible, don't you think?"

Mavis nodded. "Bud's still gone kill us if he finds out."

I handed the Bible to Mavis and continued rummaging through loose papers in the box, finding a long, slender envelope. The outside read, Come Help Us Celebrate, embossed in gold. I opened it. Inside was an invitation to church services at the newly built House of Praise.

"Can I read it?" Mavis asked.

I handed over the invitation and watched her read it.

"They probably don't want colored people."

"Why?"

"They think we're not the same as white people."

"That's silly. You're as white as me, Mavis." I held up my tan, bare arm to Mavis's, and sure enough, we were the same shade of brown.

"Not good enough," she said.

I shook my head. "Last time I used the toilet after you, your pee was the same color as mine. You're no different."

"You and I know that, but Mama said no white church in the South will have us."

"Then I don't want to go there," I said. "I'd rather stay home."

"You should go to church, Andie. It gets you into Heaven."

"It does?"

"Mama says so. First, Jesus washes away your sins, then Sunday School teaches you about Heaven."

"Oh!" I exclaimed. "Wonder why we don't go?"

"Probably 'cause your daddy wants to find the best church."

We took turns holding the Bible.

"Why can't I go with you? To your church?" I replied.

"Hardly any white folk go there, 'cept Daddy and ol' Miss Dinkens," Mavis said.

I slipped the invitation back into the pretty envelope, then laid the Bible inside the box.

Mavis's eyes sparkled as she held up a pressed flower. "What's this?"

"A rose petal!" I shouted. "Hand it over."

The heat had slowed Mavis's reaction time, but eventually, she put it into my hand.

I studied it. "The paper around it says Bud Jr.—died June 17th, 1956."

"Who's that?" Mavis asked, flashing me a curious look. Not unlike mine, nutmeg freckles marched across her light brown nose, and more sprigs of hair had fallen out of her braids.

"It's my brother," I said. "He died when I was a baby."

Mavis lowered her head and mumbled, "I'm sorry."

"It's okay." I put the pressed flower back into the box. "I'll ask Daddy to take us to this new church; maybe he needs us to ask him. After all, my mother sure needs to go. I better get this back into his closet. I feel bad for taking it."

"You jus' want to read the Holy Bible, Andie. Nothing wrong with that."

"Still, help me, Mavis, before he finds out and whips my butt."

"Wait." Mavis pulled out a kitchen knife she'd brought to peel the apples. "Let's make a blood pact."

"A what?"

"Let's mix our blood; then we'll truly be sisters. I hear Mama talk about it all the time. There's power in the blood. She sings about it in church."

"Will it hurt?"

"A little, but I brought Bactine, too."

I held out my hand and only winced as Mavis cut into my palm. Mavis gave the knife to me. In minutes, blood dripped from our hands, and we clamped them tight.

"Repeat after me," she said. "I pledge to God, fiddle dee dee, you and me, on the shores of gitchee goomie—"

"—Stop!" I giggled. "What are you saying?"

"Never mind. Jus' pledge you'll be my sister forever."
"I pledge to be your sister and best friend 'til death do us part."
"Now we have the power, Andie."

Jerked from sleep, I opened my eyes. The familiar feeling of death pressed against my chest while shadows from the oak tree outside my window crisscrossed the room. The echo of her voice, suspended in the air, pulled me to my feet. *Go now.* But no one was there. Only the sound of the wind and a sweet, sweet spirit filled the room like perfume. "Mavis?"

Go now. He needs you.

Suddenly, Dixie's scream echoed throughout the house. It broke the silence, along with Wylene yelping like a frustrated dog at the bottom of the steps. "Andie! Come quick!"

I flew down the staircase to find the hospice nurse standing by Daddy's side, doing her best to inject him with drugs and assist my aunt. Daddy's entire face, blue as a leg vein, fought for air. Wylene's heavy arms attempted to hold him still enough to secure the oxygen mask over his mouth and nose as he struggled to sit.

At her wit's end, my mother tried desperately to calm him but buckled to the floor, taking me with her. Caroline stood in the doorway watching, helpless, sobbing, and grieving to hear her daddy's last breaths. Our nightmare was ending.

Hearing him gasp for air, I let go of Dixie and pulled myself up. Crawling into Daddy's bed under the tangled mass of tubes attached to his body, I scooted close beside him, pulling what was left of his body against mine. "Daddy. It's okay. Time to go."

His hand trembled, tugging off the oxygen mask. "Forgive me," he said, gasping for air.

"Nothing to forgive, Daddy. We love you. I love you. Go on, now. Go on to Jesus."

He reached for my hand.

"It's time to go, Daddy; it's time."

Unyielding, he opened his eyes wide.

"No girl could ask for a better father. You're the best, Daddy."

With that said, he relaxed slightly. His lips parted, and his head rolled back. My mother remained on the floor by his bed. Wylene tended to her, holding her.

It was then I felt him go limp as if he were disappearing. The room swirled around me in a whoosh, like I had pulled a plug in a tub. His voice was barely a whisper; no one heard or understood him but me.

"Good men—never die—they—just fade away," he said.

I cried my heart out. "Go rest on your mountain, Daddy. Let go."

Wylene helped Dixie stand and grab his hand as he looked into her eyes one last time. I held him, watching my mother stroke his face, wordless but there.

And then, everything just stopped. One last breath, and it was over.

After some time, I slid off the bed, walked numbly past my grieving sister, and stepped outside. I stood and stared at the sky. The forecast said rain, but the sun was shining. It was a beautiful day, and my daddy was dead.

Chapter 46
A Time To Mourn
Andie ~ February 1992

We held Daddy's funeral at Tussman Funeral Home. I had become all too familiar with the place. Lula sang between crying jags. The room overflowed with flowers: bouquets, baskets of every size and shape, and vases filled with every fern and blossom imaginable.

Cold air blew from the air ducts, and I told the funeral director to turn up the heat, that it was a funeral home, not a morgue. Coot and Candace stood with me near Daddy's open casket. Neither took more than a few seconds to view his body.

Thin as a rifle barrel, Daddy's face had rutted with the wrinkles of a man twice his age. He left little of himself behind. The funeral home did well, considering what they had to work with. But nothing filled in the crevices or wiped away the ruin of a million cigarettes.

A line formed, and each mourner walked toward me, a little shy but wearing a warm smile. About thirty men from R. J. Reynolds showed up, guys Daddy worked with. It surprised me as the crowd grew. Some folks drove miles to get there, and I thanked each one for their support. A far piece from Boone, Daddy's cousins, arrived in a station wagon and two pickup trucks. Timidly, they talked about their memories of him and what a good man Daddy was. Amid their awkward embraces, I wept openly, moved by their kindness. Luckily, only Coot asked about the Olivers. I told the truth. I didn't care if they showed up. I hoped they didn't.

Wylene, relentless in her attention, held Dixie in check. Wy was a rock. Caroline couldn't get a babysitter. She chased her girls around the lobby while her ex-husbands chewed tobacco and passed a flask in the parking lot with other local men. Gracie parked herself next to Dixie and Wylene. Dillon cowered alone in the back of the room, drawn, thin, and speechless.

Caroline finally stepped in and took over for me. Finding a seat by my mother, I felt colder than when I arrived, like I'd been sitting on ice. Despite my bulky sweater and pleated wool skirt, my face and hands froze.

"Here." Candace handed me her Styrofoam coffee cup. "Wrap your fingers around it."

I shivered. "I want to go home."

"Hang in there, honey," she said, stretching her long arm around my shoulders. As she rubbed my arm, it warmed me for a moment.

Gracie had moved next to Dillon, who slouched like a lanky pup on a nearby couch, his knobby knees pushing through his pants legs. I worried. He had become rather despondent, but he perked up when Gracie began talking to him.

Gracie took her grandpa's death amazingly well, telling everyone, "He's in Heaven with our brother." But Dillon had idolized his grandfather. He tried to make his voice the same as Daddy's, even adopting good and bad habits. More than once, I caught my son with a cigarette, holding it the same way Daddy did, then stomping it out with the toe of his shoe.

Dressed in a navy jumper and a white blouse, Gracie's bargain find made her appear older than she was. Dillon wore a new gray suit and a smart-looking tie Wylene bought him. At barely fifteen, the twins showed the first signs of maturity. They both took it all in, asking only a few questions. Watching them, I saw myself at Brian's funeral years before, sitting near that same spot.

Daddy's coffin, a beautiful, engraved oak number Dixie chose the week before he passed, gleamed like a pulpit. They had laid the casket on a table in the adjacent room, and I watched as the funeral director sealed the lid. Spreading a blanket of red roses across the top, the director pulled it the entire length of the casket. *Roses—definitely his idea.* Daddy loved red roses. He said they always reminded him of me, his *Rosebud.* After reading the words imprinted on a red satin ribbon in silver glitter, "Beloved Husband, Father, Grandfather, Friend," I looked away. A suffocating sensation tightened in my throat, and I stood.

Dixie, in her black suit with pearl buttons, uncrossed her ankles. She'd hardly said two words all day. "Andie—"

"—You need coffee?" I asked.

Through a mist of tears, she nodded and attempted to smile, but her wide lips remained sullen and pale, her lipstick bitten off hours before.

"I'll be right back," I said. Dixie's color wasn't good overall. When I returned, she had folded herself over Daddy's casket, her arms spread across the spray of roses. I watched tears slip off her chin and the slow, pathetic shake of her head. Each sympathetic voice encouraging her to back away only made Dixie cling that much tighter to Daddy's remains.

But Wylene and I knew it wasn't only her husband she mourned. The world Dixie Parks was accustomed to, the world Daddy provided for her, had ended.

❧

The weathermen were a few days off in their forecast. It finally rained.

Too many people crowded inside my parents' house. Restraining their chatter, they ate casseroles and Jell-O molds, salads with ranch dressing, and little finger-whatever-foods. Aunt Wy paid for the caterer, but I managed to make a cake and a pan of brownies.

Dixie reclined in her chair, stoic and alone. I sat on an ottoman a couple feet from my mother, watching each mourner who ate free food. They stood back as if our grieving family suddenly needed quarantining. *That's right, just nod and smile; come too close, and you might catch the flu, get a zit, or lose your car keys. Catch our rotten luck.*

Feeling the dreaded obligation, I attempted to circulate with folks I barely knew who had nothing worthwhile to say. They offered pitiful, weak smiles, and I kept thinking I'd lose all self-control at the next pasty face expressing their sympathy.

But I decided not to embarrass my family. Not that it was any different from living with Joe, really. I had long ago perfected the art of walking on eggshells. What I wanted was for everyone to sob like Lula. At least she knew how to grieve, mourn, and get it out of her system. The rest of the dry-eyed faces in the house only mumbled and finished eating the chicken pies, trays of vegetables, and my cake.

Dixie coughed softly, rose from her chair, and momentarily stood with her arms at her sides, her gaze lost. "I need to wash more cups," she said. Then she pushed up her sweater sleeves and collected herself before facing the fifty people milling about her house. The grief etched on Dixie's face compounded the long and terrible night awaiting all of us. I watched her hands shake and felt the utter terror of possibly losing both parents: my only lifeline.

After the last guest licked his plate clean, we packed the dishwasher and stuffed the leftover widow casseroles into the refrigerator. I then slipped out the back door and walked to the edge of the property behind the shed, falling into a lawn chair.

Daddy's death left another gaping, bleeding hole inside me. The pouring rain soaked my clothes, and the chilled air numbed my body. I sat there, hoping the cold would also dull my brain as I bent my head over my broken heart. But when the rain had slacked to a drizzle, I stumbled back into the house, slipped into Daddy's study, and dried off with one of his flannel shirts. Sinking into his recliner that smelled of Aqua Velva and cigarette smoke, I pulled his banjo onto my lap, submitting to the racking sobs that rocked me back and forth like an oak tree in the wind.

Chapter 47

A Raging Inferno
Andie ~ March 1992

The misery of Dixie's loss lessened daily. No longer nursing a terminally ill husband, her mood improved, for which we were all thankful. Wylene had returned to Charleston to put her neglected medical practice back together on the same morning I received word Joe had sued for full custody of the twins.

I laughed, then called Dixie. Her voice blared through the line, loud and clear. "That's ridiculous! He's not getting custody. They're fifteen. What judge in their right mind would do that? I can't believe Joe is wasting good money on this!"

"He doesn't want them," I said. "I'm not worried."

"You call your lawyer?"

"I can't afford him again. And I can't borrow more money from Aunt Wy. I owe her enough." My mother suddenly realized if I needed to hire legal counsel, she would have to pay for it.

"No, you're right. You don't need a lawyer. You've always been a terrific mother. Oh, Andie—I almost forgot. That envelope you left here, you know, the big one your daddy gave you, and you taped shut. It's on the kitchen table. I boxed up everything for Lula's church bazaar and found where you stuck it in Bud's sock drawer. You might want to come get it. If it's not important, tell me, I'll throw it out."

"No! Don't! It's important! I'll drive over now."

Some women held on to their husband's things for years. Not Dixie. Daddy's clothes and personal effects were gone within the month. Silly me, I thought the envelope was safe in his sock drawer.

"What's in that envelope, Andie? It's addressed to Rupert."

"It's—not a big deal. Memories of Mavis. Don't open it, Dixie. It's mine."

"I won't open it, but come get it, okay?"

"I'll be right over!" I hung up the phone before she said another word. The envelope was safer at Dixie's house than mine, but I had to get over there in case they had tapped my phone. It was time to take everything I had on Calvin to the bank and deposit it in a lockbox.

I pulled into the Wachovia Bank parking lot, a typical suburban branch bank with a drive-through window and an interior lobby. My escort into the steel lockbox area wore her employee badge on her lapel. *Jenny.* I noticed her wedding ring and mentioned her pretty maternity dress. She thanked me and said she had six more months to go. Her first. She and her husband wanted a boy. *Excited* was the word she used.

Before I walked out of the bank, I expressed my appreciation for her help and gave her a quick smile. With everything safely locked inside the bank's vault, I felt relieved.

Months before, with a loan from Aunt Wy, I had pre-paid a bankruptcy attorney who had stalled the inevitable as long as he could. The creditors' petitions to the court had to be heard. The call came. He had completed the paperwork, filed it with the court, sent out the notices, and agreed to a hearing date.

Although the court scheduled the hearing for nine a.m., I didn't have to clock in at the truck stop until two in the afternoon. But I knew I'd be in no mood to wait on truckers buying smut magazines and traveling salesmen trying to pay for gas with maxed-out credit cards. I called off work for the day.

I staggered through the proceedings as one lost in a fog. Desperate to quit smoking, I chewed my fingernails into oblivion as the attorneys hashed out the details. In the small conference room downtown, the only creditors who showed up were Lester Gerber and his wife, Effie, who held the land contract on my house. Shooting glazed looks of pity my way, they spoke a few kind words I didn't comprehend. The only thing I heard was that because of the nature and size of my debts, my house was to be returned to the Gerbers. I had thirty days to vacate the property.

I didn't remember driving home. I parked my car in the driveway and stared at my house. A house I'd worked so damn hard for. It was an absolute disaster when I bought it. Daddy worked endless hours with me, trying to shore it up and make it pretty. I nearly scrubbed my fingers raw, cleaning it. Certainly, I'd leave it in much better condition than I found it. My loss was the Gerbers' gain.

I don't know how long I sat like a mannequin in the driveway, but it had to be the better part of the morning. Hunger, bodily functions, the weather, and emotions all eluded me. Finally, I pulled into the garage. Where would we go?

Anger. A feeling I had always held at bay, kept bottled inside for one reason or another, shot through me with such force the top of my head tingled. Getting out of the car, I switched on the light and looked around at the few tools Joe left hanging on the garage walls, tools that once belonged to Daddy. There it hung by the window. A sledgehammer.

I had ignored the padlocked storage shed in my backyard for years, caring less about what Joe had stored inside. He often made a trip to the shed on the mornings he picked up or dropped off the twins. In fact, I considered it might be empty, and he only wanted to torment me with a padlocked shed. He'd put off cleaning it out, and I hadn't cared. Until that moment.

The more I thought about Joe knowing Calvin was a pedophile, the angrier I became. The years I wasted on Joe infuriated me with sudden rage that surged through me like snake bite venom.

My dog whined on the patio. After putting her in the house, I grabbed the sledgehammer, stormed to the backyard, and took out the past seventeen years on the shed, pounding at the lock for an hour or more until my hands blistered. Nothing happened. And then, all at once, the planks holding the lock fell apart in my hands. The lock didn't break, but I busted the wood so badly the door swung open.

I stepped hesitantly into the shed and pulled the string that switched on the overhead light bulb. I blinked with open-mouthed fascination. A poster of *Farrah Fawcett* with the protruding nipple hung on the back wall. Joe had filled the twenty-by-twelve-foot shed with pornography, neatly organized, categorized, and alphabetized. Missing since the early 1970s, a decorated storage box I once used for my cookbook collection sat among dozens of other boxes, all filled with smut. New, unopened VCR tapes by the boxfuls surprised me. He had stacked audio and video equipment on metal shelving against the two longest walls. In my years of living with Joe, I'd seen that type of equipment several times, so I knew what it was.

Furiously chewing at my lip, I recalled what John Rossi had told me. *I finally put it all together. The raw tapes would have to be edited first, but the equipment wasn't in the house. Then, they'd have to send the recordings somewhere to be made into movies before selling them to adult stores...*

In that instant, the shed's contents confirmed my suspicions, and my heart sank. Joe was part of Calvin's religious Mafia. He was perfect for the job.

Quickly, I regretted opening the shed. *What if Joe is also involved in drugs or worse?* I couldn't hide drugs in a bank lockbox. And I certainly didn't want to be connected to anything illegal. I stepped over the boxes and sat on one marked *Los Angeles—Carmine's Adult Book Store*. None of it made sense, a televangelist transporting illegal pornography across the country. I searched the boxes for a name or incriminating evidence connecting any of it to the House of Praise. They had covered their tracks. There was nothing. Nowhere. It all appeared as if it belonged to me. It was on *my* property.

In the corner, a briefcase leaned against the inside wall. A large case. One like I'd seen Joe carry out the door on Friday nights. I opened it. Someone filled it with bundles of hundred-dollar bills. For a split second, I considered taking a bundle. I sure could've used it. I was also sure Joe knew precisely how much was in the case.

I panicked. Since it indeed *was* on my property, Calvin's slick lawyers would pin it on me. And in the middle of a child custody battle, I had no desire to call the police. I hurried back into the house and pulled Mavis's old camera out of the box Lula had given me after Rupert's funeral. The camera still worked fine. I drove to the drugstore on the corner for film, rushed back, and snapped an entire roll inside the shed. I had no idea if taking pictures of it would do me any good. Still, it was the only thing I thought of doing—snap a photo of every box, piece of equipment, and the open briefcase full of money. Then I wiped everything down and put it back as I found it before driving to the bank at a quarter to three, fifteen minutes before closing time.

Inside the vault, *Jenny* asked, "Do you remember your box number, Mrs. Oliver?"

"Number thirteen, I think. One of the smaller ones." I pointed and then eyed the room. Jenny pulled a card from the file on her desk. "Sign and date this."

Afterward, I handed my key to her, and she inserted the keys into the lockbox.

"Do you need privacy?" she asked.

"Yes, thanks." Looking over my shoulder again, I slipped the film and the old camera inside, followed by a quick goodbye to pregnant Jenny before dashing out of the bank.

Driving home, my heart stopped, then started with a hard thump as I turned onto my street. Joe had parked his truck in my driveway. Tapping the brake pedal, I slowed my car to a near crawl, aware of icy fear churning in my stomach, threatening to liquefy my bowels. My grip on the steering wheel tightened.

He sat in his truck, waiting. I put on my best why-are-you-here face as I pulled into the drive. My foot had barely touched the driveway when his truck door flew open, and he bounded out, slamming the door and bolting toward me. Grabbing my arm with such force my teeth rattled, Joe pulled me toward the garage. "What happened to my shed!?"

"*Your* shed? What the hell are you talking about? And let go of me!"

"Did you bust it open, Andie? What did you see? Huh? What did you do in there!?"

"I've been in bankruptcy court all day. The last time I saw the shed, you had locked the door!" The lie eased his grip on my arm. I walked into my empty garage, away from the eyes and ears of my neighbors.

"Yeah? Well, it's a damn good thing I can't find anything missing! But if someone wanted to break in, they'd take something, right? Wouldn't they?"

"Sure, just like you robbed me!"

Joe glared into my eyes like a starved predator. He hit the button that closed the large garage door behind us and threw me against the inside garage wall, spitting like a rabid dog. "You're walking on thin ice, bitch!"

"Stop it, Joe! Get off my property! I'm calling the police!" I turned around to run, but my head snapped back as if he'd jerked on my reins, which, in a way, he had. Cutting off my air, he had grabbed the back of my shirt, twisting and wrenching it tight around my neck. My arms flinging wildly, I managed to take hold of the door to the backyard patio and open it. Prissy bounded into the garage, growling and biting Joe on the leg. Joe kicked Dillon's dog and she yelped, running back to the patio.

My shirt ripped during Joe's vicious attack, and he let go. I buckled, gasping for air, my lungs hurting. "You—disgust me. I—hate you!" I said over and over from the garage floor.

Joe leaned against the wall, panting, his hands behind him as he collected himself. The plastic clock on the garage wall read 3:30. The twins would be home in a half-hour.

Without thinking it through, I reached into my shirt pocket and pulled out the one picture I kept out of Mavis's envelope. The one with which I planned to confront him. I held it up. He walked over to where I cowered on the garage floor. Like pulling a weed, he yanked me up and snatched the picture from my hand.

A fully exposed Calvin Artury had positioned himself on a beautiful bed of white down comforters beside a young Joe, whose bare back and butt lay closer to the camera. Definitely Joe, that much I knew, and I saw Joe knew it, too. Enjoying his crime with a sixteen-year-old confused boy, Calvin had even smiled for the photo.

I scooted back to the concrete floor, searching for protection. In all the years I knew Joe, I had never been afraid of him until then. He'd shoved me a time or two, hard enough to leave bruises, and even choked me once, leaving purple fingerprints around my neck. But the difference between then and now—was clear. I knew too much.

"Joe! I have all the negatives and the pictures. The ones Mavis meant for me to have. The ones you destroyed the day the mailman delivered her envelope to the trailer. I ended up with them, anyway; Rupert got the same envelope, and I swear to God I'll use them to protect our children!" I stood slowly, sliding up the wall for support, pleading. "Stop this, Joe. Don't let this happen to Dillon, for God's sake! If you love your son the slightest bit, you won't let this happen to him!"

He didn't speak. He opened the garage door instead and jogged to his truck. Bolting back inside and out to the shed with a hammer, nails, and two six-foot boards, he closed and secured the shed doors as if he knew what to bring to my house. As if an alarm alerted him to an intruder.

Nauseated, I remained standing, but had wedged myself into a corner of the cool garage, not wanting him to follow me into the house or out to the street. When his pounding stopped, fear spiked in my gut. I willed myself invisible and prayed he would leave, but he appeared in the doorway and slammed the patio door behind him. Once again, we were alone.

"Don't open the shed again if you know what's good for you. I'll be back for everything tonight," he said before slowly setting the briefcase on the concrete floor.

Only a slight shiver contradicted my outward calm. I watched the scalding fury that simmered inside him escalate into a raging inferno, but then, as if by magic, he turned into the monster I knew him to be. Knowing what he was about to do, Joe put his finger to his lips and grinned. In a split second, our eyes locked, and he hit me so hard I blacked out and wet myself.

When I opened my eyes, Joe was gone, and thankfully, the twins' school bus was late. Ten after four. I needed to clean myself up. Stumbling into the house, I sat in the bathroom, watching a new bruise turn purple beneath my eye. I held ice on my split lip and cheekbone, which had cracked and swelled like an old baseball.

Sitting on the couch in my tatty chenille bathrobe with coffee stains, I waved to Dillon and Gracie as they walked through the door and tried to explain it away as a car accident. It was a lame excuse, but the only one I thought of. They were too young to remember the last time their daddy left bruises on my body, so I figured they might buy it.

Gracie gave me a hug and promised to make supper. But the more intelligent twin wasn't always the one with the most common sense. After noticing Prissy's limp and that someone had boarded up the storage shed, Dillon pulled the car into the garage and hung the sledgehammer back on the wall.

Before Daddy died, I'd overheard his conversation with Dillon, making him promise to become the man of the family. He whispered to me after Gracie had gone to bed. "If he ever hits you again, I'll kill him myself, Mom. I swear to God!"

"Please, Dillon. This is not yours to worry about." It saddened me it had come to this, and it hurt like hell to talk. "Go to bed, honey. Everything will be fine."

"Don't let him take us, Mom. Gracie and I won't stay with him."

The bruise on my face throbbed, but I halfway smiled and squeezed his arm. "Never."

Chapter 48
Nothing But The Blood
Reverend Calvin Artury ~ April 1992

"She said she'll use them if she has to," Joe said.

"What exactly does she have?"

"She said she has every picture Mavis took. Everything Mavis meant for her to have. Rupert Dumass, Mavis's father, who's deceased, received a duplicate in the mail. We never thought Mavis was smart enough—"

"—But she was, wasn't she? She sent a duplicate. How absolutely perfect!" I held the old snapshot Mavis had taken and stiffened as though she had stuck her hand through the veil of death and time to assault me. "Call Percy. Have him come to my office. I need to find out if anyone knows about this besides Andie. I need him to send her a message from The Lord Most High."

Thou hast been my help; therefore, in the shadow of Thy wings will I rejoice! I ended a service before ten o'clock for the first time in over a decade. That Friday night in April of '92, I cut my usual five-hour service in half, finding it difficult to even pray in tongues. Eliminating the healing line, I called for the unsaved, the backsliders, and those who wanted a closer walk with Jesus to come forward for prayer. But the sight of Joe Oliver with his hands raised at the altar sent me reeling. Our meeting before church produced alarming evidence. It quenched the Holy Spirit within me.

After the service, I retreated to my church office and softly bolted the door behind me. I left word not to be disturbed. No one would dare. Stripping in the darkness, I turned to the mirrored wall. The moonlight filtered all impurities from my nakedness as I spent the night there, allowing the cleansing to exonerate me completely. It couldn't wait not another minute. I was due; it had been a long time since the last one. The last time I felt the hot breath of God searing my skin.

I pulled the ivory-handled knife from my desk drawer and sliced a line across my torso. Blood oozed down my chest, over my nipples, and collected in my chest hair and around my erection. I dipped my fingers in the warm blood and covered each scar on my body. A cleansing. To be washed in the blood, God's blood—in me. The perfect bath.

I lay across my pristine desk, moonlight covering me in God's love. Shrinking away from it, I understood its refusal to release me. He was pulling me into a vision more detailed than any I'd had before. My face stared back at me. A boy's face. The first time they washed me in the blood. My aunts had defiled my innocence with their big, sweaty bodies. The blood felt good.

"We cannot wash the sweet-sour smell of coition away with water. We must wash him in the blood," my turtle-headed aunt said. Her lips twitched upward at the corners, and her hair, what little she had, she had wrapped in a cow pile on top of her head. She washed my limp nine-year-old body in a galvanized tub filled with blood from a slaughtered hog. Her elbows stuck out like wings as she moved methodically over my tender skin. "This is God's child; we must cleanse him from all sin." She called to her sister. "Fetch a rag, Tilley. He's ready."

"Hey—hey Bea, 'member when Daddy took a shotgun to our mama and blew her to kingdom come? I 'member, sure 'nuff. Her guts 'n shit flew all over these 'yere walls. I'm the onliest one who slipped in it. Daddy laughed at me, 'member? And hey—hey, you

'member it got all over our church clothes an ever'thang!" Tilley snorted. "He made usuns clean it up. Hee-hee, I think I swallered some of it. Ain't funny. I oughtn't to laugh."

"No, dear, you should not laugh about such things. It's time to take our child to bed."

Tilley drooled. A string of spit slid down and off her hairy chin and hung there like suspended vomit. Her diseased eye rolled in its socket, and her breath smelled like spoiled meat from even across the room. Narrow-witted, her head cocked to the side, she hobbled over to hand the rag to Bea. Tilley leaned forward and looked into my youthful eyes. Her other eye had the dull look of a blueberry. Small, dark, and dried up. Her finger moved from her cracked and crusted lips toward my blood-covered face and hovered, waiting for Bea to allow her to plant a blessing.

"It's time, dear. Time to say good night to God's son."

"Can I take his picture first?"

"Not now, dear. Time to kiss him good night."

"Any whar I want?"

"Plant your blessing, Tilley. Any place you like."

❧

The rain fell in torrents the last time I saw them. I was a grown man then—a beautiful man, a young man made in God's perfect image. I remember the hot August day because it was my birthday. Approaching their peeling porch steps, I flung my suit jacket over my shoulder, undid my tie, and rolled up my sleeves. While one aunt shook with palsy and the other chewed a cud of something between her gums, I sat on the steps and read to them from the book of Leviticus. "A woman that hath a familiar spirit, a wizard, shall surely be put to death; they shall stone her with stones, and her blood shall be upon her. I'm going to preach to you," I said.

They stared through me, like a couple of deaf-mutes, as thunder rolled over our heads.

I'd come to pick a bone with two old women and to rid myself of an infected snake bite, a poison infiltrating even the most anointed parts of my life.

"Can you two understand me!?"

Both nodded in response, though I wasn't sure it was any more than a paralyzing moment of comprehension.

"Good! Then I must tell you—I have become that preacher you diligently prayed for! But more than anything, I am special to God. An overcomer!"

On and on, I preached around an invisible pulpit, raising my hands and lifting my voice in retribution to the demonic forces I faced that day. Screaming my words over the roar of the thunder, I held back what I came to do until I had fully delivered my sermon.

"Quench not the Spirit, saith the Lord! The audible voice of God speaks to me and through me daily. I once was lost, but now I'm found. You chastised me, but He *chose* me. I crossed over into the Land of Milk and Honey and found it. Despite the evil done to me by your foul and filthy hands, I found the sweet honey in the rock. Sucked out the sweetness and emptied the cone, tasted, and saw that the Lord was good. He found no guile in my mouth; no, He did not! I spend my days speaking in tongues, yes, true, the tongues of angels, and fall asleep easily every night with God's words inside me; His anointing is upon me!"

As the storm erupted with violent wind and piercing rain, my delivery escalated into a fervor of groans, slaps, and blows to their head until I thought perhaps they had succumbed to my rage. But they had not.

Lightning cracked in a furious attempt to split the sky wide open. I grabbed them up, two rail-thin elderly aunts, dragged them inside, and kicked the door closed with my heel.

"Remember those Amen enemas you gave me? Cleansings, you called them," I said, binding their hands and mouths. Pulling a chair to their kitchen table, I poured a glass of cold water and then spun my wet, empty glass around and around on the oilcloth. Licking the inside of my mouth, tasting the blood of vengeance, I traced the table's edge with my thumb, watching them rot in the heat, staring at my empty glass.

"You both fell upon my young, innocent soul like worms on a corpse. When sleep evades me in the middle of the night, I turn to the scriptures for comfort, only to hear your voices and see your faces again. This must end."

I stood and removed my belt.

"Did you know the Bible is the bloodiest book ever written? Of course, you know; you used it well. Your problem was that you had a form of godliness and denied the power. But having lived under your roof, that power and the undeniable truths of Jehovah God gave me two choices. Either kill myself or—the foul bodies who immersed me in their evil." Yanking them both by the hair, forcing their heads back to look into my eyes, I smiled. "But God gave me the power! He took it from you and gave it to me! The power, the wonderworking power to do what I do now!"

Lightning hit the house, knocking out the electricity. I found the darkness fitting for my finish. I walked around them, swatting flies off their bare, bleeding, hunched backs. Their stench was oppressive; I made quick work of the beating.

"When one is tormented, beaten—raped, the scars remain forever. When you become desperate enough to lose your past, your memory of who and why they tortured you, your body screams for the removal of the scars! Oh yes, I was an abomination before God. I looked into the mirror and saw a disfigured man, but now I see nothing. Nothing but the blood."

As I slipped a rope over their heads, the air felt like hot breath all over my body, sucking in and breathing out even under my clothes.

"I want to forget where I came from for all time and eternity."

Standing behind them, I stripped off my clothes. Thunder pounded the ground outside as I sliced my torso, allowing my blood to drip over their heads, singing aloud, *"What can wash away my sin? Nothing but the blood of Jesus. What can me whole again? Nothing but the blood of Jesus. Oh! Precious is the flow that makes me white as snow; no other fount I know, nothing but the blood of Jesus..."*

It pooled in their hair and slid down their fly-dotted faces, crusting quickly in the heat. Their eyes followed me as I picked up my knife, ran the blade down their cheeks and necks, and then jaggedly cut away at clothes, skin, and muscle.

Walking away from my aunts' den of iniquity, I sank into the parched red dirt road that had become a gushing river of mud. It flooded into my shoes, pulsating like a severed bowel. I never looked back.

Chapter 49

GOONS

Andie ~ April 1992

Between boxing up the house, consoling my twins, and promising to keep them in their school district, my job at the truck stop was a few hours of relief in my day. Keeping everybody else content left precious little time for my own happiness effort.

Wylene had come back to Winston-Salem to Dixie-sit. Diagnosed as manic-depressive, my mother had gone from elated relief to threats of suicide. After donating Daddy's last pair of pants to Goodwill, she collapsed. Caroline and I took turns sleeping at the house, occupying her mind with the semi-normal parts of our lives.

And then, Wylene announced the time had come for Dixie to sell her house. For my mother to heal, she needed a fresh start, away from the memories. I agreed, but my heart ached to think about it. Once they sold the house, my haven would be gone.

The bruises on my face healed slowly. I had told my family the same whopper I'd dished out to my kids. But Wylene spoke her mind the second she had me alone. "Next time, Andie Rose, make sure you've loaded your damn gun. It'd solve all your problems."

During spring break, the twins stayed with Dixie while I hunted for an apartment and crammed the last dozen years of my life into more boxes. The hourglass was running out. My thirty days to vacate were almost up. I doubted I could give Dillon and Gracie even a semi-normal life.

Peaceful and silent as a cemetery, my yard and the dark house appeared bleak and ominous as I pulled into the drive. Trees cast shadows on the small weed-filled lawn. Blinds and curtains drawn, the familiar home I loved had become cold and foreboding.

I parked in the garage and saw that Dillon had left the inside door to the breezeway partially open. I considered wringing his neck, but he'd been under a strain since Joe left, feeling the need to be the man in the family and to protect me.

Prissy whimpered in the backyard, scratching at the garage door to the patio. *That boy! He left his dog out, too!* I opened the door and knelt to pat Prissy, speaking in a soft, calming voice. She ignored me, whined, and tried to push past me. "C'mon, girl," I whispered, yanking on her collar. "You can't come in. You're muddy!"

But Prissy was strong as an ox. She wasn't about to budge from the doorstep. She looked at me with dark eyes like mirrors. Her paws landed on my jeans. "Damn it, Prissy, you're covered in mud! Stay, girl!" She jumped down, scratching and begging me to let her in. The frantic dog pushed her massive body forward, but I closed the door, leaning on it with a sigh while Prissy barked like her tail was on fire.

"I'll let you in later!" I walked up the two steps from the garage, tossed my purse in the breezeway's corner, and opened the door to the kitchen. Blinking in the dim house, I froze. My house was a wreck. Suddenly, two men flipped on flashlights, moving toward me in the darkness. I backed up, my hands feeling along the door for the handle. From the apparent mess, they'd been searching for something. The glow from the streetlight illuminated a third man squatting on the floor behind them.

The door handle felt cool and smooth beneath my palms. One bulging man stood so close I felt his body heat. I pulled at the handle and pushed myself against the door to escape him, but there was no room to slip through. And it was too late to run for my unloaded gun. I couldn't even remember where I'd stashed it.

"I'll be damned if it ain't the lady of the house! We been waiting for you." I recognized the voice. A House of Praise ham-faced goon. Just as I turned the doorknob, the man closest to me thrust his hand over my mouth, smothering my screams. His other arm circled and squeezed my waist, cracking a rib, but the shock of what was happening overshadowed the sudden shooting pain.

"What should we do with her?" The first man who held me, his breath hot in my ear, dragged me over to his companions. He smelled like he hadn't bathed in weeks, and his hand on my mouth tasted like grease or gasoline. A second, shorter man shone his flashlight in my eyes, and I attempted to turn my head, but he held the light on my face. "Joe Oliver always liked the feisty ones," he said.

A third flashlight to the front and right of me was blinding. While the first goon's smelly hand held me tight, man number three moved close beside me. His voice tight, he stared with the unblinking eyes of a reptile. "Mrs. Oliver. We hear you made threats to your ex-husband. We know you got something the Reverend wants and probably hid it. After all these years, why not just leave things alone? You being an ex-team wife and all, Reverend, he don't want you hurt. Not yet, anyway." His malicious grin displayed sharp white teeth. "Would raise too many questions. But he wants us to give you this message. If you show anybody *whatever it is* you got or put anything in the newspaper," he put his face closer to mine, "I promise you, you'll be dead before that paper comes out the next morning. That's a fact, ma'am. And Joe, too. Reverend's real tired of him causing so much trouble."

He rummaged through my packed boxes again, but kept talking. "Reverend wants to know. Have you shown anyone what you got?"

I shook my head furiously under the hand of the reeking man who held me, my eyes wide, the fear coiling in my gut.

"You sure you haven't told anyone? Let her talk, Hillard."

I gasped for breath as the man I now knew as Hillard took his hand off my mouth. "Only person—was my daddy—and he's dead." Hillard slapped his hand over my mouth again.

"Good. That's good. Reverend wants us to make sure you never reveal your secrets. He said there's no sense in asking you for—*whatever it is* you have. But me and the boys, we thought we'd search, anyway. Course, ain't sure what I'm looking for exactly. I don't suppose you'd care to hand it over?"

I gave no response.

"Didn't I tell ya, Hillard? She ain't obliging." He glared at me. "Well, now. Reverend suspects you're the only one who has it. Is that true?"

I nodded.

"Alrighty, then. It's your job to make sure it stays hidden. My suggestion is that you burn it. 'Cause if you ever threaten Joe or the church again, we will cut that cancerous tongue out of your pretty mouth before we shove a knife up your ass and slice out your bowels. You'll ooze all over your nice rugs here. And those kids of yours will never see their next birthday. You get what I'm saying to you?"

I nodded again, my tears flowing over Hillard's fingers as he continued to increase his hold over my mouth. Suddenly, I recognized the man threatening me as he tore more boxes apart. Silas Turlo's oldest son. Insignificant-looking, dark, coarse hair—Percy Turlo. Percy and his pals, Hillard and Delmer Becker—

cousins who looked alike. I remembered them from church—thugs I'd seen hanging around the parking lot with Percy.

I struggled when Hillard moved his massive hands to my breasts. His laugh was abrasive; his breath stunk. "Oh, baby. Baby, you got nice tits."

"I wanna feel," said Delmer.

I fell purposely to the floor as both men grappled at my chest. I heard my shirt rip, the buttons popping and hitting the floor. Delmer cursed at his cousin, "Goddamn it, Hillard, I want some! Hit her! Knock her out!"

Hillard snorted. "Fuck you." His left hand remained tight over my mouth; I could barely breathe. I felt myself getting sick. "You had the last one," he said. "I'm having this one; this one's mine!" With his right hand, he let go of my waist and pulled my right arm behind me, maneuvering me through my pain.

Prissy howled, barking non-stop at the back door. I prayed it was loud enough to alert the neighbors.

Hillard snapped at his revolting cousin. "Go get that damn dog, Delmer. Shut it up!"

Delmer unzipped his pants instead. "Shit-fire! Ain't no time for foreplay or a damn dog! Let me at this pretty lady!"

Hillard grunted. "Maybe. After I'm done with her first, now go shoot that dog!"

But as one goon held my arms, the other tugged hard at my jeans, yanking them past my hips. I kicked hard despite the pain, bucking like a wild horse, catching them off guard. They fought to keep me on the floor, cursing more at each other than at me. Suddenly, my grandmother's antique plates fell off the wall and shattered into what sounded like hundreds of pieces.

Percy slithered back into the kitchen. "You two can stop now. This ain't some slut downtown. Reverend will have your head on a chopping block. Whoa, Hillard, stop! Cool it. Enough fun, fellas. Can't do anything to her except what he said. I said, *stop*! I'm up for a promotion. This wouldn't look good for me," he laughed. "Besides, my daddy will have my ass in a sling if I screw this up." Percy bent over me as Hillard got a better hold and squeezed me tighter. "You scream again or call the cops or as much as mention we were here; you're a dead woman, you got it? If I were you, I'd keep my damn mouth shut. 'Cause Reverend, he don't make threats. He makes the promises of the Lord."

I nodded one last time, and Hillard let go. I reached out a hand on the cold linoleum as sudden and violent nausea rolled through me. I couldn't stop it. The hot bacon dressing on the salad I'd had for lunch scorched its way up my throat. Tears rolled down my face, and I spewed the contents of my stomach out at their feet.

Percy stepped back, his flashlight painting the floor with a harsh light. I crouched down, soaked in vomit, staring at the faded knees of his blue jeans. The nausea subsided, but every breath was agonizing, and I wondered if they would kill me, anyway. *Mavis. They did worse than this to Mavis.* Feeling small, I watched tears drip off my face to the floor. They laughed harder and yanked me by my hair to my feet. I winced and moaned as pain shot through my head and chest from their grip on me again.

"Aw, damn; she puked!" Hillard pushed me forward in the dark. Afraid of walking into boxes, I stretched out my arm to protect myself as they had strewn my belongings across the room. But even walking hurt.

Tripping over a stack of newspapers, I landed back on the kitchen floor. Percy yanked my head back again, his vile fist grabbing a handful of my hair. "Just remember what I said! Next time, I won't hold these fellas back."

More hot tears dripped down the back of my throat. I saw his boot for only a second. It hit my head, opening a wound, still trying to heal. In my delirium, I heard them preparing to leave, kicking my things out of their way, using my living room as a toilet, and laughing. As they walked out, they flicked their cigarettes at my head, calling me a whore. Seconds later, they kicked the patio door open, disappearing in the dark.

Prissy bounded into the room, licking my face in the dark. Moonlight streamed through the window alongside the silence where I huddled on my kitchen floor, sobbing, smelling the grimy garage stench of their clothes, tasting the grit from their hands. I couldn't move. Each breath sent pain ricocheting through my chest, ribs, and shoulder. The room swirled around me as an echo of Mavis called out my name—as if she stood on the other side of a vast canyon. *Andie, you have the power—don't let them destroy you.*

Chapter 50

I'VE GOT A GUN
Andie ~ April 1992

In the morning, I cracked open my right eye. They had either nailed the left shut with the sharp spike driven through it or glued it to the linoleum they smashed my face against. My mother/child ring sparkled in the sun that streamed through the windows. The glare hurt my eye. I rolled over to avoid it, and Prissy lay by my side, dried mud caked over most of her sleek black body. "Poor girl," I said, stroking my dog's paw.

I tried to push myself up on my elbows. Piercing pain knifed through my chest and shoulder. My arm didn't want to move, and my head threatened to explode. I fell to my side and then back to the floor. Panic rammed into my gut. Squeezing both eyes shut, I felt Prissy's head next to mine, whining like dogs do when scared. "Shhh, you're okay," I said to the both of us. Tears covered my cheeks as, twenty minutes later, I dragged myself to my feet. After letting Prissy outside to pee, I stumbled to the bathroom and stared at my face in the mirror. A thunderstorm rumbled in the distance.

Swollen and black-and-blue, my lip had split again; a tooth wiggled and bled—*ice pack*. My ribs ached. Scratches, dark bruises, and welts encircled my arms and torso. Lowering myself on the couch, I recalled the beating detail. A silent scream climbing in my throat threatened to turn me into a pile of quivering gelatin. This wasn't a guessing game anymore. The Artury Mafia had visited me. A greater alarm arose over the next hour. Had they known I witnessed John Rossi's murder, my corpse would be rotting inside my house.

Calvin didn't know I had safely stowed Mavis's envelope inside a bank vault, but it didn't matter. I always responded to fear, and once again, it worked. I had infuriated and frightened him by giving Joe that picture, and his goons had delivered his message.

I'd keep the envelope hidden to protect Dillon and Gracie. The pictures would never come to light. But how long would they tolerate me being alive, knowing I had them?

Joe had obviously given the goons his key to the front door. I thanked God I'd never given Joe a key to the back door, but I wasn't taking any chances.

Gracie's upright piano sat in the breezeway. I scooted it against the door that led out to the garage and moaned in pain as I piled heavy boxes on top and around it. Then I jammed it tight with a coat rack, placing the pole on the floor between the piano and the opposite wall.

After blocking the front entrance with furniture and packed boxes, I locked all the windows, pulled the blinds, and loaded my gun. Then I hunkered down with Prissy on the couch, corpse-still with my gun in my lap, listening to the rain on the roof.

Scorching tears once again trickled down my face. I'd not been out of the house in three days except to let Prissy out the front door on a leash to potty. I'd missed three days of work, calling off with the flu. Three days of pay—gone, and three days wasted not looking for an apartment. And I'd made excuses for three days and left the twins with Dixie again. I didn't want anyone to see me.

Immobilized with the phone off the hook, I languished inside my house. Suddenly, my head ached and my stomach growled. *Even Christ rose from the dead in three days. Guess I should come out of my tomb.*

I had two weeks to vacate my house. *Lord, how can I find an apartment in two weeks when I have no money for a deposit?* I stopped praying, unsure of how much I believed anymore. Shuffling into the kitchen in Gracie's pink disco slippers, I felt dirty. I'd gone too long without a bath and spent too much time with my mouth open. But the thought of Gracie gave me strength.

Opening the fridge, I stared at empty shelves and milk long past its sell-by date. At least Prissy had a bag of Purina, and suddenly, I wondered what it tasted like. I scowled at an empty juice carton. Slowly, after forcing myself to eat a few stale Saltines and sip warm Diet Coke from a can, the terror subsided. Somehow, I had to put the divorce and bankruptcy behind me and then get through the custody battle. I had to find a better job and an apartment for my twins and me. Move to Charleston and live near Aunt Wylene. Get away from Joe, the Olivers, and the whole blasted church. It seemed Artury's congregation infiltrated every street and neighborhood in Winston-Salem.

My children gave me hope, pushed me forward, and kept my head clear. I had to start over. Make a new life without fear.

I felt the house dissolve around me, as my parents dissolved when I thought about them. There came a feeling of letting my house go, a feeling I welcomed. For years, I fretted every month about how much money I needed to pay the mortgage. At least those worries were over. The other blessing was that I'd kept my weight off. But it was effortless. Instead of stuffing my face, I'd forgotten to eat. "Someday, this will all catch up with me." Like a slap from my hand, I had said it aloud. I never intended to commit suicide by neglecting my body, yet deep down; I didn't give a damn, which frightened me.

The doorbell rang, and my heart stopped. Like a ghost, I peeked out the front window to the driveway. No car.

A hard rain fell. I tiptoed to the peephole, hoping it was only a friend of the twins. With my door bolted, I still couldn't see the person clearly. I spoke as normally as I could. "Who is it?"

"It's Peter Collins, Andie—the chef from the Praise Buffet. You know who I am. Please, can I come in?" He coughed loudly, a wet, rasping hack like a shovel scraping sludge off cement.

Leaning against my solid door, I froze. "Are you here to threaten me? Beat me up? Because this time, I've got a gun, and it's loaded."

"No. I'm not here to hurt you. I'm leaving town, and I need to talk to you."

I opened the door a hair-width; the screen door remained locked.

He was in his mid to late forties, a large man hunched over like an elderly woman. Possibly ten years older than John Rossi, he appeared pale and in pain. Peter's massive shoulders filled his coat. His broad chest and back hinted at his former size and beauty, and he had lost most of his hair, which I remembered was golden and several shades lighter than John's. Calculating, edgy eyes took everything in as if he were looking for an excuse to run. I saw he was nervous and had probably lived the last few years looking over his shoulder.

Behind him, the rain fell in sheets, so dense that visibility was nearly impossible. A fog had rolled in. Thunder rolled across the sky and shook the trees in my yard. Peter pulled his coat collar up around his ears and gave me a look of desperation.

"What do you want from me?" I asked.

"I saw John sitting with you the night he died. I think you were the last to see him."

"No. You're mistaken. His killer was the last to see him."

"Well. You're right. But I know you talked to him. And I know what they've done to you. Please, can I come in?"

Reluctantly, I opened the door and let him slip inside.

"Still don't trust me, do you?" he asked.

I held the gun tight in my hand. "Hell, no. Why should I? Aren't you Calvin's lover?"

"No. Not for a long time. You can put your gun away. I told you I need to speak to you and then I will leave. I'm going to Florida. Sarasota. I'm moving in with my mother. In fact, you're my last stop. I'll be brief." He coughed again and then wiped the rain off his face with a handkerchief he pulled from his coat pocket. "I saw you talking to John that night at the Buffet. I stood there only a few minutes, but long enough to know he was pouring out his heart to you." He sighed. "I loved John Rossi."

"Yeah? You had an awful way of showing it. You could've saved his life and left with him years ago."

"True enough. For that reason and many others, I'm finally out. Whatever John told you is true. Did you see who pulled the trigger? Are you the one who called the police?"

I said nothing. I stared at him with my best *damn-you* stare.

"No need to answer. I know who did it." His big-knuckled hand reached inside his coat again. I lifted my gun and pointed it at his head. "Hold on; it's just a videotape." Slowly, he handed it to me. "My hobby has been making videos of Calvin's secrets. Put this with the rest of your evidence. I know you've got more. When you're ready, look at it and use it. But not until you're ready. In the meantime, if you ever need me, here is my mother's address and phone number. I'd prefer you memorize it, then get rid of that piece of paper. When they realize I'm gone for good, I should be on a bus halfway to the Sunshine State."

"Why? Why me?" I asked.

"Because I saw you with John that night. It was good they sent *me* to see if John had left for the evening. Had someone else seen you with John, they would've taken a gun to your head as well. They mean to destroy you, Andie. I can't be a Christian anymore.

Not their kind of Christian. Don't worry; I told no one I saw you talking to John. I never will."

"Why don't you go to the police with this tape yourself?"

"For the same reason you don't—threats against my family. Nobody knows who to trust there. The church is crawling with spies. Last year, they broke my nose and busted a few ribs. John may have told you that Calvin has connections in the local police department and judicial systems. They would have destroyed my evidence before any trial. Calvin and his staff would smell better than ever with new members joining the church because I was persecuting the Reverend Artury. In the end, I'd end up like John. Shot between the eyes and left in a parking lot somewhere. I don't want to die that way. My mother wants my casket open."

I didn't understand his last comment but wasn't about to inquire. "What chance do I really have? The odds are not in my favor."

"Not now. But I still believe in justice. God's justice. Someday, you'll have the upper hand. I *have* to believe that."

"Why are you *really* leaving Calvin? Lover's quarrel?"

"You could say that."

"What happened?"

"I had to find out that he's a fake."

"I could've saved you the heartache. I realized it years ago. So did John."

"I didn't want to believe it," he said. "I had to know for sure. I don't know why nobody has done this, but the idea came to me to fake a message in tongues to see if he would interpret it. I prayed first and asked God to forgive me for what I was about to do, but I wanted to know if Calvin was the prophet he claimed to be. So I babbled something I made up, hoping he would tell me it was not the Holy Ghost speaking. Instead, he interpreted it. A long, beautiful prophecy about God's will for me and how I was to forget

John, who now dwelled in outer darkness. That I must continue to work where God wants me. On and on—a load of crap. It was his effort to keep and control me. It was also the moment I decided to get out of there. But I took my time to record and edit a few choice meetings Calvin didn't know I'd videotaped. Now you have them."

I leaned against my empty bookcase, the gun still tight in my right hand, the videotape in my left. "Hoo-boy, I thought I'd heard it all."

Peter wiped the sweat from his brow. "But I never stopped caring about John. This is my way of avenging his death. Hopefully, Andie, through you."

I saw him observing my battered face. My lip, cracked and infected, had scabbed over. A yellowish-green tint covered my right cheekbone. Black rings circled my eyes, and my hair hung in a tangled, greasy mess.

"You could use some medical attention to that lip." He coughed forcefully into his handkerchief; sweat streamed from his pores.

"I know. But your cough sounds awful. My father passed away from emphysema. Are you sick?"

"I've got AIDS—advanced. Six months left, if I'm lucky." He coughed again. "This damn weather doesn't help. Calvin will never chase me. He knows I'm a dead man. He doesn't want me around in this condition. It's okay. I want away from it all. To die in peace. Or as much as I can get." Peter reached into his inside coat pocket a third time and pulled out an envelope. "Here. I know you could use some money. It's not much, but it might help. I heard you're losing your home. I'm sorry, Andie. For all you've been through."

I set the videotape down and took the envelope from his hand. "I'm sorry, too, Peter. Thanks. Thanks so much." Then I had to ask. "Is Calvin HIV positive?"

"No. Artury is clean. And so are the rest of his staff, as far as I know. We were all checked regularly. That's how I discovered I had it. He's a freak about that stuff." Peter smiled, then nodded. "Well. I should be going. If you need to contact me, you know where I'll be. Unless it's over six months from now, then you're on your own."

"Peter, how do you know they won't come after you, anyway?"

"Calvin won't do that. Not to me. If I leave him alone, he'll leave me to die alone. He'll only go after someone who can't shut their mouth. Someone who makes threats against him, the ministry, or one of his team members—as you did. So be careful. Use your ammunition wisely and only when the time is right."

I shook my head. "I'm not sure there will ever be a right time."

"You still believe in God?" he asked.

I sucked in my breath and looked away. "Not sure. I think so."

"Then there will be a right time."

He turned to open the door and leave, but I couldn't let him go without telling him. I spoke to his back. "Peter, John loved you. He did, you know. He told me. That's why he stuck around so long."

Silently, he nodded. He never looked back. "Take care of yourself, Andie," he said. With that goodbye, he disappeared down the street into a waiting taxi.

I opened the envelope. Two thousand dollars in hundreds and twenties. Enough to lift my spirits and start apartment hunting again.

Chapter 51

Pack It Up

Andie ~ May 1992

I deposited Peter's videotape into my bank lockbox. I never watched it and considered destroying everything inside the lockbox rather than paying the small monthly fee, but I decided against it. And instead of hiding the key to the lockbox in the attic again, I strung it on a chain and slipped it around my neck.

I refused to ask Dixie if I could move in with her. Going through divorce number three, Caroline had packed up her three little girls and moved in with Dixie, with baby number four on the way. My sister's recent brief fling with another pretty cowboy wore on everybody's last nerve. Dixie wasn't stable; I guessed Caroline and I had caused her too much strain. As it was, we'd mooched off Dixie and Wylene enough. I had always tried to keep the worst from my family. My current homeless situation was no different.

I begged the Gerbers for an extension, another thirty days to vacate, but they refused. Their son had taken over their affairs and was not as kind as his parents. He told me the Sheriff would be at my door on day thirty-one if I were not out.

So I walked across the street to visit my neighbors, the elderly Grissom sisters. Two years previous, Ada and Edna Grissom had fallen ill with pneumonia. I had nursed and fed them both back to health. The spinsters took pity on the children and me and said we could live on their enclosed front porch until I found an apartment, which was good because the twins needed to remain in their school district with only a few weeks remaining in the school year. The fact was, no one wanted to rent to me. With a low-wage job and ruined credit, I was a risk nobody wanted to take. I couldn't blame them.

Dillon, Gracie, and I moved across the street into our neighbors' glassed-in front porch. I allowed them to bring one suitcase, their schoolwork, and a few of their favorite things. I placed the rest of our sparse furniture and boxes in a rented storage unit across town, the cheapest I could find. We donated Gracie's piano to the Salvation Army and gave Prissy to Byron Stewart, Libby's uncle, knowing one more dog on his horse farm wouldn't make a difference to him. He loved his dogs, and he loved Prissy. All three of us cried silently, driving away from Byron's farm that day, leaving behind our beloved dog. Giving Prissy away was the worst part of the entire ordeal.

A fluorescent bulb blinked in the rust-pitted tin ceiling. Crowded with old porch furniture that someone should've burned years before, the long, narrow room sufficed. Gracie and I gutted the space and scrubbed it. Dillon painted it a soft white, and I added a lamp, a rug, and a single bed—politely refusing the recycled mattress the Grissom sisters offered. The porch was livable. Better than a cardboard box or a homeless shelter. I cleaned a small loveseat in the corner with upholstery cleaner and covered it with a clean quilt; Dillon slept on that, and Gracie and I snuggled together on the tiny bed. I told myself it was temporary, and we'd manage.

It was hardest on the twins. My heart broke, watching them get off the school bus every day and walk to the back door of their old house to wait until the bus turned the corner. Then they'd run across the street to our current address, a room no bigger than their mama's old bedroom. They didn't want their friends to know they were homeless.

At fifteen, any diversion from the norm was an embarrassment. Somehow, I had to believe it would strengthen them. Show them how delicate life is and how one wrong decision can throw everything off balance. They would learn from my mistakes.

I resolved to get through it. Most days, I drove from interview to interview before heading to the truck stop for work. I scoured the papers for a job that paid enough to rent a decent apartment in their school district. But suddenly, computer skills were more marketable than cooking skills. Competing with girls fresh out of college, I felt my frustration escalate. And I drew the line on how much I told the Grissom sisters. Although the ladies had been kind and generous, I had no way of knowing if those two were prone to gossip.

Solitude had become a commodity, something to haul home along with whatever groceries I could afford: bread, milk, peanut butter, and boxes of macaroni and cheese. Every morning, I stifled the accusations in my head to listen for a small voice I hoped existed. During my lower moments, I prayed for Jesus to tell me what to do next, clear away the clutter of life, and give me a reason to keep moving. There was no voice. Not even the slightest whisper. Nothing other than the sounds of Dillon and Gracie fighting over the spare bathroom we were permitted to use.

We took turns in quick showers at specified times of the day. I managed to hook up our little TV; it helped pass the time and warm the porch. Not wanting to impose on Edna and Ada as they ate in their dining room, we took our meals to our room.

The house had plenty of space for two families, but I insisted the children remain on the porch with me. I didn't want to give the sisters any reason to be upset with us.

Fortunately, the space was free, and we were alive. I counted our blessings. Living, at times, from hour to hour, I worked hard to make the best out of our miserable living conditions. But Gracie and Dillon felt my stress. I concluded that if we were to survive, I had to find a place of our own, and quickly.

Standing before the dingy three-floor walk-up, I wiped my puckered brow that dripped with sweat. The front door hung on one hinge, and piles of coupon magazines littered the stoop; the entire house tilted to the left. Frowning, I stepped back and looked at the building again. I couldn't believe the landlady lived in such a place. I pulled out the slip of paper with the address.

Yep, this is it.

A shot of hot wind blew down the street, and I glanced in its direction. The humidity climbed. I tried calling Annabel Boggs numerous times throughout the day to confirm my appointment, and though I recognized the name, I thought nothing else about her. Desperate, I felt my best opportunity at getting the nicer apartment at the end of the street was speaking to the landlady, but I'd reached another dead end unless I was prepared to sit and wait on the rickety stairway. Nobody was home.

I knocked on the front door again. My spirits sank. There was no time to waste. I had to get to work. Crumpling the paper, I descended the steps that swayed under my feet. Just as I hit the sidewalk, I caught a flash of hair dyed a harsh, unnatural shade of red. It belonged to a woman moving between two parked cars. She crossed the street with her head down, and it wasn't until I stepped off the sidewalk that she lifted her eyes, saw me, and stopped in the middle of the road.

"Hello," I called out, raising a hand. "Miss Boggs?"

"Who wants to know?"

"We had an appointment today," I said, hoping she was the landlady.

The woman scowled, then started walking again, much more slowly. "I don't remember any appointment," she said.

I tried to coax a smile from her but failed. She looked a tidbit familiar, but I couldn't quite place her. My eyes narrowed. Upon closer inspection, red blotches covered her forehead under a thick coat of sweat. A breeze tossed her fuzzy hair around—hair that fell past her shoulders. The woman had not aged well, having painted a new face on top of the old one; she glared at me suspiciously.

"Well?" She lifted her dome-like eyebrow. "I said I don't remember any appointment."

"I called yesterday. I'm here to apply for the apartment down the street."

Shooting me a coolly annoyed stare, the landlady walked up the stone steps and mumbled as she passed me. "I'm not interested in having you as a tenant."

"Why?" I asked sharply, suddenly behind her.

She turned around to face me. "I know who you are. You should've told me on the phone and saved us both some time."

"What do you mean?"

"I know who you are. I'm an usher at the House of Praise. I don't rent to demon-possessed people. Get off my property." She pinned me with a look that would've withered anyone else. Holding her hand as if she had a magic wand that would make me disappear, she shouted, "I rebuke you in the name of Jesus!"

Crushed beneath her heel, I refused to move. "Miss Boggs, you don't even know me."

The landlady swept a strand of hair out of her eyes. "I know enough," she said.

"Have I done anything to offend you personally?"

Her brick-red hair blew into her eyes again, aggravating her further. She pushed it away and opened her lacquered lips. "I don't like you," she exclaimed. As soon as the words came out, her cheeks reddened. She stood as still as a post, but I felt her fist in my gut.

For a fleeting moment, I thought if Annabel saw I was not a horrible person, maybe sitting down, having coffee together, and getting to know me a little would dispel her fear. I smiled grimly. "Possibly the problem is that you don't know me. You're afraid of me. Why don't we at least go in and talk—"

"—I'm not scared of dark angels like you!"

"Then why the hostility?" I shrugged. "And I'm not a dark angel."

The landlady shook her head. "I'll only say it one more time. Get off my property!"

Astonished by her hatred, I gave her a level stare. "Here's a little something to chew on, Miss Boggs. I think it's sad you believe every word Calvin says, and you allow him to control you with fear. You've not even thought to question the *accused*. Again, ma'am, I'm no dark angel. They have lied to you. I'm only a mother with two children needing a roof over our heads. And if you're an example of Christianity, I want nothing to do with it!"

She turned, stomped up the steps, rammed her key in the door, and slammed it behind her.

I sulked to my car. As I pulled away, I looked up at her apartment windows. Hate-filled eyes peered down through tattered lace with a repeated warning to stay away. I drove off, defeated, but believing there had to be a few innocent people who attended Calvin's church and knew nothing about his debauchery. I thought about Miss Boggs and how she had most likely spent her entire life dedicated to a madman and a ministry with no genuine regard for humanity. I earnestly prayed for those who still had a chance—to get out.

I did my best to quiet Dillon and Gracie's nightly sibling brawl so the two old ladies we lived with wouldn't think I'd raised a couple of heathens. After losing my temper and reprimanding my teenagers, I made tea and considered calling Dixie, but dismissed it. Anxiety, my new loyal companion, followed me as I retired to our room to read the Apartments for Rent section in the newspaper.

Nothing. Nothing I could afford. I beat my fist into a pillow, ashamed to see the small cloud of dust that rose in the lamplight. I was exhausted. I had overdrawn my energy and constant hope, just like my checkbook.

Chapter 52

Temporary Housing
Andie ~ July 1992

I *suck at this.* Saving for a rainy day was out of the question. All my days were rainy. Peter's money helped pay past-due bills, buy groceries, compensate a dentist for fixing my loose tooth, and pay driver's training fees for the twins. It was probably another poor decision, considering my pressing financial status. The Grissom sisters' little porch shrunk and grew hotter in the summer's heat. The lack of air conditioning became maddening, and the old ladies demanded more and more of my time. My twins begged to stay with friends or Grandma Dixie. I resolved to get out by the end of the month, even if it meant moving back to Shady Acres trailer park in Salisbury.

On the bright side, I had two things going for me—free rent and no car payment. My sister had signed over her Honda as an early birthday present at the insistence of Dixie, who promised to give Caroline a "little extra money" from the sale of her house. Money to move into an apartment in Charleston. Dixie would never be free of needy, forever-pregnant Caroline and her girls. As much as my mother and sister drove each other crazy, they fed off each other. There was no room in Dixie's life for my trials and tribulations, and I wondered if she gave money to Caroline and not me because my sister was Bud's daughter, and I wasn't.

What did it matter? My upcoming custody battle had ruined any plans I might have had to move to Charleston to live near my mother and Aunt Wylene, at least for the time being.

Dennis Dawson sold real estate and managed rental properties for low-income families. "It rents for three-fifty a month," he told me on the phone. "We won't check your credit on this one. If you want to fix it up, feel free, but it's your dollar. No reimbursement."

All three houses he sent me to on the south side of High Point reeked of sour milk, cooking fat, and cat pee. Seas of dirty laundry, empty beer bottles, and leftover fast-food bags littered every room. A not-housebroken Chihuahua tied to a bedpost that barked and bared its teeth greeted me in the last house, along with a cluttered backyard filled with a rotting picnic table, mangled bicycles, and rusted cars that housed two pit bulls chained to a clothesline. Overall, the houses smelled like sewers. Disgusted with the way people lived, I got back into my car. I wasn't about to fix up another place whose tenant had left it a stinking mess beyond the capabilities of ordinary cleaning.

As poor as I was, I had limits when housing my children. Driving north out of High Point, the stately homes of Emerywood were a sharp contrast to the houses I'd just walked through. They were the homes of my dreams as a young girl. Landscaped yards and gardens, exquisitely decorated rooms, and the love of a faithful husband and fair-haired children to fill them. Stupid dreams, nothing more.

Finally, I found a winner in Kernersville. It wasn't pretty, but it was clean and affordable, and Dennis was kind enough to waive the deposit. I'd been sweet to him. It wasn't until after I'd signed a three-month lease he asked me out on a date. Politely, I said, "No thank you," as he handed me the keys, and I smiled—sweetly.

I promised my twins I would work on getting them back into their school district, but at least Kernersville was better than the Grissoms' front porch. They agreed. So we said goodbye to Edna and Ada, packed up our few belongings, and moved into the tiny rental house on the edge of K'ville. I hesitated to take the rest of everything I owned out of storage. Instead, I bartered a deal with Space Savers Storage, getting my unit free in exchange for cleaning their offices once a week. That way, I could take my time as we adjusted to the little one-bedroom house that came "furnished."

But still. The furniture was typical motel furniture. Vinyl-covered and uncomfortable. A rope strung off the back porch to a nearby tree served as my clothes dryer. The place had one small bedroom and a bathroom with no tub, just a shower stall and a toilet. We brushed our teeth in the kitchen sink. It had to do. Gracie and I got the bedroom, and Dillon won the pullout couch to himself. The physically cramped *roadhouse,* as we named it, gave us the gift of a roof over our heads and not much else.

On our first night there, I didn't sleep. I lay in bed, watching streetlight shadows play across the ceiling, and the tree outside the window shivering in the wind while its rustling leaves brushed against the siding. In the quiet, a dog, moving on its chain, reminded me despite all the pressed-down, shaken-together blessing scriptures in the Bible, the decisions of my life had chained me to poverty from the moment I left the security of my parents' home. Far away, a truck geared down as it barreled up a hill. Once again, loneliness curled beside me and burrowed deeper into my soul.

A September court date loomed over our heads, adding to our insecurities. Everyone was cranky. I had seen the last of my children's good moods for a while. Gracie's inclination to cloud up and cry whenever she got her feelings hurt played like a scratched record, and Dillon played his *Pink Floyd* cassette tape over and over until all of us had become *comfortably numb*.

Although the twins wrote and mailed letters to Judge VanOrson stating their desires and reasons to remain with me, they had apparently gone unread. The judge had yet to reply.

A new school created unwanted challenges for the twins. My bankruptcy had taken the only house they'd ever known, and their grandmother's house was now up for sale. Unforeseen circumstances had turned their world upside down, even though I fought desperately against insurmountable obstacles to stabilize their lives. I had hidden more from the twins than they would ever know. We hoped the worst was over. But I knew it could always get worse.

At least there was a park across the street with basketball courts—a pleasant distraction for a fifteen-year-old boy with tons of energy and angry at the world. It seemed the teenagers of the '90s owned and played video games. I didn't know the first thing about them, and my children didn't bother asking for the luxury they knew their mama could not afford.

༄

Dillon and Gracie kept their visits with Joe to a minimum, making excuses not to go with him as often as possible.

Being the cast-off parent, Joe possessed all the benefits of the congregation's pity. Word got back to me he had boasted about being the lucky parent. Having twins without the pain and suffering of raising them. Gracie didn't understand. "So why the custody battle, Mom?" Of course, I knew why, and the slightest possibility of it scared me to death.

Raising my children alone should've denoted me as the better parent. Surely, the judge would see my dedication. That thought, and my children's voices, kept me sane in the coming weeks.

And then I heard Joe and Selma had moved into a new condominium in a picturesque suburb of Winston-Salem, close to the church, and that each of the twins would have their own bedroom. I had no words to express my rage.

I lay on my bed and rubbed my eyes, watching the wind push the curtains out from the window like a big belly. The afternoon heat should've made me sleepy, but I wasn't. I had to be at the truck stop in an hour. My unblinking eyes stared up at the blown-on, lumpy ceiling. We had settled in the best we could. It wasn't home, but as I kept reminding myself, it kept the rain off.

Chapter 53
TAKE MY LIFE
Andie ~ November 1992

Winter came early. I dreaded the twins' birthday and Christmas. Happy families forced me to remember that I had none. If I could shed the memories—if I could stay away from everybody's kids—if I could die in my sleep, I'd be okay.

I shut off the car. The air was soft and damp; the temperature hovered in the low fifties. Deliberately stopping a moment, I considered my mother's lawn bordering the narrow residential street shadowed by tall trees. The flowers wouldn't return for months. The trees were skeletal, and the grass had become brown and dormant. But there was order. There was predictability. There was beauty and structure, and energy. Considering everything I had lost, it was not a horrible thing to come home to.

Home. Something I no longer had. And there was a bid on this last home—an offer Dixie had accepted.

I slid the key into the front door and hauled my weary body inside. Chock full of antiques, the home my parents built together overflowed with security and elegance. Dixie would move some furnishing to Charleston and sell the rest. For her *retirement,* she said. Though Daddy declared himself king of his coop, Dixie had always ruled the roost. Aunt Wylene had filled the void and carried on the family traditions left by Daddy. We had turned a corner; a new family chapter had begun.

So many years before, I'd gone after the same brass ring my mother possessed, declaring to my family I would have it all someday. Someday.

My throat constricted. Well. I'd sure showed them.

At least my children weren't around to panic over; no trauma left to survive. Dillon and Grace were gone. Only silence. What more could they do to me?

A shower of bills scattered across the entryway where they'd fallen from the mail slot. I picked them up. Most of them were mine. I leafed through a few, then tossed the rest into the trash. What more could *anybody* do to me?

The Federal clock on the wall ticked softly. It gave me chills, reminding me of Daddy's desperate attempts to breathe. The house was as quiet as a morgue. No one was home. I walked into the sunroom, sank into an overstuffed chair, and closed my eyes. After the double shift I had just worked, I couldn't say I even wanted to wake up in the morning.

Dixie's note said she'd gone to supper with Wylene, Caroline, and the girls to celebrate the house sale and that they wouldn't have to vacate until the middle of January. *We can enjoy the holidays together,* the note said.

Sure. Enjoy the holidays. Then where do I go?

I would lie. Tell Dixie and Aunt Wy I'd rented an apartment— had it all worked out—I'd stay in Winston-Salem and work on getting my kids back. That I was in line for a management position at The Pit Stop. I'd—be—just fine. All lies. I wouldn't be *fine*. I'd never be *fine* again.

❦

At seven o'clock in the morning on September seventeenth, the sky changed from bright sun to smoke gray as a front moved in from the west. Custody: one last hurdle to jump through.

As the kids slept, I drank coffee and stood at the window gazing at the industrial neighborhood I had moved into. Our days usually began that way. Me, staring out the window, waiting for the kids to stir from sleep. I could hardly believe Dillon and Gracie were fast approaching sixteen. Gracie sprawled across the bed. A limp strand of hair covered her cheek. Smeared mascara under her eyes gave her a wild animal appearance. She'd been experimenting with Maybelline and Cover Girl the night before, attempting to master the art of eye makeup. A boy from school had invited her to a Friday night dance, so she'd been preparing for days ahead. Dillon's foot peeked out from under the covers. Their even breathing soothed me like one of Mavis's hymns.

Despite her new braces, Gracie had made the debate team in her new school. Braces that Joe's dental insurance paid for. Braces he'd thrown a fit over when he found out he had to pay a large deductible. Braces that Dillon should've had, too, but didn't get. But at least the tension of waiting for the results of the debate team tryouts was over.

Assured everything would be okay, I set a stack of buttered toast and a box of cornflakes, bowls, and spoons on the table. Finishing my coffee, I planned our celebration for that evening with pizza and our family debate—should a particular set of twins get their driver's licenses for their birthday?

Already running late, I hurried to dress. Dillon padded across the floor barefoot, sat at the table, and poured cereal into his bowl. Ready for my last battle with Joe, I told Dillon to dress in the clothes I'd laid out for him. His Sunday best. He complained his pants were too short.

Gracie stumbled through the living room in her pajamas, flopped into our only chair, and batted her big blue raccoon eyes at me. Her hair was a matted mess; she took deep breaths on the verge of tears. "What if that judge makes us live with Dad? I will not live with him! I'll run away, I swear!"

"Gracie. Can't you see we're running late? That won't happen," I said.

My daughter's chin rested on her chest.

"Go wash your face! I want the judge to see how beautiful you are." I smiled at her. "Tonight, we'll celebrate our victories and get pizza."

"But—mom—" Her constant whining grated on my last nerve. "What if—if—"

"—If a frog didn't hop, he wouldn't bump his butt when he walked!" I felt a sudden twinge of uneasiness and responded to her with humor instead of the panic that rose in me like smoke from a smoldering fire. "Stop it, Gracie. Get a leg up; we're late!"

❧

How foolish I'd been.

Judge Gina VanOrson severed my parental rights until such time as I successfully completed a rehabilitation program from unacceptable behavior with disreputable men, alcohol, and substance abuse, and obtained employment that could support two growing children. Then, she mentioned something about supervised visitation. It was ludicrous. I'd hardly been drunk over two times in my life. And men? What men? What substance abuse? What?

The judge was clear. "While the decision is clearly in the children's best interests, I'm certainly not a happy judge to have ruled in another mother being separated from her children. Even though Ms. Oliver knows full well that, according to the testimony of her pastor and various witnesses, she has brought her troubles upon herself. One cannot abuse drugs and alcohol and be a proper parent at the same time. Even with child support, Andie

Oliver's small income cannot properly support herself and her two teenagers. Children she has dragged from pillar to post. How did you plan to house these children on what you make?" The judge looked hard at me. "Why in the world would you put yourself and your children in such a situation?" she asked.

I blinked like a confused dog. I should've had an attorney. I should've borrowed the money from Aunt Wy—had my own witnesses. I should've gone after Joe for the spousal support he never paid. Shoulda, woulda, coulda.

John Rossi's words haunted me—*a judge in his pocket.* I had seen her in church or at the Buffet—somewhere. I couldn't prove it, but something told me this was a judge that Calvin Artury had in his hip pocket. *Judges don't take fifteen-year-olds from their mothers,* Dixie had said.

Dillon and Gracie stood outside the courtroom. It didn't matter that they told the judge they wanted to stay with their mother. After hearing their plea, the judge asked an officer of the court to retain them in the hallway. But as soon as Dillon heard the verdict, he slipped through the door at the first opportunity and ran toward the bench. "No! You can't give us to him and expect us to like it! He beat our mother! He nearly killed her! I won't go, and you can't make me! We won't go!"

Gracie followed. "Please! Please, don't do this!"

The judge banged her gavel on the desk.

"Take my life!" I cried hoarsely, in a fit of hopelessness. "But don't; please don't take my kids! Don't give them to him!" My cry made no sense. Then again, none of it did.

But the sudden revelations of Joe's temper motivated the judge to require psychiatric testing at our own expense. "You had a choice," Judge VanOrson admonished me as I sobbed while my children left the courtroom with their newly appointed Guardian ad Litem. "The pictures of you with these men do not lie. Ms. Oliver, it would be best to have professional counseling before you finish parenting these children. When I see a board-certified doctor of psychiatry has analyzed and fully treated you, I will consider reversing my decision. But not until then."

I sat in my car until the shock wore off. Until I could remember how to drive. Until I could remember the way home. Until I could put two coherent words together. When I finally stepped through the door of my rental, the question hit me like another boot to my head. *How the hell do I pay for a one-hundred-dollar-an-hour psychiatrist?*

I phoned Dan Blunden, left a message, and collapsed on the linoleum. I'd waltzed into their trap with no defense, foolishly believing I didn't need to waste what precious little money I had on an attorney. Instead, I'd wanted to save it because I genuinely believed Joe didn't have a chance. Grief seized me by the scruff of the neck and wouldn't let go. I looked at my watch. Two thirty and still no word from Blunden, who I couldn't afford to hire. "What the hell is he doing!? Why doesn't he call me? These are my kids, for God's sake!"

Within the hour, the phone rang. "I'm so sorry, Andie," Attorney Blunden said. "You should've called me earlier." How he said my name made the tear slip out—the first of many. It was too late. Too late to take my fight further. My attorney needed a retainer—a big one.

I had created a world of false optimism and blind ambition. Like Scarlett O'Hara, I had tried to find hope in an overworked field of weeds and radishes. I had failed—more times than I could count. I dialed Wylene's number. She didn't answer, so I left a message. "Tell Dixie she was wrong." *Click.*

Sitting in the darkness, I replayed the court scene repeatedly in my head. Pictures. More damn pictures. Photos of me and Hickey Gilbert drinking and kissing in his truck at an X-rated movie.

Of Jasper Wenger kissing and fondling me in my driveway, then walking into my garage in the middle of the night. Jasper, who had neglected to mention he'd joined the House of Praise a short month before we met. A slick liar, Jasper, he testified in open court, flat-out lied, stating we'd used drugs the night we had sex: drugs and alcohol.

They were the only moments of pleasure and passion I'd known in years. But Artury's team of polished lawyers made my mistakes public. Documented and recorded them—used them to destroy me. The judge also passed me a picture of some man whose name I couldn't remember. The two of us sitting together at The Purple Passion, a disreputable bar. They'd followed me more often than I'd realized and made me look like trash in front of my children.

But what frightened me most was that Calvin suddenly had access to Dillon and Gracie. According to Joe's testimony, I had raised my twins as agnostics. Unfortunately, I knew Dillon and Gracie were peacemakers. They'd never been rebellious teenagers. The cult would wear them down if they got their hands on them for any length of time. Indoctrinate them deep within Artury's ministry.

It was my fault. I fumed and boiled over at the thought of Joe's infidelities over the years. I never had the chance to bring up his severe acts of adultery in court or ask who would be responsible for the kids when he traveled every week. They knew I had no attorney, so the entire proceeding was about me. How dare they! They didn't give me the slightest chance of talking about Joe or what I hid in my lockbox, the key still dangling on a chain around my neck! Some of what I hid was evidence Joe and Calvin didn't even know I had. But once again, it didn't matter. I'd been unprepared. Calvin's lawyers were ready for the kill. Paid in full by House of Praise money. And from the look of it, conveniently brought before a persuaded judge.

I had to stay sane for the next few hours. Dillon and Gracie were on their way home to pack. Who knew when I would ever see them again?

I was nearly dark before the Guardian ad Litem, her assistant, and a police officer drove Dillon and Gracie home to collect their things and say goodbye. It barely took twenty minutes for them to pack. Suddenly, my reasons for living were walking out the door with social workers. The damnable judge's last words to my children bore into my skull. *Until your mother is well, it would be best to limit visitations. Give her the time she needs to seek professional help*, she'd said.

The court gave me two monthly visitations in a room downtown under strict supervision, but only when it was convenient for Joe. This galled me. But my heart told me these weren't small children; they were intelligent teenagers who would find every opportunity to talk to me.

Heads down, the twins shuffled out of the house. Gracie carried her bag and turned around for one last goodbye. I fell to my knees, as my legs could no longer hold the massive burden strapped to my back. Gracie dropped her bag, pulled out of the grip of the social worker, and ran back for one last hug. Dillon followed her lead, and the three of us embraced. This final devastating blow was a knockout punch, taking my breath away.

"Don't worry, Mom. We'll be okay. We'll find you," Dillon whispered in my ear.

All night, I lay on the floor where they had left me until Aunt Wy arrived early the following morning with Dixie. When Wylene pulled me toward her, I wailed like someone had doused me with gasoline and set me on fire. As I cried my heart clean out of my chest, she cradled me against her like a baby, her voice soft and repeating my name, "Andie—oh, Andie—.

I felt Dixie squat beside us, touching my face and hands, and then she went to rubbing my hair. I moaned, wailed, and cried until I had no oxygen left in my lungs, until my shoulders shook, and my breath became shallow.

While Wylene held me, my mother packed everything in the rental that was mine, which wasn't much. They loaded it into my car and moved me back into Dixie's house. The rest of what I owned remained in storage. I would stay with my mother until I figured something out. Saved money. Hired an attorney. The fact the judge mentioned she would consider reversing her decision upon my psychological evaluation bought me a small measure of hope. But there was little fight left in me.

Arriving home from their supper celebration, Wylene blew through the front door, followed by Dixie, Caroline, and the rest of her brat pack, laughing and excited about their move to Charleston. Caroline's six-month pregnant belly seemed to have ballooned overnight, and I shook my head at the extra work and worry we had caused for Dixie.

I excused myself, staggered upstairs to my room, and opened my nightstand drawer. I tossed back the last mouthful of whiskey in the bottle, oblivious to the blast of heat traveling down my throat, and thought about dropping everything and hitting the road and who-knows-where for a destination.

Surrounded by an empty bottle, an empty cigarette pack, an empty life, and what they left of my memories, I deteriorated in my room. Precisely what the monster prayed for. Calvin spared no expense or influence to see my children returned to the House of Praise. He considered it a significant victory against the *dark angel*, I was sure. Dillon and Gracie Oliver—his own personal trophies.

I should've been a better mother; I should've put the needs of my children first instead of my hopes and dreams that pushed me forward and then held me back, making me hang on to what wasn't there in the first place. I had followed every hope and dream around like the poorly paid convenience store clerk I had become, begging for a break.

And God knows I was sick to death of self-pity.

I crept down to Daddy's study while the house's inhabitants slept. Curling into his recliner with a fresh bottle of Jack, I slugged it down as if it were Diet Coke. My eyes burned. I rubbed the right one with my shoulder, switched on the TV, and emptied the bottle. A calm washed over me as the warm booze slid down and coated my insides. I blinked and tried not to think about my kids, but their faces refused to fade from my thoughts.

A drop of liquid splashed onto my hand. I looked down at the fallen tear. Remarkably, I hadn't felt them roll down my cheeks and did not bother to wipe them away. Instead, I leaned my head back and screamed out with the pain and agony I'd tried to bury since I last saw them. "I'm sorry! I'm so sorry!"

A public service announcement blared, and I nearly choked. *It is now eleven o'clock. Do you know where your children are?*

I stood and swayed slightly with a single thought: I could stand there and do nothing—or lose it.

For years, insanity hung around my neck like a talisman, dangling above my heart until it finally landed on it. I heaved the whisky bottle at the TV. It shattered. Glass, booze, and my life flew in every direction.

Chapter 54
THE BARREL'S BOTTOM
Andie ~ February 1993

A year to the day Daddy died, Dixie said her goodbyes, good riddance, and farewells to Winston-Salem. She visited her husband's grave and then walked through her empty house one final time before she kissed me and made me promise to call her when I settled into my new place.

Weeks prior, Caroline moved to her new Charleston townhouse. One that Wylene had set up for her. Aunt Wy had made the statement that my survival skills were much better than Caroline's. Whether true or not, I was happy for my sister. Within the month, Caroline would have *four* children at her feet. Maybe she'd find a new husband to care for her because somebody would have to do it, and I hoped it wouldn't have to be Wylene forever.

I couldn't complain too much about Caroline when Wy had also consistently been my financial backup. "I can refer you to a good psychiatrist, Andie. I'm sure I can get him to knock the price down; if you want to go that route, do what the judge said. I'd be happy to kick in some money for you. Of course, the court will have to approve of my choice."

"Not this time, Wy." Even at a reduced hourly rate and some money from Wy, any psychiatrist was more than I could afford. I imagined my aunt was about broke after all the money she had *kicked in* for Caroline and me over the years. No. I needed to find a place to live first, so to ease her mind, I smiled and said, "I'll let you know. Just take care of Dixie." My mother had lost a few more marbles after the court scooped up the twins and stole them away. She refused to talk about it, partially blaming me, I think.

"Not to worry, darlin'. I'll keep her busy with that old house of mine, cleaning and redecorating. She'll be in her element, and I'll be the envy of the Women's Club of Charleston!" The good doctor wrapped her thick arms around me and gave me one of her bear hugs, squeezing hard enough to leave a few bruises. "You take care. You're stronger than you know. Don't worry about the twins. I grew up in foster care, remember? You get on your feet first."

"Sure." My heart leaped into my throat, watching them prepare to leave. The big Mayflower truck, full of Dixie's antiques and furniture, was already en route to the Low Country house Wylene had inherited over thirty years before. Charleston, the birthplace of Wylene and Dixie, where they would live their remaining years. Together.

We embraced one last time, and Aunt Wy shoved an envelope into my hand. I opened it. Five hundred dollars. It would help for a while. I squeaked out a "thanks." One more amount to add to what I already owed her.

Dixie handed over her house keys to the realtor and closed the door for the last time. I couldn't bear to look back as I drove away. Tears trembled on my eyelids. I followed Wylene and Dixie to the interstate and watched them drive south.

Now what? Unbeknownst to my family, my Honda had become my home.

∽

"Quit calling! I told you they're not here!"

"Joe, please. Let me talk to my son and daughter. Please."

"They can call you at work. You telephone me again, and I'll get a restraining order."

"I'm not allowed personal calls at work; you know that! I've seen them once since you took them from me! Once! You conveniently cancel every visit. When is it convenient for you? You make the appointment. I'll be there!"

"My schedule is as tight as it's ever been. Have you stopped to think the kids don't want to see you?"

"That's a lie, and you know it!"

"Do I?"

"Why!?" I cried. "Why are you doing this? You never wanted them to begin with; why do you hate me so much—"

"—I have to go. I'm telling you one last time. Don't call here again. The twins can call you anytime they want. When I get back from my next trip, I'll try to squeeze in a visit. Until then, leave us the hell alone!"

I worked steadily at the truck stop. It kept gas in my car and a little food in my stomach. I drove I-40 and I-85 with the sun rising or setting in my windows, skimming the outskirts of tobacco fields, suburbs, and small towns—me and my memories. Wherever I felt safe enough to park the car, I pulled over, slept, and promised myself that I'd search for a cheap motel on the weekend.

I informed my boss of my situation. Not a lot, but enough for him to realize I needed to receive personal calls from my kids if he wanted to keep me. He agreed as long as I kept the calls short. By the end of March, I still hadn't heard from the twins.

The Guardian ad Litem refused to tell me anything more than they had settled in with their father and were fine. *Bitch.* On one occasion, I parked down the street from Joe's condo to get a glimpse of them, but the gated community was well-guarded, and there was no way to drive into it without an invitation. After a few hours, I left the area, feeling thoroughly defeated.

All I did was worry. *Were Joe and Selma kind to them? Did Selma give them a sixteenth birthday party? How was their Christmas?* Our first Christmas apart with no contact. No gifts. *Did Selma help Gracie with her hair?* Gracie's poker-straight hair needed special attention as it sprouted in odd directions every morning. My heart broke every single day.

All of it drove me mad. I had no way of contacting them. Of course, I wasn't sure they remembered my phone number at work. I had no address or regular phone access for them to reach me. But every day, I drove past the Magnolia Monarch Apartments and read the sign: Efficiencies: rent by the week—no credit check.

The Gerbers had sold my house on Turner Street. The new owners took down my pretty lace curtains and installed blinds, which were always closed. I drove past, straining to see inside, recalling something Aunt Wylene said. *Every ten years in a woman's life, everything changes; it turns itself inside out until you can't recognize shit.* I didn't understand her at the time, but she was right. Her remark came alive as I drove past familiar landmarks, including where my cafeteria used to be. They had leveled the building and those around it into a blacktop parking lot for Baptist Hospital. The apartment over the drugstore where the Darwoods once lived had also been gutted and turned into an insurance office. I'd lost touch with Henry and Velda Darwood. They were like any other I had loved, fleeting acquaintances I would remember fondly.

I drove past my parents' house, now owned by another comfortable couple. Children played in the castle tree house, and a big collie dog chased a bird in the front yard. Daddy would be happy if this family loved his house as much as he did. Everything around me had gone through a metamorphosis. Nothing remained the same except for the constant struggle to see my children.

As much as I hated the House of Praise, I drove my Honda in its direction, including its vast grounds, television studios, and enormous office complex adjoined by the enormously popular Praise Buffet.

Hours passed as I sat in my parked car across the street from the TV studios that towered twelve stories into the sky. The sun reflected off the mirrored windows, blinding me. I lowered the visor and slipped on Gracie's too-small sunglasses. Every half-hour, I got the urge to slip inside the studio and find Joe, but then I'd think of his wedding ring. I was not only his ex-wife but also an enemy of the church. They'd not allow me to step one foot past the door before they called the local police to arrest me.

I pulled a cigarette from my pack of Carltons and lit up. Blowing a line of smoke out the window, I raked my ringless hand back and forth across the dash and wondered what I thought I was doing. Even if he was there, he had no intention of giving me a moment with Dillon and Gracie.

Two male employees walked from their cars toward the studio. Both stocky, like Daddy. I longed to see Daddy again, eat lunch at Ham's Restaurant in the smoking section, order turkey Reuben sandwiches and homemade chips with ranch dressing, and drink sweet tea.

At noon, small groups of House of Praise employees, some of whom I recognized, walked outside. They stretched in the sun, then strolled to their discount lunch at the Praise Buffet. Smartly dressed, every one of Calvin's inner circle was also attractive. I let out a lungful of smoke in their direction. I'd never been a part of their church cliques. Three women in pretty coats flirted with the men walking behind them. Most days, I let myself feel homeless, childless, and worthless. But that day, though, that day—I felt superior to them because of living hand to mouth—something few people knew how to do.

Alone, agitated, and restless, I found myself chain-smoking until my throat was raw and sore. I inhaled the last of my Carlton and mashed it out in the overflowing ashtray. I put my key into the ignition and forced myself to think about a place to park for the night. My mouth was parched and my breath foul, but I didn't care. Once, I thought I'd never put a cigarette to my lips again. But those thoughts suddenly seemed foolish.

After another twenty minutes, my brain felt like a battering ram against my skull. My body ached from sitting up, awake, all night long. Still. I sat there eyeing every vehicle that drove into or pulled out of the church and studio lots. No Joe. I hated him and thought I might run him over if I saw him. But it was my children I longed for. I felt dizzy and finally pulled into the street, albeit without looking. A car swerved, missing me by a scant foot. It didn't faze me in the least. Not even when the driver laid on his horn. I pretended not to hear and sped away.

I was deathly sick of living in my Honda, sick of searching the highways and the hedges for a place to park so I could sleep. At night, icy fingers crept inside the car—menacing cold that crawled over my skin. I was sick of freezing, waking periodically through hours of darkness, turning on the car for a bit of heat, then turning it off to save gas. Sick of taking whore baths in gas station restrooms and washing my hair in dirty sinks. And getting out of the car to pee in the cold and dark wherever I parked was tough.

Once in a while, I was lucky enough to park in a rest area, but most nights, a clump of bushes by the roadside served as my toilet. I tried to park in safe, well-lit areas, but it became tougher to care. I awoke every day to an early-morning mist covering my skin and impaling my bones, knowing at least I had safely stowed the rest of me in a Space Savers storage unit.

When I wasn't at work, there was nothing to do but worry. Once, I sat in the public library for an entire weekend, pretending to read. I rested there, dozing on and off, until a man in dirty plaid pants and bulbous-toed disco shoes pulled out his wormy penis and waved it at me. "What?" I asked. "Do you want me to scream or follow you home or what?" Nothing about the male population surprised me at that point. I stood and pushed past him. "See a shrink, buddy." I never went back to the library.

After driving around the better part of the day and using up what gas I had left, I drove to Space Savers Storage, pulled in front of my unit, and sat staring at the number on the door. Q13. I considered renting another room at the Pinewood Inn with a color television and a remote. That way, I could take a hot shower, stay in bed, watch game shows, and fantasize about winning a million dollars. Make a list of everything I would buy. Order pizza and drink beer until I was so drunk I couldn't remember my name. Not think about tomorrow. Or next week. Lie on that bed and fade away, as Daddy did.

I didn't want to find another job. I wasn't an alcoholic or a drug addict. I wasn't addicted to men, and I sure wasn't crazy. I just wanted my kids back.

I left the storage area and stopped my car at a red light. I knew I'd gotten my hopes up to see Joe or even Selma and work something out to see Gracie and Dillon. For five minutes, at least. Five measly minutes before they took them to church. I didn't want them around Calvin, but I was no longer in control. Then again, what would I say to Joe? *Congratulations on your new condo. I'm destitute and living in my car, but hey—you certainly look great.*

I peeled out without waiting for the light to change.

I thought about calling Aunt Wylene and telling her the truth. But I couldn't. Wylene had her hands full with Dixie and Caroline.

My mother, sister, and my sister's three little girls were five extra people on Aunt Wy's plate—six after she delivered Caroline's next baby. Another girl, I'd heard. At least Caroline was smart enough not to marry the new baby's daddy.

And my mother was spending money again. "It's going through her hands like water," Aunt Wy said on the phone. I was sure Caroline was helping her spend it. Wylene attributed it to their grieving process. Whatever. I was sure Charleston's boutique shops and malls had two new favorite customers. Wylene promised to keep Dixie and Caroline's spending to a minimum. "Good luck with that," I said.

And then I told Aunt Wy another lie—a doozy. I said my apartment was decent but couldn't afford a telephone. She asked for my new address, and I said, "Off Stratford somewhere. I can't remember the apartment number or name of the place." I told her I'd call her with it later and not to worry. I was *fine,* just *fine.*

I thought about opening a post office box but then changed my mind because I, first, didn't want to pay for it, and second, I wanted no more bills, bank statements, or leads to my whereabouts. No forwarding address for creditors or predators.

Asking Ray and Libby for help was out of the question. I owed them enough. No matter how I cut it, they were still Olivers, and I wasn't about to risk any leaks to the rest of the family.

That left only Lula. But Lula was nursing a sick husband in Birmingham. I hadn't heard from her since Daddy died.

I had no one. And for the first time, there was no one to turn to, talk to, or ask for a free bed for the night. Not even Coot. He and Candace had moved to Nashville. Even the Grissom sisters had sold their home to move into assisted living.

Nobody could reach me, and not a soul knew where I was when I wasn't at work.

❦

My car slowed, and I headed north to the Dumass farm without thinking. I had no idea what I'd do once I got there. Driving past tobacco fields, yards struggling from the winter, and clapboard houses needing a fresh coat of paint, my throat felt scratchy again, and my eyes burned a little. I lit another cigarette and cracked my window, passing the *For Sale* sign at the end of the long driveway leading to the dilapidated farmhouse once occupied by the Dumass family.

I turned the windshield wipers on high; the afternoon downpour started as it had every day for the past week. After parking the car and switching off the ignition, I felt the pain of all I had lost tighten in my chest. I gazed down at my car keys and the microphone key chain Mavis had given me a lifetime ago. The gold plating had worn off. The chain clicked with the hammering rain, swaying in time with the wind. Its sound triggered a memory like the rapidly fading echo of Daddy's clock over his deathbed and a few of his last words: *avenge us all.* I knew some decisions alter your life's road while others do not. But it was then that one of those life-altering decisions pressed in on me.

My life had disintegrated to that moment. Glancing again at the now-motionless keys, I heard her voice. *Unconditional love, Andie. Hold tight to it, and nobody, not even Calvin Artury, can destroy you.*

Locked inside my stifling Honda, twenty years of unrelenting memories floated around me like flies on road-kill.

I stared at the key ring closely as if trying to remember something that passed quickly through my mind several times throughout the years, yet knowing that pondering it further would be like pulling the tread again. Further unraveling my life.

The cooling engine ticked. I leaned back and closed my eyes, whispering the apparent truth, the truth I had turned my back on. "How many lives will Calvin destroy until you do something about it? It's up to you, Andie. Time to come out of your coma." My heart raced; I felt my pulse in my neck. It wasn't easy to breathe, to swallow—to think.

I pulled the keys from the ignition and lingered over the disheveled appearance of the old farmhouse. Pebbled and weedy, the grounds needed a good raking. I remembered when Loretta and Mavis had planted zinnias and painted the barn to match the house. The farm—it was so beautiful then.

In the distance, the graves remained surrounded by a now weathered and peeling picket fence. *Picket fence.* I sighed. Tall grass and wildflowers grew around the headstones, their spindly necks reaching toward the hope of sunlight above the rain clouds. I forced myself out of the car. A powerful gust of warm wind whipped my hair around as I strolled forward on a slow ascent to the gravesite.

Mammoth pines towered across a distant ridge. A scattering of faint images appeared out of nowhere. A little boy from a lifetime ago played near the site. Why? It was Mavis's resting place. *Brian. His name was Brian.* I straddled the little fence, then on bended knees, pulled a few weeds, and brushed dirt from the grassy graves that no one had tended since Rupert died. I stood, and the soaked earth pressed up through my shoes.

Stiff breezes whistled through the pines that surrounded a giant oak locked inside the fence to stand guard over the graves. The sky grew threatening. Dark clouds changed shape every few seconds. I shook my head and dropped to my knees again; maybe I *was* crazy. A voice echoed over the tobacco field as another gust of wind rushed through the pines. *He killed Mavis.* It startled me.

The wind whispered more names. Names of the dead. Names that had battled the monster in life. Names the monster devoured. *Ted Oliver, John Rossi, Vivian Artury.*

"Vivi?" I asked aloud.

Yes, the wind said. *Even Vivi. And Bud. Shall I go on?* The wind paused.

"No." I could only imagine the list of names, sure to include many people I never knew. Standing with renewed strength, I wiped my eyes and shook my head. On the crest of the sacred hill, the wind preceding the worsening storm blew through my hair and clothes. And then, a single sun ray sliced through the dark clouds, piercing the air with golden-yellow and white light. Suddenly, another great stretch of sunlight broke free. Explosions of light, one after the other, split the Heavens open and rolled over the landscape. God had uncurled His fist and extended His fingers to shoot streams of pure radiance out of the clouds and touch the ground where I stood. It took my breath away.

I don't remember how long I stood there before the clouds smeared the bruising colors of war overhead, erasing the light. Rain hit my face when I finally came to myself and picked up my key chain. I had witnessed something achingly and overwhelmingly beautiful.

God, in His way, had spoken to me.

Calvin Artury had stolen my life. My loves. My breath grew short. Calvin meant to break me, and so far, he had done an excellent job. But I had one last card to play.

I brushed the dirt off my rumpled coat and wiped away stray wisps of unwashed hair from my forehead. After straddling the fence, I walked purposefully to my car. Looking back at the graves one last time, I faced the turbulent skies. "Time to end it," I said.

It was my turn to prophesy. I made a simple vow.

To kill him.

Chapter 55
DO AS I SAY
Andie ~ March 1993

While I scribbled my resignation, something about leaving town, my boss asked for my forwarding address—a place to send my last paycheck. I gave him the address of my divorce attorney. A check for three-hundred-fifty dollars wasn't worth the worry. If I were lucky, maybe the twins would end up with it.

Evening approached as I drove to my storage unit. The relentless rain made it difficult to see. *Q13—there it is.* I winced, getting out of my car as sheets of rain bludgeoned my body, attacking me for being an unfit mother. I kicked the door open and rummaged through my stuff. Lamps, chairs, boxes, and more boxes. Bedroom furniture, the little black-and-white TV, Dillon's basketball, Gracie's books and board games, dishes, and small kitchen appliances. All of it stared back at me as if I'd lost my mind. I searched through the memories, making myself sick to my stomach. The photo albums—I had to find them, the blue afghan, and the gun—*where is Daddy's gun? What box did I put it in?* I knew how to shoot—I was good at it. *Ah, bullets. They'll come in handy. And vodka, where's the vodka?*

On the way out, I handed my storage unit key to the manager and told him to sell everything. I couldn't clean his office or pay for the space any longer, and I had no way to dispose of its contents. He wasn't happy: I didn't care. I imagined my worldly possessions as income for some thrift store or garage sale—a source of comfort for the next needy woman's desire to design on a dime.

I stopped at a gas station, bought a liter of Dr. Pepper, and then drove to the pay phone. Carefully cleaning the area on the dashboard where I had eaten a light supper of Twinkies and a bag of chips, I composed a script for my phone call to Joe.

Taking one last deep breath, I felt a great weight lift from my chest. Killing Calvin was a drastic step, but was the only possible protection for Dillon and Gracie. I had lost it all and would end up in prison, but I concluded—it was worth it. Worth every second to save my children from a madman. Waiting two years until they were of legal age when they could return to me on their own would do no good. It'd be too late. I knew all too well the mental pull and brainwashing of Calvin. By then, I would have lost them to the church, and God knows what else he planned for them.

I had no choice.

I flicked a few specks of dirt off my knees as the calm after the storm entered my soul. There was no hope left. A new husband would tire of my baggage and kick me to the curb or begin his own cycle of abuse. I had nothing to bring to a new marriage. Nothing but poverty and utter hopelessness. And yes, I might survive needing no one's help and perhaps someday find a degree of happiness, but any way I looked at it, it was fleeting. I couldn't live like that, and suicide was not an option. But if I had to live, then he had to die. He had swallowed my family whole, and I was determined to have the last word, even with a future behind bars.

For decades, the monster had handpicked each unsuspecting soul to fulfill his fantasies. Money meant power, and power brought fame and control over any man or woman, boy or girl, of his choosing. He had allowed Evan Preston to create a Mafia, making it easy for him to enter into his own cruel and perverted indiscretions. He wanted Dillon and possibly Gracie. The monster wasn't getting what he wanted.

And to attack them without a plan, they would find any means to discredit my story and destroy my evidence. They would use any method to prove I was lying, but once Calvin was dead, what did it matter? My children would be safe. That's all I wanted.

I might as well be drunk when I call him. I took a long pull on the vodka bottle and wiped my mouth on my coat sleeve. Scooting to the passenger seat, I dialed Joe's number. I had to concentrate; the number was already fading from my memory.

It rang only once. "Joe?"

"What the hell are you doing calling me again? What do you want?"

"I need to talk to you. Give me just five minutes, please. It's important."

"You've got one. I'm on my way to the studio."

"Tell Calvin we need to meet. Just him and me."

Joe laughed. "Why would he meet with *you?* God, Andie. Calvin Artury is the most watched and beloved televangelist in the world. Haven't you listened to the news lately? We beat the numbers in Billy Graham's last Crusade. President Bush and half the Christian Coalition attend our services in Washington. People love Calvin Artury, and nothing you do can hurt him. He won't meet with you."

Indifferent, I smirked. "I don't have a TV, Joe. I don't care how big everybody thinks he is. He's pond scum to me. Tell him this. Tell him I'm living in my car. I'm at the bottom of my barrel—the end of my rope. Tell him I don't give a damn anymore. I'm prepared to expose him unless I get what I want."

"Are you drunk?" The acid in Joe's voice came across loud and clear.

Driven to a new level of rage, I felt it course through my body, a violent scraping inside my skin. "I've got proof. I know who killed

John Rossi. I saw it. I was there. I watched Evan pull the trigger, and Silas Turlo was with him. I'm the caller the police looked for, begged to come forward. I can give them details. Peter Collins gave me a videotape on his way out of town. I've no idea what's on it, but I'm sure it's good. Oh, and by the way, I still have the pictures and letter from Mavis. I'm sure he had her murdered. And when I broke open the shed that day, the day you beat the hell out of me, I took pictures of all of it, including the money in that briefcase you carried. I've got the evidence I need, Joe. I know about the church's illegal activities. I have evidence to put Calvin away, destroy his ministry, put the rest in prison, and maybe—even you"

Joe's voice slowed; his intention to cut me off—gone. "Okay. What do you want?"

"Certainly not you." It was my turn to laugh. "I want Calvin. Alone. I want him to meet me alone."

"Andie, damn it, I demand you tell me what you want from him!"

"You—cannot—demand—ANYTHING from me! YOU TELL THAT BASTARD TO DO AS I SAY! I'm not explaining myself to an ex-husband who owes me thousands in child support and alimony, while he lives in a beautifully decorated condominium with a scrawny wife! I heard Calvin allows Selma to travel with you. Sleep in the same hotel room. Probably to keep you faithful. Right? HOW DARE YOU MAKE DEMANDS SITTING THERE WITH PLENTY, even *if* you bought it all with dirty money. You kept me in trailer-trash hell for seven years, doomed to poverty for the rest of my life. It was ME, not Selma, who did all the sacrificing and risk-taking so *you* could party for weeks at a time with Calvin, you son of a bitch! And don't you even threaten me. You can't make threats to a woman living in her car!"

My head hurt most every day. Dehydrated, I had no appetite or thirst, and my bowels were a mess. I was sick with grief and hadn't showered, changed my clothes, washed my hair, or brushed my teeth in over a week. Delirium stalked me as I lost track of time.

"Calm down. I'm sure we can work this out."

"I'm not working out a thing with you, you fucked up moron! I want to talk to Calvin. Alone!"

"Let me pray on this, okay?"

"Well. After you *pray* on it, call your attorney. You're going to need one."

"Okay. When do you want to see Reverend?"

"As soon as possible."

"Listen, Andie, I swear to Almighty God, he's on his way out of town. He's probably in the air right now. He won't be back in Winston-Salem until next month. It's a four-week trip. I'm leaving tomorrow myself—to Zimbabwe. The church bought a jet. A 747 to travel the world and save the lost. It was the last prophecy God gave, through Reverend Artury, to be fulfilled before Jesus returns. The rapture will take place soon. You know that. Why don't you give your heart back to the Lord?"

"Yeah, it seems to me I read that somewhere in the Bible. Something about Calvin and his big-ass jet in the end times: grow some balls, Joe. God never said that." I laughed.

"You never believed, did you?"

"I believe that you and Calvin stole my life. I believe Calvin and his mob are pedophiles, murderers, and God knows what else! And I believe Calvin wants to devour our children, and *you* will sacrifice them. That's what I believe, you sick, twisted sack of shit!"

Silence.

"Dillon and Gracie, they're doing well, you know. Do you want to see them? I'll set it up," he said softly.

I hesitated and clamped my hand over my mouth so he wouldn't hear me cry. "Tell them I love them," I squeaked out. I couldn't take the chance.

"Sure, Andie, sure I will." He stalled for time. I heard him breathing hard.

"Tracing the call? I'm at a pay phone, you idiot."

"Andie! Listen to me! You can't make threats like this! You can't see him alone! They'll kill you! Reverend is worldwide. Untouchable. You saw John die; you *know* what they'll do to you. Do you want our kids to be without their mama?"

I laughed again. "What do you care? You took them away from me!" I lit a cigarette and took a long drag. "Strange, seeing how you never wanted them to begin with. So tell me now. What day does the murdering boy-fucking bastard return from his trip? And you better tell me the truth, or I swear to God I'll find you. You've seen me shoot, Joe. You know I don't miss," I said through a plume of smoke.

"His plane lands in Greensboro on April sixth, early in the morning. What are you planning, Andie?"

"Plenty if he doesn't show up."

"What if he refuses? I can't guarantee he'll—"

"—I'm only saying this one time, so listen up! Tell Calvin to meet me alone at noon on April sixth. Meet me at Tanglewood Park, by the tennis courts. Rain or shine. They're busy all the time and wide open. I'll wait exactly five minutes. If he doesn't show up, I've duplicated every bit of evidence several times over. It's packed up and ready to go to TV stations, newspapers, and more than one police department and judge. I'm sure there's a judge out there who is not on his payroll. I'm going to nail him, Joe, nail him to his own cross unless I get what I want."

"Andie, please—what is it you want? You want the kids back?" he asked, softening.

I want him dead. "I will tell him what I want when I see him," I said.

"Okay. Tuesday, April sixth at noon. Tanglewood Park tennis courts. I'll tell him."

"Right. And Joe?"

"Yes, Andie?"

"First man or woman I see from the House of Praise, between now and when I talk to Calvin, the packages get mailed." I slammed down the phone.

⌒⌒

I had duplicated nothing. I couldn't afford to *duplicate* anything. I didn't even know how or where to start. But they didn't know that. Not for sure. I planned to let my attorney clear out the lockbox before my murder trial. Once Calvin was dead, who'd care anyway? Fuck them all.

I pulled into the Magnolia Monarch apartments, parked in the back, and rented an efficiency apartment. I had enough money to last until April sixth. And then it'd be over.

Chapter 56
Spirit In The Sky
Reverend Calvin Artury ~ March 1993

I massaged the back of my neck, feeling Evan's glare. My exhausted body longed to be anywhere other than locked inside a plane with Evan and Silas. At 63 years old, I worked harder than any televangelist in history. Parting seas, moving mountains, and blazing trails into nations barely touched by the Gospel, I had perfected the efforts of my competitors. Like Moses, I had to remind myself to *stand still and see the salvation of the Lord!*

It was my appearance that suffered the most. I had traded in my recent baldness for a beautifully coiffed toupee matching the blonde locks of my youth, but there was nothing to be done about my sagging chin and drooping ear lobes, saving surgery. And who had time for surgery? I had hoped to age like a fine wine. Instead, my bloated body found plenty of youthful energy when I hit the pulpit. The strength of Jehovah-Jireh! The Lord our Provider! My faith in God gave me power from On High to withstand the extended services. But on the trip to Zimbabwe, I had hoped to relax. Instead, I sat in an emergency meeting at 37,000 feet.

"She's bluffing!" I crossed my legs and laughed.

"I don't think she is, Reverend." Evan cleaned his Ray-Bans, then placed them on his head, gazing out at the clouds below and then back at me.

"I'm not cowering to the wishes of that tramp! I did it when Mavis was alive; No piece of white trash is going to blackmail me!" My voice thundered throughout the cabin as I intended.

My private jet had stopped in Atlanta for business before heading to Africa ahead of the team. By the time my meeting at Bank of America Plaza ended, a frantic Joe Oliver had tripped over his tongue, desperate to reach me, and I suspected, to make himself look important. Evan intercepted the call and found the entire House of Praise office staff and ministry team riled up and speculating about a possible attack on the ministry.

Evan removed a notepad from his pocket, then pulled off a pen cap with his teeth. "Get Joe on the phone again when we land, Silas. I want to ensure he's cooled down before the team boards the 747. I don't want him spilling his guts about this."

If my voice was the thunder, my eyes flashed with lightning and bore into Evan. "So, what do you suggest we do?"

"We have to do something about Oliver. He's got to go."

I laughed again, an explosive sound that shook my seat. "There's nothing wrong with Loverboy." Leaning back, I gazed out the window. "I've known him a long time." Quickly infected by the thought of him, a curious moan escaped my lips. "I can get him to do anything by throwing a beautiful woman into his lap. He's been with me since he was a kid, Evan. And he's been loyal, as you know. Done everything you've asked him to do."

Staring at Evan's tight jaw, I needed more than Joe's loyalty to convince him. "You must realize, Evan, never in my ministry had I felt Hell's flames licking the soles of my feet more than the day I rescued Joe from his wife's grip. I stood at the edge of *Gehenna* to yank him away from her! To this day, the experience burns in my soul. Knowing someone you love is about to land in Satan's pit—

it's horrific. To feel your body burn as you pull him away from a wife who has sold her soul—no—I can't lose Joe now. Not after what I experienced to hold on to him." I folded my hands behind my head and stretched out my legs.

Evan shrugged. "It's difficult taking care of business when your boss has visions."

I pretended not to hear his disrespect and peered over my sunglasses. "Did you say something?"

"I said Oliver can't concentrate. And now he can't keep his mouth shut. He wants everyone to see how valuable he is. He's created too many problems. Demanding Fannie to get you on the phone. What an ass!"

"He knows the consequences of his actions. He also knows what will happen to him if Andie goes through with this."

My eyes narrowed into ice-blue slits. She could've circumvented what was coming to her. She could've had a better life had she stayed faithful to the church. The reality was I adored Andie. But she had avoided me from the time she was little. Even though I orchestrated her marriage to Joe, my plans to bring her into the upper echelon of the ministry ended shortly after. She never knew how I felt about her because she had allowed herself to be taken over by Satan as a young woman. Ahh, yes, as God once loved Lucifer, who fell from grace, so was Andie Oliver loved by me, only to become my dark angel.

I had lost her, but God gave me something in return—her children.

I glared at Evan. "I think she's still in love with him, so I say she's bluffing. She wants Joe and the kids back, that's all."

Evan returned my glare. "I disagree. It's bigger than that. It's *obvious* she knows everything. We have to eliminate her and whatever she's got as evidence. Right away. We should've done it when we took her kids away from her."

"We would have, except *you* didn't want it to look *obvious*, remember?"

Evan smiled. "I'll call DeSanto when we land, have him send out a few of his men to look for her. She has to be in town. She won't be far from those kids. I'll ask Joe the description of her car and where she works; maybe her employer can cough up an address." Evan turned his attention to Silas and grinned. "Do you think Percy would like to make some extra money?"

Silas had been quietly chewing his toothpick. He looked hard at Evan and wiped his sweaty forehead with his hand. "My wife and I would rather you leave him out of this."

"Come on, Turlo," Evan said. "The boy's got more guts than anybody I've seen lately. Besides, we got him a pretty wife, didn't we? Wouldn't you love to see Percy advance in position? Sylvia loves her new daughter-in-law, doesn't she?"

Silas and Sylvia treasured the dark-haired beauty Percy married. Barely eighteen, the girl had attended the Rochester, New York Crusade, along with her family. Like a love-starved hound dog, Percy fell in love at that Crusade. Since Percey had proven himself valuable in service to the Lord, I prophesied over the girl's family that it was God's will for them to move to Winston-Salem. There's not a better perk than a divine one. The girl's family sold all they owned and quit their jobs in New York but became destitute in North Carolina. It was, of course, the perfect scenario. Their only hope of survival was employment within my ministry. In return, they allowed their daughter to marry Percy. He got his girl. Of course, I paid for the enormous, televised church wedding and Praise Buffet reception. No, the Oliver disaster was not a job for a brute like Percy. I needed a professional.

"I'm not in the mood to clean up after Percy again," I snapped. "No, Evan. This is a job for Pastor DeSanto and his people. Percy's good, but he's not an expert at this. We need people who know how and where to look for her."

Silas slumped backward in his seat, stuck his toothpick into his pocket, and sighed heavily.

I needed a drink. "I think you're right, though. I believe Andie knows everything. Evidence that could bring us all down, including the ministry. You want that?"

"Of course not," Evan said. "I will let DeSanto handle it then. What if he can't find her?"

I thumped my hands on my chest, tilted forward, and stared straight into the eyes of my top brass. *"Watch ye therefore, and pray always, that ye may be accounted worthy to escape all these things that shall come to pass.* You two better hope he finds her before I return to the States, or I guess I'll have to play tennis at Tanglewood Park on April sixth. With Andie Oliver."

Chapter 57
If God Be For Me
Andie ~ March 1993

On the first night in my rented basement efficiency at the Magnolia Monarch, I sat and planned his last breath. Dropping to my knees beside a mattress covered with greasy sheets discarded by a former tenant, I pushed the gun to the side of the bed. My fingers landed on a photograph. A white beach shaped like a crescent moon surrounded by an azure sky reflected onto an ocean as smooth as sapphire glass. A string of tropical hotels banked the beach. A young woman with honey-blonde hair and a man with sad eyes lounged on a straw mat, arms locked together. Printed neatly on the corner—*Andie and Joe, Hawaii 1987*—words now surreal. I stared at the snapshot.

Flies swarmed over the overflowing dumpster outside my door. A multitude had made their way inside the airless room and tickled my skin as they fluttered over my pale legs. A rusted refrigerator with no handle vibrated next to a stove that had most likely seen its last scrubbing in the '70s. The stale scent of cigarette smoke rose from the floor where someone had swept butts into a corner, and the pungency of urine reeked from the tiny bathroom. Gold napless carpet yielded the stench of feet from years of poor tenants. But the smell from the dumpster seeped in and filled any odorless space.

A roach wiggled out of a fist hole punched into fake paneling. The walls dripped with mold and mildew. There was no closet, just an old set of drawers with chipped paint and holes from a TV bolted to the top a lifetime ago.

A sooty, vague darkness soaked the room, and my eyes strained to adjust. I stood and opened the draperies, once gold, now faded and water-stained. Dust flew into the air. There was no lamp. Just an overhead fluorescent I couldn't bear to switch on. But the dump was cheap, and I could rent it by the week.

I surveyed my remaining possessions. I'd brought all I had left to that foul-smelling hellhole: photograph albums, the blue crocheted afghan, a few clothes and toiletries, a pair of shoes, a liter of Dr. Pepper, and a loaded gun.

I lit my last cigarette, then picked up my .380 automatic. My daddy always said the phrase, *he needed killin'*, was a valid defense in the South. I figured Hell would be worth seeing Calvin's face as I pressed the gun to his head. The world would be a better place with one less dirty televangelist.

Moving to the edge of a metal folding chair, I sat wrapped in the afghan as the sun moved behind the drapes. Shadows crawled about the room. One of them belonged to me. The dark silhouette of my body dragged across the wall, inch by inch, stretching me into a brutal abyss—it seemed fitting.

Calvin had slowly stripped from me the strength of endurance I once possessed. How could I reclaim it when he dangled his holiness in front of the world, shouting scripture? Was killing him the only way? Would I ever be able to expose him as the monster he was?

I could hardly wait for April sixth because I had come to an end. There were no safe places. I unclenched my hands and looked down at a crumpled note I'd written to myself, as if I could read the words in the dim light of dusk. *Only monsters kill.* Would I be one if I killed one?

I stepped to the small kitchenette sink and lit the note with Daddy's Zippo, watching the paper blacken and disintegrate, and releasing the air I hadn't realized I was holding in my lungs. The room's stench overtook me once again. The urge to stop breathing settled on my chest like an anvil. A peculiar quiet passed through me. It expanded from the center of my body. I wanted to speak and put the world in motion, but I couldn't find my voice. I felt suspended in the silent room, like drowning in deep water. My voice had dwindled to nothing, and I pressed my palm flat against my heart, checking for a beat. Possibly, I *had* died and gone to Hell.

A poem filtered through my head, surfacing and then vanishing. A poem, half-remembered. Something about strong women. Blurred words at the far end of a long corridor in my memory. Words that seemed almost liquid or smoke. There, but fleeting. The body of the poem beyond my reach.

Another hour passed, maybe three. Suddenly, it was like God had given me the gift of sight. I looked down at my crusty feet, at the pants I'd worn for a week; maybe it wasn't the dumpster I was smelling. Disgusted, I wiped tears from my dirty cheeks and shoved my matted hair behind my ears. I pulled Daddy's old family Bible from under the stack of photograph albums, traced the words, and choked out a desperate laugh. *If God be for us, who can be against us?*

The room sank into darkness. I sat there for some time and then said to God with all the sincerity I could gather, "I've been told my entire life—great is Your faithfulness. Where is Your faithfulness to *me*?"

I realized suddenly that contrary to what my parents had brought me up to believe, the prayers of the spotted, the wrinkled, and the flawed never made it past the gates of Heaven. That, possibly, Calvin was right. God had finally turned His back to the cries of the damned. But the dim light in the room suddenly brightened as if someone had switched on a lamp, and it startled me as the power of my determination and defiance softened, filling me with peace in my chest, as gentle as a fruit fly.

Perhaps the answer was even simpler than I imagined. Had God's faithfulness actually disappeared? Maybe it had all come down to this moment, and all I had to do was ask.

Continued in **Vengeance Is Mine**, Book 3,
in the *Televenge Trilogy*

Author's Note – *Televenge Trilogy*

Although there are many similarities, this book is not about me. All the characters are fictional. They are not based on any person dead or alive. While many scenes were inspired in part by real life, all events and dialogue are entirely imaginary and/or wishful thinking. Any resemblance to real people or events is entirely coincidental. Although it was difficult to revisit many dark places in writing this story, it does not change the purely fictitious nature of the work.

Sorry We're Open Diner does not exist, but there is a town in North Carolina called Welcome, and Mount Zion Baptist Church in Winston-Salem is not the same church as described in this trilogy.

Southern Fried Women, a book of short stories, contains spin-offs of scenes in this trilogy, or minor characters who tell their own story: *Pigment of My Imagination*, *Beach Babies*, and *Punkin Head*.

Though it is true this book is about the dark side of televangelism, it is also about the true light of unconditional love. Writers write about their passions, what moves them, what they know. My key inspirational force is my spirituality. I wrote the *Televenge Trilogy* to reflect the realities, the long-lasting devastation, and the horrific effects of legalism.

For those who have left a manipulative situation or are thinking about it, you should know the great plan of redemption belongs to us all. No matter how desperate your circumstances, you can come out of a dark place, and into a life that is calling your name. God's mercies are truly renewed every morning, and He never, ever turns His back on us. No matter what anyone preaches from their pretentious pulpit. And that is why I wrote this trilogy.

—Pamela King Cable

For more information or to purchase go to **GracelynRose.com**

Books by this author:

TELEVENGE
Book One of the *Televenge* trilogy

AVENGE US ALL
Book Two of the *Televenge* trilogy

VENGEANCE IS MINE
Book Three of the *Televenge* trilogy

SOUTHERN FRIED WOMEN
a collection of short stories

THE SANCTUM

On her fifth birthday, Neeley McPherson accidentally killed her parents. Thrown into the care of her scheming and alcoholic grandfather, she survives by her quick wit and the watchful eye of an elderly black man, Gideon. In 1959, as equal rights heats up in the South, authorities accuse Gideon of stealing a watch and using a Whites Only restroom. Neeley, now thirteen, determines to break him out of jail.

When the infamous Catfish Cole, Ku Klux Klan Grand Dragon of the Carolinas, discovers their courageous escape, he pursues Neeley and Gideon into the frozen Blue Ridge Mountains to a wolf sanctuary. There, Neeley crosses the bridge between the real and the supernatural. Giving sanctuary, the healing power of second chances, and overcoming prejudice entwines, leading Neeley to tragedy once again but also the desire of her heart.

The Sanctum is a coming-of-age Southern tale dusted with magic and set in a volatile time in America when the winds of change begin to blow.

www.ingramcontent.com/pod-product-compliance
Lightning Source LLC
Chambersburg PA
CBHW020324010826
48973CB00005B/1120